THE SERAPH

The Seraph

Jane Goodrich

THE SERAPH

Copyright © 2026 by Jane Goodrich.
All rights reserved.

www.janegoodrichauthor.com

Printed in the United States of America. No part of this book may be used or reproduced in any manner whatsoever without written permission from the author except in the case of brief quotations embodied in critical articles and reviews.

ISBN 978-0-9758920-2-2

7 6 5 4 3 2 1

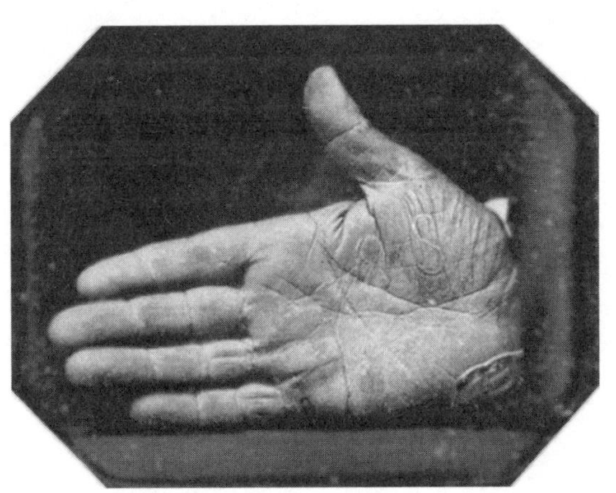

“There was a being whom my spirit oft
Met on its visioned wanderings far aloft.

A Seraph of Heaven, too gentle to be human,
Veiling beneath that radiant form of woman….”

Percy Bysshe Shelley
Epipsychidion

SPIRITUALISM!

Phantomatic Whispers
Soul Reading
Further Evidences of the Love of God

MRS. CORA CARTER

WILL

LECTURE IN TRANCE

Lyceum Hall
Wednesday evening October 10, 1856
at 7 1/2 o'clock

As was her custom, she fixed her eyes on one man. An older gentleman, It always had to be an older gentleman, seated in the middle distance. Like the others, he was to be a man unused to female admiration. Like the others, he was defenseless. Yet, he would be her guide.

The hall was a large one, blind-windowed and tiered, and filled on the main level with an audience of hundreds. In the curved balcony, decorated with cupids and flowers, even more faces appeared, rows of pale smudges in a darkened cave. When the door to the vestibule opened, admitting a latecomer, it blazed with a slow explosion of dazzling light. Somewhere above her an organ played softly, a tune in B-flat.

She sat, straight backed, in the ornate chair provided for her in the center of the stage. She kept her face composed and calm, with the tiny smile she had practiced. Her loosely clasped hands lay in her lap. From her raised position the smells of the audience came to her. They were always the same: leather, perfume, sweat. The room was full of a velvety heat, and if she had held out the palm of her hand, she believed she could have measured the weight of it. It was anticipation, she knew, the same way she knew the audience would shortly shift in their seats all at once, in unison, as flocks of birds do when they bolt from a single place all at the same time. Just after this moment is when she stood.

She stepped forward to the apron of the stage, her gown gathered around her in an air of careless grace. The limelights before her hissed in their little chambers, making the glow she moved in luminous and overprecise. It fell slanting and resplendent upon her. She turned her head slowly, knowing this brightness highlighted her golden hair.

The voice came in a dark blur, the way it always did. She never knew whether the voice grew from the low murmur of the audience, or out of her own head, but the sound shaped and reshaped the words she was going to say, forming itself into sentences, phrases, even rhymes. She could feel the presence of the sound behind her eyes, hear the resonance it would make in her throat.

She closed her eyes, and listened for a mere moment, then took another step forward and raised her arms toward the audience with her palms upright. The organ played a little louder and faster. She opened her eyes and placed them again upon her chosen gentleman. He had already begun to fluster under her gaze. Then she began to tell the lie.

The Platform

1857–1858

Cora
1857

I unbuttoned my stage gown and let it slide down to the floor, kicking away the ludicrous heap of silk and lace, leaving it to lie where it fell.

The theater dressing room was garishly lit and well-mirrored, the flickering of the gas lamps bouncing anxiously from one silver surface to another, from the wall oval to the tilted cheval, to the hand mirror laid flat on the dressing table. A room for preening, stale with the sweat of a thousand others, sweet with the ointments of subterfuge.

A battered screen stood in the one dim hollow of the room, concealing a chamber pot with a green scum line around its rim, a chipped washbasin and a discarded hairbrush coiled with dark greasy hairs. A velveteen couch disgorged a wad of stuffing from a torn seam; a curve of wallpaper drooped away from the dado in a water-stained corner. In every theater, these rooms were all the same.

Benjamin and Lovey were not awaiting me as usual. Since I could still hear the creaking seats and bursts of laughter of the departing audience, I assumed my husband was out in the front of the house. His fur-collared overcoat was tossed over the back of a nearby chair. Lovey could be anywhere.

Still wearing my chemise and corset, I drew Benjamin's coat around me and sat in the chair. As always after a lecture, I was exhausted, and I rested my head against the chair back and closed my eyes. The silly ringlets into which Lovey had curled my hair tickled my shoulders.

The remains of a meal sat upon the small table beside me. Evidently Benjamin and Lovey had eaten their supper. Two plates nestled together, an empty glass and a cup ringed with sludgy liquid, either cold tea or chocolate. My stomach cramped. I'd not eaten since the forenoon, and it was now near 8 o'clock. One of the plates sported a few crumbs of something which looked like cake, and pressing my fingers onto the still-moist fragments, I tasted them. Spice cake. Closing my eyes again, I sighed.

I always hoped my familiar spirits would visit after I had finished a lecture, but they never did. During the lectures given in trance, I was beset with voices of strange spirits, and after exposing myself to these others I wished for the comfort of the ones I knew. I liked the feeling of being surrounded by their benign, affectionate presences.

Hollis especially was missed, the friend of my childhood, the one person I'd known both living and dead. His was the first spirit whose voice I ever heard, but he spoke less frequently now in the year since my marriage. I feared Hollis disapproved of my choices, even though he knew better than anyone the hard choices life insists upon. Not everything I told the public was a lie, but it was not all true either. For one thing, spirits could not be bidden. Hollis and the others came and went as they had in the living world, in their own time.

A stumbling lurch heard in the outside hallway startled me, and I pulled the coat to my chin, until the next sounds were Benjamin's voice and Lovey's shriek of laughter. The pair entered the room without grace, barging through the door with an air of excitement.

"Such a crush!" Lovey exclaimed, as she strode directly to the oval mirror and began gazing closely at her face and touching her pouting mouth with a fingertip. The girl was twenty years old, three years older than me, with a lush, fleshy body and a trilling laugh. When she entered a room one could always smell the warmth of her. Indeed, whenever she stood close by, winding my hair into rag curls or helping with the fasteners of the stage gowns, her odor rose from her, sweet and milky and not at all unpleasant. Lovey also possessed a bustling manner, with some part always in motion—currently the feather bobbing on her pert little hat in the mirror's reflection. *Miss Lovicia Gale*, I'd once seen written on the envelope of a letter she had from her mother, but Benjamin always called her Lovey.

"Another triumph my dear," said Benjamin as he leaned to kiss the top of my head, "and good work with your mark. That fellow in the center stall was well on his way to apoplexy. More than one husband will have a surprise for his wife tonight!"

Benjamin laughed at his own joke and Lovey tittered, but I was in no mood for his ribald humor. Among the many things the platform had stolen from my youth was my own girlish laughter, and it seemed I always now spoke in the measured cadence of the lecture hall. "I am looking forward to having my supper," I said, just feeling relieved the performance was over.

"I have marvelous news." Benjamin replied. "We are invited to a reception at Judge Edmonds' at Irving Place in the next hour. Many a New York celebrity will be in attendance. Horace Greeley and his wife are to be there!"

"Ben, I can't, not without eating something beforehand," I said, shaking my head.

"That's just it, my dearest, you'll be singing for our supper. A feast is to be laid, and it has been suggested to me that Mrs. Greeley is longing for a séance."

He stood over me with his wan, indulgent smile and one eyebrow cocked in question. I drew his coat even more tightly around me.

"Go ahead," he said, gesturing to the dress upon the floor. "Put on your gown and let's go."

"Not in that stage costume surely." It was one of a pair Benjamin bought last spring. I'd heard the whispered comments. They were too showy, too revealing.

"Why not? It certainly cost me a fortune." Benjamin was agitated now. His eyes dimmed with menace, and a heavy lock of dark hair tumbled across his forehead. Only months ago, such quarrels dissolved into teasing and laughter, but now such words stayed in the air like poison smoke, making it hard to breathe.

"No." I said.

"You are a minx," he hissed through his teeth while jabbing his finger in my face. "Do you know what these people might mean to your career? We've finally landed on our feet and you spoil it."

I knew what the reception meant, and the thought of a real supper tempted me. I knew who Horace Greeley was and of his famous newspaper. *The New York Tribune* was read all across America. "My good day-dress will suit just fine," I answered, this time emphasizing every stridency in my tone.

"I've even hired a carriage for tonight. What is wrong with the gown?" Benjamin turned his eyes from my defiance and looked at Lovey. She knew me better than he did and wordlessly shook her head in the negative, warning him from his insistence.

Benjamin grabbed the gown from the floor and tossed it toward Lovey. "Get her in something decent and out to the carriage in half an hour," he commanded, before leaving the shabby room and rattling every mirror with the slamming of the door.

I passed Benjamin his folded coat as we prepared to climb into the waiting carriage. After he'd forgotten it in his rage, Lovey ran a brush across it, then helped me into my green silk day-dress for the reception. I chose to go bare headed with a single sprig of flowers pinned behind one ear.

"He's just nervous," said Lovey, holding my own coat for me, but I said nothing while slipping my arms into the lightweight sleeves, hoping only that it would be exchanged with something more substantial before the winter came.

The conveyance was a surprise, a lavish touch unlike Benjamin, who usually insisted we walk about the city, sometimes requiring me to trudge a mile or more to my speaking engagements from whatever corner of the city he'd managed to secure our residence. I knew he was intent on making a good impression, knew he was already constructing an elaborate evening of deceit.

"The guests at this reception are select," Benjamin began, talking in a high, fast voice. "Very select. Editors, newspapermen, powerful political men. Judge Edmonds himself was on the State Supreme Court. They've heard of you and will be watching you closely, and their wives even more so. Perhaps that plain dress was a good idea after all. Don't treat the men like your mark. That's for lectures. Smile and be sweet. Saying very little will be best."

I ignored him. I'd sat silently through hundreds of these admonitions—Benjamin's reminders of how I should behave—and knew his instructions. I was accustomed to his lies now too, but did not like them. They made me feel badly, and I was forced to keep track of them. Yet, I had allowed myself to be led here by the hand. The blame was my own.

The streets outside the carriage windows were quiet and nearly empty, the few passersby appearing only as shadows fluttering in the orbs of the gas lamps positioned in every block. How quickly the darkness gathered on these late autumn nights. Behind the softly lit curtains in the brownstone windows, I imagined ordinary lives. On nights like this I tried to work out how I might possibly find my way back to my own ordinary life, as though there had ever been anything ordinary about it.

"...of course people say she's mad," I suddenly heard Benjamin say.

"Who?"

"Mrs Greeley. I think she is called Mary. Aren't you listening? Anyway, she's the one we want."

"How will I know her?" I asked.

"We'll be introduced, I suppose. We've been asked to give a seance after dinner with a handful of guests. I'm told Mrs. Greeley places great store in those who talk to the dead like yourself," Benjamin said, chuckling. "She kept Kate Fox nearly captive in her house for months, making the poor girl contact her dead son, Pinkie."

"Pinkie?" The carriage had drawn to a stop before an impressive brownstone. A tall set of steps led up to double doors inset with claret-colored windows.

"Pinkie is the one." Benjamin said as he waited for the driver to unlatch the carriage door.

"You give Mrs. Greeley "Pinkie," and I'll wager Uncle Horace will give you a column in the *Tribune*."

Select or not, the guests at Irving Place were as curious about me as anyone else. My contact with people followed a familiar route. Some thought I was a fortuneteller; others hinted at predictions or wished me to locate objects they'd misplaced. Many seemed to want simply to touch me, and I was accustomed to their hands, plucking and insistent as though some clutch would result in a benediction. Every living being was seeking something, something lost and mute to their searching.

Most people were admirers, of course, and I was beginning to understand, as evidenced by a reception like this, that I was becoming famous. In the dining room, chafing dishes were warming croquettes of chicken and a frosted Charlotte Russe sat on the sideboard. Oysters glistened upon a bed of ice in a silver bowl. The two dozen guests were distinguished: Judge Edmonds, the host, bespectacled and precise and devoted to promoting Spiritualism but also his pale-eyed daughter, Lydia; Mr. Peabody, the banker; and Mr. Dana, the celebrated columnist. Still, I'd come to see my audiences as all the same. I felt as a mother bird before a nest of hatchlings with their faces upturned and their beaks always open, waiting for me to feed them. They all wanted the gift of miracles without the work of faith. All I could do was bring them every scrap I could find.

I recognized Horace Greeley at once, knowing him immediately from caricatures in many publications and had to admit he more than resembled even the unflattering ones. He was a sallow, short-sighted man, with translucent eyelashes like a spiderweb's filament and a pink scalp gleaming through wispy remnants of hair. He wore a shabby coat with one collar turned up and folded into the fabric of his badly-tied cravat. As much as Benjamin annoyed me, had his own cravat been so askew I would not have been able to resist a proprietary wifely gesture to straighten it. Perhaps Mrs. Greeley was mad, or at least, distracted. I had not seen her yet.

Standing with Judge Edmonds as I was introduced, Mr. Greeley greeted me in a high-pitched but enthusiastic voice and raked me with an eye that was experienced in scrutiny. I knew it would be a mistake to conclude that Mr. Greeley's mind was as carelessly tended as his costume.

"Have you a prediction for us, Mrs. Carter?" he asked jovially.

I smiled, hoping my ardent hunger was not too apparent. "I predict a lovely supper."

"Ah! Too much meat and not enough greenery, I suspect," Greeley said, elbowing Judge Edmonds.

"You'd have us eating tree bark soaked in tepid water with Reverend Graham and his vegetarians," the Judge countered with a smile. "We'll see where you are when Lydia serves the Charlotte Russe. We were just admiring Mr. Greeley's new prize. Show Mrs. Carter your new watch, Horace."

Mr. Greeley fumbled at his waistcoat and brought forth a great gold watch attached to a lengthy chain. "It was meant as a tribute from the typesetters and pressman at the paper," he explained, as he extended the gold chain and displayed the novelty of its links being fashioned in the letters of the alphabet. "Twenty-six letters and the ampersand! Everything we writers need to make fools of ourselves in print."

"Or we lecturers in speech," I said, while reaching out to touch the fob from which dangled another set of charms, a quill, an inkwell, and other printer's tools in miniature. "Why, you even have a tiny composing stick."

Horace Greeley's eyes narrowed in interest. "How does a young woman of the spiritual platform know of a composing stick?"

"I spent many hours sticking up type while working on *The Beacon* in Hope Grove."

"An Association girl!" Mr. Greeley said. "I might have known it. So you were a member of Reverend Asher Lyman's Practical Christian community?"

In the instant Mr. Greeley spoke these words, I sensed a change in him. His interest proceeded from curiosity to kindness, and I felt as if I'd walked from a cool place into a warm sun. "Yes," I answered. "I had two jobs as a child in Hope Grove. I tended chickens and worked in the print shop on the community paper."

But as quickly as I'd basked in favor, I felt the old editor's emotions drift to a different place, his thoughts wandering to a former world, the days before Hope Grove and the other idealistic association communities began to falter under the brute force of pragmatism. "Asher Lyman is a noble man." Greeley said. "His ideals for society are of the very best, but I understand he is retired now."

"The sad business with the son," Judge Edmonds added. "dying so unexpectedly while at school. Certainly he was to be Hope Grove's spiritual heir."

"Hollis," I said.

"Yes! Hollis," Mr. Greeley exclaimed. "That was his name. The lost son, he was..." But he did not finish the sentence and seemed abandoned by his intended statement, his eyes glazed with emotion. *Pinkie*, I remembered. *It is of his own dead son he thinks*. I watched the man's mind struggle like an overloaded horse and then catch on the strong legs of his own formidable brilliance to become lucid again.

"Perhaps that accounts for your eloquence on the platform, Mrs. Carter," Mr. Greeley said. "The influence of typesetting the words of Reverend Lyman's *Beacon*."

"I learned much from Reverend Lyman," I answered, "but the words I speak on the platform come from the spirits. They belong to no one living. Once I've finished speaking I do not even know what it is I have said."

Horace Greeley smiled and regarded me with eyes which were soft with fondness. "Then I must learn to blame the spirits for my editorials," he said, "as I am often accused of having no idea of what I have written."

Benjamin had arranged the séance table this night as he always did, with the theatricality he preferred, preparing the sitters with a sonorous voice, darkening the room, lighting a single candle, and advising the holding of hands. To me, these preparations were unnecessary, as I had seen spirits in bold sunlight and in the clamor of a railway station, but also knew these arrangements never failed to be appreciated by the sitters, who always sat nervously glancing at one another.

He'd placed Mrs. Greeley at my opposite with the best view of the proceedings, though whether to honor the lady or remind me of what he expected of my séance I could not tell. The wife of the most famous newspaperman of the day was a small woman, thin and fretful with an unsettling gaze. After being seated and regarding her fellow sitters blankly, Mrs. Greeley resumed staring at a remote and vacant place far beyond my right shoulder. A feature of my strange trade was its acquaintance with grief, and I in no way believed the lady to be a madwoman. Grief had odd effects, especially on those with no relief from it. Mr. Greeley's business insured he'd only so much time to devote to mourning a lost son. A lady like his wife would have day after empty day.

The spirits came like deer through the mist, reminding me of the deer in the autumn orchards of our farm in Cadytown whose cautious steps brought them out from the forest haze seeking dropped apples before the snows came. Altogether different than spirits who came at lectures, séance spirits approached tentatively, and I could never tell whether they were wary or curious as they appeared in my mind's eye. Like pieces of a lost memory slowly surfacing to view, becoming clear and wonderfully detailed, they stepped forth from either the murk or a glittering light, often bearing with them some object of secret significance. They carried many things: jewelry, letters, confessions, pets, dead children wrapped in shrouds—and clutched tightly. Occasionally they arrived empty-handed, puzzled or astonished, and sometimes seemed fearful, an event which perplexed me, as I wondered what could be fearsome after death.

Comprehending the voices of these dead was more difficult, even in the complete silence of a séance room. I had to enter another sound to be able to hear them and usually relied on the murmur of the audience, but if it were quiet listened to my own heartbeat or the ringing of my ears. Then came the sickening feeling of falling, just as in the moment of descending into sleep, but rather than snapping awake, I always felt panic while straining to hear the voices, afraid they might abandon me. But they never had, and arrived again as always, speaking in soft whispers as though I'd held a seashell to my ear and could indeed hear the sea.

"Hod," the elderly female spirit said, and I repeated this word which seemed to be a name. Mr. Greeley, who'd been seated to my left with his eyes shut tightly, shuffled his feet and straightened. "One of two of the same name, the spirit says," and knew from the rate of Mr. Greeley's breathing he recognized the spirit woman. I could see the lady spirit seated on a small trunk or valise, dressed in a bonnet of fifty years before. Her countenance was weary, but she seemed pleased to be able to speak.

"My mother," Mr. Greeley said, almost in a whisper. "There was an infant son who died before me also called Horace. I was always called Hod."

"I feel your mother has traveled much, as she shows me her trunk," I said. "She has often traveled without wishing to, and she is glad to be rested now. She is proud of you."

The old woman stood slowly and spoke again, and I passed on her words. "Heed contentment," your mother says, "for there is nothing beyond it."

"There is truth in it!" Mr. Greeley exclaimed suddenly, but as he spoke his mother disappeared, and I wondered if Mr. Greeley understood her words were less proverb than warning. In any case, I'd no time to ponder as my own heart quickened with what I next detected.

Faintly, in an evocative tug from my childhood, a scent emerged. The tallowy smell of ink and the stinging odor of linseed and machine oils. The printing shop in Hope Grove! Hollis was coming, after being gone for so many months. His appearance was often preceded with the scent of the room where I'd met him, and I relaxed into gladness. Hollis would help me. He always had.

Six years ago on a June day, I'd been sent to the Reverend Asher Lyman's house to fetch a copy of *The Beacon*. My father had written his first article for the paper and wanted one to send to a friend. Thus, I found myself for the first time pushing aside the heavy blanket nailed into the doorway between the Lyman homestead and the printing shop built on the rear of the house.

The shop was bright and bare-walled with many windows. Presses with big levers stood in the middle and a heavy stone-topped table with metal frames on its surface sat illuminated in a long slash of sunlight. Some pages hung from a line suspended from the beams of the ceiling.

These things I noticed in an instant, before my eyes fell and rested on the figure at the end of the room. Hollis Lyman I surmised, the only son of the Reverend, perhaps eighteen years old, recently back from the State Normal School in Bridgewater where he was studying to be a teacher.

He'd not heard me enter and stood with his back to me before a drawer filled with little compartments for printing type. In his left hand, he held a composing stick and his right hand fished in the case for the letter he sought, making a pleasant shuffling sound. He'd hung his jacket on a wall peg, and wore an apron looped around his neck and tied at the small of his back. Beneath the apron he wore a yellow waistcoat, an unusual color for a Hope Grove boy. Dark hair swept across his collar in a soft curl.

Hello, I meant to say, but "Hollis?" was the word that came out.

He did not startle, as I thought he might, but turned slowly, squinting a bit to see who'd spoken. He smiled at me. His face had a gentle look, an earnest lucidness which made me feel I'd been pleasantly observed. His teeth were nice too—none of them missing or dark.

"Well, hello Cora, how are you?" were the words he said, stepping toward me to close the distance between us.

"I've been sent by my father for a copy of *The Beacon*," I said. "Are you back from school for the summer?"

"Yes," he said brandishing the composing stick, "and straight to the printing works."

I'd never met Hollis before, I only knew him by sight and reputation, which was how I supposed he knew me. I liked his yellow vest and yearned to ask him about it. He looked so friendly I thought I might dare.

"Do all the boys in Bridgewater wear yellow waistcoats?"

"Do you like my coat? They wear all colors in Bridgewater. The fellows there are a bit more colorful than those here in Hope Grove, but my father says there is no place in a print shop for a yellow waistcoat."

Stepping upon the bottom rung of a wooden stool beside the stone-topped table, I leaned upon my elbows to look at his composing stick. I could see the letters he'd placed there, all sitting upside down and backward. "What are you typing?" I asked.

"It's called composing, Cora. I am composing type. Take a look for yourself."

Carefully, so I would not upset the letters, I slid the stick nearer myself. It was quite heavy for something so small. "We are ready to enter in good faith any plan of union." I read aloud.

Hollis' eyes widened. He seemed amazed at how fast I'd read the reversed letters of the sentence. "Good gracious, Cora, you did that perfectly! How about this?" Hollis reached across the table and pulled over one of the large metal frames filled edge to edge with hundreds of the metal letters.

I noted the familiar but backward headline. It was obviously the front page of *The Beacon* and I said so. "That's easy."

"But can you read the text in the columns?" Hollis asked.

I crept forward on my elbows and peered at the letters. They were tiny and differently shaped but seemed easy to read. "All correspondence to be sent post paid to Asher Lyman, Hope Grove, Mass," I read quickly. "Those are slanted letters," I added.

"Italics!" Hollis exclaimed. "They are used to stress key points. I've never seen a printer of any age read so quickly and accurately. Can you read more?'

I placed my finger in the center and began to read again. "God is a *Spirit*. What is the grand leading idea expressed in the word *spirit*? As understood with reference to God and intelligent beings, a spirit is an…" I came to a word I did not know, but tried to sound it out. "…incorp, incorpra…"

"*Incorporeal*," Hollis said to help me. "It means having no material body, like a ghost."

"Cora!" I heard my name but did not know who'd spoken it. Snatched back from my reverie to the reality of the séance table, I opened my eyes and looked around. The sitters were quiet, grasping the hands of their neighbors, all with closed eyes except for Benjamin who watched me stonily, the shivering uplight from the candle casting louring shadows on his forehead.

Closing my eyes again to concentrate, I was rewarded with the vision I most sought. Hollis appeared wearing the familiar yellow waistcoat of which his father disapproved but peculiar in the way all spirits were, as though what I was seeing was a mirrored reflection, a likeness both real and unreal. He had a young boy by the hand who I supposed was the Greeley's son, Pinkie.

"Hollis is here." I said aloud, and sighed in deep relief. "The Reverend Lyman's son. He has brought a young boy to us." Several chairs creaked and I had everyone's attention but dared not open my eyes and face Mrs. Greeley's longing.

The boy twisted and pulled on Hollis' hand but was held fast. There was no doubt the child had been a rascal and was probably spoiled.

"An impish child, perhaps six or seven years of age," I said.

I heard an indistinct groan or cry nearby, followed by rustling movements and sympathetic noises from those at the table.

"The boy is Arthur." Hollis said, but noticed the child stomped his feet and slapped at Hollis' legs in protest. "Mama knows my real name," the child suddenly said.

I repeated what I'd heard. "Hollis says the child is named Arthur, but the boy disagrees. He says his mama knows his real name."

A soft mewling sound arose, unmistakably from Mrs. Greeley, and my heart twisted in such pity I opened my eyes to regard the woman. Mrs. Greeley still clutched Benjamin's hand but had drawn the other from Judge Edmonds' grasp and covered her weeping eyes.

A small gleam to my left caught my eye, and I shifted my focus to Mr. Greeley's midriff. Here his watch chain lay, an arc of twisted letters with only two facing upward in legible fashion, the N and the O. No! Was it Hollis? It would be like him to speak using type—but what was wrong? What was no?

"Tell them Mama—tell them my real name," the child said, and Hollis pulled the boy's squirming form against himself holding him tightly in a cross-armed hug to quiet him. He then crouched down and whispered something in the child's ear. Smiling and holding his small hand to the side of his face, the boy whispered something in return to Hollis. *Hollis would have been a wonderful teacher*, I thought, but I'd no idea what words had passed between them.

"The boy is called *Pickie*," Hollis said, "A pet name his mother gave him."

"Pickie! Pickie! Pickie!" the boy shouted in joy, clapping his hands.

I was confused. Benjamin had told me the name *Pinkie* in the carriage. Was this what the warning of *no* meant? I was pausing too long, and I could feel Benjamin glowering at me. *Pickie* or *Pinkie*?

Both the boy and Hollis then disappeared, and though there was nothing before me but darkened air, I could feel Hollis had come closer. Six years ago Hollis had explained the word incorporeal, and now he himself had no material body, but his spirit was somehow regarding me with an unavoidable look of insistence. The eyes of two men were boring into me.

"You must choose, Cora." Hollis said gently.

I felt full of turmoil and terror and pierced with a shiver of shame. Yes, I must choose. Did one lie always have to lead to another? How long would it be before my life was a false tangle which could never be undone? I was tired of being party to Benjamin's habit of deceit. Hollis had never lied to me, and the information Benjamin gathered in advance was likely to be incorrect.

"Pickie!" I said, raising my chin in defiance. "Pickie is the name his beloved Mama gave him."

A great sob erupted from Mrs. Greeley like the rending of a hank of cloth, and all eyes at the table opened, each sitter drawn back from her as though in alarm. "Pickie...my son...my son," she cried, grasping her head in both hands.

Benjamin studied me for a mere second in puzzled disbelief but collected himself as he was not about to let a moment of drama go to waste. Using a trick of his breath he caused the candle at the center of the table to gutter and flame out, leaving each person in the circle in their own stunned and transfigured darkness.

Benjamin was whistling a few days later when he returned from being out. Each morning since the séance he'd risen unusually early and left our lodgings to haunt the newspaper stands hoping for news of victory. Returning thus, with a folded paper beneath his arm and a new malacca cane draped over his wrist, I knew he'd found it.

Earlier, I pretended to be asleep as he rustled through our trunks, cursing softly as he stubbed his toe on the washstand, then peering uncertainly over his shoulder to see if he'd awakened me. Through half-closed eyes I watched him, fastening his cuffs and collar, combing something new and bad-smelling through his thick dark hair. Down the stairs silently, then chirping a greeting to our hostess. I could imagine his nervous smile, agile and buttery with insincerity, convinced as he always was that his charm could erase the fact of our overstaying our welcome, convinced as he always was that his charm could do anything.

Once I was sure he was outside, I rose and stepped to the window to watch him go, crossing the street, his footsteps a trail of grey ovals in a scant wet snow which had fallen overnight. Searching through the trunk for my robe and seeking the upholstered chair in the corner of the room, I sat and drew my legs up beneath me. How hopeful I'd once been listening to Benjamin's plans for our future, plans which I now knew were beyond him, and depended solely on me. Nothing was as he promised. Nothing he said before our marriage was true. I sat for several hours in silence and self-reproach, observing the melting snow falling from the tree branches outside the window and the grainy light moving across the walls of the room.

"Let's go to Delmonico's," Benjamin said when he stepped back through the door, tossing the newspaper in my lap. "Soon you'll be so famous we won't be able to go anywhere."

It was the *Tribune*. Mr. Greeley had repaid the favor of the séance.

Shivering, I placed my eyes on my husband directly, hoping to see something, though not sure exactly what I was seeking, and certain I was not finding it. Even though I earned our living, Benjamin held the money, and I'd be obliged to ask if he'd remembered to send any to my Mother and baby brother Edward upstate. I'd have to persuade him to buy me a heavier coat. I had no choices of my own. I felt an ironic smile cross my face. I'd been such a fool.

Looking away, I fingered the tasseled cord which secured the robe and let the newspaper slide to the floor. Benjamin regarded me darkly, with an uncomfortable scrutiny.

"Aren't you going to read it?" he asked.

I knew what the newspaper said. New York was, quite literally at my feet. For all my new life had taken away from me, this is what it gave.

The Spiritual meeting on Tuesday evening was a large and attentive one. In recent months the speaker, Mrs. Cora Carter, has created an unusual sensation, and astonished audiences with her extempore lectures delivered through trance and which she attributes wholly to spirits. On Tuesday last she certainly performed wonderful things, whether she did it under the influences of higher intelligences or not. Those interested would profit from going to listen themselves, for hearing such reasoning and powerful eloquence without being convinced that there is a higher power connected with it, is at least worthy of a candid investigation.

—*New York Tribune* October 1857

Hollis

1857

After my death five years ago, I crossed a river. It was not the River Jordan or the River Styx as all the teachings led me to believe but just the Mill River in Hope Grove which had been my home. It halved the town in a long curve, sluggish in every season except freshet, barely quick enough to power the machinery which named it.

At the low end of the common pasture, where the river eddied, lay a small footbridge over which I watched my coffin trundle, borne on the shoulders of six of the townsmen stepping unsteadily through the snow. I had been dead for three days.

It is a strange business watching one's own funeral. Stranger still, the stoical acceptance with which I viewed it, as though I'd merely passed a restless night and woken to an ordinary morning, a morning bringing a hundred mourners, all of them following a box which contained...me. Me! Or what was left of my body after the typhoid fever had wrung the life away.

Typhoid. I'd heard the word at some point, proclaimed in the little chamber where I lay dying by some elder male voice, a doctor I assume. I have no clear memory of him, only of his voice, like God striking me down. In those hours, I was lost in sweat and senseless dreaming, but the word sobered my drifting mind and fixed my belief that I was done for. *Why me*, I had thought, when I just spent the week in the company of other fellows who were perfectly sound? We'd all eaten the same foods and passed through the same weather, in the same classrooms. Why indeed? Even now, even here, no clear answer has ever been given me.

What an odd untethered time were the days when my death was fresh. How strange it seemed then, what I now take for normal—the standing within my own absence, the walking with footsteps which make no sound. How simple to travel like a breeze to the forehead of one who mourned me. How strange to riffle their hair, know some of their thoughts, coil around their fingers and yet be unable to touch them. That lost sensation gone and so foreign I can barely recall it; though there are times now when I think I would welcome pain, just to see if I would recognize it, for it is both forgotten but still somehow felt.

As the son of a minister, I was familiar with spirits, and they are all here with me now, just as father's sermons promised they would be. There are others too—those he would never suspect—as the sorting of saints and scoundrels does not follow man's imagined plan. No, the world I now inhabit—this heaven, this Summerland, this feared and longed-for dwelling place—the Reverend Asher Lyman would have no near idea of it.

My funeral was that of a prince, for Hope Grove was to be the kingdom I inherited, the already faltering dream of my father, the king. For years, he'd hunched over his little desk and in his firm handwriting worked out his aspirations for an ideal practical Christian community. Residents who wished to live in Hope Grove had to forswear violence, voting, lawsuits and liquor. Just as in the plans he drew on foolscap sheets, the streets were laid out. There were stores, a post office, community gardens and machine shops, and a small factory which made parts for fabric looms. Neatly delineated squares represented plots for the modest homes of amicable and industrious families who would live in unity and equality. Our own home was on the corner of Peace and Hope Streets.

That February of 1852 was light on snow but savage as to cold, and the forlorn group who accompanied my coffin included my parents, now huddled beside the newly dug hole I was to be placed in. My father was especially stunned and stood with his winter muffler askew and dangling pitifully off one shoulder, grim and defeated for a hundred reasons.

I had been sent to the Normal School in Bridgewater to pursue an education in teaching; I was to learn the new methods, garner the latest ideas and return to Hope Grove to implement them. Father had already named his new school the Hope Grove Educational Institute and was at work on his plans for the organization and curriculum. I was to run the school and save the failing town's finances by teaching the local children and taking in boarding students who paid tuition.

Father always spoke of education in the most reverent terms, often in rousing words, as though giving one of his sermons. Using phrases like "fertile young minds" and the "spreading of wisdom", he presumed if all people only had an education they would understand, and once they understood they would believe, indeed agree, on a moral society. He saw it like the task of burning over a field. One blade of grass would light another, and the job would be done. He never foresaw human nature, or death, or my own reluctance.

Hope Grove would change, as I'd known all along, and father had to bury his aspirations along with me. Competition rather than cooperation would win out, and the old man's days would now shrivel and bow asunder. Hope, for all its virtue, has eyes that are bigger than its belly.

Gloved and veiled in black, my mother rearranged my father's disheveled muffler. Lucy is her name; she'd been an Emerson before her marriage and more of a lady than the duties of her life required of her. She'd certainly not been expecting the heavy physical labor of the communal living of Hope Grove but wielded the heavy crockery, the laundry and garden shovel without complaint. I realized then, as I watched her adjust the woolen strip around father's scrawny neck, that it was a performance they had enacted many times in myriad ways, which I'd witnessed without noticing. It was the women of Hope Grove who made the village work. While the men envisioned schools and by-laws, special diets and water cures, the wives farmed and loomed and tended the citizens. They even managed, mostly, to keep from fighting among themselves.

After mother replaced the muffler to her satisfaction she lifted her arms across her chest and began absentmindedly rubbing her forearms with her gloved hands. In the raw cold of the morning, the movement seemed to denote only the chill, but to me, it was a habitual gesture as familiar as her own face. In past kitchens of my boyhood, she would pause and straighten and clasp herself thus. I'd often wondered if her arms ached as I watched her rubbing them, but I'd never asked. Now I understood they did ache, not from hauling laundry or hoeing gardens, but from a lifetime of holding the string to her husband's kite.

The day of my funeral was not my first visit to the little cemetery. Oh no, I'd arrived for the first time the night before, drawn by the fire burning on my grave.

There is nothing that attracts a spirit like a flame, no jewel brighter or more welcome to our lifeless eyes. Strike a match in the dark and one of us will be there; each small candle in every corner of the world is attended. The lone fire of a travelers campsite will be watched by several of our band, and when a city burns, a host of us come to warm ourselves on the lost experience of being human. Wherever flames burn the living can be found, and the presence of a spirit is more likely around a glowing hearth than any lonely graveyard, but in my case the two were one and the same.

I died in February, and in normal practice, my coffin would be stored in the ice house to await spring. Unable to bear the thought of burying his future twice, my father ordered the ground in the cemetery to be thawed with a bonfire so it could be dug right away.

After the typhoid and the hands of the stranger who closed my eyes, I entered a place of darkness and warmth. Everywhere was silence and enveloping heat, so thick and comfortable I felt suspended in it, floating in a lambent radiance, surrounded by nothing I could recognize. How long I dwelt thus I could not have said, it could have been moments or years. I was simply there, and whether transfiguring, dissolving, healing or perishing, I did not care. Instead, with an inexplicable feeling of rapture I drifted away from myself.

How astonishing then was my perception of the flicker of light, and my immediate passage toward it. I have been told since that the newly-dead often visit their home place, and knew immediately my surroundings, the circumstance, the thawing of the frozen ground above my grave. Slipping through the bare branches of the treeline, I sat nearby the fellows tasked with the burning, Hiram Page and Dan Barton, stirring coals into showers of sparks and adding wood to the flames in the darkness.

Hiram, who stood this night with the collar of his jacket turned up, was to be dead himself two years hence. At the time, I knew him only as the work-shy father of the clever girl who sorted type with me in the press room. He'd not yet made the hungry pounce for fortune which would be his undoing. I have not encountered him since, if "encountered" can be considered the proper word. Yet, if I were to come across him now in some dark corner of our new and common universe dolefully begging forgiveness, I would not be surprised.

I listened for the men to make some mention of me, but they worked in silence, their movements brisk and even cheerful. This omission stung like a rebuke, but I realized then that remarkably, I somehow knew parts of their thoughts and could feel a measure of their own exertions. Their pants were wet through at the knees; Dan's hip was aching where it always did since he'd fallen on it years before. They both just wanted to get the job over and done with; the wood burned clean, the ashes swept aside and the hole dug. Another hour or two and they would be back across the pasture and asleep in their own beds. Neither man was thinking about me.

With a dizzying speed, I witnessed the glow of the graveyard fire break free from the ground and become a growing sphere of its own separateness, whirling toward me in utter silence with brilliant beams flashing from within it. Engulfment was inevitable, and I found I could travel these pathways of light to the human eyes at the end of them, who were also watching the fire from far away.

The first of these was Eben Bancroft, who'd looked up alarmed at the flames while forking hay in his barn, and then reminded himself *It's just the burn to thaw the grave for Lyman's boy*, before resuming his labors.

The next were eyes in the very house I'd lived in. My father in one room and my mother in another, pausing by separate windows to note the flames in the graveyard far across the pasture from their doorstep.

My father averted his eyes from the view and quailed at the

gnaw in his heart which signaled the loss of his life's labors. How ruthless he was soon to be in trying to retain these dreams I did not yet realize. My mother stood in a reverie of the past, remembering a day in a former decade when she was a young woman with an infant son and a life of promise.

None of these people were thinking of me, not the me who'd lived only days before. They were all either grateful not to be grieving or grieving a person who was a stranger, even to myself. In my amazing ability to travel so close to those I'd known, I still came to an ending, some kind of closed door. The thinnest barrier remained between us, translucent as clear air, but impervious all the same. There seemed to be no place my spirit could find an opening, no place I could go and be recognized.

As quickly as the light I then was, I entered the second floor window of a different house nearby. Through lenses of eyes that were blue like my own, I suddenly found the vanishing point, the very center of what I perceived, where everything I saw led. Never before in my life, if it could still be called my life, had I ever felt so up against the immensity of what seemed to be the universe. A leap of radiant euphoria and I heard the floorboards beneath me creak as I landed in the little chamber.

I could see myself now when I looked down the length of me, standing on the unfamiliar rag rug, but in the clothing I wore while working in the printing shop at home. Here were my normal trousers, my long apron tied around me, and incredibly, my yellow waistcoat! Bought on a spree with some other fellows from my class while in Boston last spring, it was my favorite article of clothing, one which I was sure lay folded in the drawer at my home, as my father would never have allowed my burial in it.

Alerted by the sound I'd made on the floor near her narrow bed, the small blue-eyed girl who'd stood in the window in her nightdress watching the fire turned toward me. I assumed she had been looking out for her father. Could she see me I wondered? She did not seem afraid, only curious as she proceeded toward me with an uncertain expression, coming closer than I would have wanted to allow, and then passing through me! An extraordinary shock possessed me, an odd diminishment as though I'd been struck a blow. My knees, if I had had them, would have buckled at this profound intrusion, for my being took on a trembling confusion as I felt her stepping through me. It was the last time I ever tangibly felt anything, and had I known it then, would have paid the sensation more mind, but I was not thinking of myself. I was watching the girl. She stopped at that moment, turned and raised her eyes upward as if she had somehow detected me.

"Hollis?" she questioned the emptiness, in a voice just like the first time she spoke to me.

That the one pair of eyes which saw me, the one person who could let me in was little Cora Page was really no surprise. I'd spent many hours working with her in the printing shop the last summer I was alive.

I can still recall the day she stepped through the door, and addressed me in a voice so pure and pretty it disquieted me. *Hollis* was the only word she'd said, but the tone always stayed with me.

That same summer day, Cora revealed to me her amazing facility for reading and identifying printing type, and by some unspoken agreement she began coming to the shop several times a week to work with me. Again and again she stopped by, only eleven years old, in short dresses and pinafores with girlish braids fastened together at the bottom in a little loop down her back. I set up a stool for her by the cabinet, tied an apron around her waist, and she sorted type, as fast and accurately as anyone I'd ever seen.

Of course, this all happened in the hours when my death was new. In the days when I had not yet learned how to walk without feet beneath me. Before I'd fully lost myself and become an inscrutable presence, a darting shape in the corner of someone's eye. Before I had spoken any words to Cora from a dead throat.

In church sermons of my youth, I'd always been told tales of God's plan. We were all parts of God's larger plan, small but necessary cogs on which other gears turned. This news put me in the mind, as I am sure it did others, that we were to face upcoming tests. Situations lay ahead like hidden snares which would require avoidance or escape. I did not understand then, as I do now, that God has plans for us even after our deaths. It is only now, these five years later, that I realize Cora and I have been walking side by side all along.

Why the two of us? Why were we, so far apart in age, fitted so well to converse with one another? God is just as silent about his plans now as when I was alive, so I can only use my memory to form an answer.

It was the end of summer in the printing shop on the last day we ever spoke in life, when Cora with childish wisdom coaxed a confession from me I'd never even allowed myself to hear.

The heat of the summer broke that day, and an early fall rain had swept in, soaking grass and soil which had been dry for a month. The calendar still said August, but the best of the season was behind us.

Humidity rose from the earth outside which was good for printing as it softened the paper; so, I had cracked the windows of the shop to take advantage, allowing indoors the spattering sound of the rain. Cora sat on her stool immersed in her type, and I remember the calm dignity of her face when deep in concentration. There was the rain, the clicking of the type and little else.

I looked beyond her shoulder and through the window. The rain was steady, and a bale of thick mist lay above the river in the far distance. The green of the trees was becoming muted, as though being rinsed out to make way for the bright dyes of autumn. "I'll be going back to Bridgewater in a week," I said.

"I know it," Cora answered quickly as though wishing the summer to stay.

We sat for a few minutes in silence, before I rose and crossed the room busying myself taking down the last handful of *The Beacon* from where it had been drying overhead. Cora had resumed her sorting, but I wanted to say something more to her, some sort of acknowledgment of how much I'd enjoyed working with her these months. In another year I would be her teacher, once I'd finished my term at Bridgewater and returned to Hope Grove to start the school my father dreamed of.

"You'll always be my best pupil," I said, smoothing the printed sheets and running my folding rule across them as I saw Cora smile.

"Did you always want to be a teacher?' she asked, striking at the concealed but salient point.

"It was more my father's idea," I replied, "but I seem suited to it."

"What would you do if it were only up to you?"

"I'd like to run a store." A dream I had built a thousand times but never told anyone.

"Like our store in Hope Grove?"

"Certainly not," I said with a snort, thinking of the dull, poky wares of our local mercantile. 'In my dream, I would sell only things people don't need. Games, novelties and lots of toys."

"Then I would rather shop in your store than attend your classroom," Cora said laughing, "Why don't you do it?"

"Father wants me to teach; he says it is the best profession."

"Why isn't he a teacher then?" Cora asked, a question I'd often asked myself.

"His own father disapproved. He didn't value books and education."

"What sort of work did his father do?"

I remember well my short stiff laugh. "He ran a store," I answered.

Just like that Cora learned my secret, pried it from me as deftly as a lawyer in a trial room, and worse, left it in the open for me to see. I remember sitting silently, folding and stacking the remainder of the papers in a thick pile. A large ball of twine rested on a spindle on our worktable, and I pulled out a length and knotted it around the papers, heaving them onto the mailing table. My father's printed words ready to go out again to the waiting world. Even that day, the old man was sitting in his study writing more words and dreaming more ideas and plans for me to follow.

Cora pushed away the form she'd finished and was wiping her fingers on a rag. The rain was still beating down, and I would shortly have to help her with the heavy drawer of type and lend her an umbrella for her walk home. As I circled the room closing the windows, a feeling of bitterness grew inside me. I tried to imagine my grandfather's store, but I'd never seen it. My father spoke of it only with contempt. A mere merchant who only cared for commerce. Asher Lyman had left home and become a minister in protest. On that day, I wondered if I was being encouraged to Bridgewater just to prove my father's point.

"I could work with you in your store," Cora said, removing her apron.

"Alas, I am the only son, Cora, and I am to embody my father's ideals." I said this while closing the last window with more force than I'd intended. Some rain had wet the windowsill and I wiped it aimlessly with the edge of my apron, unable to imagine any escape from the future which suddenly seemed like an iron cage around me. How odd it seemed at the time to be making this confession to a child, but now I know some of the strangest conversations are the most important and that those words were the first paragraphs in the long dialogue we have shared ever since.

"The thing of it is," I continued, "I am not always sure if I want to spend my life being my father's example."

Now I am waiting. Waiting to see if my recklessly blurted command at the séance has sundered Cora's life. Waiting to see what the action of choosing, which I so thoughtlessly urged, will reveal. I resented seeing Cora forced into a corner by her circumstances and that shiny-haired varlet of a husband. Still, what business had I in demanding such a thing, knowing as I did that Cora's troubles began because I spoke to her first?

My entry into her little chamber on the night my grave was burning was a refuge, and our conversations, thereafter, were filled with my descriptions of the joy of this world behind death's curtain, the amazing knowledge that life does not end and is more than just blind happenstance. Dead though I am, I still have the sense of moving among the living, and perhaps, have paid too scant a heed to the consequences of my spectral chatter.

Yet, I fear it just as likely I have been too quiet. Certainly I said nothing when Cora began to confess with childish amazement to her elders of the presence of my voice and my spirit, repeating to them my depictions of heaven which come to her in trance and dreams.

Silent too was I when my father recognized my own speaking tone in Cora's words and knew my spirit communication with her was real. With all the soft sawder of a seducer, he encouraged her trances, honed her eloquence, transcribed her nascent lectures for *The Beacon* and even placed her in his pulpit as a "new organism in the world of Spiritualism," planning all the while that through her he might regain me, and thus save Hope Grove. What his plan might do to Cora, he gave nary a thought.

Inevitably, Hiram Page intervened, but I was quiet then too. I ignored the glitter in his eye and reacted with no astonishment when he spirited—now there's a word—his daughter away from Hope Grove and the graspings of the Reverend Asher Lyman and placed Cora on the speaking platform at fifteen cents a head.

Yet, what could I have said? Cora was twelve years old, and I was neither her father nor her brother. I am not even alive.

So begins my own transcendence—if that is not too grand a word—the long inclination toward perfection which is the task of those both living and dead. I now believe I was wrong to try and re-direct Cora's life by forcing her choice at the seance and shall not attempt such intervention again. In this new world, I am privy to many mysteries, and though I can now see quite clearly the warp and the weft of the universe, I cannot always understand the raveled complexity of things, the large pattern of hidden significance. Just as when I was alive, there is a tangled picture I am too close to see, but cannot step back from and understand.

Cora

1857

I was wary of the gathering Benjamin had insisted we attend from the very start. Once arrived and seeing our destination was a shabby structure located in the Bowery and just two doors down from a raucous beer garden, I knew just what to expect.

The scene got no better once we were inside, escorted by two small and consumptive-looking young men who were possibly brothers. But for a single gasolier, the interior was lit to near blackness, and I was so intent on watching my step while shuffling along the gloomy foyer I barely realized when we entered the séance chamber.

Anticipating something bigger, we instead stepped into cramped quarters with the usual large table circled with chairs. The entire space was so closely surrounded with drapes of dark velvet they brushed the backsides of those being seated, an audience of larky couples most likely lured from the beer garden grounds.

Directly, two of these draperies parted with a flourish, revealing a portly impresario resting his meaty paws on the back of a tall chair in which a woman sat tightly bound in coils of stout rope. The woman was an elderly personage with a white chalked face, rouged cheeks and copious hair combed back and captured in an elaborate sparkling snood. She regarded her sitters with a glazed and indifferent gaze. A small candle burned on the table before her.

I'd never witness Benjamin so intent on another human being as he was on the stout showman, locking his eyes on the man's flushed and shiny face when he began his introduction. I even believe Benjamin might have been trying to memorize his words.

"This is not a magic act," the man bellowed, his lengthy mustaches jiggling across his overfilled shirtfront as his jaw worked up and down. "After years of careful study of the subject of Spiritualism, Mrs. Beckwith has mastered the secrets of spiritual manifestations and will present the most startling of them here for you tonight!"

All then watched intently as the two wan young men who'd been at the entrance slithered from behind the curtains and began to tie the wrists of Mrs. Beckwith to match the bondage of her body.

"All is veracity here and, to attest to these claims, Mrs Beckwith regularly submits to the restraint of her person prior to her demonstrations," the showman proclaimed. "The spirits in these rooms come direct from the heavens, not from some sham sleight of hand."

He disappeared behind the draperies then, presumably to count the fees of admission we'd paid upon our entry, and Mrs. Beckwith began to speak.

Hers was a voice flutey and faint, as though it hadn't much breath to ride on—doubtless because her corset and pinioned condition prevented little but a gasp of air.

She invoked a mother figure first, a gentle woman "gone too early to her reward" and killed by a pain in her chest. Half the sitters perked up at this, as half the dead population fits this category. Moments afterward, a heady and cloying perfume filled the room, and these same spectators gasped and murmured their recognition of the motherly fragrance, despite the unlikely fact any woman of their acquaintance ever carried such an aroma.

Then in a voice with more lilt than gurgle, a drowned sailor was described and made himself known by rocking and tilting the séance table as though in a storm at sea. This effect alarmed and disturbed the sitters, probably to prepare them for the "fond hands of ancestors" many then felt touching their shoulders, which heightened their jumpiness and caution.

The finale of the evening came as Mrs. Beckwith summoned the great-grandmother of the most overwrought of the sitters, a young woman who'd arrived at the séance already addled by beer garden beverages.

"Your beloved sends you a token my dear," Mrs. Beckwith squeaked, and a floral bouquet fell from the ceiling into the sobbing woman's lap. I admired the aim of whichever seedy son had flung the flowers with such accuracy in the darkness. Neither had appeared to have the strength to manage it.

At the last when the lights came up, Benjamin rushed to the foyer where I saw him pumping the impresario's hand. Meanwhile Mrs. Beckwith, released from her ties, remained on her throne selling her autograph on little cards. I took note as she stealthily slipped a few of the coins she received into her sparkly snood, an act I presume the fat man knew nothing about.

"That was marvelous!" Benjamin said, throwing himself into an armchair when we were back in our own rooms.

I gave him a doubting look. "It was a complete fraud."

"That goes without saying," he said rolling his eyes. "But did you notice how the audience lapped it up?"

"Most of them were drunk," I countered.

"Pfft, audiences usually are, but their tricks were very clever."

"You can't be serious," I said. "The deceit was obvious."

"Perhaps to you my dear, but you are a creature of the stage yourself. With that old witch trussed up in her hawsers and those cadaverous imps plying their hoax unseen behind the curtains, the sitters were convinced."

"It was awful."

Benjamin steepled his hands beneath his nose. "A bit artless perhaps, but imagine how much better we could be. Why we've a professional stage, with trap doors and flies!"

He was getting excited now, standing and flapping his arms about. "That Mrs. Beckwith had them weeping over a soggy bouquet. We could manifest a thousand things, lost objects, unexpected inheritances, even flying doves!"

I closed my eyes briefly and sighed. It was the same old argument we always had, and I knew now it was never going to change. "Why do you continue to insist me to lies and spectacle? Neither myself or my spirits can do such things."

"It is spectacle that sells tickets, you little fool," he spat out at me. "What is wrong with you, don't you want to succeed?"

Benjamin stood behind the armchair now with his hands gripping the back of it. His chin was raised in indignation and his chest puffed out. It was no great leap to imagine him as the fat impresario and myself as the woman tied to the chair. This was where my future led, and I had to find a way out.

For now though, I could only defy him. "I succeed well enough with the truth," I said.

"Close your eyes," I urged, as I placed my hands gently over Lydia's eyes. "It helps to have your eyes closed in order to see."

Lydia wrinkled her freckled nose. "It makes no sense," she replied.

"Most people say seeking the dead makes no sense."

We sat toe-to-toe on the sofa in the parlor at Irving Place, our bulky crinolines rustling around our legs, our tea cups set aside and the pot grown cold an hour before. The bland sunshine of early winter was extinguishing into a soft purple evening. This last of the day's light glimmered on the inlaid table, the silver tray and the mahogany bookcase which reached the full height of the tall ceiling.

"Still, I should like to see mother again, as father does," Lydia said.

"You must sit quietly," I instructed. "Most important is clearing your mind. Strive to think of nothing, and make an empty space for your mother to enter." I took Lydia's hands and continued, "Breathe deeply and count your breaths as they come and go. When you lose count is when you should be able to see or hear the spirits."

I continued holding Lydia's hands and regarded my new friend. Lydia's twenty-five years sat lightly upon her, and she seemed nearer my age rather than eight years elder. How pale and delicate she was sitting in complete stillness, lost in the act of counting! Her gentle face was neither plain nor pretty, but her grace and bearing were striking and her eyes a remarkable pallid blue, the color of watered ink.

With Lydia's long tapering fingers nestled in my palms, the warmth of them seemed a symbol of their owner's heart. The fine townhouse was one thing, but it was impossible for me not to see the goodness of the family who lived within. Since the night of the séance with the Greeley's, my friendship with Judge Edmonds and his daughter had grown far beyond what I'd come to expect in my relations with people. For a city family of some rank, the Edmonds' nonetheless held radical beliefs which reminded me of my former neighbors from Hope Grove. Lydia's family were supporters of women's rights and attended the national conventions in Worcester. They also promoted the abolition of slavery and followed the custom of the free produce movement, allowing no slave-produced goods in their home. I was certain the sugar in the tea I'd drunk that afternoon was bought from the West Indies, where no slave had labored to harvest it.

Our sympathies were so in tune, and we all talked so pleasurably together, I longed for the hours spent at Irving Place, and as Benjamin approved of my mingling with those people he called "select," I knew he encouraged my time here.

So, once or twice a week, Benjamin dropped me at the doorstep before he was off on what he called his "rounds," and I slipped across the threshold into this place of peace. Here was virtue, permanence, order, and perhaps even a bit of dullness, but it seemed a heaven to me compared to the erratic nature of my own life: different lecture halls and boarding houses each week, scanty meals and sometimes none at all. This and the incessant fear, which I tried to push to the back of my mind, that something Benjamin might do on one of his "rounds" would require us to flee with just the clothes on our backs.

"It's no use," Lydia said, releasing my grip and dropping her hands into her lap in defeat. "I haven't your gift."

"The spirits come as they please. You cannot will them." I said this to console Lydia but had known all along there were no spirits in the room today. Over time, I learned to sense their presence and could feel them, the small change in the weight of the air that gave them away.

“Father says he speaks with mother nearly every night. He says she comes and sits on the edge of his bed. Do you believe that Cora?”

“Yes, of course. Spirits often come to us where we are comfortable. You know my first spirit, Hollis, came to me outside a hen house. Perhaps you should ask your mother to visit when you are in bed, too.”

“I’d be too frightened to try alone.” Lydia said.

I shook my head. “You know your mother would never hurt you. Don’t let fear hold you back. You must try again another day.”

I knew what vexed Lydia. She was the youngest daughter, and the only one living at home when her mother died four years ago. Since then, Lydia was her father’s constant companion, but a change had arrived in the person of Mr. George Austin, Esq., who appeared quite often at the front door with his hat in his hand and his hair carefully combed. He was a young lawyer working in the state offices and a favorite of the Judge. It was clear what Lydia wanted to talk over with her mother.

“Why do you think mother speaks with father, but not to me?” Lydia asked, the remarkable eyes marked with a sad and puzzled curiosity.

“Perhaps, as a parted husband and wife, they have much to talk over,” I suggested but could not resist reaching out to tug one of Lydia’s coiled plaits and smile. “Or perhaps, as far as a frequent visitor is concerned, your mother is telling your father what you don’t dare tell him yourself.”

Lydia looked down at her lap, her face coloring. “Don’t tease me so,” she said.

We both grew quiet and shifted back into the cushions of the sofa, each retreating to the thoughtfulness of our circumstance. Lydia was no doubt ruminating on George Austin, but I was allowing myself the pleasure of the mood, the warmth of the twilit room resting upon me like a blanket. Everything I did not have lay before me, a home, a fire, a supper, and…dare I say it…a sister.

I knew it would be foolhardy to think Lydia’s goodness made her blind. I assumed she could see my own situation as well as I saw hers, and I'd finally come to a point where I could ignore my shame and confide in her.

The Bowery séance had reset my view. I suggested to Benjamin we might sell my autograph at lectures. Not to be outdone, he brought me to Mr. Brady's photographic studio on Broadway and had my photograph made. Now after every séance, I was tasked with selling both my image and my autograph, just as I'd hoped. Business was brisk enough. Lovey and Benjamin had to assist in the selling too, and following Mrs. Beckwith's sly lead, several half-dollars found their way into my own boots each evening.

I had a cache of them on this day, sewn into a pouch made from the cotton rags I used for my monthlies, where I was certain Benjamin would never stumble upon them. Yet they were accumulating, and I was fearful of discovery.

I drew the pouch out and held it toward my friend. "Lydia," I ventured slowly, "Would you keep these for me? I fear leaving them unguarded in boarding house rooms."

Lydia took the heavy parcel and judged the weight of it in her hands. She fixed those pale eyes on me, and I relaxed in relief as I saw a complete understanding in them.

"Of course," was all she said, crossing the room to place the pouch inside her desk and returning to me on the sofa, where we sat for some minutes in silence.

"Is it so really different, being married?" Lydia finally asked.

"Yes, it is different."

"Was he very handsome? Lydia asked.

"I suppose that is one of the reasons I married him."

"Oh, no, I'm sorry. I didn't mean Mr. Carter, your husband. I meant the spirit who visited you first at the hen house. You knew him before he died, yes?"

"Hollis? Goodness!" This question was unexpected. "I don't know whether he was handsome or not. I was just a little girl." Closing my eyes, I tried to picture him as he appeared on the first day of our friendship. "His smile was nice."

* * *

Even though I now understand miracles are commonplace for those with the eyes to see them, the day I first saw Hollis' spirit remains singular. It was the last day of a barely recalled stillness, a day in which worlds bled into one another, and the flat silence of my childhood was interrupted by the first of many voices.

The wind was blowing from the southwest that first mild day of March 1852. I was out early in the hen house, shoveling out the dirty bedding and heaping new wood shavings inside. Freed from their confinement, the chickens were eager to get outdoors, flapping their wings and pecking at the bare ground. The coop had a long row of windows, and, now the days were growing longer, there were more eggs to be found in the nest boxes. I moved down the rows, placing them carefully in a basket.

A fluttering sound came, and the graze of a small wing brushed against my shoulder. One of the banty hens I thought, startled from its nest, but my eye caught a blue flash and heard another battering noise in the rafters. Turning toward the sound, I watched as a small bird landed in the mound of shavings and sunk within it. Pouncing on the bird with my apron as a net, I trapped it within the folds of the cloth. Lifting and parting the apron, the tiny head appeared. I held its body firmly, brushing away the sawdust from its feathers. I'd seen bluebirds, but never this close. He was as bright as a cornflower and his ruddy chest and dark eyes almost as notable. The pretty bird struggled in my grasp, and I decided to release it. I could feel its heartbeat against my fingertips and its moving feet beneath the fabric. The bird dashed away when I shook it out the open door, moving with great speed toward an exposed ledge in the distant field.

It was almost a spring day, but the earth had not yet let go of winter. The sun of the early morning had changed to a sky concealed in soft shifting clouds. The field was a hazy grey but for the particular spot where the bird had flown, which glowed in a single ray of radiance broken through a patch of cloud. A dash of brilliant blue in the dry grass near the ledge made me think the bird landed again, and feeling I wanted to see it one more time, I lifted my skirt hem and ran toward the color.

Shadows fluttered in the beam of sunlight, and I slowed my run to a stalking pace, hoping not to startle the pretty blue creature.

"It is your gift, Cora.' Hollis said, in a whisper not so different from the mild wind, as my attention veered from the bird to the familiar voice. For it was Hollis, seated on the rough stone of the ledge in the beam of sunlight, smiling at me!

Stopping still, I released my skirt and let my hands fall to my sides, trying to make sense of the sight before me.

Just as when I first met him he appeared, in his rolled shirtsleeves and yellow waistcoat, but how could this be as I'd seen him in a coffin just over a month ago? It passed through my mind that some other boy had been buried in the coffin, but his were not clothes for the outdoors, and this was not a person who was real.

He was not human, but he was not frightening and he sat casually, with his knees pulled up and his arms draped across them, his back resting against the ledge which rose higher behind him. He held a small stone in his hands which he turned over and over.

Watching him handle the stone, I wondered whether there was fidgeting in heaven but could say nothing in reply to him, as I was stunned into muteness. I stepped closer as though a smaller distance would give the encounter some sense. The glimmer rising from the grass created a strange nimbus which surrounded us, a glowing corona making an enclosing chamber.

"It is your gift," Hollis repeated.

I could not see Hollis talking. His only movement was the worrying of the stone. His lips made no motion, but I heard his words in my head nonetheless.

I was confused, but it was true. Hollis was not really talking, just as I knew he was not really sitting on the ledge. The chickens had wandered away from the hen house and were moving around us. They scratched and searched the ground as usual. If Hollis were really seated before me, they would not come that close.

As if Hollis read my mind, he cast the stone he'd been handling among them. The chickens did not scatter, and when my eyes searched the ground, there was no stone.

The hair on my nape rose, and I felt the urge to run; but fear freed my voice from its silence, and I betrayed my apprehension only by stepping back one pace. "Are you a ghost then?" I asked, almost in defiance.

Hollis had returned to his state of motionlessness, with only the calm smile on his face.

"Incorporeal," he said. "Do you remember the word, the day you found it in the type?"

"Having no material body." I replied.

"Your gift is your ability to see and hear me, Cora. No one else can."

His words entered my mind as though he were whispering, just as if we were conversing, but I knew I stood alone in silence where nothing but wind and peeping chickens stirred. Looking upward to the odd sunbeam which fell in radiance around us, I felt a strange knowledge from the past shifting within me, and it seemed Hollis and I had been talking about things for many lifetimes—the eternity of our discussions beyond counting, and just outside the boundary of recalling—as though I had eavesdropped upon our sentences and just caught a few words.

"Why?" I cried. "Why only me?"

But he did not answer, and as his face began to grow vague, I realized he was disappearing. "Listen for me, Cora."

I was silent but for the sound of some incoherent emotion. I wanted to reach out and hold on, but to what?

On that day, I did not yet feel older, or transformed or profoundly changed. I was still just a young girl in a brown dress and apron, standing alone with a flock of chickens in a muddy field.

In the parlor at Irving Place, Lydia watched me with wide, believing eyes. "I would have been terrified."

"It may seem so, but it is not frightening," I replied. "When your mother comes to you in spirit it will be just as we are now, sitting together and talking."

Lydia smiled, her smile like an open door, warm and yielding, and I felt something twist in my stomach. Life is such a mystery, that we each possess a magic the other feels without. Why is it some singularities keep us apart while others bind us together?

"What of your other spirits? Tell me about them." said Lydia.

"There is a young man and an elderly woman, but unlike Hollis, I do not know them, although the woman seems familiar, like I've seen her before."

"Maybe she is an ancestor from long ago?" offered Lydia.

"I don't think so," I said, "as she speaks with a French accent and dresses from our own time. She seems like a farm woman. I smell pipe tobacco whenever she appears, which I also cannot account for. The young man is a complete mystery. He never comes into focus and does not speak, but his presence is strong. I think he was a soldier, or someone very brave. He stands just at the corner of my eye, almost guarding me. I feel protected."

"And comforted?" Lydia asked.

"Yes, very much so. The old woman even touches my hair and kisses the top of my head."

"Isn't that strange? Lydia asked looking doubtful.

"It's all strange," I replied.

And so it was, as I strode the boards of the stage at Dodsworth's Hall stepping along the limelights and raising my palms to the audience before me, waiting for the rustle of their movement and the muffled hum of the sound inside my head.

I stood entirely still, my mind remote and detached, but my body taut and shivery with sweat already prickling between my shoulder blades and underarms, where Lovey had sewn pads to keep my gown from staining.

No longer did I choose a man from the audience. That had been Benjamin's idea, and I was wise to it now. Instead I concentrated on the patterns of light gathering in my vision and the rushing of something electric passing through me, like a frail lightning bolt, crackling from the top of my head to my toes and pulling me away from consciousness. In explaining my gift to myself, I believe I must possess some form of electric transmission, like a machine through which come the voices of spirits, just as men of science use the telegraph to pull words from thin air.

Immediately came the terrible falling sensation as I plunged—and there was no other word for it—into the great river of spirit voices. This was no cautious, hesitant visit from a séance spirit coaxed from their gentle and somnolent space, but a deafening din, a raucous babble. As though wading in the waters of a true torrent, I felt the debris of a thousand souls rushing past me, voices chattering, raving, some in foreign tones and others in an English spoken from a time so ancient I could not fully understand it. Men, women, children, all garrulous, incessant and jostling to be heard.

The presence of this Babel of thousands was so palpable it sometimes felt as if I might be standing among them—indeed, I often feared I was,—but pressing against their mighty insistence, I forced myself to hear just a single one.

Before my even stepping to the stage, Benjamin always announced to the audience the identity of the spirit I was to contact. It was almost always a "man of local esteem who has passed to the spirit realm," but sometimes, if he deemed the listeners "rubes," he would tell them the departed personage was George Washington or some other famous worthy. In either case, this was the lie, the falsehood told nearly every night.

In reality, the voice was whatever clear and articulate expression I could grasp from the cacophony besieging me. Half the time the "man of local esteem" was a woman, but this was part of the lie I was willing to live with, for there is no reason a woman from the spirit world would not have just as important a message to impart as that of a man.

From this teeming hoard of strangers, I snatched a single voice, and once my mind had attached to it, all other sound fell away, even the organ music disappeared, and I became the receptacle of another human soul. This was the trance state, and the words of this other soul came from my mouth in my voice, without a trace of hesitation.

"*Across the bridge of death, into the region of our spiritual existences, we invite you to wander. Your departed loved ones are here. Their lives are fashioned as your own, of complicated wishes and desires, of impulses born of the spirit. They have made for themselves the habitations which they enter here. Their lives have been clothed and adorned with their own wishes and aspirations. They have been received by kindred spirits into habitations prepared for their reception by those who have loved and gone before them....*"

Simultaneous with speaking the spirit's words, I waited, suspended in the air of this other world which was both strange and familiar. Light blazed beneath my eyelids, I could see the words I was saying while speaking them, as though reading them in a book. Invariably engulfed in a slow annihilation, lost in a state of both being and not being myself, until the sound grew more distant, weary and faded.

"*...and these souls in their stages, in groups or circles, like spheres within spheres, passing one above the other, are your disembodied dear ones, each striving in some way to minister to some other soul, and thus point out the pathway that leads to those heights where the brightness is too intense and the glory too surpassing for mortal vision to behold!*"

Impossible to describe the jolt at the ending, like being thrown down from somewhere above in the flies and barely landing on one's feet or being coughed up by some demon and sent staggering back to the platform floor. At this moment I often wondered how long I would be able to endure the great rending of my person being wrought by these trances. Two years? Five? Yet the audience suspected nothing. To them, I appeared as calm and deliberate as a sleepwalker, stepping backward from the apron of the stage and letting my arms fall slowly to my sides. Then I became aware of an imperceptible sound, the same sound heard an hour earlier, just before beginning to speak, drawn out like a whisper then followed by a roar. Applause and cheering, seats groaning with the weight of people rising from them, men with canes and walking sticks drumming them on the wooden floor.

The evening had been another success. Once again, I'd somehow entered the spirit world and brought forth a voice which pleased the people and gave them the hope and comfort of knowing their loved ones were in God's heaven. The people had their solace, and with the coins I was secreting away, I would someday have my safety.

Benjamin
1857

It was her feet I noticed first—yes her feet—to all you fellows who cut me a knowing grin when presented with her youth and my old age, though I am not so very old, just thirty-four this birthday. Still, this makes me more than twice Cora's age, and whenever we walk out, no one is goggling at me.

The fateful setting was Hemlock Hall, a building whose appearance can be imagined from the euphonious name it bears. The structure of rough bark timbers had sprung up on the site of one of the summer camp-meetings common wherever a stream babbled in the bucolic groves of western New York state. Camp-meeting devotees have such a nature impulse. It makes them feel closer to Eden, I suppose.

At any rate, I frequented these gatherings of the gullible in those years, finding them ideal places in which to mingle and distribute my cards hoping to lure patients to my rooms back in Buffalo. "Doctor Benjamin Chandler Carter, Physician," the cards proclaimed. Five small words and none of them true.

"Friends of Human Progress," the Hemlock Hall flock called themselves, and they were of the usual stripe. Free thinkers, crank radicals, and lapsed Quakers of the Hicksite bent. They arrived in wagons or on the new railroad; prison reformers, abolitionists, and the drab doves of the women's rights clubs, all eager to hear the assembled lecturers. Only the few free-love couples stood out, or at least to my practiced eye. The men with gilded buttons and the women fluttering elaborate fans, their eyes roving for others of their kind. These women made good patients for me, quite willing to submit to my physician's fondling hands.

All these were assembled, sweating and squirming on their hard benches, before the raised platform festooned with bunting and wildflowers where sat my darling girl. The youngest she was amidst that gang too, positioned in one of five throne-like chairs with the others that August day.

To her left sat the star of the show, a grim-faced uncle with a shock of black and grey hair standing starkly back from his forehead. An emancipation darky no doubt, with eyes as bright as a razor. From his perch, he regarded the audience with a baleful gaze that almost approached rebuke. He looked as though he'd been pleading his cause for a good many years and was tired of explaining himself. In his place I might feel the same, I suppose.

To her right were a more prosaic pair, one of the sapphic sisters of suffragism, high collared and decorously dewlapped, and a lath-thin mesmerist with a greasy quiff combed over his balding head. How well I knew all his tricks! I even spotted the girl he'd planted in the audience for his upcoming demonstration. A shopworn Aphrodite fifth row back, wearing a red silk rose pinned to her plunging neckline, slumping drowsily in her seat and scratching at a bug bite on her forearm. I don't know why I noticed her especially, but I have been acquainted with all sorts of dubious people and like to make sure I can still take their measure. I smiled at her, as I must always keep in practice.

Still, my attention kept returning to the girl on the platform and her pretty little feet and would have stayed there but for the amazing personage that was the current speaker.

She stumped across the stage, setting the boards to groaning, an elderly and giant negress, an Amazon of her race, truculent and probably disputatious. I certainly would not want to be tasked with preventing her from an objective. A head taller than me with broad pink-palmed hands which she swept through the air, she kept up a rambling oratory which resembled a berating and joke-filled sermon. Those who allowed themselves were laughing, and the others hardly knew what to make of her. Hag-ugly and hell-bent on her message, one almost expected to see casualties writhing and bleeding in her wake, but instead, there were smiles. *Sojourner Truth* she was called, a stage name surely, but I had to credit her. Camp-meetings were never known for their humor, and she absolutely knew how to work a crowd.

There was something else about her too, which prodded at my hardened heart. Miss Truth, and surely she must be a Miss— had no accent of the plantation south. No drawl bred below the Mason-Dixon line came from her mouth, but rather the hacked and harsh consonants of the old Dutch tongue. I heard Valatie in her words. Valatie, of all places. But I am getting ahead of my story.

Cora's feet, ah yes.

How beautiful she was, alone in youth and innocence at Hemlock Hall. For there was no doubt of her innocence, or in a devil like myself recognizing it, as innocence can still undo me.

The chair in which she sat was too tall for her, so she held the toes of her little white boots balanced on their tips, and as she curled her ankles a lascivious shudder ran through me. When she stood to speak, my stomach plunged heavily to my lower regions. She hesitated a moment, glancing briefly over her shoulder to the platform side, searching for her minder probably, or whoever managed her, oh lucky man he!

Her voice was supple and persuasive, deep for a young girl, and delivered with upraised eyes in the attitude of trance, so beguiling to those of us who think in terms of seizing and possessing. The words themselves were platitudes. It is perhaps needless for me to admit I never believe anything I hear, but the sight of her was made to quicken any pulse.

A head of copious blonde ringlets bounced happily on her shoulders as she stood, tense and poised, bathed in her display of vague dreaminess, of delicious submission to whatever muse she served. Her hands dipped and fluttered and as her words poured forth; her near-perfect form insisted itself beneath her chaste and formless dress.

In a trance myself I was, watching her with a ravening gaze until I returned to my senses and turned my eyes away, alarmed I might be observed by the audience for already defiling her. Yet, when I glanced around me, I was likewise astonished. In addition to my own attention, my little Cora was the object of hundreds of prurient stares.

Now, I would not expect her charms to be overlooked by the free-love males in attendance, but what of the other men, what explained their lecherous leers? There they sat, nearly panting and licking their lips, the soft-hearted sympathizers and equality idealists, even the pure-thinking preachers. Cullions, all of them. All of us, I mean.

Later on, when Cora fell so haplessly, so providentially, into my eager hands, I could barely believe my luck. Fate shifted in the strange ways only it can master, and I became Cora's minder, charged with managing her engagements, her fees and audiences. Since then, I have stressed to her the value of keeping these adoring men as her advocates and taught her to choose one during each lecture to keep her eyes on, to be her mark, if you will. Thus far, the results have been gratifying, and I am amazed fate has gifted me with so willing an accomplice. I would never have imagined it that day at Hemlock Hall. Yet, I knew then exactly what I was seeing. An enchantress, just fifteen-years old, and worth a fortune.

"You must go forth, Arie."

My father spoke this way, in the throaty and dissonant locution of the New York Dutch. It was the same un-charming sound which I'd heard in the palaver of Sojourner Truth at Hemlock Hall, the lingua franca of Valatie, the town where I was born.

I'd wondered about her then, the oddness of a Dutch-accented negress, but supposed she'd been one of the slaves of the old patroon families in the days before New York abolished the custom. I knew nothing about that. On our starveling Hudson Valley farm, my family pushed its own plows.

Wynkoop was my surname, Arie Wynkoop the inharmonious whole. I have since learned the name means wine cup, a more than fitting moniker for my father, who'd been in his own cups regularly since my mother died.

“I’ve no money to keep you,” the old man said, his bleary eyes betraying no hint of whether this admission troubled him. I knew it was probably true. Since the panic earlier that year of 1837, no one had any money on the local farms. Crop prices had crashed, and many banks had closed their doors.

I had an elder brother, a simple-minded brute nearly as large as Miss Truth. He could eat like two men, but work like four, and since all my father’s suggestions I take up an outside job had come to naught, I knew my living situation was precarious.

So after the last hay was in, I was bundled off. My father drove me in his wagon to the stage in Valatie, where he purchased a one-way passage to Albany. I had a change of clothing, a wedge of cheese and an apple in my traveling sack. I felt fortunate my father had also given me a silver dollar to take along, and considered this the only sign he might have a sliver of sorrow in parting with me.

I climbed aboard the stage, and while passing my sack to me, he spoke for the first time since we’d left the farm. “The ticket can be forgotten, but I expect that dollar to come back to me when you’re able,” he said, and turned away.

There was no one to say goodbye to. My witless brother was left leering and waving back at the farm, and my father never turned around again as the stage and I left town.

Fourteen years earlier my mother died giving birth to me, and I suppose the old man had finally avenged the killing.

My eyes prickled and throat tightened, and I might have started sniveling if it had not been for my reluctance to let others in the stage witness it. By the time we were a few miles out my sorrow was replaced by anger, and I got down at the next stop in Schodack. Wheedling back part of my half-dime fare was probably the first act of flummery in my life. I could walk to Albany myself and save the money.

That my choice of walking would necessitate sleeping overnight in the open air gave no pause to my youthful bravado. I followed the Post Road a few miles and when dusk began deepening decided the stony corner of an old cellar hole I spotted would be a suitable place to pass the night.

There I sat against the crumbling walls of what once had been a dwelling and rested while my doubt returned. I did not know what I was going to do, poised between panic and joy, floating in a sort of euphoric misery.

Overhead, a great bowl of stars appeared and with my hands clasped behind my head and lying against my traveling sack, I regarded them; the speckled and sparkling arc of all that presumably was. Giddy and dizzy, I was sure I could feel the very turning of the earth.

Cora has since told me when she felt lost as a youth her spirits came to comfort her. Such stories are claptrap, of course, for cowering in that cellar hole any spirits hovering over me were resolutely tight-lipped. It was that night when I started to go bad, I suppose. No one spoke to me, and with the world so rapidly turning, all I felt I could do was try to hang on.

How easy it is to sleep in such a state. A crowded calendar of small worries can cause a man to walk the night, but weigh him down with real distress, and he will sleep like the dead. For a brief moment there had been the resplendent stars and the earth groaning beneath me, but a wiser young man would have noticed the turning of the weather before the turning of the earth. I fell asleep, and after what seemed just moments, woke again with rain on my face and water soaking into the seat of my trousers.

Now I sometimes wonder what difference it would have made if it hadn't rained that night. Such pondering leads to relentless speculation. How many futures are altered simply by avoiding the rain or any minor obstacle? The bobbing and wind-tossed futility of life. It is really too awful to contemplate.

How dark it was that dismal night! I gathered my sodden traveling sack and scrambled back to the road straining to see anything in the murk. A thick forest lay a quarter mile off, and I ran for it, slowing only when I was startled to see a tethered horse and bow-roofed wagon pulled to the verge and sheltering under the same trees. I'd not heard any such vehicle pass earlier. The horse snorted as I approached, and the springs of the wagon creaked as someone inside it moved about, but I decided to risk it. I crawled beneath the dry underside of the rig. A few hours sleeping here and I'd be gone, with no one the wiser.

Dr. Titus Meacham poked me hard with the toe of his boot. "What do you think you are doing under my wagon?" he snarled.

That he was standing over me with a club was no surprise, but otherwise, he cut a risible figure looming in the clear dawn. Clothed as he was in flannel drawers and a long silk coat embroidered with moons and stars, he resembled some sort of disheveled pasha.

My eyes were gummed with sleep and my throat too dry to bring up any words, but I rolled out from under the rig and took grateful note as his hand relaxed on his weapon. "I thought you were a pile of rags, boy."

"I am walking to Albany," I said, knowing it was at least ten miles away.

"You aren't walking," he replied.

Judging that humility would serve me best, I replied in a feigned tone of shame. "I took shelter last night. I'm sorry, if I startled you."

Dr. Meacham sighed, ran his hand through his tousled mop of wildly hennaed hair and tossed his club beneath the seat of his wagon. "There's always some damn trouble on the roads," he grumbled, as he stomped behind the vehicle and began to take a loud piss.

I ached to do the same but feared turning my back to the man, so instead, cautiously approached his horse and stroked its muzzle. The gelding stood with great dignity, regarding me with the same doleful eye as his master.

I then got a good look at doctor's wagon. It was painted a bright yellow, with doors, drawers and cubbyholes. Elaborate curlicue brushstrokes adorned nearly every angle. "*Dr. Meacham's Celebrated Medicines—Tonics and Elixirs for all Ailments of Humans and Animals—Blood, Liver, Kidney Panacea—Restores Youth*"

"That's Ptolemy," Dr. Meacham said, returning from his toilet, tugging at his drawers, buttoning his flies and scratching. He reached for the bucket hanging from the wagon fender and passed it to me, rattling its bail for emphasis. "There's a stream a quarter mile ahead of us on the left."

When I returned, Dr. Meacham had fully dressed and shaved himself, but nonetheless rinsed his hands and face with the water I'd brought, and gave the remainder to Ptolemy. The remarkable coat with the moons and stars was gone, and he looked a prosperous gentleman in his cutaway jacket and foulard cravat as he latched the wagon's back doors. "*Phantasmagorical Wonders*" and "*Magnetic Healing*" were the words painted there.

Of course I knew he was wily and unscrupulous, but I got in the front seat with him anyway.

He spoke little on the journey, treating me with a watchful friendliness. Once in Albany, he bade me to help him load his supplies, which were stored in a warehouse on the riverfront. I'd never seen the city before, never seen so much bustle and commerce, but tried to disguise my goggling lest I appear the rube I was.

"I don't work the cities," he said as I passed him the last of his clanking crates which seemed filled with bottles. "That would be asking for trouble. I load here and move on." Stepping down from the wagon he shook my hand. "I don't think I caught your name boy, back there on the road."

Of course he'd not caught it because I hadn't given it. "Benjamin," I replied. I'd always coveted the name as it seemed so—so English.

"Is there another one behind that?" the doctor asked.

I'd not expected this and glanced around the area in panic. *Briggs & Hazen Haulers and Carters* the sign on the warehouse said. *Herrick Chandlers* was painted on the building opposite.

"Benjamin Chandler Carter," I answered, prideful of my quick thinking.

Dr. Meacham eyed me narrowly. "That's a long name for a boy who's never been west of the river."

He had me. I'd never been west of the river before. I did not know then as I know now it was part of Dr. Meacham's job to spot weakness in others, or how important it is to recognize the crack of dupery in every person so you can enter it and dupe them first. I also understood, probably with the part of myself which had grown bad since my father put me on the stagecoach, that Dr. Meacham's statement was a challenge.

"Until today," I countered. "I'm west of the river now."

Titus Meacham's face registered a slight smirk, and his eye slid over me with appraising speculation. He stood quietly, drawing a finger back and forth across his chin. "John I'll call you then, John Cheese."

Jan Cheese, Yan-kees. I recognized the slur on my Dutch farmer antecedents, but let it pass. As far as I was concerned Arie Wynkoop was dead.

"Besides," Titus Meacham said, "in our line of work real names can be a liability."

For the next two years I slept under that wagon and occasionally in it, if the weather was particularly inclement. Titus and I went from town to town all over the eastern states, and I watched with awe and admiration as he palmed coins, shortchanged customers, and kept up his improvised monologue of mendacity.

His voice was large and dexterous as he pranced on his makeshift stage with all the strut and glitter of the mountebank. It began in lower octaves as he transported his audience to the jungles of India where he gathered rare herbs for his elixir. It moved to a higher pitch as he bartered for bark and berries in the Amazon, and rose to a piping climax as he rolled up a sleeve and displayed the razor-straight scar on his forearm he'd told me he received from a sharp-edged barrel hoop. Yet, before his wide-eyed onlookers, it became a graze from a poisoned arrow as he pursued the coveted Shia root in Java and cured with the very medicine he was purveying.

Eventually, his voice would soften to a sympathetic purr as he questioned his purchasers of their ailments. Cancer to croup, the contents of one of Dr. Titus Meacham's bottles promised mysteries and miracles.

It was an odious elixir, as I knew from mixing it myself. We brewed it on off-days, pulled over in some out of the way spot. Grain alcohol and laudanum were the primary ingredients, occasionally flavored with sarsaparilla, but Titus had an aversion to bottling anything that tasted good, convinced his clients only trusted results from something painful to swallow.

On one occasion I found him stirring in a quantity of turpentine.

"Won't that kill them?" I asked, aghast.

"Precisely why medicine is called a "practice," John," Titus replied. "Even the foremost in our field must admit it is all trial and error. Besides, this will get rid of their pinworms."

Nonetheless, our set-up was an impressive sight in these dreary farm towns. The gaudy yellow of the wagon stood out, its doors flung open revealing rows of bottled tonics beneath our large canvas banner, "*Sick Made Well. Weak Made Strong*." Charts of human anatomy fluttered in the breeze, along with a skeleton hung with its jaw dangling in surprise and grotesque creatures and specimens swaying in stoppered jars. These were the "phantasmagorical wonders" advertised on the wagon's rear doors, which Titus charged folks an extra penny to gawk at. The most hideous of these was a hunk of flensed and wrinkled flesh floating in a greenish liquid Titus claimed was the brain of the Balor giant.

His wagon did hold true wonders however. Wrapped in soft cloth and tucked under his sleeping pallet, Titus had a set of books I yearned to spend my time with. *The American Dictionary of the English Language* they were titled, and he let me read them whenever my hands were clean and his mood expansive.

"Articulacy, John Cheese," he would say. "It sets a man apart."

Titus did possess much in the way of knowledge and sensed straight away what each town required, so in some places he dispensed with his exotic tales entirely. In these towns he'd don his magic coat, the same outrageous garment in which I first saw him. Thus enrobed in his silk galaxy, he would perform simple magic tricks to call in the crowd.

Occasionally, he'd not sell elixirs at all but spend the stop laying healing hands on paying customers. "Magnetic healing" he called it, and he'd simply pass his hands over his patient who would generally shake and shiver and get well. That these patients were often good-looking women was not lost on me, and I often wondered why old Titus bothered hauling bottles all over the countryside when he could have made the same money soft-talking and flapping his hands around.

The hours I most enjoyed were the quiet ones. The long evenings when Titus still held shop but sat outside by a small fire awaiting customers. It was then I was most likely to be trusted with the dictionary, and Titus took to playing an instrument he carried in his wagon, an odd bulbous thing he called a "mandolina."

This was the hour when the hard cases came out, lurking with their coins clenched, eager to obtain a bottle of what they called their "remedy." Titus always timed his stops so he arrived in towns a month behind the bigger medicine shows, to "give customers time for their symptoms to return." Such customers often sat at the fire too, sipping their tonic slowly, growing dull and dreamy. Titus mellowed on these nights too, playing his mandolina and singing softly, with his eyes fixed on some far horizon, as though he were trying to make out something too distant to see. His innocence, for instance.

Whether I was just trying to hang on to the turning world or had gone bad was debatable, but two years on the road with Titus did nothing to dim my eyesight in watching for the main chance. So I could not imagine he was surprised at what happened next.

For chance it was, the day I stood beside him as he flourished a handkerchief doing one of his magic tricks. Chance it was, I heard a metallic clank when the hem of his starry cloak hit the hub of the wagon wheel during an exuberant gesture. Chance it was again, the unusual sound and my knowledge he slept in this coat every night collided and told me he'd hidden something there. A month passed before I had an opportunity to get near the magic coat, unravel the seam and prise out the contents. Three gold eagles tied crisscross with twine. Thirty dollars.

When he discovered them missing, Titus lit into the only rage I ever witnessed, rummaging his bedclothes and stomping about the wagon. Tossing me against the wagon box, he made me turn out my pockets to reveal them empty, but as he rousted me there was a timorous speck in his eye. I suspect he was a little afraid of me as I'd grown taller than he was by then, and in another month he seemed resigned to his loss. I'd let time pass on purpose, of course. It eased his suspicion and allowed me to travel with him to a larger city.

Chance too, that we were back at the same Albany warehouse where I'd joined him when I slipped away, after plunging my hand into the stinking bottle where the Balor giant's mucid brain had hidden my purloined eagles. I like to think Titus would have applauded the treachery of John Cheese if he'd known all its details.

I miss old Titus, I really do. I suppose.

Since then I've played a version of his game by my own rules. I am a doctor now too, by his definition. Rather than rattle the roads, I see patients in my rented rooms, keeping to one city for a few years before moving on to another. Quackery is, after all, a reputation that gets about. I've also no desire to see the likes of gouty farmers, so I have specialized. "Professor of Theory and Practice, Obstetrics and Diseases Peculiar to Women," the advertisements I place in newspapers state. Yet I purvey the same opiates Titus did, along with paragoric, ergot, and catarrh snuff, with the same results.

It is with his procedures of magnetic healing where I have made improvements. I too, pass my hands over the bodies of my hysterics and hypochondriacs and lull them with honeyed words but using manipulation techniques I have developed and a pair of warmed magnetized rods, have produced even greater results. There has been only one angry husband a few years back in Ithaca, which occasioned my hurried removal.

So you can imagine my interest in young Cora and my delight to find, after discreet inquiries, that she had no minder at all. No impresario trailed in her wake, no manager arranged her performances, there was not even a father about. At Hemlock Hall, she was accompanied only by her mother, a heartsore and recent widow with a baby clapped on her breast. Well, the Devil always takes care of his own.

I began at once the task of beguiling the mother but underestimated her willingness to share her sorrows. Zilpha, she was called, a wraith-like woman but with arms like twists of rope, indicating to me who'd been the workhorse of her family. I had merely to push the pump handle of sympathy, and her woe came pouring out.

Cora's father, Hiram, was apparently a great reader of pamphlets and tracts and inflamed by this reading sold the family farm in nearby Cadytown, a baleful little burg not far from Hemlock Hall. From there, he dragged them all to one of the radical utopias outside of Boston, and all went well until, as Zilpha related with a catch in her voice and the babe jiggling on one knee, "Cora's sight opened."

The community leader, a Reverend Asher Lyman, promoted Cora's visions and encouraged her to repeat the spirit voices she claimed to hear before his own congregation. Hiram had other ideas and went west to Wisconsin seeking land to begin a utopia of his own, envisioning himself as the leader and Cora as the oracle of his prairie Delphi. Hiram had every plan in place, except for the summer cholera which killed him. The baby, named Edward not Hiram, Jr. I noticed, was born four months after his father's funeral, and the three survivors returned to Cadytown with few resources and reduced to renting the farm they once owned.

So I was not the first to see Cora's potential. I can well imagine that scheming duo of her childhood, the New Jerusalem Reverend and hapless Hiram struggling for dominance over their newly discovered prize, but what of Cora herself? I had the advantage of Titus' dictionary, but how did she come by her remarkable fluency? The Reverend? Possibly, but her words lack the self-aggrandizement of the morally certain. Hiram? If so, he'd have been counted an unusually erudite farmer.

It gives me a fearful pause to think it is she herself, her own impressive theatrics. She never leaves her character, insisting on the truth of these spirits and even giving them names. It certainly serves to make her performance so believable. I cannot forget the night at the Greeley séance when she pulled the correct name Pickie out of the air, after my informant had given me the wrong one. I still don't know how she did it. Of course, like Eve, all women have something in common which men must beware. Nonetheless, the skill of Cora's "improvisations" cannot be gainsaid.

But once again, I digress. Pondering Cora has that effect.

I spun my seduction all that winter, countering Zilpha's pathos with fabricated tales of my own. My burgeoning medical practice in New York City, the famous and fashionable I knew there, and Zilpha lapped it up with an avaricious smolder in her eyes. Baby Edward was dandled and a bill or two quietly paid. Cora herself seemed to enjoy my nosegays and my gentlemanly kisses.

We were married last year, taking the train directly to New York after the wedding. I knew no one in that city, but I'd arranged for a single performance for Cora at the Lyceum Hall with more openings promised contingent upon the success of the first one. Zilpha and little Edward waved us off at the station. She'd had her daughter's trunk packed for months.

Today, I am a happy man. The lectures are going well, we've landed on our feet, and the money is piling up. Of course, I am careful with expenditures and much else.

Naturally, I yanked myself raw during the months I was courting Cora and must admit I grasped her a bit roughly once I finally got hold of her, but of late I have become more circumspect. A pregnancy would foil all, and I believe there is some Biblical precedent about not binding the mouth of the ox who treads the grain.

Happily, my problem in that quarter was solved by the fortuitous appearance of the winsome Lovicia Gale. I discovered her booted-out and blubbering on the street before one of our boarding house accommodations, unable to pay her rent. Not overly particular where her coins or pretty clothes come from, she follows us about, ostensibly helping Cora with costumes and hair dressing. With a hot and heavy-breasted hoyden riding me of an afternoon and cool Cora purveying her Orphic charms to a full house in the evenings, I am a satisfied man indeed.

Still, problems creep in.

The promoters of these speaking venues are a larcenous lot, full of chicanery and always demanding something new. For those who think I do not hold up my end of our matrimonial bargain, I will have you know wrangling with these men is a full-time job.

Latterly, they have been complaining that mere speaking is no longer enough and point out others of Cora's ilk who materialize spirits. Bouquets delivered from beyond the grave, tilting tea tables, all effects Cora claims she can not and will not make happen. Such is my contrary consort. I should hate to think I've placed all my money on a dog that knows only one trick, but Cora is a clever girl yet.

Perhaps, we should embark on a tour of the lesser provinces where audiences have not yet become so jaded. Or maybe, I should bring Cora in person to these promoters to remind them why her audiences are two-thirds men and that materialized spirits offer nothing like she does for visual contemplation. I shall have to think of something, I suppose.

I must be careful. Cora is becoming a sensation and will be an altogether different horse to race if she realizes her fame has loosened my grip on her bit. I must also learn to interpret her spells of moody insolence.

Take, for instance, that indecipherable day when I brought back Greeley's *Tribune* telling of her triumph. Cora was asleep when I left, but on my return, I found her coiled in a chair and regarding me with a grim watchful stare. Neither of us knows the other very well, but I'd always thought that neither of us cared to, so I cannot imagine what occasioned such cold observation.

She didn't glance at the newspaper and warmed slowly to my suggestion of lunch at Delmonico's, a mystery to me, as she is always complaining of being hungry or cold. Rather, she held me in a gaze that was provocative and discomforting, her eyes scanning my face as though she were looking for something, until finally venturing a small smile.

For all that is said of truth and beauty, it is odd that in a face where beauty is so evident, truth is obscure. I must remember to keep my head. From the moment I changed my name in Albany, nearly twenty years ago, I have set myself on playing the long game. Perhaps my darling Cora is playing one that is even longer.

A young gentleman visiting New York wrote home:

January 24, 1858
Stevens House Hotel NYC

I had scarcely put my foot on New York soil when approached by a stranger, asking if I had heard of the wonders of Spiritualism. I replied I had, and would be interested to investigate its claims. Then said he, "Come with me to a Spiritual church meeting, and you will see Mrs. Cora Carter, a celebrated trance speaker.

I acquiesced and accompanied my newfound friend to a spacious hall, filled with an intelligent audience of both sexes. Imagine my pleasure and surprise at seeing, on the rostrum, a woman—a bright young woman, divinely fair with clear cut features and sweet blue eyes, which seemed fixed directly upon me, radiant with beauty, purity and intelligence. She stood, her head crowned by a profusion of pretty blonde hair, falling in graceful ringlets upon her shoulders, with a voice orating in sweetest tones on the love of the Infinite, the glories of the universe and kingdom of the soul.

And oh! How the entrancing eloquence did uplift my soul and make my heart throb with emotion and gratitude to the Spirit realm. Such exalted thought and charming oratory and such feminine loveliness, on a rostrum I had never seen or heard before.

To possess such a lovely fairy mortal—for her intellect and genius—I would have given a kingdom or braved a world of dangers. Lost in wonder and admiration, I could only weep with tears of joy, and bless the stranger who'd led me to this shrine of Spiritualism, where, for the first time, my ears were greeted with a voice of inspiration, direct from the world of Spirits.

Cora

1858

Memory speaks the same way the spirits do, but oftener and with a louder voice. It is perhaps our oldest companion and certainly our most constant. Invariably, it attends us—teaching, teasing and reminding. It barges in unexpectedly with words to a song long thought forgotten, or a scent from years ago. It gently touches our shoulder and points the right direction on a path not trod since childhood. It saunters in with any number of fond recollections, an old love's smile, a picnic on a perfect day. Yet it slithers too, bearing our worst terrors which resurfaced seem like a warning, a footfall heard behind us on a dark and otherwise silent street.

I was fourteen years old when I hid in the closet at Wager's boarding house in Utica. Crouched in that small space beneath the stairs, I'd laid my head on my knees and wept. My pantalettes were soaked with blood, my dress stained and my elbow sore from the place where the woman at the Genesee Lyceum clutched it.

With a glint of amusement, the fair-haired woman had grasped my elbow and dragged me roughly away from the small group of admirers assembled after my lecture.

Indicating with her eyes the blood-stained cuff of my pantalettes, the woman whispered in a sweetly scathing tone, "You may want to attend to yourself, dear."

"Not now daughter," was father's reply when I tugged at his sleeve a moment later. He was speaking of Wisconsin with a group of men and barely met my pleading eyes.

Wisconsin I despaired, *it is all he ever thinks of*, as I hurried out to the street and ran to the place called Wager's where we had lodgings.

It was only when I reached the steps of the large frame house did I remember, the key to our room was in father's pocket.

Entering the front hall, I glimpsed the slant-topped door beneath the stairs, and finding it was a closet, secreted myself within.

I cried for a while, but it made no sense to be long at it, so my mind turned to practical things. I knew what happened of course. I'd seen the blood-stained cloths from mother's monthlies in the laundry. I even knew the rudiments of why it happened, as mother had told me, but never imagined it would come so suddenly. I'd always assumed there would be some sign beforehand. I never thought it would come when others might see and was miserable with humiliation.

Nor could I work out what to do. There was no cloth, such as my mother used, in my traveling trunk. I'd have to tell father, the thought of which shriveled me with shame, and he would be cross. We were expected in Rome the day after tomorrow and Oneida after that. We had been traveling all month since the heavy snows melted. If only we could stop. If only we could just go home.

The odd noise sounded like the scuttling of a mouse at first. Or had I dozed and been dreaming? It was a problem for me now, sorting sounds and voices, whispers from spirits, memories, the discourse of my own conscience. Often it was hard to tell them apart, but again I heard the sound clearly. Earlier, I'd been startled by the heavy footfalls of someone climbing the stairs above me, speaking in an angry voice and slamming a door. This sound was something other, something softer. Something beyond the boarding house, beyond everything, a tiny imperfection in the quiet space.

Again I heard a faint rustle. A breeze? A sigh? I didn't know but began to smell something, tobacco and another familiar scent I recalled from past days but could not quite identify, unreachable like a word forgotten but still on the tip of one's tongue. It was not from Hope Grove or a scent from the farm. It was something from further back, from long ago, perhaps before I could remember.

A breeze and a shower of blossoms swept across the eye in my mind, and suddenly, I gasped and gulped for air. I was so intent on listening, I'd been holding my breath in silence. A springtime meadow and orchards appeared, and a soft laugh from an old woman standing in them. The woman's sleeves were rolled, and she had blood on her wrists and hands, as though she'd just stepped from a murder or a butchering into a pretty pastoral morning. The leaves of the trees trembled, falling blossoms twisted and fluttered in the bright air. Despite the blood, I did not fear her. Quite the contrary, as what I felt was relief, inhaling deeply a cool fresh air with the odor of warm earth and grass.

Wearing a worn apron and a skirt of dark fustian, the woman was not any person I recognized, but the familiar feeling was strong, and moreover, I knew I could trust this elderly lady with the placid and imperceptible smile, her entire being bathed in the faint glow of strangeness in which all spirits travel. An eyebrow then arched over an old and rheumy eye, which rested in a crease of her papery skin, as the woman drew close, until she seemed just beside my shoulder.

"Mon ange," the old voice whispered, words I did not understand, but then I felt calloused fingers stroke my hair and a kiss placed on the top of my head. The tobacco odor filled my cramped hiding place as well as the curious remembered smell which was warm and sweet, like love.

"Get yourself out of there!" a new voice commanded, as the closet door was snatched open.

Mrs. Wager, the landlady, had no doubt expected someone entirely different inside the closet when she caught the whiff of smoke. She didn't allow smoking in her rooms, a rule she stated emphatically to my father when we arrived. "Don't even try to light up," she said. "I will sniff you out and show you out." Now here I was, hiding while probably being sought by father all over town. I guessed it was him in the house earlier talking too loudly and stomping up and down the stairs.

"I smell smoke," Mrs Wager said, looking down at me with a suspicious eye.

"I-I'm not smoking," I stuttered.

"I can see that, but what are you doing? Don't you know your father is searching for you?"

By way of answer, I stood and lifted my short dress exposing my bloody pantalettes.

Mrs. Wager pulled her lips into a thin line and sighed. "Is this your first?" she asked.

The landlady made a brisk, but not unkind, business of helping me out of my stained clothes and tore up some cloth rags for my use. In between chattering nervously about chasing smoking men out of her front closet, she offered some terse instructions about monthlies. "Lord knows it's been twenty years since I've given any of that mess a thought."

When father and I were reunited, he sat with me in the front room with a manner more impatient than repentant. Although he tried to hide it, he was as cross and snappish as I'd predicted. "I can send a message to Rome and Oneida if you want to go back to Cadytown," he said, jiggling the knee of one leg so nervously a door of a cabinet rattled behind us. "Why didn't you just tell me what the trouble was at the Lyceum?"

"I was ashamed," I replied. "Everyone saw. I asked if we could leave." He gave me a blank stare and knew he'd no memory of my request. Sitting with his indifference made me wish for the safety of the closet again and for the hand of the old woman on my hair.

"No one saw anything." he declared. "I searched for you for half an hour at the lecture hall. They held the building unlocked for me. It was embarrassing. I had no idea you'd run for home."

Home. My heart tightened. Father called every boarding house "home." I knew he loved me, but ever since the family left Hope Grove and he talked of starting over in Wisconsin, I'd felt we were all in danger. He thought every new idea would help him dodge disaster, but something huge and unavoidable was lurking, I was sure.

"On to Rome or back to Cadytown?" he asked, obviously hoping for the former. "All is fine now? Mrs. Wager has helped you get everything, uh, solved?"

I knew what he wanted but knew what I wanted too, and my anger grew larger than any sense of obligation. I was tired of rented rooms and lectures, the waiting for trains and traveling and especially of people watching me, wanting something from me. With a conviction which surprised even myself I spoke."Cadytown," I said. "I want to go home."

As we started up the stairs to our beds, Mrs. Wager joined us, and father paused with the landlady as I continued to climb. Stopping on the highest step I looked down on the pair, my smarmy father with the expanding patch of bald on his head and a fierce Mrs. Wager with her index finger pointed at his shirtfront. Her words were whispered, but the sound traveled clearly upward to my hearing.

"The shame should be yours," Mrs. Wager scolded. "That girl should be wearing long dresses."

Back at home in Cadytown, I was shocked to overhear the same words. My parents were arguing, as they often did since father had "had words" with the Reverend Lyman and we'd removed from Hope Grove. My parents had changed in the months since our return and taken to quarreling and making up dramatically in performances I found embarrassing to witness. One moment father was shouting and in another mother giggling and batting away his kisses

"Cora should be wearing long dresses now," mother said firmly.

"Just a few more months Zil, please," father answered. "They pay more for a little girl, and the crowds are bigger. If we go until summer, we'll have enough for the land in Wisconsin."

More than his request, it was the tone of his voice which frightened me, the weak wheedling which caused me to realize my terrible situation. From now on I would have to take care to interpret every voice I heard, and I recognized this awful pleading. I'd heard it in the Reverend Lyman's voice, too. I'd never been safe with any of them.

Now four years later, with father dead and myself a married woman, such memories served only to underscore the unreliability of the hands which currently held me.

Benjamin came into my life with all the flash and dazzle of a summer thunderstorm and in hindsight, with more than a hint of its malevolent possibility.

A tall figure in a frock coat, Dr. Benjamin Carter's clothes were expensively made, his collars were turnover and almost ostentatiously white. Every four-in-hand was silk, and on each of his waistcoats, he'd left the bottom button undone in the latest fashion. No Cadytown farmer was he.

He recounted how a slight weakness in the chest obliged him to leave his medical practice in New York City during the hot summer months and how he enjoyed journeying the upstate communities so congenial to the reform movements which interested him. Here, he chanced upon Hemlock Hall.

At first I thought Benjamin came around to court mother, as the two were near the same age. Indeed, it was mother who paced and counted the clock the several times he was delayed from his promised arrival, and mother who flushed in his presence and preened beforehand. Quite often my brother Edward was looked after by a neighbor on "Dr. Carter's day".

"He is a gentleman with much education," my mother said over and over.

Benjamin did have an impressive manner of speech. He often used words I didn't understand, which compelled me to secretly commit them to memory and learn them so he would not know more than I did.

Still, there was a false quality to his language mother did not seem to hear. His words were deft and agile, scurrying like a thief being pursued or smooth and aiming to charm. To me, he often sounded like one of the doctors who traveled in a wagon with a medicine show, rather than a doctor with an office in New York City.

By winter, I realized that I, not mother, was the object of Benjamin Carter's interest. Furthermore, it was apparent mother approved and encouraged his suit. Benjamin's eyes stalked me, his countenance both alluring and threatening. If we stood in close proximity, he brushed against me, the skin of his hands oven-like against my shoulder or the small of my back.

I felt myself the innocent in some fairy tale who might soon be seized and eaten but could not picture what form such an assault would take. I imagined some awful scene in which Benjamin grasped me and in which I would be required to resist. I imagined some sort of struggling or wrestling. The thought was not entirely unpleasant.

The day I decided to marry Benjamin was a Wednesday in late June. Mother had prodded me outdoors with a packed lunch and a parasol and onto Benjamin's proffered arm.

It was a day of hot sun and racing clouds, and we proceeded walking along a wooded path to a pretty pond that lay nearby the farm. We first talked of silly things, but a quarter mile along when the trees grew close around us, Benjamin spoke. "I should like you to continue with your lectures, if that is your wish," he said.

Surprise stopped my heart and my walking, and I turned to face him. "If we were to marry." he continued.

Sure my face was coloring or showing some reaction I did not want him to see; I turned away and stared at the ground. "Are you asking?" I replied.

"Yes, I am, I suppose. I wanted you to know I believe a woman should be able to speak on a platform, just as a man does. Your ideas are just as important to express."

"They are not my ideas. They are the words of spirits."

A hint of skepticism crossed his face, and I watched him conceal it. "Yes, well. Whomever is the author of your words, I would never forbid your speaking them. I would encourage it."

I'd never thought it possible to give up lecturing. The spirits never advised me. Spirits seldom made requests. It was the living who insisted I had a duty to share my gift. The Reverend Lyman explained the phenomena of Spiritualism and pronounced me one of a special few girls who had the ability to connect with the Summerland. There were some sisters in Rochester who could translate the rapping sounds of spirits into messages and some who claimed visions, but it was only me who heard articulate proclamations of those in life hereafter. Reverend Lyman gave me lessons in elocution, and father certainly compelled me to the platform after we left Hope Grove. In recent years I'd had no choice. My lectures were the sole support of the family.

Nor did I think about marriage. I perceived of it as a state all women desired, to have a husband, a home and children, and hazily expected it to be part of some distant future. I always assumed I would be able to do both but was not truly certain I wanted to do either.

So I did not give Benjamin any answer, and we said little more as we continued to the pond, found a shady spot beneath a large willow and ate our lunch.

But for the occasional note of a bird, the area around us was silent, so quiet I could hear Benjamin breathing. I'd removed my bonnet, closed my eyes and sat resting against the tree when I heard him uncross his legs and scoot toward me.

I shivered with the expectation he might kiss me, as he'd done thrice before on other days, twice on my hand and once on my forehead. A tiny foreboding whispered as I imagined his dark eyes now intent on me and his possibly planning some form of seizing but kept my eyes closed, refusing to award him any reaction.

What he did was unexpected. He lifted my one extended leg and placed my foot in his lap and began to unbutton my boot. Eight small buttons were there, and he undid them slowly before removing the boot.

My stockinged foot in his lap, Benjamin began to stroke it faintly, maddeningly, in small circles with the tips of his fingernails, like a soft light scratching. My foot jerked once involuntarily, and he quieted it, holding it gently, stroking all the while, and something deep inside me turned over, almost causing me to make a sound.

We sat together thus for some time, his hands moving from my foot up my leg to my garter which he undid and pulled my stocking down, continuing the same movements up my bare calf and in a particularly sensitive spot behind my knee. He drew closer, and I trembled, feeling precisely the distance in the air between us.

It was wonderful and terrifying, and I was sure, quite unwise to give in to this. I kept my eyes closed and pondered my vulnerability. I was on the ground, wearing but one shoe and encased in the cage of my crinoline. Yet I allowed him to do it, missing, I often later thought, the last moment when I might have come to my senses.

Only when his stroking hands moved higher did I object. High upon my leg and far beneath my petticoat he was when I pulled away from him.

"Don't," I said tugging my dress down over my feet with both hands, and he sat back on his haunches and smiled at me. It was an awful smile. He cocked his head, like a dog listening for a sound, and his mouth crumbled into a crooked line, one side sweet and one side cruel, a slit of inscrutable intent.

Then he grasped my wrists and spun me roughly around with my back to him. I pulled and tried to get away but he held me tightly, twisting my arms behind. Dr. Benjamin Chandler Carter had never seemed an overly vigorous man, and I was surprised at how strong he was. He pulled my arms to painfulness and then relaxed them, just to remind me of his capabilities.

He kissed me from behind, in the devouring way I'd long imagined, his head falling heavily onto my shoulder with his mouth against my throat, his dark forelock spilling across my cheek, before brushing his lips along the lobe of my ear and pulling me even closer. "You certainly know how much I admire you," he whispered.

I'd never been so close to a man before, his man smell, hair oil, steamed cotton, and something raw and keen, something awful, something which made me understand his strangeness and otherness from me. I felt his whole body and all of its hazardous possibility, an intimacy one could desire and then die in. Yet how could I be hurt by a heartache I already expected?

He then gave the edge of my ear a painful bite and spoke in a dark undertone. "I perhaps neglected to tell you: I will see your mother and brother are provided for."

For a moment my mind was erased to a vast blank space, and again, something within me moved, but this time as if it simply collapsed. There was every possibility of confusion in this scene of apparent mercilessness, but I had never felt as certain or more clear of a message.

I was finally confronted with something that was as it appeared to be. This was no nebulous spirit seeking detection and no paternal elder urging my duty to produce his desire. It was an exchange, a wretched exchange, but at least this time, I believed I knew both sides of it.

Aboard the train to New York City after my wedding, I thought of my father. The drumming of the wheels seemed to count every foot of distance between me and Cadytown, and I recalled my first journey on a train when we moved to Hope Grove. How father had brought a map and showed me the route we were taking. He was a different father then, different than the man now dead and in a grave somewhere in Wisconsin.

After the incident in Utica, a small distrust of my father seeded itself in me, and I was more inclined to disobey the man I'd always loved and obliged. I balked at the constant lecturing which made me feel like an act in a circus. Other girls did not have to go about and stand on platforms, and I knew many people mocked and disbelieved me. The awful result was: when father died, I did not grieve him.

Now in recent days seated with Lydia at Irving Place and knowing of her desire to hear the spirit of her mother, I retained a secret. Since his death, I had never perceived any message from my father. I'd never had to go to Wisconsin. His death had mercifully ended that notion. Yet I felt guilty about feeling relieved and worried my lack of grief somehow barred his spirit. Did I owe father my obedience, or was he the selfish one?

Nor had I any inkling of his death before it transpired. Why did Hollis and the other spirits say nothing? All was silent, and I did not know why.

So in leaving on the train with my new husband, I hoped I was done with spirits forever. I would be a wife. Benjamin assured me I need not lecture unless I chose to but asked me to give one more performance for a gathering of his friends in New York City.

"They have all read so much of your marvelous gift in my letters," he'd said. "Everyone is eager to hear and welcome you."

Thus I relented, but looking at the face of the man I married that morning raised an awful presentiment. The day Benjamin grasped me in the woods, I believed I'd finally made my own choice, but on this wedding day, I was not so certain.

While saying goodbye to mother earlier that day, at the train station, she whispered some parting words into my ear. "Don't give your husband any sass," mother said.

In the end, perhaps I had done everything I'd been told to do.

March 20, 1858
New York

Dearest Cora,

I suppose you must be packed and ready to leave tomorrow. I hope this letter reaches you before then. To think you will be traveling for two months and as far away as Maine!

I do think Benjamin has made a good plan for you to carry the Spiritual messages to smaller places where people might otherwise not have the opportunity to hear them. It will at least give a pause to your routine at Dodsworth's and make a change of scenery.

I can understand your fear of practicing Benjamin's new method, but I think having the audience pose questions directly of the spirits, who then answer through you, will silence the skeptics and further bind the faithful to our beliefs. Perhaps the spirits do not appear at one's bidding, but you have <u>never failed</u> to make contact in the past, and I don't believe your guides will leave you voiceless on the platform.

I <u>am</u> disappointed you will miss the National Women's Convention. I had looked forward to us attending the sessions together and am anxious at the thought of hosting such famous orators in our home! Wish me luck. I would give anything to have you meet them and hear their wise words.

I almost forgot to say I saw one of your new broadsides yesterday. The engraver did a fine job with your likeness. No matter what you think, you do not look stern. You look lovely and <u>just like yourself.</u>

I will write as often as I can and will miss our teatime afternoons. Good luck and safe travels to you, Benjamin and Lovey, and I know father and Charles wish the same.

Keep well, and much love, Lydia.

Mrs. Beaulieu

1858

I am a figment in my orchards still, a small trembling in the trees, a quiver in the empty air. I stroll and speak their names, *Pendu*, *Pippin*, *Fameuse*, and the *Spy*. Even the nameless white winter apple of which I made my tarts is greeted. "You," I say running my absent fingers along its branches no bigger than a pipestem. "I know you."

Mon Dieu! My orchards were the finest thing Octave and I had on the farm, and I loved them in all the seasons. Raining their pale and bee-covered blossoms in the spring, sleep-heavy with fruit in the summer, and especially in winter, when the absent leaves revealed their true natures each tree was peculiar—this one sullen, this one kindly, this one shy.

Ma chere Octave was a soldier, come from France with the Meurons in DeWatteville's regiment before the war on Lake Champlain. He'd fought across the sea in the land of Spain as well, and when his years fighting came to an end, he wanted no more of them.

We met in the store in town, each tending to errands we both forgot on the day we saw one another. I remember no joy, no rapture, just the arms of a calm man, deliberate and slow, who moved easy in the world. My maiden's eyes believed he would be good to me, and good he always was.

For seven years, we worked the land Octave had been granted for his service in the military, but in the winter evenings, we often talked about going to the West. The Canadian land was not prime and the water from the well unreliable in the summer. More than once, I had watched Octave as he stood straight, rubbed his back and gazed toward the sunset. I had watched as his mouth formed a scowl when one of my six brothers offered advice on how to farm. Octave had fought wars; he had crossed the seas. I had married an adventurer.

"What about New York, Rosa?" he one day asked. "I'm not sure I want another season of Lucien telling me which day I should get the hay in, and I like the Americans. They were good soldiers."

We left La Prairie on the feast day of St. Joseph. Pierre, Adelaide and Jean-Baptiste stood by my skirts. Marcel and baby Almira held each of my hands. The little tree roots were tied in canvas on the quay with our other belongings. I was an adventurer, too.

Now I am dead these four years, and Octave goes along without me. I am still here of course, for the living have no idea of how the world endures, invisible, weightless, yet ever poised.

He will die in another two years in the week of the Day of All Saints, his calm mottled hands cranking the cider mill next to the orchard we planted in 1824. Death will spring out at him from a root of a tree he placed there. The end, the beginning. For me, it becomes impossible to tell the difference.

After my tenth child, women began to ask me for help with their own birthing. My gardens were like Eden, the boucané from my smokehouse praised by all, and my roots and herbs second to none in our valley, but it was the ten healthy children playing in my dooryard the women noticed. Why Octave and I were overlooked by the death angel who plucks the children of the earth, I do not know.

The women who sought me out must have thought me either wise or lucky, but I know now I was both. Wisdom comes from observation, but luck is a form of magic, and in the world where I now travel, I understand magic is never in short supply.

It almost always happened the same way. A frantic husband would appear at the farm in his wagon. I would gather my kit and my pipe, for Octave had taught me smoking, and I found it the perfect companion for sitting out a long labor. Sometimes I would be gone from the farm for two or three nights, but I was held in high esteem and well paid for my duties.

I will remember forever the night Emeline Chamberlain began her labor at her home down on Rushford Flats. Miles Chamberlain had knocked on our door in some hour past midnight, and I made to gather my things as quickly as possible. Bleary-eyed and in the light of Octave's single lamp, I fumbled through my cupboard seeking the packet of lobelia I felt I needed and had misplaced. Impatience overtook me, and I began to fuss when I was unable to find it, slamming the cupboard door harder than I meant to and storming about.

Still in his nightshirt, Octave grasped me and pressed me against the dry sink with more speed and force than I'd ever known of him. "Rosa! Rosa!" he exclaimed as he shook me by the shoulders. "Stop this!" I gazed at him in the colorless half-dark and watched as his eyes widened with a look of startled awe.

"Emeline does not want your root cures. The women don't want your herbs. They want you; they want Rosalie Beaulieu. They want you because you are brave.

Of all the love words Octave had ever praised me with, none were as sweet as these, and I climbed into Miles Chamberlain's wagon with tear-blurred eyes.

Little Abel Chamberlain slid out of his mother that same morning by the time of cockcrow, an easy birth, and a mirthful child he was to be. He had a nose like a perfect button so *mon Bouton* is the name I have given him.

He and the hundred others I have seen into the world are now my care. I am the shiver in their air, the sudden slamming of the door before a storm, the fleeting pressure on a small shoulder. Mine was the hand which held them first, as mine was the hand which guided them from their first dark to their first light.

Like vague smoke I swirl around each one, touching them, as they are the small strings on which my fingers still want to make music. *Mon Bouton, mon Chaton, mon Hibou, mon Ange*. "You," I tell them in my softest whisper. "I know you." Each child peculiar. This one sullen, this one kindly, this one shy.

A squall line lay heaped up on the far horizon that May of 1840. I eyed it warily from the window of the milk house where I'd been that afternoon straining the yield of the day but decided the storm was hours away and would perhaps not even arrive until after nightfall. Still, the dark line pressed heavily up against the pure overhead blue, and the leaves in the orchard were making a fretful nervous sound, turning their undersides upward in the prickling excited air.

And oh, the blossoms! Tumbling like the flakes of a snowstorm, a gale thick enough to obscure the sight of Hiram Page's wagon as it came down our farm road alongside the orchard.

It was Zilpha's time, he said, and as I rode away with him in the sleet of petals, it seemed as if we were figures in a pageant or some marvelous procession heading off to war or glory.

An hour later when I leaned over Zilpha in her childbed, a single pink petal fell onto her from somewhere in the folds of my dress. At the time I brushed it away, but from where I live now, I know it was a sign.

Cora emerged from between her mother's knees encased in a bloody shroud, her face pressed against the murky skin as though to a dirty window. La coiffe! Born in the caul. I had heard of such a thing, but never seen it, and tried at once to think calmly in the roar of two women moaning. Zilpha, given to excess in any weather, was wailing about giving birth to a monster. Her sister, Ellen, had bolted from the room sobbing. Thanks be to God, Hiram was somewhere out of doors.

The little babe, born in the sac she had grown in, was supposed to be making her first lusty cries, but her mouth opened and closed silently like an expiring fish and her little hands pushed at the balloon of skin surrounding her.

With the small knife I used at all my births, I pricked the frail skin, sliding it away from the face of the babe with my heart in my throat. She made a small gasp and opened her remarkable eyes to me. It is strange how the exact look of a moment stays forever in memory. A kind of radiance came from the child's eyes, a curious energy as though she were on fire, and something like an amazement passed between us.

That the girl would be a beauty I immediately understood, and I knew with a certainty that felt much like pain that her beauty would bring her many things, both wonderful and terrible. Yet I was unprepared for the resolute features I saw on a face only moments born. A determined set of the jaw which seemed like anger, but was not, a virtue which appeared strangely solemn on her sweet, alert face. Otherworldly she was, as a messenger sent from God.

"Mon Ange," I said aloud. My angel. Cutting again at her navel string I held her aloft for her mother to see. "La coiffe, born in the veil!" I exclaimed smiling. "A lucky girl she will be."

I would have thought my pipe would be forbidden in heaven. I am surprised now to find an endless twist of the finest southern brightleaf in my pocket when I reach for it. I still pack the bowl slowly, draw a flame-warmed breath and puff the smoke into swirls around my forehead. I even believe I can savor the taste, though whether I can or am just remembering is another matter.

My babes are my care, and when I saw mon Ange crying in the closet far from her home, I had the remedy. That Mrs. Wager never knew the pleasure of a pipe and was set against smoking, so I blew a wave of smoke under her nose as she cut up her meat pies in her kitchen. She did her best by Cora. I'd have brewed the poor girl a cup of blackhaw tea, but Mrs Wager was a city woman who would know nothing of that.

I guide them as I can, touching them as I am able. My babes. My trees. I wonder how long I will have my hands on their souls, and when they are finally taken, what else my eyes will be watching.

Cora

1858

Their laughter echoed throughout the hall like the warning growls of a dozen surly dogs.

"Which proposition of Pythagoras do you wish me to discuss?" I asked the standing man, the obvious leader of a group who had assembled themselves in the front row of my evening lecture in Lynn, Massachusetts and proposed I discuss the Pythagorean Proposition.

The man was exactly the sort Benjamin once goaded me to use as a mark.

"When they look at you like a man in love," Benjamin had in those days counseled, "then you know you are doing all right."

What did a man in love look like? I was sure I did not know and also sure this man standing before me was no lover.

"The very learned spirits ought to know without any inquiry." the stranger said, turning to his peers, smirking and raising his eyebrows in mock exasperation, causing them all to laugh again.

For the first time ever on the platform, I fought back the urge to stammer. I'd no idea what the Pythagorean Proposition was; I could barely pronounce the word. Furthermore, I could not hear the spirits while someone else was speaking. This was the problem with taking questions from the audience. It took time to slip into the stream of the spirit speech, time to ride the sound to its source, discern a single voice from the thousands and let the trance envelope me. Nor did I dare glance at Benjamin, for his frown and outsize expectations would surely undo me.

I could but rely on my own resources and trust the spirits. Raising my head I lifted my gaze toward the rafters, until the hum of heartbeat began swarming in my ears. As always, many voices came blaring which caused my soul to waver. This time many of the voices were foreign, words I did not know and could repeat but not translate. I caught the word "theorem" and "geometry" and understood the questioner in the audience was positing something mathematical, but did not know what. The spirits never spoke of mathematics. They did not talk of such things.

An image of an older man entered my mind, a stooped and weary stranger who rose and stood with difficulty in my vision, pressing his hands hard against his thighs in the effort. It was his voice I heard most clearly, and I fell into it as though through a trapdoor, where the sound, as always, caught and held me.

"Spirits, in their distinct essences, perceive not by time or external space but intuit the elements of existence, and they work through the means of internal form and identity into the human brain. Those who are deeply learned in science, probably each of you, has become so interested in your external identity, to sometimes forget the spiritual essence within and imagine that the external brain—the intellect—is everything and acted only upon that principal. The scientist may understand the spirit is a power which governs matter but comprehends it only in its external manifestations. Such studies and means of education produces a human race so much externalized that they know nothing except by positive, external proof. What follows? That the spirit of man, in thus becoming exteriorized, finds itself unable to manifest the divine essence within. Faith cannot be subordinate to man's devices."

The sting of awareness jolted me back to the stage where I wavered a bit, deafened for a mere moment as the spirit voice receded to the chorus of thousands and then withered into the thin high-pitched whistle I always thought of as silence, or at least as the absence of sound.

The audience sat in puzzlement. Someone coughed, and there was a single unsettling laugh. Another problem with the method of answering a question from the public was I'd no exact memory of what I had just said to them. I scanned their faces for some reaction.

The questioner met my eye with a look of sour mirth then swaggered to the edge of the platform and turned to face the audience himself. With a hand that seemed as wide as a paddle he struck the wooden stage, and I startled. I could not help it, the unexpected move thwarted my practiced stage-calm, and the audience startled too, regarding the man with a bright-eyed anticipation. A tear trembled at the edge of my eye, and I blinked it away.

"The lady," the man began in a thunderous voice, drawing out the word "lady" to dramatic effect, "or rather "the spirits," accompanying this part of his statement with an incredulous look, "have entirely misunderstood the subject. The Proposition of Pythagoras is purely a mathematical one, being simply that the sum of the squares of the two legs of a right-angled triangle is equal to the square of the hypotenuse."

The men in the front row scoffed and chuckled, and a hot flame of anger rose within me. I was protective of the spirits and did not believe they misunderstood things.

"I understood your question to be a mathematical one," I stated, "but you did not ask for a definition. The spirits discussed the Proposition as you requested. Venturing a look in Benjamin's direction, I noted his smile was twitching.

With this, another of the fellows from the front row arose, flailing his arms toward the audience. "Not one sentence uttered by Mrs. Carter could," he shouted, "by the greatest ingenuity, be tortured into the most distant allusion to anything ever put forth by Pythagoras!"

"Indeed!" another of the group assented. "All she has uttered has as much to do with any views held by that philosopher as it has to do with the views of Tom Thumb."

Malevolence swelled in the room, and scornful laughter spread from row to row like a flame given air. The faces of the assembled took on a savage tone, their eyes wild and mouths opened in laughter and shouting, countenances which could not be distinguished for mirth or menace.

By this time Benjamin had risen from his seat in a fluster, holding both his palms toward the crowd. The lights had come up, and I stepped down from the stage and stood behind him.

"Here, Here!" Benjamin said. "You've no call to submit my wife to such an outrage."

"Can't she stand up to a bit of scrutiny?" the original questioner growled.

"Scrutiny is one thing, my friend, and abuse entirely another." Benjamin replied. "She can't be obliged to battle three of you."

"She should be obliged to prove her claims!"

The four men had stepped closer to one another. Benjamin was nearly in their faces, the men's vests only inches apart. I backed away toward the door to the dressing rooms.

Benjamin lowered his arms, but his voice had changed. Tonight, it took on a shrill note I'd never heard, and the men still regarded him doubtfully.

"Cora—Mrs. Carter, cannot be rough-housed. Her inner organization is delicate. She is an instrument of the spirits, as sensitive an instrument as any used in science," said Benjamin.

"She may also be a fraud," one of the men shouted.

"You, sir, are a bulldog!" Benjamin retorted.

Benjamin lurched another inch forward, clenching his hands into tight fists. This was it; I was sure, the moment I'd long feared. The downfall. A scream leapt into my throat which was just as quickly extinguished by a hand covering my mouth and a sharp tug pulling me backstage. For a moment, I imagined the hands of an audience mob, but these hands were Lovey's, dragging me and tossing a large scarf over my hair. "Run!" Lovey commanded.

Together, we scampered down the hallway and through a door into the alley which ran beside the large granite lecture hall. The air was chill, and I felt suddenly relieved at the coolness, until I realized Lovey had not draped my head with the scarf because of the weather but as a disguise.

For the next ten days, I lived like a married woman, or at least in the way I envisioned normal married women lived. Benjamin canceled my performances in Framingham and New Bedford and sent Lovey on ahead to prepare for our final performance in New Haven. He then focused his every attention on me.

He took rooms in a respectable hotel in Boston; we ate thrice daily and attended a play. We even went shopping. He purchased a new bonnet for me. Yet, I was not so purblind as to misunderstand Benjamin's smiles as anything other than appeasement and did not wait long to voice my concern. On a morning stroll in the Boston Common, I made my announcement.

"I will never again lecture to a question from an audience."

"That gang of troublemakers in Lynn was hostile to Spiritualism," Benjamin answered. "I don't know how they received front row seats. It won't happen again."

"No," I agreed, stopping on the pathway and looking at Benjamin directly, "it won't, as I refuse to do it."

"I've done my checking," he said. "Other than a single negative review in the *Courier*, I don't think anyone has taken any notice. Besides, I've been advised those man were academics"

"What difference would that make?" I questioned.

"The college men don't want to lose their own racket, of course."

"It is not a racket!" I said, turning from him in disdain, while an uneasy feeling quivered in my chest. I did not like to remember there were those who regarded me as a purveyor of deception. Yet, I knew I was often disbelieved. How could I not be, with people like Mrs. Beckwith and her tricks. My spirits did not behave in this manner. Why would they when they could speak to me plainly?

Benjamin coiled me in his arms and drew me close."We can dispense with the spontaneous questions," he said, kissing me gently on the forehead, "if that is your wish."

Just at that moment, a large flock of crows shifted in raucous commotion from the branches of a tree overhanging the pathway so forcefully it seemed the tree itself had tossed them into the sky.

I was too inexperienced to know spirits did not always speak plainly, and too young to realize a kiss is not the same as a promise.

The placard was displayed prominently in the window of the New Haven Confectionery, just around the corner from the Tontine Hotel. With less than two hours before my lecture, I'd left the hotel seeking to buy a packet of the horehound drops I used to soothe my throat before a long evening of speaking. I approached the candy shop worried only that the proprietor might have difficulty making enough change for the three dollar gold piece Benjamin sent me with.

I'd grown accustomed to seeing the broadsides announcing my lectures displayed in all manner of places. The engraving of my likeness preceded all our travels, just as this one propped up among the black jacks and sugared almonds in the shop window. It was the words printed below my image which froze my heart.

"An Invitation to the Investigation of Spiritualism"
We invite the assembled to propose any
question or topic for elucidation.
The answer to be delivered from the spirits
entirely in trance by Mrs. Cora Carter.
For this opportunity, we will meet you
at the New Assembly Rooms on Thursday evening
May 13th at 6 o'clock."

"When exactly did you intend to elucidate me you had broken your promise!" I snarled at Benjamin behind the slammed door of our hotel room.

Tensely seated in a corner chair, Benjamin uncrossed his legs and dropped his steepled hands from their plotting position beneath his nose to fall heavily in his lap. "You'll find I have not" he replied.

"The broadsides say otherwise." I snapped. "We agreed in Boston I would never again lecture to questions."

"Spontaneous questions, my dear one," Benjamin said, "which I recall was the exact wording of our little pact. Tonight you will know the question in advance."

"But that would not be truthful," I replied.

Benjamin stood with his hands on his hips in exasperation. There was less than an hour until the lecture. "You might have considered truth before you took up a profession which barters in illusion. Your spirits must still provide the answer. What does it matter when the question is posed?"

"Who will ask the question?"

Benjamin regarded me contemptuously. "No promoter wants a repeat of our debacle in Lynn. Our host at the New Assembly Rooms will have his nephew in attendance, third row center, with a buttonholed carnation. Tonight you'll be asked to discuss the subject of man's moralities."

Moralities? I did not know whether Benjamin was being outrageous or merely cruel. "You've agreed to this?" I asked.

"Of course," he replied, moving toward the wall mirror where he tidied his hair and flung me a bright-toothed, rueful smile. "It is a grand plan."

"Then you have made a liar out of me!" I cried.

With a quick, sharp look he stepped toward me, snatching the placket of my dress and pulling me close to face him. "I'd say you made that choice long before we ever met. You, or your father, or that mercenary minister—or all three, for all I know."

Rage and misery possessed me, but Benjamin held fast, very nearly lifting me off my feet, the toes of my boots grazing the floor. When he relaxed his grip, it was as if he meant to toss me aside.

"Go and get dressed," he growled.

I waited to catch myself, but as I was dropped to the flat of my feet, I tore away from him, rushing toward the door. "I won't do it!" I exclaimed, wishing to get away so the performance would have to be canceled.

He grasped the fabric of my skirt, and as he towed me backward, I heard a seam in my dress tear. The urge to weep overcame me, but when he twisted me to face him again, words spilled out instead of tears. "I won't," I repeated over and over, although I was not sure how many times I said it, because when he raised his hand to me everything stopped.

You really do see stars, I thought, remembering a time as a child in Hope Grove when two schoolboys were fighting in the road by the Mill Pond, and one warned the other with the threat "I'll make you see stars!"

They flickered against the back of my eyes, not unlike the lights I saw during trance, but glittering with fire and pain, a prickly sparkle which traveled from my nose to my ear.

Raising up on one forearm and then onto my knees, I held out one palm in Benjamin's direction to ward him away from me, though I could not see him through the twinkling galaxy around me. Something wet ran down my face, either blood or tears, and I swept it away with the back of my hand.

Moons appeared in my vision and a flying comet against a night as black and shimmering as silk, and improbably, I felt this firmament sweep across my face with all the smoothness of a sumptuous fabric curtain. The sensation served to steady me, and as my eyes focused, they rested on two men in the room, Benjamin and another. My first fear was my husband had enlisted another man to entrap me, but I realized the new presence was a spirit, and one only I could see.

I was still on my knees when this unfamiliar spirit brushed the side of my face with the sleeve of his fantastic costume, a robe decorated with the stars from my vision. He was an old, crafty-looking man and held in his palm three gold coins. I had the idea he was a magician or some kind of dubious showman, as he manipulated the coins as a trickster would, palming them, letting them roll across his knuckles and disappear. Finally, he put them in the pocket of the star-covered coat and jingled them, twisting his face into a shrewd smile and commencing a vengeful laughter. He seemed to be enjoying our fighting.

Benjamin stood beside the spirit regarding me with a savage face which looked almost like grief. He did not hear the laughter or sense the ill will directed at him from the sinister ghost at his side. There was certainly more than one quarrel in the room, and I wanted no more of either.

With the last bit of ferocity in my body, I stood, feigning a stagger and pawing the air with my arms as though trying to regain balance but actually in search of the doorknob. I lunged when in range of it, and my heart despaired as Benjamin gripped my skirt once more, yet the door opened without my touch, and I was amazed to see the old magician holding it for me. Benjamin gasped and released my skirt, and I did not hesitate. I slid past the starry robe and was gone.

A hundred choices were made while hurrying along the hallway, and I felt exhausted, almost too tired to seize my own freedom. Still, I could not leave without Lovey. Benjamin would likely dump the girl penniless somewhere, now the lectures were over forever.

As always, Lovey's room was some distance away. I never understood why Benjamin did not request adjoining rooms, but what had been inconvenient in the past was a blessing today.

"You're late," Lovey scolded, not looking up as I entered. "I've put out the blue dress and crimped the ribbons that go with it." she continued, "We don't have much more than half an hour."

"I have all the time in the world," I replied, my voice sounding different now, strange even to my own ears, as though Benjamin's beating had altered something in its tone.

Roused by the unfamiliar sound, Lovey looked up and then ran to me.

"Cora! My God!" Lovey placed her hands on my shoulders and with the girl's touch I thought again of her warm and ample body, her motherly gestures.

"I'm leaving him, Lovey," I said, and as soon as the statement left my mouth, as soon as I saw Lovey had heard and accepted it as true, I knew I was sure of it, too. I was leaving Benjamin, and I was leaving tonight.

Lovey stepped back uncertainly and examined me keenly. "What happened?" she asked.

"I won't be party to his lies any longer," I replied, "and surely don't intend to be beaten again for standing up to him. You must come with me."

"Come with you?" Lovey questioned with her face averted, moving toward my costume dresser where she opened the drawer and pulled out one of the cotton rags I used for my monthlies. The money I'd been secreting during the tour was hidden deeply beneath them. Thank God I'd hidden it here in Lovey's room, and Lydia had the rest.

"Of course," I said. "There will be no more lectures."

Lovey took my arm and pulled me closer to the dresser. She dipped the rag in the water standing in her washbowl and blotted at my face. "Hold still now," she commanded.

I realized then I had some injury. The wet cloth made my eyebrow sting, and when Lovey wrung the rag out in the water of the basin, it turned pink. There was blood, quite a lot of it, and the grim little room suddenly seemed overly warm and close. Trunks stood open on their ends, disgorging Lovey's stockings and flouncy dresses, a flashy beaded handbag hung from the inner doorknob. My stomach felt quavery. When Lovey came close, her sweet familiar smell now seemed rank and feral. There was concealment in the girl's silence.

Finally she spoke, in a brittle cheerful voice. "It's clean now, but it may bleed again if you're not careful."

"Lovicia," I said, but the girl was intent on rinsing the handkerchief, so intent it seemed she wanted to keep her eyes turned away.

"Where is he now?" Lovey asked.

"Fabricating some lie about my absence at the lecture hall, I would imagine. We should pack and clear out of here before he returns or, I daresay he'll be hard on both of us."

"I can't," Lovey said.

"Lovey, he is a bad man and liable to cheat or abandon you. He won't want you anymore without me." I said.

Lovey took a step away from me and folded her arms tightly across her chest. "Oh yes, he will," she replied, with the smirk of a rival.

It was as though Benjamin struck me again, the realization, the obvious truth of what had been right in front of me. I closed my eyes, wavering where I stood. My stomach still felt sick, and the entire room seemed to tilt and list. "I see," I finally said.

For a mere moment, I thought to slap Lovey or grab her hair and tear at her, but what would I be fighting for? Certainly nothing I wanted. I opened my eyes and looked at the bed. In this room? In this bed? And how many others? It had been a long chicanery.

I raised my eyes to the window. There was a pleasant park with flower gardens across the way, carriages and people moving in the street. The candy store where I'd been, in what seemed a lifetime ago, was to the right, as was the lecture hall. I would walk out of the hotel and go to the left.

But first, I snatched the gaudy handbag from the doorknob, plunged my hand into the open dresser drawer and withdrew the three pouches of money I'd hidden there. Lovey watched me wide-eyed as I stuffed them into the mouth of the purse.

"Good luck then," I said to Lovey, pushing past the girl and departing her room.

It was only when I was out of sight of the hotel that I began to run.

Shame was probably the only emotion I did not experience on the train to New York, but it made its appearance when I arrived at the bottom of the steps before the house at Irving Place.

Long before the train even neared the river, I could make out the glow of the distant city, but now all was made darker by rain. As my hack pulled up to the townhouse, it was falling in a harsh slant, billowing in lush curtains along the street under the steamy light of the gas lamps. Fallen tree buds collected in the gutters borne by a wind muffled by the purling of water along the cobbles.

Just as when Benjamin and I came a year before, the hallway lamp illuminated the pair of claret-colored windows in the door. Just as then, behind lace curtains, the shadows of figures moved, but instead of longing for the ordinary lives I believed existed within, I now wondered what those same lives would think of me.

My dress was wet and torn; my eye was swollen badly enough, I could no longer see from it. As Katie the maid gasped but recognized and admitted me, I considered for the first time how awful I must look.

Katie, adopting downcast eyes and trying her best not to look askance, led me into the parlor which was full of women who were soon trying not to look askance themselves.

The National Women's Convention! I had forgotten entirely about it. I'd wanted to attend, had spoken of it excitedly with Lydia for months, but the lecture tour prevented it. Several of the prominent orators were to stay with the Edmonds family during the two-day event and here they all were, gathered around their coffee and staring at me. I tried to identify them with my one good eye. Some were strangers, but Lucy Stone was here, Eliza Farnham, Lucretia Mott, Mrs. Post from Rochester, and Sojourner Truth from the camp meetings at Hemlock Hall.

Shame nearly withered my resolve, but I faced them all directly. I was sure of Lydia and Judge Edmonds, but not of the rest. Somehow, I'd escaped from my distress to what could be either the most sympathetic or unsympathetic parlor in all of New York, but I did not know which to expect.

Sojourner Truth

1858

Done up in her nightdress and robe, Mrs. Amy Post crept into the bedroom she was sharin' with me balancin' a glass carefully in her hand.

"Do you have your hot milk, sister?" I asked, sittin' on the edge of my bed while braidin' the long end of my hair.

"I do, Belle, though the glass is a bit overfull and too warm yet for drinking. I shall need it to get any sleep tonight. We've never had such a contentious convention."

Amy callin' me Belle made me smile. Isabella Baumfree was my real name, but I started callin' myself Sojourner Truth when God told me to begin my platform speakin' and preachin'. Only those from the old times still called me Belle. "It was surely a day for argument," I agreed, "and that girl showin' up at the door with her face all blood at the end of it. That is the work of a man's hand, you see if it is not."

Amy wrinkled up her nose in question and tested her milk temperature with her smallest finger. "I do not take your meaning," she said.

"Why that blinker!" I exclaimed, "the damage to her face. A girl like that will say she fell down or bumped a doorway, but that mark came from a father or a beau, to be sure. I know the results of the back of a man's hand well enough when I see it."

"Mrs. Carter is a married lady," Amy said.

"Married? As young as she is?"

"I'm afraid so," Amy replied, tucking her hair into her nightcap.

"Pah!" I said as leaned over and turned down the lamp. "Then I s'pect that young girl has jus' had her first taste of love."

TROUBLE AMONGST THE SPIRITUALISTS

THE CARTER DIVORCE CASE—Mrs. Cora Carter the spiritual medium, in N. York has commenced a suit of divorce from her husband, Dr. Benjamin Carter, on the ground of ill treatment. Her allegations state that they were married upstate in July of 1856, he having represented to her that he was a practicing physician in the city of New York with an income of $10,000 a year; that notwithstanding these representations he had not practiced as a physician since their marriage, but has depended for his support upon her labors in lecturing, that during her lecturing; he has had control of the exchequer and has deprived her of many of the necessaries and comforts of life—even to flannel underclothes and proper food. Mrs Carter consented to give the lectures on the condition that he should provide for her mother, to which he assented, but has paid her very little, and left her too in the want of the necessaries of life. He has given his wife little spending money, and frequently neglected to provide board for her, but accepted invitations to private houses where he stayed until she was subjected to the mortification of knowing that the welcome was worn out. In addition he has frequently brought her into association with immoral characters of both sexes; has been guilty of indecent and immoral practices in her presence, and that he was a hard case generally. This case bids fair to rival the infamous Bennett case of 1855.

—*New York Tribune* August 1858

His Terrible Swift Sword

1858–1867

Hollis

1858

During the time Cora recovered at Irving Place, I sat curled at the foot of her bed as a sleeping cat. Not that I appeared as a visible feline of course, for I did not intend detection, and still remain hesitant to assume the shape of creatures, although in death I now possess the talent to do so. I certainly used it with success when I appeared before Cora as a bluebird and have made cautious attempts with other mild and innocuous creatures in the years since. Flight and feathers, the ability to leap twice my height, four sets of sharp claws, and my tail. A tail! Long enough to curl around my body and touch my own nose. The entire experience is quite unnerving.

The talents available to spirits are as varied as those they possessed in life and seem to be somehow related. My love of animals may account for mine, and the hours I spent observing them in life. Mrs. Beaulieu is likewise skilled, and the shocking quantity of shameless tricks Titus Meacham is capable of no doubt rival those of his earthly profession. Such mischief will certainly retard his progress in our sphere, but we all laughed when he opened the door for Cora at the Tontine Hotel.

I merely felt I should be with Cora, if in my state I can rightly call it being. I spoke many words of encouragement both in her dreams and her ears, and though I remained invisible, I wished I could be more tangible. A vigil was how I saw it. "Calf-love," was what Rosa Beaulieu said, with one eyebrow raised and a suggestive smile, but she is prone to such blunt pronouncements.

In any event, I was hardly Cora's only visitor. In her first days at Irving Place, her room was filled with every sort of sentinel, spectral and otherwise, and my harmless dent in her coverlet was completely overlooked.

Mrs. Beaulieu was there from the first, casting a doubtful gaze on the ministrations of the household women, relaxing her watch only when Cora was in the presence of Sojourner Truth. Old Sojourner seemed to have taken an interest in Cora, as evidenced by the long hours she sat with her, sometimes in silence and sometimes softly singing one of her wonderful improvised hymns.

"She has the common sense of a country woman," Mrs. Beaulieu declared, but I suspect her sympathy was encouraged by the presence of another woman with a clay pipe in her pocket. Indeed, it was endearing to see from my invisible vantage two elder women sitting with Cora and puffing away.

How pleased we all are here in the spirit lands with the first name Sojourner has taken for herself. How perfect an epithet "Sojourner" is, for the state of every soul is certainly temporary. To name oneself "Truth" however is a different thing, and mortals would be wise to avoid such absolutes. Sojourner's heart may be pointed in the right direction, but as far as humans are concerned, truth can only be aspirational.

Another spirit came and went cloaked in a glow of fantastical quality. An advanced and partly transcended soul, he yearned toward Cora in a way which seemed both detached and intent. I say "he" because although I felt it was the spirit of a man, I could not be sure. He moved like a patch of marvelously bright sunlight gilding the little chamber wall, invisible to those on the human plane. Nor could I fully see him, could at best only discern his outline, and I harbored the thought he was hiding himself thus. The one time I believe I glimpsed him, I saw large strong hands covered with scars, a sorrowing gaze and clothing so shabby as to almost appear as rags. But this may be an embellishment of my own making.

They move freely but solitarily in my world, these advanced spirits, and are as much a mystery to me as to the living beings they follow. Descending from a higher sphere than mine and largely silent, they are almost always visibly indistinct. They seem to have crossed from a curious distance which is neither time nor space.

Curious too was the visit of yet another of our kind. From my corner of Cora's counterpane, I almost did not recognize him as he made his one-time foray into the house. Captain Jonathan Walker's gesture was familiar though, as he reached out and rested his hand in Cora's sleeping palm. The image was just as I'd seen it years before when he and I were both alive.

On that well-remembered day, Captain Walker let Cora touch his hand where his wound had been. She'd crept up to him quietly, when all had become dusky and languid in the evening, after most everyone had returned to their homes. Only a few of us remained clustered around the dying fire, some softly singing the old Hope Grove hymns.

She took his hand from where it rested on his knee and turned it palm upward. He did not resist and regarded her with a gentle weariness, the lines in his face made deep and apparent in the flickering orange light. I watched astonished as Cora traced the shape of his scars with her finger, two letters *S* just beside the thumb. I wondered if her child's mind fully understood the awfulness the scars represented, but I imagine she'd just been compelled to come to him, take the damaged hand in her own and hold it. No one stopped her, no one said anything as she eased down beside his chair onto the grass and kept her small hand upon his, as the mellow tone of the hymns rose into the air along with the ebbing flames.

It had been an exciting day in the village, Anniversary Day, when we celebrated the anniversary of the emancipation of the slaves of the West Indies. That glorious day of freedom had happened back in 1833, but even seventeen years later abolitionists like the citizens of Hope Grove used the occasion to urge both the United States and the world to universal emancipation.

The shady grove near the curve in the river for which the town had been named was filled with several small tents and a large number of chairs and blankets brought from people's homes for the event. A platform had been constructed, and the trees dangled with with paper stars and lanterns made by the Children's Committee. A great circle of ground had been prepared for the evening bonfire. There had been a picnic, speeches, games and contests, sermons and the singing of hymns. But the highlight of the day was the appearance of Captain Jonathan Walker, the man with the branded hand.

Late in the afternoon, a large crowd had assembled and sat chattering and fidgeting in their seats. I can remember the cooking smells from the picnic and still hear the sounds of the music teacher and her pupil tuning the violins they'd brought to accompany the lecture. A man sauntered among us selling pamphlets.

"Take the story of Jonathan Walker home," the man repeated quietly, as he walked among us, shifting the stack of booklets on his hip and jingling coins in his pocket. "Five cents only for the inspired words."

Like the other children, Cora spent the day running all over the vicinity, so by the time Captain Walker ascended the platform, she was seated beside her parents in the grass, with closed eyes and her head on her father's lap.

Climbing the steps, Captain Walker didn't look like much. A tall paunchy older man with a listless face and straight thin hair combed over his head. Alone on the platform he looked almost trivial.

With a quick gesture, he held out his hand—the hand—facing the audience, a neat trick as everyone quieted and craned forward trying to get a glimpse of the brand. He stood silent for a long moment sweeping the hand in an arc before him, so all could have a view, then holding it straight and still once more. Suddenly a dramatic and deep-toned voice tumbled forth recounting the vivid tale, the appeal of the desperate fugitive slaves, the ready assent of Captain Walker to carry them in his vessel to freedom in the West Indies. One could feel the anxious escape from the Florida coast in Walker's tone. Storms and sickness and fever were described with the same wild look in the eyes the storyteller must have possessed while experiencing them. The despair of their capture and the filth and terror of the prison were evoked with stirring phrases. Heat, mosquitoes and leg irons entered the tale. A lengthy foray into the monotony of the trial, accusations, pleas, sentencing, enticed the audience for the salient part of the story. All eyes were on the figure of the Captain. Cora had risen from her father's lap to a kneeling position of attention. The tying of the Captain's arm to the rail, the slow approach of the red-hot iron, and the branding itself, described as great pain and a spattering noise, like a handful of salt thrown on a fire. *SS* seared into the skin. Slave Stealer.

Some of the women wept, and men approached the Captain after he'd finished speaking and clapped him on the back. Six years before, when the Captain was finally released from the Florida prison, John Greenleaf Whittier had written a poem about him which had been put to music, and many in the audience took up the words and sang them with the violins, as Jonathan Walker made his way slowly and wordlessly through the Hope Grove crowd with his hand extended for all to examine.

"Then lift that manly right-hand, bold plowman of the wave!
Its branded palm shall prophesy "Salvation to the Slave!"
Hold up this fire-wrought language, that whoso reads may feel
His heart swell strong within him, his sinews change to steel."

Hours later, in the last light of the day, it was Cora who held the careworn hand and gazed into the fire, spellbound. I wondered if she perceived the terrible pain. Did she realize then how wicked the world was? The world she was to live and grow in?

In the far meadow, fireflies had started to rise. Much like the sparks twisting upward from the fire before us. In the same way, Captain Walker's words had been cast into the air, the seeds of an awful fire to come.

No doubt Cora was meant to hear the Captain's words. The ugly story of brands and slaves and shackles. Why else would the hand which had passed through those fearful experiences have come to rest in Cora's own those many years ago? Why else would it return again in spirit form, and after Cora's own terrifying escape, to resume the same place? I could ask Jonathan Walker but have the idea he intends to keep himself scarce. I am also perhaps too shy.

Indeed, I am in awe of him still. In awe of them both if truth be told, though I must remember my own advice about absolutes.

Cora was unusually quiet the next time we worked together in the print shop. It was the high of summer, with ardent blue skies spattered with ragtag clouds, and the air was heavy and sweet with the smell of the last cutting of the hay. She worked in peaceful concentration, her small head bent over the typecase, her braided pigtails sprouting little tufts of escaped hair, which detracted nothing from her rather majestic bearing. Such was the force of her personality even then.

I longed to ask her about the evening of Anniversary Day, when she'd sat with Captain Walker, but it was this very force which stopped me, that and some invasion of her privacy I did not dare. Yet I'd seen the remarkable interaction with my own eyes, we all had. The way Cora approached the famous man with a demeanor both bold and meek and simply held his branded hand.

A moment after witnessing the stunning act, I turned to look at my father's face, intent too on what was before him.

"She has taken his hand the same way God will surely do," the Reverend Lyman said quietly, and it was true.

Like everyone else, I regarded Jonathan Walker as a hero, but went one step further and envied him too. The man had been tested and proven; he'd done the right thing and lived to tell his tale. I wondered if placed in a similar circumstance whether I would succeed or fail? Would I make it to elder manhood with a lifetime of good decisions behind me? Would I meet such trials with the same courage and rise to the same distinction as Captain Walker? How nice it would be to have already run the race and run it well, I thought. To have God or Cora take my hand.

Well, God took my hand all right, and in a way I never expected. I needn't have worried about running races or for that matter, manhood. Perhaps this is sad. There is sadness in heaven. Bad news for those who think in death it will disappear. I often forget I am dead, and even find I miss the act of weeping. But sadness in our world is altogether differently felt. As you will see.

* * *

"What is the name of the device made by our factory here in Hope Grove?"

It was Cora, looking up from her task at the print shop. Her first real words of the day interested me, as I knew they would relate somehow to the evening with Jonathan Walker. "It's called a loom temple."

"What does it do?" she asked.

"It keeps the fabric in the loom stretched just right. It is designed so the weaver can run two looms at once. The work is done twice as fast."

"Then slaves must have to pick twice as much cotton." Cora said frowning, revealing in her words the thoughts which were troubling her.

"Yes, I suppose they do," I answered.

"How can we be against slavery and make a tool which causes slaves more work?" she pressed.

I paused my own work and considered my future teaching career. Is this what teaching was to be? Not the recitation of tables and stanzas but a profound question from one presumably too young to ask? How many times would I be called on to answer such a question, one which I could neither answer nor claim I'd ever even asked myself?

There were many small enterprises in Hope Grove, but the factory where the loom temple was made was the most profitable and the Draper family who owned it, the richest family in town. Indeed, without the support of the Draper enterprise, Hope Grove could not exist. My mind then followed the same pathways Cora's had. Hope Grove depended on the loom temple, the loom temple needed cotton, and cotton needed slaves.

I pushed aside the chase I was locking up and slid my own stool closer to Cora's. She turned to me, taking her ink-smudged fingers away from the type and placing them flat on her apron-front.

"You ask a good question, Cora, and it is one I cannot answer," I said. "I confess, I myself have never made the connection."

"It seems wrong," Cora said.

"I am certain the man who invented the loom temple had no desire to burden slaves," I told her, "just to make a better loom. I think both he and Hope Grove can only be judged by their intentions."

"Are you saying we can do bad things, as long as we claim we really mean to do good ones?" she asked.

"A bad deed can't be hidden that way, Cora, but we are all small parts of a bigger world. How else are we to proceed except by following our good intentions? What else do we have?"

Cora's brow furrowed in contemplation, and I knew she was not convinced. Nor was I. Nor am I still. Is intent really enough? Or, is it not more like truth, a slippery and changeable thing? It is no simple question, and I fear that any answer which presents itself will still answer nothing.

Jonathan Walker
1860

Dusk time, from my prison window I could see the crows homing. Reeling and darting like smut from a chimney, small shreds of life which always made my heart flare with a brief joy.

You would think tropical Florida would nurture a fairer bird—something with red plumes and golden crests for instance—but no, I saw only crows, as black as the men I tried to rescue on my ship—blacker, and more clever too, as all crows are more clever than men. They are always two tricks ahead of us. Perhaps if I had been a crow, I could have avoided the prison cell but of course not the scorn. Crows are scorned everywhere, but whether it is because they are black or because they are clever, I do not know. Pity such creatures that are both.

I went to Hope Grove in the summer of 1851 from my home in Plymouth. It was a two-day journey, by the Old Colony Railway and the stage. I was well past the age of fifty years by then and such bone-rattling travel made me tired and sore.

It was one of the experimental towns, a bit raw with newness, but set aside a river with a decent fall. I'd visited a number of the like, with populations held together by ideals of a better world. Most were followers of temperance, others anti-violence, all were abolitionist, and I knew for them I was a figure beloved. Each time I'd lectured in one of these towns they invariably asked me to take up residence with them. In Hope Grove, the Reverend Lyman broached the subject less than an hour after I'd stepped off the stagecoach, but I'd seen too much to believe the innate goodness of men was going to take root anywhere.

I was not even sure how I arrived at that place in my life. I'd been tossed one way and another for half a dozen years, famous because I made an unwise journey with a bad end. The world thought me brave, but I shuddered at the folly of it. Setting sail in an open boat with seven escaped slaves, all the while with a wife and children who depended on me.

I never dreamed we would all be captured, but I was angry enough at the time to do anything. Angry at the treatment of the Negroes. Angry enough to ignore good sense. That we survived at all was a miracle, but the men I tried to help were no better off than before, and likely worse. Their fates still caused me sleepless nights. I wondered if they were still living, if you could call their lives living. I had worked for abolition all my life, but who had I ever saved?

When abolitionist friends from the Northeast got me freed from the Florida prison, I arrived back in Massachusetts as an unexpected hero. I'd been praised and feted, taken to a photographic studio so my famous hand could be daguerreotyped, and somehow I'd ended up on the lecture platform. I learned exactly how to tell the story, what to emphasize, where to pause for best effect, but good men still languished in bondage.

After I'd taken the brand and was thrown back in my prison cell, I worried about infection and gangrene. I'd seen men lose limbs from far lesser injuries. Yet after I had lectured for those many years, I wished I could cut the hand away entirely, leave it and all it represented behind me, where it could exist only in the gold-encased daguerreotypes, unattached to me.

For the long months I spent in prison, I thought mostly of two things, my family and fruit. I'd dreamed of my wife and children often, but with the unhealthy swill I'd been daily fed, I also imagined wonderful fruits, apples, plums and pears. If I survived, I would move to the West and plant orchards. Only a few more lectures, a few thousand more pamphlets sold, and I would have enough for a farm of my own.

* * *

The child came to me after the lecture, when the day was over, in the pleasant hour of the evening when I and some of the others remained seated by the shrinking bonfire. Down by the river, fireflies sparkled in the long grass, and some of the assembled began to sing hymns.

"We have come from various quarters,
both parents, sons and daughters.
We have come from various quarters,
to live a truer life……."

The sweet-faced girl arrived by my side furtively, as children often do, with the quick and silent movements of small animals. She took my hand and turned it over to the palm. Children often asked to see my hand. Girls squealed, and the boys would laugh or proclaim wonder; all of them I believe, preparing themselves for the reality of cruelty and evil, as it was sure to come in some form into each of their lives.

The girl did not ask however, she simply moved my hand and held it, sinking to a seat in the grass beside me. The child's hand was so soft, so unspoilt, the gentle clasp of it like a sanctity or a blessing. The top of her head was close to my knee, and I noted the small parting in her pale hair, which reminded me of my own daughter. I missed my children when I traveled away from them. My throat thickened, and I felt an agony of tenderness and the long-ago day of my own innocence. I withdrew my hand from hers and placed it gently on her head, cradling it in a soft, pleasurable clutch.

"I have a daughter just your age at home in Plymouth," I told her.

My hand felt warm and heavy at the crown of her head. The child shifted and let herself rest against my knee, and I closed my eyes to the hymn being sung, which became a distant sound like murmuring, and then like the splash of the rushing sea, slave voices on my boat, and the snap of the wind filling the sail. My hand was still resting on the girl's head, holding it fixed and still in a place of complete safety, but I could also feel the ships wheel running through my fingers and turning both our souls to face a new direction.

"Maria," the girl said.

"Yes, my daughter is Maria," I replied, wondering how the child had made the right guess.

When she then turned to me, her face glowing and as translucent as a tiny wraith, I saw an absolute verity in her eyes, some vital message which called to me from a place far beyond the girl herself, yet inexorably connected to her, and which I suddenly understood. This was it. Hope Grove would be the last. I would return to my family and seek my fruit trees in the west. I would never lecture again.

I wasn't many years on my new farm before my life disappeared, and only since I've shed it, do I realize how heavy it was. My guilt is gone, my anger is gone, and everything that went before seems shadowy and unreal and as if it all may have happened to someone else. What balm to my troubled heart to rest now in this silent place; a wonderful and waiting stillness I have no desire to disturb.

Thus, a more reluctant revenant has never pierced the veil of heaven, but I must return sometimes to Cora if only to renew our fated touch. I visit her without words, as I do not seek to be another voice in her murmurous air. The footfall she hears is mine, prowling her night in dim and blessed anonymity and because there are bonds which exist which turn the mysterious works of the universe. I must still rest my old and terrible hand in Cora's unscathed palm, for each person is born from parents other than the two which share their blood.

Sojourner Truth

1861

I was both right and wrong. That girl Cora who'd come to the Edmonds had been thrashed by a man, but she wasn't shy about tellin' who'd done it. 'Twas her own husband had taken his hand to her, splittin' her eyebrow and knockin' her to the floor with one hard blow. She ran away after that, escapin' through a locked door she said a spirit opened for her. Now I don't know if that part is the true, but in her place, I'd have done jus' the same. I've been owned and knocked about by five different men, and when I finally had the chance to get away I took it.

It didn't take long before I recalled the girl either, speakin' the words of the spirits at Hemlock Hall back in the 50's. She was jus' as pretty then and had all the menfolk gawpin', so I don't imagine she'd far to fall into the arms of a scoundrel husband.

Even in those days, I had no doubt the spirits spoke through Cora. I've been a good deal around seekers of the spirit and seen many people seized by spirits, though I never took most of them for the true. The right preacher pumpin' his bellows can make big men quiver and twitch and set off women who might seem as sober to shriekin' and howlin' like wet cats. Some places I've even seen 'em throw themselves to the ground and blubber in foreign tongues. Now God commanded that His people "watch and pray," so I can't see how He would have any doin's with any such carryin' on. Cora is quiet and listenin' always, and when the spirit of God or His dead come to her you can see their presence pass across her face and the corners of her eyes sparkle with tears. God don't live in a place of commotion, but I know well that He does live at the point of tears.

I was stayin' at the Edmonds' that night three years ago because we'd all attended the Women's Convention which'd finished up that same day. I'd been upstate in Rochester for a month that spring makin' a visit at the home of Mrs. Amy Post, and she and I had come down to New York together for the event. It was a rowdy proceedin' with much quarrel and fuss, and when Cora stumbled into the parlor, some of the women present were still smolderin' from the squabbles of the afternoon.

I will say right now not every woman in the house that night believed in the spirits, and I heard some scoffin' and hard words toward Cora. Women's rights was a common cause, but we hardly all of us thought alike. A good many of the women were so taken up with protestin' man's laws, I felt they did not put God's laws to the fore. Some few like Mrs. Farnham did not believe in God at all. Now I can't go along with that. In tryin' to gain our rights, we must all put our shoulder to the wheel, but it won't move until God gives His own push. The way I see it, we must all push and pray.

This made me feel as kin to Cora. We'd both been years on the platform and had both stood before the people testifyin' as much as firebrandin', speakin' of God's word as often as man's. I'd heard the words of God in my own ears and followed what He asked me to do. I'd changed my name and left my home when His Spirit called me. Though Cora's speeches came to her from common spirits and mine were the professions of an old and simple woman who the Spirit'd commanded, we spoke of the same things. We were more alike than most of the women at the Convention, and I wondered if Cora's spirits spoke to her in the same way mine did to me. The night she came I resolved to find out. All the other women in the house talked of men as their foe, but I was more than sure Cora and I were the only two who'd ever known the hard lesson of a man's fist.

So I stayed at the Edmonds' after Mrs. Post and the other women had left, and it was Judge Edmond's daughter Lydia and I who sat at Cora's bedside. We dressed the eye and talked over whether we should stitch it. I'd a twist of fine silk thread in my reticule that would have done the trick, but Lydia was afraid it would make a scar. *Jus' a reminder of a bad decision*, was what I thought of that, but in the end, Cora remained asleep and the eye was left to heal itself. Lydia and I took turns in the room, and I sat and worked on my knittin'. Sometimes I smoked. Sometimes I sang.

"It was early in the mornin'—
it was early in the mornin',
jus' at the break of day—
when he rose, when he rose, when he rose
and went to heaven on a cloud."

Cora stirred beneath the bedclothes and opened her good eye. "I'm tempted to pretend sleep and stay here all day listening to you sing," she said.

I smiled in return, for I was glad to see her stirrin', and always glad to hear good comments on my singin', but I knew the girl was wakin' to a fearful future. "It's no easy thing to wake to a bad mornin'," I replied.

"Who is here?" Cora asked, rising against the headboard.

"Jus' Lydia and I, the hired girl Katie and the Judge."

Cora then glanced about the room, as though searchin' the corners. That mornin', I thought she might jus' be testin' her eyesight, but over time, I came to know that look she got about her. All eyes and ears, heedful. I know now there'd been spirits in the room.

"The other women from the Convention have left?" she asked.

"They have all gone on, as of yesterday afternoon."

"But you stayed," she said, givin' me her own small smile. "Has anyone come to the house?"

"Not who you might think, but Lydia said there was a newspaperman hangin' about. The Judge drove him off."

Cora sank back into the pillows and sighed.

"Might be he was here lookin' for Miss Stone or Mrs. Mott."

"Pfft! Not if there is something bad to report." Cora said, reachin' up with one finger to touch the bandage on her damaged eye.

“That man of yours gave you a right smart blinker and split your eye wide open. You might have a nick of a scar in your eyebrow, but no more than that.”

Cora shrugged and waved away my remark, pullin’ back the covers and slidin’ to the edge. “A souvenir of an unwise journey,” she said.

I almost thought to take the girl into my arms and praise her good sense and bravery but was struck instead by a great streak of sunlight which jus’ then entered the room through a crack in the curtains and surrounded her. I’d never seen such a tone of gold, dancin’ on the walls of the room, and I could only think it was a sign Cora’d been blessed and rescued by God. It gave me a scare to think what evil might otherwise have befallen her. “You are lucky it wasn’t worse. I once saw a man beat so bad, all the bones in his face were broken,” I said.

The beam of sun moved between us and lay like the edge of a sharp and shiny thing along the wall and the floorboards. I should have thought it would have blinded her, but Cora took no notice and instead looked to me with a question on her face. “Was the man a slave? Did he live with you on a plantation?” she asked.

Now it was my turn to scoff. “I’ve lived on no plantation. For near thirty years I was bondswoman in this very state of New York! Yes, Robert was a slave too and subject to every whim of beatin’. There was slavery here in the North, and not so long ago. When I was half your age, I was sold with a flock of sheep for a hundred dollars.”

Cora shook her head slightly as though she was clearin’ her thinkin’. “I’m sorry,” she said. “These days one tends to think of the South.”

“The sin of slavery has lived in every corner and the South is the worst, but Lord knows even if the serpent’s head is cut off in the North it looks to grow back in the West.”

The girl sat quietly for some time. The bright sun disappeared as quickly as it’d come, and I felt some shame about speakin’ so wrathy. Cora’s eye was bandaged. Her hands lay forlorn in her lap. Her nightdress was not even her own.

“Did Robert live?” she eventually asked.

"He was never the same. His self was beat right out of him, and he died soon after."

"How did you get away?"

"I walked away when my freedom was due me with nothin' but my clothes in a handkerchief."

"I'm a bit better off," Cora said with another sad smile, "as I have some monies I saved from the lectures."

"Judge Edmonds will help, and Lydia is as your sister."

"It is still reliance on others. How can any of us be free until we can do for ourselves?"

"You can still travel and speak," I argued.

"Yes, by the arrangement, or the behest, or the permission of a man."

I knew Cora was right. Though I always kept it to myself, I had the same uneasy notion as I made my own way in the world. Slavery of every kind still ruled the land, and though I truly believed God would someday put an end to it, I often wondered which would be the last to pass through the door of freedom—my color or my sex."

Cora was a good girl. She helped wherever she was needed in the Edmonds' household and made herself 'specially valuable to me. I had never learned to read or write, so'd made a habit of askin' friends in various places to make and send letters for me and to read those I'd received. It was about a month into my stay when Cora and I sat with a stack of finished letters she'd written for me in the thick fancy paper the Judge had on hand.

Cora's handwritin' was so neat and pretty, and even though she knew many more words than I did, she promised not to use any of them. It was a relief to me to have someone put down my words jus' as I'd spoken them. I knew others often changed what I said to sound more proper and people have told me that some of my letters don't sound like me a'tall.

Cora had some new dresses, and her eye'd healed almost to the not noticin', and though she seemed a different girl than the one who arrived in the rain the month before, I knew she was still heartsore.

"Why do you think your spirits didn't warn you?" I asked.

Cora lifted the clutch of letters and squared them with a small tap on the tabletop. "There was too much to warn," she said.

"But why didn't they at least protect you from your husband's attack?"

"It is not the way of the spirits. I don't think they can shelter us."

"Yet the one spirit opened the door for you so you could escape?"

"Yes," Cora agreed, "but I do not know who he was, and it seemed less that he was helping me than thwarting Benjamin—if that makes any sense."

"Not to me," I replied. "When the Spirit told me to leave my home and go east, the command was clear. I spent no time in wonderin'."

"Perhaps it was God Himself speaking to you," Cora said. "I only hear the voices of mortal souls, and they do not always make themselves known by speech."

I went silent then, but I could have made an oath there was somethin' there with us, somethin' as quiet as a sigh, and it made me shiver and strain to hear. "Are there spirits here with us now, Cora?"

The girl closed her eyes as if listenin'. "They are always here," she said.

"God Almighty!" I exclaimed, feelin' all-overish and wrappin' my arms around myself and drawin' my collar tighter. "I don't know if I like that notion. Who is here?"

"Hollis, just as regular as daylight, and the old woman who often attends me. A man must come along with her as I smell his tobacco whenever I see or feel her."

I dug into my pocket and produced my pipe. "What manner of woman is she? Maybe she is doing the smokin'. Doesn't take a man to enjoy a pipe."

Cora breathed in deeply. "Then the two of you smoke different tobacco," she said, smilin'.

As quick as she'd said it, I felt the hair rise on the back of my old neck, and swore to the feelin' someone had run their hands through my hair risin' sparks, though whether this was the true or jus' my own brain makin' mischief I couldn't say. I jumped and looked around all corners of the quiet room.

"I wish I could hear them."

"You've heard God," Cora answered.

We sat together for some time in the grand room, until the mornin' sun crossed to the street side of the house takin' the hard edges off the light, and Cora spread the letters we'd written out before us.

"You've all your children we've been writing to. Who was their father, Sojourner? You never speak of him."

The reminder troubled me some, and I was unsure of my answer. I loved my children, but not the one who'd been my man. "Thomas, he was called," I said and then paused. "He was neither bad nor good."

"Was he your husband?" she asked.

"Slave husband," I said. "Not a man of my own choosin'."

Cora was quiet awhile thinkin' on what I'd said, an awful condition for any woman, but not so rare as I believed back in the day when Thomas was forced upon me. Many kinds of women find themselves with no choice.

"Now that Benjamin and I are divorcing," she began, "there are those who say I should not do it. Lydia and Judge Edmonds favor my actions, but others say differently."

"What do these others say?" I asked.

"They say marriage is sacred, that I have a duty to obey my husband's wishes. They say divorce will ruin my reputation."

"What reputation comes from obeyin' a scoundrel?"

"My mother says Benjamin deserves a second chance."

Cora's mother—ho! I'd never met the lady, but I think I knew the sort of woman who would say such a thing to her daughter pretty well. "What do your spirits say?"

"My will is always free, so they are silent. But even if they were to speak, I don't know if I'd hear them over the noise of my own indecision. What do you think, Sojourner?"

Shocked I was and at first did not want to speak. In all of my long life, I don't think any White woman ever asked for my advice, and I was not sure how to give it. So I put my hand atop Cora's before I spoke, as the words seemed awful hard.

"Snake sheds his skin, but not his stripes," was all I said.

Now, three years later, the woe I long predicted has beset the land. Praise God for He has finally pushed, Fort Sumter has fallen, and the great war has begun. It is as if the sky has opened and released the fury of Heaven. At first, my heart was happy. My people would have their vengeance yet, and if the slaughter were terrible than so be it. The punishment of the slaveholder had at last found its hour as all evil returns to the begetter.

Now I feel more fearful. The Rebels have whipped our Union boys at Bull Run and I scare to think of the blood that will soon be runnin'. Still, I come out in front of my home when the regiments go marchin' by and wave my handkerchief and hoo-ray with all the rest. Back indoors I keep prayin'. If I have to fight myself, I will. I am jus' as much a soldier as any of them. My legs are not so limber as once, but my arms, which have bound ten thousand sheaves of grain, are as strong as any rebel.

I have not seen Cora or Lydia since last winter in New York City. Now with the war I don't know when I ever will, but the girls write to me and I hear of their doin's.

In January, when I was last there, the talk of the house was of marriage and divorce. Cora had finally got loose of that no-good husband, and Lydia had said yes to Mr. George Austin who'd courted her for so long.

It was a strange day, and whether it was the war so close in comin' or the conversation we had I don't know, but I won't forget it. Georgia had jus' been the fifth state to secede, but the war still seemed impossible, or even if it were to happen, it would not be somethin' where men would die.

The girls seemed so young that day and sat on the floor like children talkin' about dresses. Patterns, scissors, and a pile of Lady's

Books were stacked around them. We had a pot of chocolate, and Cora and Lydia had gone silly, gigglin' and carryin' on, pullin' bits of fabric from a basket and tossin' them all around so the floor looked as though it were covered with a scrap quilt. They asked my opinion on one dress or another, but what could I say? I'd never been a bride, and my sewin' skills were jus' for simple.

Sometimes in my life I'd felt mean over things I didn't have—freedom was the worst of it. Other times, I wished for nice clothes or spendin' money, but on this day, I felt other things I had lost. In watchin' the girls I remembered the girl I once was and did not like to think of her.

"Pamela sleeve or Pagoda style?" Lydia asked, holding up two colored pages from the Lady's Book for me to inspect. "Which do you like, Sojourner?"

"You girls are being silly," I said with some sternness, for that was it. It was not my gone youth which made the hole inside me but the loss of silliness. I'd never been silly. I never could.

"Lydia's in love," Cora said. "You'll have to excuse her enthusiasm."

"It's true," Lydia said. "Love makes me foolish. Tell us when you were in love, Sojourner."

I scowled and rolled my eyes.

"What about your husband?" Lydia asked.

"Pffft. Certainly not him." I scoffed.

"There must have been someone, when you were a girl," she insisted.

It was hard to remember, girlhood. Was it even possible I was young? I remember bein' stronger, healthier. I remember when my children were babes, liftin' and carryin' them. I remember some man showin' me how to pack a pipe, when I was owned by the Schrivers and worked at their tavern, but I did not love him. It was another man, one I met in secret in the woods. One I saw beaten nearly to death in the dooryard, because his master did not want him visitin' with me.

"It was Robert," Cora said.

That Cora was a smart one, but the minute she spoke I panicked. Had she remembered our past conversation, or had she heard Robert's spirit speakin' and know? If there is anythin' slavery teaches you, it is to hide your emotions, and I kept calm. Robert may have been beaten into line, but he would never tell what he knew, even in death, even to Cora.

"No man ever asked for me, and I never wanted one either," I said.

Like a flash of summer lightnin' a beam of sunlight streaked through the window, brightenin' the books and furniture and fallin' across our faces in a harsh glare. The same light as three years before on the day Cora and I spoke about Robert. Cora said not all spirits came as voices. Was this light Robert's spirit? I wanted to believe it was.

I am often asked what was most difficult about slavery, and what was the worst work I'd ever done. My answer never changed. What is most difficult is the same for everyone, slave or free. Faith is difficult, and belief is the hardest work of all.

That first day I saw the beautiful golden light, Cora did not seem to note it, nor did she take a special interest in it this second time, except to raise her hand to her eyes to shield them from the glare. Lydia too, was turnin' her head away, droppin' her dress patterns and risin' from the floor to close the curtains.

"My goodness," Cora said, blinkin' once behind the shadow of her hand. "That sun is awfully bright." But I watched her as she paused, her ears pricked like a horse, her eyes narrowed as she seemed to surmise the air, almost sniffin' it like a dog. "It's just as if..."

"Jus' as if what?" I asked.

Cora shrugged and shook her head slightly. "Something...I don't know."

Parlor Receptions

A valued correspondent reports that Cora Carter is receiving friends in mediumship circles Saturday evenings at her residence at F Street. After each circle she speaks in trance on a different subject, unique in character and phenomenal in versatility.

It is further understood that she will accept calls for weekday evening lectures at different points within a five mile radius of Washington City. Now is the time for the friends resident at adjacent points to listen to those beautiful inspirations with which from the commencement of her public life, and wherever she has been, her spirit guides have elicited to the esteem of the believer and the wonder of the skeptic.

—*Banner of Light* Spiritualist Newspaper, Boston.
Saturday, April 26, 1862

Cora

1862

The vision of the hand frightened me at first, the sudden appearance of the palm with fingers pointed skyward as if in readiness to strike, as well as the way it appeared morning after morning in my final moment of sleep. Was it some replaying of Benjamin's beating, or another sort of warning? There was never time to study the vision before it startled me awake, leaving me shuddering and sweating in my little room at F Street.

This was hardly the only portent to decipher in the already overheated Washington City spring. The constant presence of sick and maimed soldiers in the streets and makeshift hospitals, the sad death of Willie Lincoln and the White House draped in black, and just last month the carnage at Shiloh, a place presumably named for peace, where thousands of voices were stilled in a single day. The advent of the awful hand in my dreams and these discomfiting events seemed related, but what did it mean?

Spirits could be as clumsy as children, especially the newly dead. I believed many were just as tongue-tied in heaven as on earth, or perhaps confounded by their incorporeal state. I knew spirits did not mean to be confusing, so I often only had to repeat my question, and they would speak in a different way as to be understood.

The next time the hand woke me, I spoke sternly to the unknown spirit. "Bearer of the hand, stop frightening me and let me sleep," I commanded. "If you have a message, please state it more clearly."

In some measure, the spirit obeyed, and though no clear message was offered, the hand of my morning nightmares disappeared. Yet it returned at other times, palm forward and fingers splayed, insistent in its inexplicable significance. It appeared behind the head of the Negro vegetable seller in the market. It hovered in mute beseeching above the table at my spirit circles. I saw it often in my mind's eye, indistinct but somehow reminiscent of the past, like a memory, which perhaps it was.

I appealed to Hollis, but on the subject of the hand, he paid me no heed. Rather, he continued to speak as he always did, his words seeping from his world into my head just as though they might be my own thoughts. Encouragements, stories, and memories from his own life, his presence so rich, it sometimes seemed as if I were talking to myself.

Whether he could not or would not speak of the hand I didn't know, but there are some questions the dead refuse to answer. Each time I implored him, his reply was opaque. "Just because you have forgotten something does not mean it has forgotten you," was all he would say.

I stood in the light of the partially opened bed chamber window unpinning my hair, letting it fall to my shoulders. I wore it more simply now, foregoing the elaborate ringlets of my New York days.

While brushing it, I took in the view from the second floor of the house on F Street. Here I rented two rooms, and this, the back room where I slept, was the smaller of the two. Outside was the slope of the roof covering the porch of the lodger below, and the small yard where Mrs. Ludlow, the landlady, kept a tidy garden. Mrs. Ludlow owned two houses side by side and lived and cooked the meals for her boarders in the one opposite, but kept the yards fenced together. This was a good plan as the numerous groups of free-ranging pigs were thus kept from grubbing up the vegetable beds. It was nothing like New York.

The principal streets of Washington City were paved with cobbles, but many other roadways were little more than furrows of mud. The houses seemed bland and insignificant, while unfinished government buildings including the Capitol dome rose in a contradictory and half-hearted glory above it all. Sometimes the grand

Capitol, for a brief moment, relinquished its ill-favored surroundings and one could imagine its future majesty, but more often, it appeared just truncated and forlorn. Even without the war and incomplete structures to give credence to the thought, one could see a United States was more easily dreamed of than done.

Nevertheless, I thought my two small rooms were like a palace and my removal from New York, a chance at a new and free life on my own, and I was managing. There was little money, but so far there had been enough.

Still in my dressing gown, I walked to the front parlor of my lodgings and opened the interior shutters. The room had been a small office before the war, and the former tenant left behind a threadbare carpet and a rather grand six-jet gasolier which lit the room to dazzling.

I'd covered the worn spot in the carpet with a single table, and the twelve chairs I possessed for my receptions circled this and lined the four walls at two against each. I draped the mantle of the fireplace with a lambrequin I'd sewn myself and decorated the bare walls with framed views of Roman fountains and gardens found at a removal sale last year.

Raising the window a few inches, I felt the gentle cross-breeze waft by at my waist to the window in the back bedroom. A man with a handcart rumbled by on the street below. I pressed my forehead to the cool surface of the window glass. The coming heat of the day was already rising.

The clatter of traffic on the cobbles never ceased, livestock rambled the streets, damaged soldiers idled, and coffled groups of Negros with despairing eyes tramped behind wagons, but I'd never felt such peace. Pestilential heat and rains brought fevers which flared and extinguished, and a hostile army was encamped less than fifty miles away, but it had been years since I felt so safe.

Benjamin, the tattling newspapers, the divorce and relentless lectures were finally behind me. Without the funds once dispatched to Cadytown, my disappointed mother had been compelled to move from the farm, but she and little Edward were suitably housed with my aunt and uncle Page. Mother's grumbling letters continued to arrive, but after a quick perusal, I tore them in quarters and threw them away. I'd given her most of the money scavenged from my lectures and now sent money home whenever I could.

Fumbling for the hairpins in my pocket and placing them in my mouth, I grasped the brushed length of hair with one hand and twisted it upwards, fixing it firmly in place. Where did my determination come from? How did I find the strength to proceed with things others either forbade or ridiculed? Faith was part of it and my certainty in what I sensed; although I was unsure whether I sensed these things with my heart or my mind, and if that distinction made any difference.

Either way, I was grateful for my calm new days, hours which I arranged and ordered myself. Everything which had always been unstable and transitory was still at last. It was as though my whole life had finally stopped to take a breath. I owned a trunk of clothing, some used furniture and a vast and beautifully blank future.

May 5, 1862
Irving Place, New York

Dear Cora,

I wanted to send this letter right away and enclose the article I clipped from the latest Banner of Light. It seems word has traveled as far as Boston of your receptions in Washington City. I thought such a notice would please you after the lies you've endured at the hands of some of the other papers. You see your old friends have not forgotten you, and those who know you esteem you for both your work and yourself.

It goes without saying how much you are missed here in New York, and how I wish you were here to see how little Mae grows and grows. I cannot describe how she pleases me and how every little change in her seems so monumental. She smiles and has learnt to roll over by herself in her little cot. She will be 4 months in another week, and it seems impossible how much has changed in just a few years. Married and a mother, with a husband off to fight in this terrible war. I can only hope some real good will come of it all.

Charles leaves with his regiment at the end of the month, he thinks to Camp Hamilton in Virginia. How I worry—but am no different than a thousand other women. Between Mae's short nights and my thinking of Charles, I sleep very little and it shows. Father worries as well, and he often sits up with Mae. I sometimes hear him talking with her. Hearing his voice across the hall is a comfort. I suppose he talked with me in the same way when I was a babe, and some interior memory is brought forth by the familiar sound.

Write to me dear, of all you are doing. Don't tell Father I told you, but he rather thinks of you as a protege and advises all his political friends to call on you when they are in Washington City.

With love from Lydia and Mae Cora Austin

A year ago at my first parlor reception in Washington City no one came. No one except my landlady, Mrs. Ludlow, whose appearance I first feared might indicate the woman's disapproval of seances in her establishment. Yet, the elder lady arrived bearing a tray of sweets which I realized was offered as a form of payment and a request for help in locating some lost papers. It was a common request, and one I always dreaded.

"The spirits don't keep us in a constant vigil," I warned Mrs. Ludlow. "They often know no better than we where we've tucked something away."

"But what if he hid it himself?" Mrs. Ludlow asked. "I've hunted those deeds to these houses for four years since Eli…er… Mr. Ludlow died."

"Then our results might be better." I said.

I bade Mrs. Ludlow sit in one of the chairs around the table and carried a lamp from the entry. I no longer cast the room in the pitch black Benjamin preferred but lit it softly. Still the room seemed vast with just the two of us at the table, and the single light made our silhouettes loom like a pair of large twins against the wall.

Mrs. Ludlow clutched the table's edge and looked warily around her. "Ohhhh. I've never done anything of this kind." she said.

I took the lady's hand. "They'll be nothing fearful," I promised. "Just close your eyes and think of Mr. Ludlow. Ask for his help in finding the deeds."

"Eli," Mrs. Ludlow said timidly.

"Mr. Ludlow?" I asked the air.

We'd both spoken at the same moment, and in an instant, a man appeared in my vision. I'd never seen a spirit so fast or forthcoming. It was as if he'd stepped in from another room, which I suppose he may have done, except he was not standing. He was sitting, with his shoes off and one leg crossed over the other, scowling and rubbing a stockinged foot with a meaty set of hands. He seemed annoyed to be interrupted.

It was hard not to laugh. "Did Mr. Ludlow have problems with his feet?" I asked.

"That's him!" Mrs. Ludlow answered, slapping one hand on the table. "Never did find a pair of boots that fit him. Eli!" she shouted out, "Where are those deeds?"

Mr. Ludlow ceased the foot rubbing. He frowned and a large crease appeared on his forehead. Sighing in exasperation, he pointed one finger toward the ceiling. "Up." he said.

"Up?" I questioned.

Mr. Ludlow appeared out of patience. He jabbed his finger twice more in the direction of the ceiling. "Up attic," he said tersely. "Safer away from the kitchen." Then he continued the rubbing and disappeared.

Sitting back in the chair, I exhaled deeply and opened my eyes, signaling to Mrs. Ludlow that the contact with the spirit was done.

"Did he look well?" Mrs. Ludlow asked.

It was a surprisingly common question, especially considering the subject was dead.

"He looked as though his feet hurt."

Mrs. Ludlow shook her head. "Eli was always cross when his feet were bothering him. What did he say about the deeds. I heard you say "up."

"Mr. Ludlow indicated the deeds were in the attic."

"They can't be," Mrs. Ludlow said. "I've searched there a dozen times."

"I believe he means the attic of this house," I said.

"But we've never lived here. These rooms were always let."

"Nevertheless, I think he means the attic above us. He said they were safer away from the kitchen, and you've no kitchen in this house."

Mrs. Ludlow stood from the table and waved her hands in disbelief. "It's all foolishness, but I will get my keys and have a look."

At the next of my receptions, people had to be turned away.

While Mrs. Ludlow and I stood at the doorway greeting the first of the gathering, Mrs. Ludlow smiled. "Your reputation has spread through the boardinghouse dining rooms."

Of course, the landlady herself was responsible for the spreading, as by this time the entire city knew of Mrs. Ludlow's good fortune. The missing deeds, discovered by "spirit intervention", were tucked on a beam in the unused attic in a green baize-lined box. That the box also contained an entirely unexpected fifty dollars in gold specie was a part of the story Mrs. Ludlow told only me, but such a windfall put both the lady's finances and cheeks in the pink, and she was delighted with the notoriety I brought her premises.

Now a year later, I always left a chair reserved for Mrs. Ludlow, and each week there appeared a modest but tempting array of eatables, for the landlady was a fine cook, and a pitcher of either lemonade or cider for the expected gathering. We settled into an unplanned routine, with Mrs. Ludlow acting as a sort of hostess to the receptions, greeting arriving guests and flustering in the presence of the many notable ones.

For notables there certainly were, and those in my parlor often made up a distinguished company, Republicans mostly, nearly all anti-slavery and curious about Spiritualism. Each week there arrived many men of note, senators, representatives, judges and their wives. Early in the war, their attendance had a mood of a restless fear and excitement, but now they were more weighted with gloom. Death had become a frequent caller in Washington City, and there was an increasing number of homes where it left its black-edged card. Now during my receptions, the spirits were most often implored with questions on the fate of the country.

One such was Daniel Somes who attended with his wife Laura and three other guests on a late November evening in 1862. A Republican lawyer from Maine who'd been in Congress until the year before, Mr. Somes was, like most of his political fellows, an abolitionist—but also a pacifist—and heartsick the nation had come to a state of war. He'd spent his last days as a member of Congress in vain, trying to abate the impending bloodshed as a delegate to the fruitless Peace Convention. I had the idea he felt personally responsible for the conflict as he and his wife attended my receptions nearly every month, hoping with bright-eyed expectation that the spirits would have some word of termination or victory.

Unfortunately, there was little I could say to Mr. Somes or anyone like him. I certainly believed the Union had the favor of God, but in trance and at seances, I heard the voices of those killed on both sides. In visions, I saw their pale shapes, felt their unsettled energies and realized with some surprise that in death they still retained their division, though like all spirits the present day seemed transcended, no more important than anything past or future. Spirits regarded the war with indifference, and though they might venture McClellan was a coward or some Secesh a grey-backed louse, they were more concerned with communicating solace to their bereaved and confirming the afterlife. They spoke of little else.

"I can say, Mrs. Carter," Mr. Somes said while shaking my hand, "that no other evening could give as much pleasure or thoughtful instruction as one spent here, and I have brought three friends who are anxious to make your acquaintance."

"Thank you. I am always glad to see you and Mrs. Somes at my table," I replied while eyeing the three strangers. The trio seemed to be one family; an imperious and well turned out lady accompanied by her more carelessly dressed husband and a daughter about my own age. They were silent during the earlier séance, which was not unusual as many people attended out of curiosity and wished only to observe.

"Mrs. Margaret Laurie of Georgetown," Mr. Somes said, gesturing to the elder lady whose eyes flicked across my face with an assessing interest.

"Your gifts are quite pronounced," Mrs. Laurie said, while pressing my hand in her cool dry palm in greeting. "Of course we've long heard of you from your days in New York. Certainly Washington City is fortunate to now have you."

"Indeed," Mr. Somes said, "and please meet Miss Nettie Colburn, Mrs. Laurie's protege."

"I saw you once in New York," Miss Colburn said with a broad smile.

The young lady could not have been much more than twenty, her hair a dark brown version of the same ringlets I'd now given up. She wore a cloak of heavy wool as she stood in the hallway beaming with excitement and pleasure.

"It was at Dodsworth's," Nettie went on. "I was so impressed. You were no older than I and standing before hundreds of people speaking in trance. This was before I came under the spiritual influence myself."

"It seems Miss Colburn and you have followed similar paths," said the un-introduced man. "Both of you beginning as untaught children and passing to the success of the speaking platform."

"I'd better introduce Mr. William Chaney now," Daniel Somes said laughing and shaking his head. "A son of Maine himself, and perhaps the most radical Republican I know. He was a newspaperman before he landed here."

"Ah," said Chaney, a short man with a puffy face and hard, nailhead eyes which resembled a pair of tiny buttons pushed into a sofa cushion, "that was long ago, but I still write now and again. I'm here to do a piece on Miss Colburn for the Spiritualist press. I hope to make the acquaintance of all the noted mediums in Washington City."

"I'm pleased to know you all," I said, "and thank you for attending my reception," but I'd taken the measure of this group immediately and rejected any future close relation. The young lady Nettie seemed innocent enough, but I knew two promoters when I saw them. There was even something of Benjamin in Mrs. Laurie's appraising eye.

"We have our own small circles at my home on First Street in Georgetown," Mrs. Laurie said, "and sometimes in other locations. I'd be pleased if you would join us Mrs. Carter. I'll let Mr. Somes know when we meet next. We're a modest group, but select."

Select. It was more than four years since I'd heard that word from Benjamin's lips, and it sounded just the same as it had then.

In less than a fortnight, Mr. and Mrs. Somes appeared at my door again, this time on a frosty December evening which threatened snow.

"There's been a sudden invitation to Mrs. Laurie's seance I think we should not miss," Mr. Somes said, rubbing his bare hands together in the raw air to warm them and gesturing to the couple's carriage awaiting in the street. "Won't you come with us, Cora?"

It had been a quiet day. I was mending a tear in a chemise. I had no desire to face the cold weather, or the company for that matter, but hated to disappoint good clients. *I'll go this one time and have it over with*, I told myself, as I put on my coat.

Once inside the carriage I had misgivings and turned to Mrs. Somes. "I'm not sure my dress is fancy enough for a Georgetown parlor."

Mrs. Somes patted my hand. "My dear, your natural beauty will go a long way before any dress. You look fine."

"Besides, we aren't going to Georgetown," said Mr. Somes.

"Where are we going?" I asked.

"To the White House." he replied.

Cora

1862

That I would be transported in the space of an hour from my own small room where I'd been repairing a torn undergarment to a parlor in the President's mansion was more than I was prepared for. While trying to talk myself out of nervousness, I barely heard the excited comments of Mr. and Mrs. Somes during the carriage ride to our destination.

The Somes' hoped for my impression of the upcoming proceeding and the decision to hold the spirit circle was sudden. Although Mrs. Laurie had given seances for Mrs. Lincoln before, on this night the president himself was expected to attend.

All was cold and silent as the carriage rolled along the curved drive to the large columned portico where a lone guard opened a gate and motioned for us to pass. A slither of brumous wind slashed at my ankles while descending to the chill stone pavements and making my way with the others to the steps. From this vantage, I saw another carriage with its privacy curtains drawn waiting in a wedge of shadow beyond the portico. I supposed it belonged to the Laurie family, as the horses were newly arrived with steam from their sweat rising from their backs in the frosty air.

Once at the top of the steps, I could not resist the desire to stop and look back in the direction we'd come, across the winter raddled grass and young trees and then overhead to the starless sky, so dense and black it seemed it might indeed fall from its own massive weight.

This was the most famous building in the world, with some of the most famous occupants, but I succeeded in calming myself. I'd been famous, too, and had also stood before cheering crowds of hundreds. So I knew well that despite the adoration and envy, the gawking and notoriety, every famous person was in their own heart a small vessel of doubt, no different than the obscure. The President and his wife were just people after all.

Inside, we met a sleepy attendant who never rose from his chair and directed us to a door beyond a large darkened vestibule. The interiors were sumptuous but seemed flat and hollow, little different from the many theater stages I'd stood upon, where the cornices, mirrors and doorways were either false or merely painted on.

The rooms smelt of stale cigars and disuse, or perhaps, more rightly, of overuse by a thousand people who had no love for them. I was reminded of the death of young Willie Lincoln last winter, but the president's house was a somber place in any regard, and I shuddered at the sorrow I felt seeping from the gilded walls which seemed as though they remembered many things they might rather forget.

Just then I saw it, in a tall mirror in the columned vestibule, initially just at the corner of my eye and then in full view. The hand of my nightmares, hovering in a vague and peculiar light in the center of the glass, large as the face of a clock and giving me the longest glimpse I'd ever seen of it.

It was a man's hand, callused and hard worked, not the smooth and tapered fingers of Benjamin. Yet there was something odd about it, and I instinctively turned to look behind me, to identify the hand's owner.

Of course there was no one behind me, only Mr. and Mrs. Somes. "Lovely mirror, isn't it?" Mr. Somes said. "I daresay many of these furnishings are quite old. Perhaps from the time of President Madison."

Mr. Somes placed his hand gently at the small of my back and steered me toward the door the attendant pointed out earlier. "It's the Crimson Room where we are headed," he said.

We crossed a broad hall and entered a room where a more domestic scene could be found. My heart resumed its fretful dance as I scanned the space for the President or his wife, thinking I would recognize them from engravings in the periodicals, but realized there was much to observe in the ornate room—and even more to comprehend.

The dimly lit space was a bower of blood red walls and lush furniture profuse with gold ormolu which caught any speck of the silty light and scattered it, making the room both tranquil and unsettling. A grim-faced portrait of George Washington loomed over the huge yet claustral chamber, clad in black and gesturing with a weary outstretched arm toward a corner, where Mrs. Laurie sat at a grand piano playing a nondescript tune.

Nearby, before the marble mantle piece, in the demi-jour of a low burning fire, a set of chairs and couches were clustered, and I saw Nettie Colburn seated with another young woman I later learned was Mrs. Laurie's daughter, Belle. Nettie retained the girlish aspect I remembered from our first meeting, with her shy gestures and artless speech. Belle possessed the same dark, scrutinizing eyes as her mother but also a sharp vulpine face, like some creature peering from a burrow and apt to bite.

Almost invisible in this grouping was the lady I took to be Mrs. Lincoln herself, draped in mourning garments of crow-feather black, upright and immobile in her place on the couch, as though she were some unwanted lamp or vase covered with a piece of dark velvet by a housekeeper. But for her tiny sound of greeting when introductions were made, I might not have recognized her when she took both of my hands in hers and spoke.

"My dear, it is kind of you to come and sit with us," Mrs. Lincoln said in a toneless voice.

Despite her troubles, age had scarcely touched Mrs. Lincoln and I looked upon a face frank and pleasing but resolute with grief. It was impossible not to recognize how vulnerable the President's wife was or how isolated in her quest for solace. The searching eyes, the dazed and vague air of one who lives with nothing but the thought of an absence. Mrs. Lincoln's countenance put me in mind of the long ago séance in New York with the wife of Horace Greeley—what had been her name?—Mary, yes—just as Mrs. Lincoln was also Mary. Both lost beloved sons. No doubt both women had inattentive husbands. I could only speculate on how consumed the President must be with the war, and how susceptible this made his wife to the unscrupulous. I was not yet ready to pass judgment on the entire company but did not like the look of Mrs. Laurie so cold and fierce, or her crafty-faced daughter, Belle.

"Our friend Cora who joins us tonight is a medium of remarkable ability," Daniel Somes began.

"Certainly we know of your work in New York," Mrs. Lincoln said, and with this, my confidence faltered. Still shy of the outrageous falsehoods reported in the newspapers during the divorce, I'd already scanned the room for the presence of the cruel-eyed newspaperman William Chaney, who accompanied Mrs. Laurie to my rooms last month, and found his absence reassuring. Was Mrs. Lincoln making a judgment? Scrutinizing the lady's obliging tone, I decided she was not.

"I saw Mrs. Carter years ago myself at Dodsworth's Hall," added Nettie, "and have never forgotten the performance. It has inspired me ever since."

"I doubt New York will ever forget Mrs. Carter," Belle said with a sharp adversarial smile, which made no secret of her opinion.

"I understand the entire Laurie family are under the spiritual influence," I said, trying to divert the conversation while at the same time looking directly at Belle.

"Time and again they have brought me my son," Mrs Lincoln declared. "Both Mrs. Laurie and Belle are exceptionally sensitive to spirit visitors. Through them, I know my little Willie is still beside me."

With this statement barely finished, Mrs. Laurie abruptly changed the tone of the piano music she'd been playing from the soft refrain to a tune which resembled a military march, and shading a candle in the palm of his hand, Abraham Lincoln stepped into the room.

Blowing out the flame which guided him and setting the chamberstick upon a table, President Lincoln paused before us silently for a moment, and it was as though the room caught its breath at his presence.

Against Mrs. Lincoln's diminutive stature and youthful unlined face, the president made a contrast. His tall frock-coated figure appeared hard-used and gnarly, like a tree at the edge of a forest which suffers the brunt of every storm, the marks of a permanent fatigue carved into him. Wan and weary, he received his guests as though he was familiar with every sort of sorrow and tired of them all.

Plain and informal the great man seemed to be, but his body was also enveloped in a strange atmosphere I knew was only visible to me. As President Lincoln moved, the air around him seemed to collapse and re-assemble, and the very edges of his being were blurred and dissolving, just as if his spirit were a color running in the rain. His was a soul on a threshold I realized, poised for withdrawal, impatient and ready to be off and away, but I could not account for it as everything else about the president seemed both hale and resolved.

My attention returned to the gathering when I heard Mr. Lincoln address Nettie Colburn. "Is this our little Nettie we have heard so much about?" he asked.

"Yes sir," was all that Nettie managed to answer, though I would probably have no better reply myself in the presence of such an esteemed man. President Lincoln bid Nettie to sit on a large ottoman near a chair which had been left empty for him, and once they were both seated, he laid his hand upon the girl's head.

It was a large hand, easily covering the entire parting in Nettie's dark hair, and I imagined the weight and warmth of it as something familiar, something tender and solicitous from my past, appealing to be remembered.

Captain Jonathan Walker!

As though awakened from a significant dream, my mind returned and brought with it the memory of Hope Grove and the night I held Captain Walker's hand. The bonfire, the singing, the praise lavished upon him by the citizens. I'd been a child then and remembered how his terrible tale touched me. I remembered, too, that while everyone applauded and admired him, no one thought to comfort him, and this I tried to do at the end of the evening when the excitement of the day was over.

That a vision of his hand had traveled through time to return to me in Washington City, while the war raged and the promise of the emancipation of the slaves was almost in sight, made all the sense in the world. Sadly, it also meant that Captain Jonathan Walker was now a spirit himself, and the man who once placed his hand on my childish head was likely dead.

All at once, Nettie's voice erupted in a harsh and throaty growl from her place on the ottoman, and we all looked at one another in astonishment. No circle had been formed or hands joined in the customary preparation for a séance, just the girl herself speaking with great vigor and sitting tensely with a strange and frozen expression.

The President sat in the chair beside her with his fingers interlaced across his lap, self-contained and reserved, as though listening to one of his fellows, which it seemed to me he perhaps was. For the deep voice from Nettie was that of a man, speaking of affairs of state, using officious language. Was Nettie in trance? Had some strong and masculine spirit overtaken her?

If so, it was like no trance I'd ever seen or experienced and I detected no spirits in the parlor. Something seemed wrong, some detail was out of place. Slowly Nettie spoke, with great strength and force, but in a manner that seemed recitative, even rehearsed.

"As to the upcoming proclamation of emancipation, you sir, are charged with the utmost solemnity and force of manner not to abate the terms of its issue."

Nettie's tone gave great weight to her words, but excepting the President the remainder of the party seemed shocked at her temerity—if her temerity it was.

"You are advised not to delay the enforcement of this proclamation beyond the promised date of the first of the year. This decision is to be the crowning event of your administration and, indeed, of your life."

Daniel Somes turned in his chair and cast his eyes upon the portrait of George Washington, and I knew at once he believed the voice emanating from Nettie was that of the first president.

I considered this and recalled the many times Benjamin had evoked the spirit of George Washington to the audiences he called 'rubes," insinuating the voices I repeated came from the famous man. It was the lie I once allowed, and even now a shaft of shame pierced my conscience to recall it. Was Nettie up to a similar trick?

A shuddering quiver of nausea went through me, and I lifted my eyes to the portrait. The tall familiar president in luxurious surroundings, black-coated, silver buckled but with a face impassive and so…inaccessible. His spirit was not in the room. Then, the well-known swarming of the blood pulse in my ears, the tickly prickling along the skin of my forehead and the single hum whispering in my head—urgent, sibilant, but always unintelligible, coming from its far and unknown region.

A small spot of reflection on the varnish of the portrait flashed and split into two fragments and then into more swirling shapes which glittered and sparkled like broken sunlight growing into a luminous space where I floated among the billions of flickering sparks, feeling my way in the blinding brightness until I took hold of what seemed to be a long buried memory.

At once back in the chair in the Crimson Room and with my eyes still fixed on the portrait, I found Washington gone and in his place another man represented. Ragged and worn, with clothing rent with holes and tatters, he appeared. A Black man, with a square of old blanket tied across one shoulder and his torn shirt foul with a bib of blood. He did not need to say his name.

It was Robert, so known and strange all at the same time.

"Robert," I whispered, though whether aloud or to myself I was not certain.

He stood with his hands clasped loosely and with a kind of radiance rising from all sides of him, regarding me with placid interest and a contentment I could not fathom. Robert had the otherness of all spirits, but also a shimmering quality I'd never seen before and which set him apart from familiar visitants. I saw his rough, scar-covered hands and remembered the feel of Captain Walker's branded hand in my own, the letters *SS* raised beneath the smooth tips of my childhood fingers, and realized I'd carried that moment at the bonfire through the last decade of my life, precious and ineradicable.

Unlike my other spirits, neither Robert or Jonathan Walker had ever spoken or made a sound, and I knew they never would. They were different than Hollis, and they expected me to understand their message was more important than words. Something beyond language. Something whose meaning was eternal.

Nevertheless there was a voice, a sound from the present world. Nettie still speaking as if in avid prayer, her words sure and masculine and heavy with portent.

"You are being counseled by strong parties to deter the enforcement of the proclamation. They hope to supplant it by other measures and to delay action, but you must in no wise heed this council, but stand firm to your convictions and fearlessly perform the mission for which you have been raised up by an overruling Providence!"

Nettie went quiet, sighed deeply and hung her head as though exhausted for as long as a minute, then recovered herself and glanced around the room with eyes which were wide and candid. We all sat rapt and stunned at the majesty of her utterance.

President Lincoln received her words with silence, but Daniel Somes could not contain his amazement. "Mr. Lincoln," he said, gesturing to the Washington portrait on the opposite wall, "Did you notice anything peculiar in the method of Miss Colburn's address?"

"Yes,' the President said, "and it is very singular."

"Would it be proper to ask?" Somes continued, "Has there been pressure upon you to defer the enforcement of the proclamation?"

Abraham Lincoln looked about him as if to ascertain he was speaking to a group of friends. He nodded gravely and replied," It has taken all my nerve and strength to withstand such pressure."

He then turned to Nettie and smiled. Taking her hand he said, "My child you possess a very singular gift, but that it is of God I have no doubt. I thank you for coming here tonight. It is more important than perhaps anyone can understand. I must leave you all now," he continued as he stood, "but I hope I shall see you again." He bowed to all the company and withdrew.

During the carriage ride home, Daniel Somes spoke solemnly. "We have witnessed history tonight," he said. "The spirit of our greatest president come to council the current president at our moment of national crisis. What were your impressions, Cora? Did you not sense President Washington in the room?"

I knew I had to choose my words carefully. "Nettie and I do not hear the same voices. It is likely we are served by different spirits."

"Am I then to understand you don't think the message came from Washington?" he asked, clearly disappointed.

"I could not say one way or the other. I am not sure it matters where the message came from as long as it is vital and true." I recalled the calm and kindly face of Robert. No wonder Sojourner loved him. I thought, too, of the bloodstains which his spirit continued to carry. "It is quite possible the message to President Lincoln came from a common person. Nettie did not identify who was speaking."

"Surely you can't think a common man could possess such language,"Daniel Somes said, "and Nettie herself would never have such vocabulary."

His statement rankled me, and I endeavored to conceal my anger. Somes was a radical Republican and a broad-minded thinker, but like every man of his station, he discounted those below him in rank or sex without even being aware of it. It was the eve of possible emancipation, and as far as I could tell, the only spirits in the White House with President Lincoln that evening were a slave and a farmer, and the only person speaking was a woman unable to vote on any ballot. It seemed to me the most powerful man in the most powerful building on the continent was attended not by the time-honored and august but by the beaten and the belittled.

My question was whether Nettie's address came from the spirits or herself. Despite Somes' trivializing assessment, I knew I would be capable of giving the oratory heard tonight and guessed Nettie was capable, too. So, was the girl in trance and contacting spirits or was she pretending, using the freedom trance would allow her to speak her own opinions? Seen as guileless and innocent, she could attract the attention of everyone—even the president of the United States.

Certainly Nettie and Mrs. Laurie had Mary Lincoln convinced, but they'd only to bring the grieving lady a whisper of her dead son to gain access to the president and then to a séance in the Crimson room where they could inveigle political ends.

I supposed I could do it too—speak for slaves or women in the guise of the dead—and wondered if this was what Robert and Jonathan Walker's presence counseled. I supposed I was a radical

Republican too, sharing their beliefs in emancipation and universal suffrage. But would it be right to use a lie to tell the truth, or would such duplicity make the truth into a falsehood?

Daniel Somes spoke again as the carriage drew up to my home on F Street. "In any case, I pray to God Lincoln holds firm on emancipation," he said. "but I must know Cora, do you believe President Washington could come back?"

"I believe no spirit has ever left," I truthfully told him, but my mind was already beyond his question and deep into a question for myself.

In all the years of repeating the voices of the spirits, had I lost my own?

Sojourner Truth
1865

In betwixt the proclamation of emancipation and Appomattox, my hopes rose to the clouds, but now President Lincoln has gone to his long home. He was struck down unsuspectin' when our joy at the end of the war was only a few days old. Now jus' four months later even that joy seems bygone, and for us of the colored race, the war is not ended.

In my heart I already expected his death, for I had met the president once—was taken to his chambers in the White House where I'd seen the man with my own eyes. I don't know what I'd imagined beforehand, some warrior I suppose, but he was jus' another man, none too considerable, and I thought at the time probably no match for his task.

He was half a hand taller than I was to be sure, as most men are not, but he was fagged with trials and worry and surrounded by devils of all kinds. He was Daniel in the lion's den, and I told him so and how I feared he'd be ripped to shreds. He laughed at the time; but there ain't much of nothin' comes without a sting in the tail, and twas the lion that laughed in the end.

I'd come down to Washington City from my home in Michigan jus' after Atlanta fell in '64 to offer help. I'd done what I could earlier in the war to encourage the colored men to enlist once they were allowed to and to gather supplies for them, and I am well pleased to say my own grandson joined with the 54th Massachusetts.

I'd heard of the desperation of those escaped slaves the government called "contrabands," ones who'd made their way to the safety of Washington City and were now crowded up in rough-built camps. I was told missionaries and others from the North had gone to the camps to teach and nurse the people, so I thought I should go too. Of readin' and writin' I am ignorant, but for my own brothers and sisters, I can work and pray and counsel. My lessons come from my heart. I know more than any missionary what it means to walk away from slavery with nothin'.

So before the year was over, I was livin' at the Freedman's Village outside Washington City in the Greene Heights part of Arlington. I was there during Appomattox; I was there when Lincoln was killed, and it was from there I went into Washington to watch the Grand Review parade of our victorious army along with the rest of the celebratin' crowds. Yet, the very next day, I was reminded that for my people the war nowhere near won. When I tried to return to the Village on a public streetcar, it would not stop for me because I was colored.

It has been hard livin' at Freedman's Village. People are hungry, supplies are scarce, and this past winter, shelters were always frigid because of old cast-off stoves that barely held heat. Sickness sometimes swept through. The pox carried off more than two dozen late in the spring. All kinds are crowded together, both the bad and the good, those desperate to work and the shiftless. I've tried to talk plainly to the people and give them hope, encourage them to do what they can for themselves. "Get off the government and prove your value," I tell them. "If you sit and take what is handed out, you will find yourselves worse off than in slavery."

I've been workin' in the hospital there but also with friends in the North like Mrs. Post and Judge Edmonds to help with re-settlement. Most all freedmen are anxious to work if they can get employment, and we are sendin' as many as we can to farms and households upstate that are glad to have them. Young and single men and women have the best chance, but it is for the families who wish to stay together I feel the most sympathy. No one wants the children or the old. Not many farms in the North can afford to take on whole families, and those few poor souls who managed the miracle of stayin' together during the war or have reunited are now faced with being torn apart again. Here I feel the government should step in. With all the land available in the west it seems the United States could part with a mite of it. So many families are stuck here as in a prison but for the want of a few acres and a small start.

I wish some of the great men would speak out, for my own voice is only that of an old Black woman, and few pay me any heed. I am beginnin' to see neither old age or freedom is dependable.

In June, when I visited Cora in the city, she wrote a letter for me to Mrs. Post, and I told her to put my plea in 'specially as Mrs. Post and Frederick Douglass both live in Rochester. "Where is Frederick that his voice is not heard from in this tryin' hour?" I asked Cora to write. "He is needed to instruct his people and lead them to freedom."

I visited with Cora often enough at her little headquarters on F Street. The girl was makin' a small livin' with her talks and circles, and I gathered she was still sendin' what monies she could to that mother of hers upstate. She was poor as Job's turkey, but I admired her pluck in standin' on her own. She wrote letters for me sometimes, and we talked of our old friends and the times before the war. It does me good to talk with someone from the North, 'specially one who knows the Edmonds' and Mrs. Post. Our meetings always felt like a comfort, but when I saw her jus' after Independence Day in July, we both had a surprise for each other.

When I entered her doorway I was all done up. I'd been good for nothin' for a week because my arm was in a sling which caused everyone to inquire of my injury.

"An incident on the streetcars," I told Cora.

"But how were you hurt so?" she asked.

"After I'd boarded the car, the conductor told me to step down. I told him I would not as I knew the law as well as he did, and I'd a right to ride. He tried to push me off, and I was jammed against the door mighty hard."

"Good Lord! Is your arm broken?"

"Lucky for me, Mrs. Haviland the hospital inspector was there, and we went right away to the Campbell Hospital. The doctor said my shoulder was misplaced, and he and Mrs. Haviland wrenched it back into position."

"How awful!" Cora said, "That beast of a conductor should be punished."

"As he may well be," I answered, "I am not done with these streetcar companies yet, but when one is colored, injury is always possible. I've known that all my life."

Cora got quiet then and made herself busy unwrappin' a plate of biscuits and pourin' some of the tea she'd been brewin'. Even when she finished and sat down, her fingers still twisted nervously at a button on her shirtwaist.

"I have never seen you ailing before and hope you are not in pain," she said.

I looked down at my sling. "No, just a little sore."

"Your injury reminds me. I have something I have long wanted to tell you but don't know what words to use."

I could not imagine what Cora was gettin' at. Modest Cora was, but never without words.

"I s'pect plain words will do jus' fine," I said, my thoughts full of curiosity.

"You met President Lincoln," she said.

"Yes."

"Well, I have met him too."

This was a surprise. Cora'd never given me any account of this.

"At the time, I thought it best not to repeat my story. President Lincoln didn't need any more hostile gossip around him, but now I cannot see how it would do any harm."

The more Cora spoke, the less I understood, but I said nothin' and let her go on.

"There was a séance in the White House," she said.

"You gave a séance in the White House?"

"No, I attended one," she said, still fiddlin' with her dress button. "It was back in '62, just days before the Emancipation Proclamation was due to take effect. I know how important the proclamation was to you Sojourner, but you cannot imagine the agitation this caused in Washington City then, and the pressure upon Lincoln to change his mind about it. The séance was given by a young girl named Nettie Colburn, if you could even call it a séance. The minute the President entered the room she started speaking, in a deep masculine voice, urging—no, it was more than that—commanding the president to ensure the proclamation became law!"

I couldn't imagine such a thing, a young girl commandin' the president of the United States to do anythin'. "Thank the Lord she was on our side, but was she the true?" I asked, "What sort of spirit had ahold of her?"

Cora shook her head slightly and ran her finger along the rim of her teacup. "Sojourner, I don't know the answer to either question. There was a big portrait of George Washington in the room, and, of course, all those in attendance believed his spirit was speaking through Nettie offering advice to Lincoln, president to president. It makes for a good story, but I did not sense George Washington in the room. In fact, I sensed no spirit when Nettie began her discourse; it was only until later..."

"Later what?" I interrupted during her pause, unsure of what any of this had to do with me.

"Later when I saw a spirit in the room. A spirit I am sure was showing itself only to me."

"Who was the spirit?"

Cora said the name softly, as though she thought it would be too heavy for me to bear.

"Robert," she said. "It was Robert."

For half a moment, I did not know who she meant, but she was lookin' at my face for the first time since she'd started her tale, right in my eyes, and I understood.

A hundred thoughts went racin' through my head at full chisel, but the old habit of hidin' my emotions took charge, and it was this habit which spoke out. "How would you know him?" I said in a contrary tone I regretted the minute I heard myself.

"I wouldn't, but I just knew," she replied.

"How did he look?

"Calm," Cora said, "and gentle. Raggedly dressed and with a

great bloodstain on his chest. Perhaps that was how I recognized him. You told me he'd been badly beaten."

"Many Black men have been badly beaten," I said. "How was his face?"

"Fine," Cora said. "More than fine. That's just it Sojourner, he looked God-like, different than any other spirit I've ever seen."

This was just humbug, Robert lookin' God-like, when in life he was no more than a hard used slave. Maybe the spirit Cora saw was some kind of impostor. Maybe spirits tell lies too, and death don't change folks much after all. "Different how?" I asked.

"He is not like Hollis or the others I know. He travels in a curtain of light, so bright it blinded me at first. He seems to be made up of a million pieces of gold. His hands were covered with scars, and he wore a piece of torn blanket across one shoulder, but he was transfigured all the same, come down from some high and heavenly place."

I felt a jump in my heart as I thought back to the odd and beautiful light which had come around us years before at Irvin' Place and the scrap of greasy oilcloth Robert always tied across his shoulders when he was obliged to work in the snow or rain. I also knew as well as my own face the scars that lay across the backs of the hands I once held in my own. "What did he say?"

"Nothing," Cora answered. "Not a word. I don't think he was there for me, he was there for President Lincoln. To advocate for Emancipation. I think all spirits seize their chance. Perhaps the words Nettie spoke were Robert's."

"Robert was not one for words. Why would it be him in the White House?" I argued.

"Why would it not?" Cora said rather sternly. "He could testify as well as any, and with just as much right."

I reached up with my good arm and uncurled the temple bow of my spectacles, first from one ear, then the other, folded them, and set them in my lap. I pressed my fingers into the sockets of my closed eyes feelin' the hot tears pushin' behind them. How long had it been since I cried? I could not even remember. Years probably, and certainly not in front of others.

"Why doesn't Robert show himself to me?" I finally asked.

Cora scooted her chair closer to mine and placed her hand on the fist I'd closed over my eyeglasses. "I don't know Sojourner. Spirits have their own methods. Despite her attempts, Lydia Edmonds has never seen her mother, and my father has not appeared to me. Robert was bold at the White House, but usually spirits are skittish. When they show themselves it is almost always with hesitation. They seem to be afraid, and I have never been able to explain why."

To me the answer seemed obvious. "They are afraid they won't be recognized," I said. "They fear they won't be remembered."

Yet I remembered, and gave silent thanks to God. Robert in gold light with his face healed. Robert in the White House to free our people. My dear Robert. Father of my first child.

"...and with me, in the sphere I now inhabit, are all those who have successfully plead with legislators and counselors of nations for the uplifting of any class of persons from bondage; and we urge those still in earthly life to continue this work.

Here we have Cobden, Wilberforce and Peel still carrying forth their aims, and a million million common men adding to the call. Abraham Lincoln, recently risen to our estate, who signed the Emancipation Proclamation might not have done this but for a voice that came from our sphere of risen souls and gave him the strength that human legislation hesitated so long to give.

Yet, the great work of human emancipation and elevation is not political merely; it first becomes narrowed down to the limits of the State, but then to those municipal laws and local legislations. Here it is narrowed down to the very small compass of the individual human life, for in order to have proper legislation we must have proper legislators. Human life shall everywhere be held sacred; and no human being shall arrogate to himself the right and privilege of taking away that which he cannot confer upon his fellow being.

The abolition of slavery has been bought with human blood, but the great nations of the earth carry on toward freedom, as the highest work of man becomes the assistance to his fellow men..."

Though I was sittin' in the fine parlor of Congressman Somes, I could jus' as well been back in homely old Hemlock Hall as I listened to Cora speakin'. Closin' my eyes I could almost smell those piney forests, feel the creakin' floorboards. Cora was the same as in those days. Eyes shinin' in the lamplight and her face in rapt entrancement, her voice strong but sometimes a little quivery. Jus' as pretty too, unmarked by any age, 'cept for a small line between her eyebrows when she was intent with listenin' to the voices of the spirits.

And oh, how I loved to hear her! Pourin' out the eloquent words of our dear ones who've gone on to their long homes. How brave it makes my heart to know the invisibles pay heed to politics and fight along beside me in our common cause.

We'd come a long way the both of us, Cora and I, to the fancy parlors of these powerful men, but we are strange creatures in a strange land. We are welcomed to be sure, and these people are good at heart, but their favor is still purposeful.

Cora is a fine thing to look at, but I wonder if she ever tires of the gawpin', if she gets worn down havin' to always sing for her supper. In places like this, less is required of me, but by puttin' me at their table these men and their wives get any guilt wiped clean. Still, in this day and age, neither Cora nor I can afford not to take what we can get.

As far as spirit circles go, this evenin' was a large one, with more than thirty people around two tables pushed end to end. Cora called up spirit ancestors for the better part of an hour, and after a short rest stood and spoke in the trance I so enjoy hearin'.

The room was full of big bugs, and afterward, as they nosed about the buffet supper, I put a closer eye on them. There was Mrs. Haviland, who'd brought me, and several more from the Freedmen's Bureau includin' straight-backed General Howard who headed up the whole works. Reverend Pierpont was here, as old as Methuselah, and lookin' 'bout like him with his long grey beard. He sat with a plate of oysters balanced on his belly, suckin' his fingers after eatin' each one. Mr. and Mrs. Somes circled the carpet, keepin' up the conversation, and Representative George Julian rooted around in the fricassee chicken.

I stood around to the edges of the room holdin' my glass of cider, and it was not long before a couple who'd been earlier introduced approached me. The man was Senator Benjamin Wade. He'd furry eyebrows and a fixed scowl but was friendly enough, as was his wife, a woman called Caroline who was so wee in height I felt like I'd a long ways to look down at her.

He placed his hand on my elbow and spoke. "Mizz…uh… Truth, my wife and I wish to congratulate you on your success in your suit with the streetcar company. You had every right to have that fellow brought up for assault and see that he was punished."

"We both hope your injury has healed," Mrs. Wade said.

I'd been without my sling for a few weeks and lifted my elbow and flapped it like a wing to show it worked. "I thank you. Twas a small injury to a good end. I can only hope before long the insides of the cars will look like pepper and salt."

Senator Wade laughed as did others within hearin'. "It took grit," he said, "and I commend you for it."

"That was more than grit," said a man's voice behind us. "That was courage."

I turned to have a look at the man who'd spoken, and saw that, though he was a stranger to me, he was a man I'd been watchin' all evenin'. I'd hardly moved my eyes from him when he first arrived—not because he was so special, but because of his companion.

Cool, he'd been, and aloof, which made his sudden comment even more surprisin'. I'd surveyed him at the séance, and since then he'd tucked himself and his consort into a pair of chairs catercornered to the side of the room where Cora sat with Mrs. Haviland. Here he gave himself away to this wise old watcher, for as as reserved as he was, his eyes never stopped followin' Cora wherever she went.

He stood from his chair and reached his hand out to me, and the girl beside him stood also. "Sojourner Truth needs no introduction," he said. "I am Nathan Waldo Winslow and this is my daughter, Sophia."

A three word name, a high falutin' accent, and a bluenose so sure of himself, I knew he was sired in Boston before his famous surname even turned the gears of my brain.

But the girl, oh the girl! Somethin'd flashed in the air between us when I first saw her, a thing that'd crackled like lightnin'. She'd fine clear brown eyes, bright with thought and a warm smile, but there was somethin' broody about her I was certain hid a fierce soul underneath. Her complexion glowed, almost as dark as mine, but with all the bloom of youth, as she'd passed no more than eighteen summers.

His daughter! Now that was some far-fetched gum, but I could not cipher their relation. All I knew was I'd never seen a colored woman so well turned out in my life-or so proper. They were a Boston couple this father and...daughter. Not a speck of anythin' flashy like one might see in New York or Washington City. Her silk was fine but not too fine, her flounces simple, her lace mitts first-rate. He was soberly dressed too, but his gold watch chain was as thick as my little finger.

Sophia
1865

I've seen him brave, seen him follow a whim, seen him angry, seen him peevish, but I never expected to see him fall in love. Yet, there he was, moving about the room after the seance so he could keep his eye on the woman he fancied. Not that I disagreed with his choice, as the trance medium they called Cora Carter was certainly a beauty, but he was doing more than watching her. He so scarcely spoke to anyone else and kept his attention so trained in her direction, I knew he was listening too. Such is the way we place ourselves into love's hands. In just one evening, his eyes and his ears undid him.

In the past two years he never asked me to call him "father." This is fortunate; as I doubt I would be able to with my true father's face still so fresh in my mind. "Mr. Winslow" is my name for him.

My father was a soldier, enlisted in the Louisiana Native Guards, Corps de Afrique in 1862 soon after New Orleans fell to the Union, when I was fifteen years old. Days after he was mustered and hoping to see him a final time, I sneaked out to the Touro Barracks on the levee to search for him. I picked him out of the mass of men at once, standing in the shade of one of the great archways of the structure. The wet heat of the summer was not yet over, but the sheen of sweat on the walls and cobbles of the little alcove seemed altogether different from the normal rising damp of the river, secluding the two of us in a small cool vault of freshness between the stinking bodies of the soldiers, the rank air of cooking and horses, and the perfume from the fallen and trod-upon blossoms of a huge jasmine growing along an opposite wall.

"You shouldn't have come here," my father said, looking splendid to my eyes in his blue uniform and new shoes. "There are good many rough men about."

"You look so fine," I said, fingering one of his gold buttons.

He smiled and patted the front of his jacket. "I suppose I will soon have my chance to get dirty. We'll be moving out at any time."

"I know; I just came to tell you good-bye again."

He looked at me with the calm gentleness I'd known all my years as his daughter, smiling with the familiar crinkle at the corners of his eyes but then drawing his lips into a determined line. "See that you mind your mistress," he said. "Do just as Mrs. Menard tells you and work hard."

I'd wrapped my hair in a scarf that morning before I'd set out for the barracks, but a single curl had come untucked and lay against my cheek. My father reached out and touched this strand, handling it lightly, letting the individual hairs sift between his fingers. I knew what he was thinking, could hear the name in my mind just as if he spoke it aloud, for he'd so often remarked on our resemblance. "Lissy"—my mother—died of fever eleven years back along with my only sister, and before I could remember the face of either one.

I knew there was something deliberately not being said, and as I studied his face I saw there was something he regretted, some failing he could not repair. I now suppose he must have feared he was looking for the last time at everything he'd ever loved, and I was all that remained of it. I was young at the time for that sort of thinking, but I certainly knew his searching gaze was memorizing me, as I was memorizing him.

"I will miss you," I said, and my words seemed to shake him from his brooding, as he let the coil of hair fall and placed his hand beneath my chin.

"It won't be long," he said, leveling his gaze into my eyes. "With colored men now in the brawl, this war will be cleaned up in no time. I expect I we'll be together again before the new year and in a whole new circumstance."

A dark haired White man in the uniform of a Colonel stuck his head around the corner where we were standing. "Pol," he said, addressing my father, "can I get your help with that company loading rails for Opelousas?"

My father nodded his assent without speaking, and the Colonel allowed his eyes to pass over us for a long moment. "Take your time," the Colonel said, before stepping quickly away.

I did not know it then, but he was Colonel Nathan Waldo Winslow, and it was the last time I ever saw my father.

"It was the yellow jack that felled him," Mr. Winslow told me once he'd returned to Boston after the war, "but not until after your father had distinguished himself at Pascagoula. My God he was brave! I saw him there with my own eyes, walking steady through a rain of fire with others falling all around him. It was later on Ship Island when the sickness came. Others had the fever too, but your father died peacefully. I sat with him myself, and that is when he told me all about you."

Mr. Winslow frowned and looked down at his lap, picking at his fingernails as he always did when he was anxious. He was lying of course, and foolish in thinking he could tell anyone who lived in New Orleans that a yellow fever death was peaceful. There was no one from that vicinity unfamiliar with the writhing, the vomit, and the bleeding noses and eyes, but Mr. Winslow's words were meant as comfort, and I took them as such.

"There was no other man like your father. Never another man like Pol," he said.

Never another man like Pol. Mr. Winslow repeated that sentiment often in the time I'd known him, squinting his eyes and casting his mind off into whatever fond memory he nurtured. I agreed, there never was another man like Pol, but my experience in losing him was altogether different.

Late in the summer of 1863, a Union lieutenant so young and green his flushed face was still covered with boyish spots, came knocking on Mrs. Menard's door. He explained my father's death in a stammering voice and bade me to accompany him to the city docks. It was my father's dying wish I enter the care of Colonel Winslow he said, and to this end, Colonel Winslow was having me sent to the safety of his own family in Boston as soon as possible.

Colonel Winslow! Who was this man… and Boston? I knew nothing of either one and saw no reason I was compelled to obey a boy not much older than me, even if he did wear a Federal uniform. I was not even sure I could believe my father was dead. Grief rose inside me, and my tears and anger came fast. "You lie!" I shouted at the lieutenant, trying to glare at him though my crying eyes.

Reaching inside his pocket he withdrew a folded letter which he passed to me. "No," he said in a voice which sounded as old and sage as God and seemed almost laughable coming from such youthful lips. "I do not lie."

Anguished I was, and my helplessness made me rage. I slapped the letter out of his hand. "I can't read that!" I shrieked at him, and it was true, I'd no idea what the words on the paper said.

Bending down, he calmly retrieved the paper from the floor and unfolded it, glancing at it briefly. "It says just as I have told you," he replied. He then refolded the letter and let it fall from his fingers back to the floor, regarding me with a look of inscrutable puzzlement.

How strongly his strange gesture affected me! I shall remember it always. There was nothing impatient in it and certainly nothing saucy or pitying. The dropped letter struck at our feet and glided across the room, stretching the space between us into a long silence. It seemed as though I was losing something forever with the tiny tap of the paper on the floorboards. As though I was witnessing a death, as though I was breaking a promise.

I looked around the room which seemed almost unfamiliar now. Just another place in the world where my father no longer walked. Was this Colonel Winslow of Boston perhaps the man who'd interrupted us at the Touro Barracks on the day of our parting? I had no memory of his face, but his words were recollected. "Take your time," he'd said, giving us a chance for our final embraces. I was grateful for that.

I stepped to the rude pallet by the stove in the back kitchen where I slept and gathered my extra dress, camisole and scarf, folding them inside my only coat and tying the bundle tight with the arms. I'd never spent a night here in which I wasn't either too hot or too cold and always too tired to care.

Back in the front room, the long bolt of fabric I'd been hemming before the lieutenant's visit remained lying on the table, the spool of thread and my thimble atop it. Mrs. Menard was wringing her hands and complaining, but she wanted me for no more than the sewing work I did for her, ten hours a day and longer when the light was good.

"I don't care if you are the Federals! How am I going to get another girl, that's…" she was saying as the lieutenant and I stepped outside and closed the door.

Louisa Murphy, the woman who was appointed to accompany me on the ship to Boston was no more kindly disposed to me than Mrs. Menard had been.

"I won't be sharing with a colored," I overheard her telling the lieutenant in the shipping office on Poydras Street, but after we'd climbed the gangplank of the *Sallie Foster* and I saw our tiny two-bunk cabin I knew Mrs. Murphy had lost that battle.

I took to sick almost at once on the journey, and when I made the mistake of complaining, she chided me with a sour rebuke. "You think you're the first green-hand sailor?" she scolded. "Keep yourself lying down and watch what you eat."

To be fair, I was not Mrs. Murphy's only charge, nor even her main one. The raw-faced Irish widow was an army nurse and had the responsibility of two dozen sick soldiers on the deck above us, but she spared little sympathy for me. Before the *Sallie Foster* had even slipped her hawsers, the surly woman had erected a bed linen barrier between our bunks, sealing her own little sleeping space away from mine, and recited a list of rules for me to follow.

I was not to mingle with the soldiers or the sailors or even go above decks for the good chance of being swept away. Meals were at the long table, but it would be best if I ate with my tongue silent. Best too, if I kept out from under her feet altogether, and I was to take charge of my own chamber pot. "I'm no lady's maid," Mrs. Murphy said.

So for the next two weeks, I remained in the tiny cabin, shaky and sick in the airless space lit with a single round window which often leaked with the waves of the outside sea. It might not have been as bad except for the nights, when Mrs. Murphy returned to the cabin muttering and exhausted, shambling about in the cramped quarters or tossing and snoring in her bunk.

Worse was when she started telling her tales in the dark of midnight, her voice growling out from behind her pinioned bed sheet. Descriptions of Confederate commerce raiders, ships far faster then the *Sallie Foster*, loaded with guns and hell-bent on finding lone vessels like ours filled with the spoils of war and then burning them to the waterline, slitting the throats of all aboard. At first her nattering made me angry, but when I realized she was talking away her own fears, I grew fearful myself. I'd seen the spars of the Federal fleet on the Mississippi River as they descended on New Orleans. I knew how fierce the explosions coming from warships could be.

Most nights I cried, my face pressed into the mattress to keep myself silent. My stomach was queasy; nothing around me was solid; the ship would creak and shudder with the endless sound of water rushing along the wall of the cabin, and voices sometimes moaned in pain above me. I knew not where I was going or how long it would take or what sort of promise two men had made to bring me here. I was trapped in a small dark space surrounded by decks of sickness, hogsheads of confiscated sugar, and a thousand bales of seized cotton. It was just as though I were being sold.

When the *Sallie Foster* finally approached Boston and I was allowed to the main deck, my eyes dazed and blinking as my vision adjusted from the days of darkness, my feet would not place themselves as I intended. My body continued to sway as if it were still on the ship sailing, and it took some time before I felt steady enough to descend the plank to shore. The air was sharp and cool, with a crisp wind. I took a good look at the buildings of the city not unlike those of the American side of New Orleans but built on both high and low places and with a large yellow-domed building rising atop the rest. Where I would end up in this place? What room, what window would be mine?

Mrs. Murphy's scowl had not disappeared even with the end of the voyage, but she uttered a great sigh as we stepped on the wharf. A few of the soldiers in her care shouldered past us, headed for awaiting wagons. Most were wounded or lame, some with crutches, and some being carried by the sailors on stretchers.

"Your party's to meet you here," she said, but I was barely listening. I was staring beyond her at a sight I had never seen before. Between two of the buildings a tall stand of trees was growing. The trees' leaves were not green as those in Louisiana, but red and orange as if they were afire, colors which seemed impossible, even false.

"Did you hear me girl?" Mrs Murphy asked, glaring at me as if I were foolish. "What are you gawping at?"

"The trees." I said, both as question and answer.

The soldiers had come off the ship by then; only a final stretcher remained bearing a blanket-covered man who'd apparently not survived the voyage.

The old nurse followed my eyes back to the trees. "Didn't you know," she said, "in New England the leaves turn color before they fall off for the winter. They're beautiful before they die." Mrs. Murphy eyed that last stretcher passing us and then turned away herself, offering me no backward glance and shaking her head."Just like everything else," she said.

How quiet the home of Nathan Waldo Winslow was! Looking back, that silence was the first thing I noticed when standing on the front steps with his sister Mrs. Eliza Eliot, who'd come to collect me at the wharf in a fancy carriage with fine fittings.

As the carriage pulled away, Mrs. Eliot spoke. "The carriage belongs to the household, but the stables are located down on the flat of the hill. This is Mount Vernon Street, your new home."

The street was in half-shade by that hour of the day, and the banquettes were clean swept but for a few of the brightly colored leaves, fallen from the trees and scattered along the gutter. The departing carriage clattered on the cobbles, but teamsters unloading a crate from a wagon further up the street worked in purposeful silence. There were no groups of children playing, no street vendors singing the quality of their wares to the windows of these sober brick-faced houses.

Inside, the hush was even deeper. Mattie the hired girl who'd appeared on the threshold offered a cheerful greeting, but the great heavy door closed behind me with a final sound, sealing me into an unexpected world.

From a tiled floor just inside the door, a staircase rose to the unknown upper quarters, straight up and down with no hint of curving. To the right was a sumptuous parlor with polished wood floors sunstruck in afternoon light. It was a high-ceilinged room the color of dry mustard with tall sash windows and a fireplace mantle carved from a dark and swirly stone that looked like the angry sky of a cyclone. Books filled nearby shelves, decorative china and ornaments were arranged on tables with claw-like paws. From some unseen corner, the shivery peal of a clock chimed three notes. I'd not seen such finery since the years I was at the big house at Belle Clair on the River Road.

At the edge of my vision, Mattie and what seemed to be another housemaid scurried through a door beneath the staircase stifling giggles, but I felt their eyes still on me. It was a feeling I was to become familiar with in the coming year. Eyes watching, eyes wondering.

"Pay them no mind," Mrs. Eliot said smiling. 'They are silly girls, but kind ones, and ought to be down in the kitchen anyway."

I followed Mrs. Eliot up the stairs, still clutching the small bundle of clothing I'd brought from New Orleans. I knew good fabric and admired the crisp silk of her fine dress as it swept the stair treads before me—stair treads so immaculately clean one could have climbed them dressed in white cambric without picking up a speck of dust.

The second-floor room where she led me sat in the middle of a long hall. The walls were papered with a flowered print, and a big tester bed dominated. It had four posts covered with a drape of lace where the mosquito curtains ought to have been, which seemed unwise to me but very pretty.

Just as at home, the room smelt of river but a different kind of river, and I noticed the two windows along the outside wall were open halfway, and the curtains swayed above the sill in the soft breeze. I could see a river in the distance, blue-grey rather than mud brown, and held back my urge to close the sashes against the bad air.

It took nearly a year of living in Boston before my battle with the housemaids about opening and closing windows was resolved by my eventual understanding. Northern people had their own awful fevers, wasting away and coughing blood in stale and smoky closed-up rooms. In Louisiana, fresh air was the bringer of the yellow jack but for the northern fever, it was the cure.

"This was my room when I was your age," Mrs. Eliot said, interrupting my goggling at the windows. "Of course I live on Chestnut Street now, or I will be as soon as the war is over, and Mr. Eliot returns. For the moment, I am staying here with mother... and you."

"Thank you," was all I could think to say. *Thank you for the room and the pretty bed and the nice end to the awful voyage*, was what I was thinking, but I did not know this woman or how to start a conversation. I was still holding my parcel of clothing but reluctant to place it on the clean covers of the bed, so I set it down on the rush-seat of a painted chair near the door.

Mrs. Eliot looked at my humble belongings and took my hand. "We will soon see about getting you some things," she said.

What an understatement that was, for in a fortnight, I had a cupboard full of dresses, a mauveine jacket, five pairs of shoes, three bonnets and a fancy snood, a crinoline, a coral necklace, a Bible and a book of Wordsworth, two tutors, and no idea what I'd done to deserve any of them.

Of course, my new life altered me. I loved my lessons and Abbie Giles, the woman hired as my teacher. Only a few years older than myself, and as pale as I was dark, I'd never seen anyone with hair as red as hers. Just the same color as the trees I'd seen on my arrival. Abbie was patient and persistent and showed no temper as I struggled in those early days with my reading and writing. She'd come to our house from a college in Worcester and lived in a room upstairs, and thus was my closest companion. She remains with me still, even here in Washington City, and her efforts have greatly increased my abilities.

The women of Colonel Winslow's house were kind to me too, though they presented a different puzzle. Mrs. Eliot came and went and often took me on outings or shopping, but Mrs. Phoebe Winslow, Colonel Winslow's mother was both the hardest and softest woman I have ever known.

Old and heavy enough not to be very active with a doughy face which smiled often but laughed seldom, I knew I moved constantly before her shrewd and watchful eye. There was nothing fearsome about her; in fact, she was kind and encouraging, often patting my hand lovingly and taking an especial interest in my daily lessons.

Long evenings she spent at her desk in the front parlor with her own bookkeeping and accounts, but at days end, she would always call me to her. "Sophia," she would say, in her deep, lush voice that was nonetheless cut with aristocratic syllables, "show me your lessons."

Her eyes would progress rapidly and thoroughly across whatever papers I handed her, and she always found an achievement to commend. "If you continue to do this well with your figures, you'll soon be able to run our family paper mills yourself," she might say, or "With handwriting like this, you'd make a fine amanuensis."

"A man what?" I might answer and the easy smile would be bestowed.

"When you come across a word you do not understand you must consult the dictionary," she would advise. Mrs. Phoebe Winslow was warm-hearted, but I knew one had to earn her good opinion.

Yet, what Mrs. Winslow never inquired of was myself. No one in the household did, and thus I discovered candor was discouraged in the habit of their relations. So I never once recounted anything of my family, my background, or my life in Louisiana. It was as though my arrival on their doorstep had been a natural thing, and I was as untouched and worthy of care as a foundling babe.

I suppose I made many missteps in my first days in Boston, but there was one which provided the best lesson of what the character of my new home was to be. Days after my arrival with Mrs. Eliot at my side, we visited Madame Walsh's at Bowdoin Square. Already excited after being measured for the marvelous mauveine jacket, I was perhaps overeager. Madame Walsh sold beautiful bonnets, from which I was urged to choose three, and a tempting array of floral hair combs and false hairpieces. A particularly fetching cascade of pink flowers and dark ringlets suspended from a tortoiseshell comb caught my eye, and I gasped "Oh!" as I lifted it from the counter. Without even facing Mrs. Eliot directly, I could feel the chilly rebuke and the swift but silent correction. Finery was fine, but frivolity was not going to be tolerated.

It was Colonel Nathan Waldo Winslow who remained the greatest mystery to me as well as the nature of his benevolence. He'd stayed on in Washington City after his war duties ended, working to help establish the Freedmen's Bureau, so I'd yet to see him, and his first letters to me had to be read by Mrs. Winslow. Once my skills improved, he sent some short and simple letters, but no doubt forgetting I was not a child, they were of a very basic language. It was not until I wrote him letters of my own that he replied in a tone appropriate to my age, but his responses were still terse and unrevealing: the weather, his daily activities, his desire for me to study and learn.

I had been treated with such generosity I could only conjecture my father had done the Colonel a great service or perhaps saved his life, but I didn't know. It was only three months ago, just after Mr. Winslow returned for a short visit, when I chanced upon a possible reason.

That Mrs. Henry Merrihew was arriving from her London residence on the steamer *China* was the talk of the household in June of 1865, but I gathered not everyone was looking forward to her visit. In the weeks prior to her arrival, I pieced together all the information I could by listening carefully.

“She is Mrs. Winslow’s sister-in-law, “Mrs. Eliot explained to me. “The late Mr. Winslow’s sister and the auntie of both myself and my brothers, Nathan and John.”

“She apparently wasted no time in Boston as a young woman and went off and married abroad!” Abbie Giles let slip during one of my lessons one day. “I’m told she is...well...colorful.”

“At least she’ll be staying at the Parker House for the duration,” I overheard Mr. Winslow say one evening when he thought he was alone with his sister in the parlor.

“Nathan!” Mrs. Eliot scolded. “You’d better keep that sort of opinion to yourself. You know we all really love her.”

“And you know how she is,” Mr. Winslow replied with a sigh.

As luck would have it, I was the one to see Mrs. Merrihew first. On a sunny forenoon, just as Mrs. Eliot and I were passing across the entryway, I noted a shadow through the sidelight windows of the doorway. There was a brisk knock, and the visitor opened the door herself and stepped in. “Halloo!” the lady shouted out.

She was a tall woman, keen-featured and imperious. At least as elderly as Mrs. Winslow, she was nonetheless of a whole different make, her age unashamedly wrapped in the remarkable attire of a fashion plate. Daringly bareheaded, her grey hair was unadorned and center-parted and her bronze-hued skirt was of costly shot-silk with a braided border, but upstaging it all was her remarkable periwinkle blue dolman wrap with long pointed sleeves, each with a little tassel sewn onto the ends.

“I’ve walked from the Parker House,” Mrs. Merrihew stated. “It’s a lovely day. Finally fresh air, after being hutched up in that steamer cabin.”

“Sophia!” she then exclaimed, coming toward me and taking me in an embrace, “I’m so pleased to meet you.” This was entirely unexpected, and while held in her grasp, I noticed Mrs. Eliot making a pained face. Mrs. Eliot had expected to make an introduction.

Mrs. Merrihew let me loose and took note of Mrs. Eliot’s uncomfortable look. “Oh for goodness sake, Eliza,” she said, removing the lovely wrap and hanging it on the hall tree. "You've written me about the girl, and it's obvious she isn't one of John's vast brood. Is he still up north managing the Maine mill? Is Sarah expecting again? How many children do they have now? Six or seven? I can't keep count. You'd think they were Catholic."

I smiled. Mrs. Merrihew didn't expect an answer to any of her questions. They weren't questions. They were opinions and observations tossed into the air for anyone willing to catch them and with an edge kept sharp for emphasis. I understood at once her bluntness was not unlike the bold hairpiece at Madame Walsh's and just as discouraged. Mrs. Merrihew was a woman who said what she thought, and I liked her from that moment onward.

"Besides," Mrs. Merrihew continued, entwining her arm in Mrs. Eliot's elbow, "I suppose you and Mr. Eliot are busy starting your own family now he's home from the battlefield."

Mrs. Eliot reddened and rolled her eyes almost imperceptibly. "How was your voyage, Aunt Susan?" she asked.

Later that evening after a too heavy supper, the family gathered listlessly in the parlor. It must have been close to the longest day of the year, because the light seemed to overstay its usual hour casting the room in a dusky blush. The top sashes of the windows were open, the single tree across the street moved its leaves drowsily in the extinguishing light.

As he often did, Mr. Winslow asked me to play the piano for the family and show off the results of my music tutor's efforts, and once I'd finished, I hurried back to my corner of the sofa next to Mrs. Merrihew, my newfound friend. The lady had sunk down in the cushions a bit, joined her fingers at the tips and allowed her eyes to wander the room. "That was lovely Sophia." she said. "I'm so grateful we have all been spared in this terrible war, Nathan and Mr. Eliot especially," she said nodding to the two men, both seated across the room, "and of course, Sophia."

"There were times when I wondered if we would ever be together again," Mr. Eliot said as Mrs. Eliot smiled and took his hand.

"Yet, from the look of everything, the paper mills have prospered," Mrs. Merrihew said.

"Prices were never higher than the week of Gettysburg," Mrs. Winslow agreed.

Mr. Winslow sat quietly as was his custom, combing his fingers through his beard, frowning as if vexed with a problem, and waiting for so long to speak that it placed everyone in anticipation of what he was about to say. I sometimes wondered if he did this with intention. "Every hollander was pulping rag as fast as we could get it," he finally said. "We did run some of the cheap manila when the supply got slack, but with the rag boilers working overtime, the quality was quite good."

"Well, my Henry did his part," Mrs. Merrihew said. "We sent half a dozen shiploads of rag from Liverpool. Will you go up to Maine now, Nathan?"

Mr. Winslow gave Mrs. Merrihew a courteous and patient look but picked at his fingernails while his hands lay in his lap. "Five shiploads it was Aunt Susan, and no, I believe John can handle the management at Winslow Falls. My brother steered the family ship well enough during the war, and Mr. Eliot promises to lend his financial experience now he is back."

"I am eager to lend any hand necessary to the Winslow Mills," said Mr. Eliot.

"All of Nathan's care is directed to the Freedmen's Bureau and the work of Reconstruction," Mrs. Winslow added in a measured voice.

"It is true," Mr. Winslow agreed. "I find I am devoted to the advancement of the colored man. It is my avid hope this ill-starred race will be able to take their place in the world's machinery their God-given rights entitle them to. I will return as soon as I can to Washington City and continue my labors to inaugurate a system in which the nation may extend to the Negroes the protection and education due them as citizens. The South especially must be brought under the laws of the Republic!"

I'd heard Mr. Winslow speak this way before about such issues. In all else he remained taciturn and cool, but for the rights of my race, he was ardent. Something changed in him when he fell into such declarations; his costive nature left him, and he became almost fervent, almost...happy.

"Well," Mrs Merrihew said studying her nephew openly, "you are quite an orator, but I have lived long enough to remember slavery was not the sin of the South alone. Have you forgotten Toby?"

Mr. Winslow threw his aunt a glare, and I watched her jawline harden in determination. That the two did not like one another was obvious now, but I wondered with approval where she got her toughness and the vinegar which allowed her to talk business like a man and stand up to her nephew.

"You mean Grandfather Winslow's man?" Mr. Winslow asked.

"Grandfather Winslow's slave," she answered.

Mr. Winslow sputtered now. "I-I've never heard this. The two men were devoted to one another. Grandfather depended on Toby for everything."

"Precisely," Mrs. Merrihew said.

"A slave in Winslow Falls, Maine, how ridiculous! A Black man there in those days would be almost unheard of!"

"My very point. Do you think Toby just grew there, like some errant seed windblown from the South?" Mrs. Merrihew's last words were lobbed out with some humor, but for me, they carried a strange weight.

"I know better." Mr. Winslow growled, "Why we all loved Toby. He is buried at Winslow Falls in the family plot."

"He is buried in the same part of the cemetery with your grandfather's dogs."

Distressed at the argument, Mrs. Eliot interrupted. "It just can't be. I was too young to remember any Black man, but I played in that cemetery every summer. The dogs' gravestones were all by the white lilac bush. She closed her eyes briefly, then opened them again, remembering the row of stones as she counted them on her fingers. "Minna, Tigo, Felix, Jack...Toby! Toby was a man?"

Mr. Winslow slashed the air with his hand, as if this gesture could end the unwanted conversation. "It is a lie! No Winslow of our family has ever been a slave owner!" He was almost panting in anger and almost certainly lying; his cold virtue brought to boiling by an aging woman who now regarded him with a face closed and remote like a stone statue.

"It is the lie in one's heart that counts," she said hoarsely, almost in a whisper, but regained her vigor and began again. "And be that as it may, ten thousand mudsill Frenchmen are coming overland from Canada, and there are steamships crossing the waters every day with wretched consumptive Irish families packed below decks. Once here, they won't even have time to wash the dirt from their boots or the salt from their hair before some mill like our own will put them to work, even the tots. How many of our pulp beaters are run by children? Is this not slavery too?"

"Aunt Susan, stop!" Mr. Winslow commanded. "After all, Sophia is here."

Mrs. Merrihew snatched at my hand and held it, and pulled me close to herself in a hug. "And no doubt in a better position to judge injustice than any of us," she said.

Mrs. Merrihew paused, and I felt her body loosen; she had made her point. She turned to face me directly, now ignoring the others in the room who sat looking both startled and uncertain, and she ran her hand lovingly across my forehead.

"Such beautiful serrated hair," she said. "I could only wish to have such a head of it myself. Why you would be a prize to any Pre-Raphaelite, but your tresses need a comb of flowers to set them off. We will go out tomorrow dear, and I will buy you one."

It was as if the room itself had gasped. I hardly dared turn my head to look at the others, but I did, meeting four sets of astonished eyes across the parlor, none of them like my own, but all the same blue color as the veins in their wrists.

The following August, I watched as Mr. Winslow fell in love in the fancy parlor in Washington City. We'd returned as he said we would, he to his work at the Freedmen's Bureau, and I to my lessons with Abbie. We often attended these types of evening soirees where I would usually be asked to play the piano, but on this occasion, Cora Carter was the star.

For my part that evening, I was taken with the presence of Miss Sojourner Truth, and I will always remember her majestic bearing. Arriving in my best Prussian blue with the white lily hair piece Mrs. Merrihew had given me, I felt quite grand, but standing beside Miss Truth, I knew I was small.

I'd heard of her of course, even back in New Orleans—the Black woman who'd won a lawsuit against a White man, and more importantly to me, one who spoke boldly to audiences of hundreds. Looking at her in Washington City, I could see her power. Her eyes were dark and lively, and I am sure she noticed me for at least a moment. Tall and queenly, with her grey hair covered in what I first thought was a tignon but later saw was just a simple white cap, she nonetheless astounded me. How brave she seemed and how unflinching, a myth of my childhood now come before me as real!

Mr. Winslow found a different person to adore, and I am sure he fell in love with Mrs. Carter's words as much as her lovely face. She was beautiful, but seemed curiously disinclined to make any use of this fact, which would have made only a secondary effect on Mr. Winslow regardless. I don't think he'd any ability to separate his idea of justice from his idea of love, and in Mrs. Carter, he saw both. He had found a woman who applied his convictions in melodious and skillful speech, and a beauty who embodied his ideals.

We were apart on most days, as I attended my lessons, and on some evenings as well, so I've no idea how he courted her. Indeed, it was difficult for me to imagine him courting anyone, as he was always so aloof and reserved.

So, I was surprised when he called me to his desk one afternoon to show me his plans. I'd seen him working there for several hours with scissors and a pot of glue but hadn't asked his reason.

"Sophia, what do you think?" he said as he held out a tiny paper puzzle for me to examine. Made of many small cuts and intended for movement, he demonstrated how the puzzle opened to form a small dome, with a place for a hidden message inside.

"It's called a cobweb," he said. "One of the officers I knew received one from his sweetheart, and I thought I would try to make one for Mrs. Carter."

He passed the cobweb to me, and taking the fragile object in my hands, I opened and closed the puzzle to see how it worked. Penciled inside the puzzle in Mr. Winslow's handwriting were the words *Will you marry me?* I felt awkward and nearly dropped the puzzle, for it was not what I expected or was prepared for.

"Do you think she will like it?" he asked.

I wanted to reflect for a moment before I answered but felt he might be offended so I let my tongue overrule my heart. "I'm sure she will," I said, and indeed, I suspected she would be overjoyed, for in the little I'd observed of Mrs. Carter she seemed to share his affection.

Perhaps then, it was only my girlish romanticism that felt the gesture was without passion, yet, it was so like him and made me uneasy. Mr. Winslow had just managed to advise me of his intentions without any explanation, and he was about to ask Cora Carter to marry him without actually saying the words.

Nathan

1866

Of course the first thing I noticed about Cora was her voice, given our initial meeting was in a room darkened for a séance. It was rich and emotive, but precisely clear, and caused within me the same shiver music can sometimes do, and which would have made me turn away bashfully had I been within anyone's seeing. I raised my hand to my forehead to hide my face and was shocked at the warmth of my brow, like a fever, but it was only fluster. Her vocabulary was refined and polished, the words warm and lush and easy to hear, like a lullaby. Her expression was in every way alluring, and I strained to keep it in my ears, for just then nothing mattered but the sound of her.

She'd stepped into the shadowy chamber after everyone was seated, and I was so far down the length of the joined tables that my view of her was vague and ill-defined. It was just as if I were watching her furtively, spying as it were, which perhaps gave a heightened pleasure to the effect she had on me. I closed my eyes involuntarily then, and her presence disappeared wholly, leaving me stranded with nothing but the darkness and the timbre and vibrations of her voice, and that is how I gave myself up.

I should perhaps explain that in my past, women were never absent. There have been any number who were either presented or presented themselves to me. Here I must make the discomfiting admission, I have always probably been too self-conscious and disciplined. A deep habit of constraint steers me, and I have always feared what a wrong step might precipitate. Twice I have been out of bounds—once in college and another time in the army—the first at the urging of my fellows and the latter after an evening of too much drink, but I don't wish to recall these episodes overmuch.

Beyond the beauty of Cora's voice was the meaning of her words. In the early part of the séance, she brought forth the voices of dead relations of those in attendance. I am unsure about the truth of Spiritualism having had no time to deliberate or investigate it, but in this new age of electrical invention, it would be folly to dismiss invisible powers.

Cora's statements that night were gentle and candid, full of the sort of things the grieving were probably listening for, and when she finished, her reputation in my eyes remained unimpugned.

It was when the lights returned and her séance had ended, and she began speaking before the party in trance, when my yearning was transfixed. I cannot forget how her lovely countenance was in perfect harmony with her words. She seemed a woman both heroic and exquisite. Reaching across into the land of spirits and coaxing out what must have been the words of one of the old abolitionists, Lovejoy or Reverend Parker perhaps, and recounting a discourse both tantalizing and inspired on the subject of universal suffrage, and the rights of all humans. In a melodious tone of absolute conviction, in her eyes a subtle communication, she spoke as if making a promise.

Time does stand still, after that evening I am sure of it, for I saw her audience huddled together in the dusky gaslight as she boldly advocated for the cause. It put me in a strange mood, and I wondered if I were allowed to teach her all I know, if she might somehow join with me and help me become more of what I wished myself to be.

Her words lifted and fell in meaningful beauty; she stood both studied and impetuous, insisting and also yielding, and when she finished and dropped her head to her chest and arms to her sides, her words lingered in the air like perfume on a coat sleeve, and in the powerful silence, those in the room looked to be trembling. I wanted to seize her.

January 4, 1866
New York, New York

Dear Cora and Nathan,

How strange it seems to write Mr. and Mrs. Nathan W. Winslow on the envelope! And how wonderful from all this war and sorrow and confusion you two have found and made a happiness. We are all blessed, coming through these years unscathed, and with our families intact. *So many others have not been as lucky. I cannot but keep thinking of poor Mrs. Lincoln and the thousands who have lost their beloveds. I shudder sometimes to consider it, all the death and destruction, and so many places which lie in ruins.*

It brought George and I so much pleasure to make the trip to Washington City for your wedding. It was little Mae's first long journey by train which seemed to fascinate her. Of this I am glad, for it seems our children will be great travelers in the coming years, now that the railroads are sprawling everywhere.

Father was in his element as well, greatly enjoying having Mae on his lap for hours pointing out the sights as we rode along. It gave him quite a grandfatherly *feeling I think, though the sight of Reverend Pierpont made a bolder impression on Mae, as his long white beard and great head of white hair caused her to ask him directly if he were Santa Claus! I suppose it was the nearness of Christmas which put the idea into her head. The things four-year-old children say, but you will find this out for yourselves soon enough!*

In any regard this is just a note to let you know we have arrived back home at Irving Place safely and enjoyed in every particular attending your wedding, seeing old friends again and meeting new ones. We thank God for our many blessings and wish the same for you both in 1866. May peace really have come to earth.

With love,
from George, Lydia and Mae Cora Austin

* * *

It was strangely silent for a church in which the pews were overflowing. Men and women, both Black and White, filled the seats in the Asbury Methodist Church as I climbed the stairs of the platform to speak. The quiet unnerved me, but I told myself it was merely anticipation and continued on.

I was unused to speaking. Since the war I had written many articles for the Anti-Slavery Standard and other weeklies, but also for newspapers like the Rochester Express and New Orleans Tribune, but standing before an assembly was new for me.

I could smell the audience, the human odor of breath and bodies, and also the scent of the wet wool overcoats tossed over the backs of the pews. Outside one of the light snowfalls of the Washington City winter had begun, flakes falling and melting drowsily.

The subject of my discourse was "Rights, Qualifications and Injustices of the Colored Freedmen of America," and I meant to relate my personal experience among them as a citizen and soldier and declare their rights to be the same as our own, but it is different speaking to men when one is out of uniform. I fear I began awkwardly, clearing my throat several times and stuttering my first sentence.

When wearing the braid and the badges, one feels responsible and determined, but in my plain sack coat and britches, I felt as though I were merely extending a courtesy or a platitude. I hoped they could see my ideal intention—my genuine desire to amalgamate—and not just someone stiff and ceremonial. I hoped I could tie a thread of my life to theirs.

Soon enough though, I found my footing when I began to recount the heroism of my regiment of colored men on the battlefield and remonstrate against the daily atrocities being committed upon these same people by Reconstructed traitors and slave-holders of the South. In the end, I believe my remarks were received with favor given the applause of those in attendance.

After me, it was Cora's turn. Of course, her fame far surpasses my own and most of those in attendance had probably heard of her, but Cora remains like no other.

She ascended the platform placidly, never seeming to feel uncertain. Though I hoped I'd spoken gracefully and knew my words were uttered earnestly, Cora was authentic. Beautifully balanced in her trance state and with an expression of utter goodness, she repeated the words of whatever venerable spirit unleashed himself from the ether to illuminate us, and I was set to marveling as always, at the curious energies which existed in her head to allow her to hear these invisible beings.

One could hear the audience stirring in their seats, see the fixed expression in their eyes as they observed her, the craning of necks and concentration of hearing. No doubt there was much which sounded studied in my lecture as I had practiced it for many days, but Cora's words tumbled out unrehearsed, precise and elegant, and without even the slightest tone of argument or persuasion advised all in the room that human inequality must be rejected.

We were the among the last to leave that February night, stepping from the church together into the velvet-soft silence of the darkness. The snow had sharpened into small stinging crystals and it was in the air—the smell of cold weather coming.

The trees on the street were motionless, and we stood side by side in the sallow light seeping from the church doorway and spilling across the stone steps. I turned to my wife in her dark wool cloak at the same moment she turned to me and felt a flash of euphoria and fate.

I had courted hope for many years, through the dark days of the war and even before, and I knew at once what transpired that evening at the Asbury Methodist Church was meant to be. This is what Cora and I were born for. She lifted her eyes to me and then her mouth to mine, with little flakes of snow sparkling in her hair.

Cora wished to return to New York to have our baby. Not the city, but Cadytown, the home of her childhood. This I understood, as I supposed any woman might want the counsel of her mother when carrying her first child, but Cora spoke more often of her desire for her Aunt Ellen and Uncle Arthur and some inscrutable belief she should give birth in that region.

"I can hear my spirits more clearly there," she would say, but offered no other explanation.

I took her request seriously and mapped out the location, finding it would be a fine place to spend the summer away from the bustle and unwholesome climate of Washington City. Sophia had already returned to Boston just after our wedding and would be spending the summer with the Eliots and my mother at our cottage by the seaside in Nahant. It had been my intent that Cora and I would return to Massachusetts and join them, but her pregnancy changed those plans.

Cadytown was located in the southern tier of New York state, near the Genesee River in the old Seneca territory. As Uncle Arthur Page's household was already full to brimming with Cora's mother and young brother Eddie in residence, we needed a headquarters of our own. Ellen Page made local inquiries and a solution presented itself in a matter of days.

"The old Beaulieu farm in nearby Black Creek," Ellen wrote. "Will Beaulieu and his family had outgrown the farmhouse his parents had built but still worked the land on the property," she explained, "and the house is as neat as a pin."

"There's mighty good fishing," Arthur advised.

So it was decided. A season of country living would benefit us both.

What a season it was, May to October, six months in a timeless world. Day after day passing unhurried and sweet, the afternoons lasting forever. The farmhouse, tidy and foursquare and surrounded by flourishing greenery. A vine covered veranda, pink hollyhocks pressed against the clapboards on the sunniest side, insects humming in the trees. The dense lilac hedge beside the milk house, the pasture-land on all sides where the wind cut fickle paths through the grasses. Behind the house a fine orchard of old and well-pruned trees, biding their time until harvest, sloped down to the dark-watered creek which gave the place its name. The empty barn, somehow holy with its heavy beams and dappled light, where Cora and I spent one evening in the loft lying in a drift of hay as a thunderstorm thrashed and spattered overhead.

We planted a small garden in our first week. I clearing sod with a shovel in my shirtsleeves and cutting willows by the creek for a pea-vine trellis, while Cora laid out and seeded rows with her skirts hiked-up and tied around her waist.

Soon enough, we became accustomed to what at first seemed like unnatural stillness and learned to relish the drowsy silence. We began to order our days according to whim, rising sometimes from our bed as late as midday, flushed and tousled, or giving ourselves over to some other sort of indolence.

One particularly sticky day, we even bathed nearly naked in Black Creek, with a pair of Will Beaulieu's cows standing up to their bellies in the water downstream as our only witnesses. I lifted Cora out from the water that day, her soaked chemise plastered to her rounded belly and laid her on the grass of the bank.

That our bond of flesh would be so irresistible, I never expected. Encouraged by our unbroken days of aloneness, there was such luxury in measuring time by our pleasure and wonder at new things as they became familiar.

I watched as Cora undressed, layer upon layer falling to the chamber floor as the tail end of twilight scarcely illuminated her shoulder blades, her collarbones, or the backs of her thighs. Sleeping beside Cora and listening to the sigh of her breathing, turning to one another in the night and feeling the heat of her as she took my weight and held me, while I silenced her little cries with kisses. The way our hands, fingers, mouths found their natural places. My palm on her hip or the small of her back, her fingers sifting through my hair, my lips questing her tongue and the hollow of her throat.

How on waking she would let herself be kissed again, as she washed herself with soapy hands at the standing basin. Her wet fingers would linger on the curve of my jaw, her hands stroke my chest, and her voice—the same remarkable instrument whispered in my ear as in platform oratory—would cause my heart to twist and tremble.

My previous need for things to be precise and ordered, my lifelong task of reticence was tossed aside, and I was utterly transported by the overflow of feeling and the fearful and exciting notion I was recklessly exposing my heart. That this was all emergent from the same possibly dangerous and slow-burning place where all my convictions of human equality and morality lurked, I already suspected. However, I hadn't foreseen physical passion would feel like this, possessive, addictive, and insatiable, or that surrender to it would be another kind of troth.

That marvelous summer brought other understandings, and I will always recall a day I espied Cora unaware and from afar.

I'd been on my knees weeding our garden, wearing an old straw hat I'd found in the milk house and straightened, placing my hands on my thighs as I heard a voice of greeting. Cora was seated in a wicker chair on the veranda shelling peas in the shade of the trellised trumpet vine, her hair simply braided, her figure in a lovely repose.

Visitors were infrequent at Black Creek, but Cora's relations sometimes stopped by on a Sunday afternoon, and she enjoyed their presence, cooking special treats for them and exchanging garden vegetables. She especially fancied her Aunt Ellen and could easily fall into a spell of gossip with the lady, talking of some common acquaintance or situation from the past. It was only with her mother where I sensed a slight, odd coolness I could not account for, but as Zilpha treated me with a regard which bordered on the lavish, I did not fear the cause of their constraint was due to me and did not care to consider the situation overmuch. Women nurse tensions between themselves man can never fathom.

The visiting voice that summer afternoon was of her brother Eddie, a sturdy and cheery ten-year-old boy who much resembled his elder sister but for freckles along his brow and forearms.

He'd trotted into the dooryard riding bareback and barefooted upon his pony, Blackstrap, dismounted and slid to a seated position on the porch floor beside Cora. There I observed the two in conversation, their heads bent and close to touching, examining something Eddie held in his hand. When I saw Cora hunting in her apron pocket and taking Eddie's hand in hers, I instantly knew the reason.

She carried a needle case there, and when I saw Eddie squirming and trying to hold the hand steady, I smiled. How many splinters had my mother removed when I was boy at our cottage at Nahant? And how beautiful sister and brother looked while intent on their objective, Eddie poised and Cora deliberate until she dropped his hand and smiled.

I could see the future mother in my lovely wife, feel the softness of her hand as I saw it pass across her brother's forehead, pushing his hair away from his eyes. He pointed something out to her in the far pasture, and they talked and laughed together, comfortable and easy, as if they had not been siblings with ten years and many miles between them.

Was this the way it had been with myself and Sophia when I first returned to Boston from the war? I hoped so, but had my doubts.

Now a boy with a splinter is not the same thing as a colored girl-child seized from a place of slavery and war and deposited in the foreign world of a northern city, where none of her race are even common. Yet, by the time I returned with the war waning, Sophia had lived for many months with my own family, and I hoped she'd begun to heal and adjust.

Indeed, I'd been told the girl had gone from strength to strength when I first saw her, already becoming genteel and poised, flourishing in her studies under Miss Giles, the tutor I'd selected from the Oread Institute in Worcester. By all accounts and in my own observation, she was forging ahead with her languages, music and even mathematics.

Yet I was obliged to give her an account of her father, and the story was a terrible one. I emphasized his bravery and character, both of which were above reproach, and tried to speak of his awful death with scant description. Dear Pol, what I would not have done for him, and how solemnly I accepted his request I find and care for his daughter!

I have done my best for Sophia and made her as my own, even to the legal particulars, as she is my daughter now in every aspect, so she might forever benefit from my estate. I've outlined for her all she can expect from the Boston world with its nearly limitless promise but also what this world will require from her, so different, no doubt, from all she has ever known. It was not an easy conversation, and I confess I lack Cora's tender tongue.

Sophia reacted as anyone with a pure heart would, giving voice to both emotion and gratitude, but some partly concealed sentiment flickered across her face, and though her smile remained in place, something cowered behind it. I found I could not meet her eyes for a moment, a moment I knew then would grow larger and larger for the remainder of my life. There was obedience in Sophia's face, an expression I dreaded observing on the face of a colored person more than any other.

Since that day, I have tried to put our first exchange out of my mind. I did not intend to dictate and hope Sophia will only remember my good intentions.

The day before our child was born, I spent the morning fishing. Cora remained at the farmhouse, as her time of delivery was at hand, with Zilpha, Ellen and Lydia Austin who'd come the week before on the train from New York.

With a stout hickory and hairline pole lent by Arthur, I tucked my trouser bottoms in my boots and made my way through the back orchard now dense with fruit ready for harvest. On my way, I plucked a half dozen apples to accompany my pocketed sandwich, noting for the first time how many varieties there were.

It was the finale of summer; the foxtailed grass rustled beneath the trees, crickets sang, and butterflies grazed from flower to flower. I ducked through the willows at the bottom of the orchard, crept carefully down the rise of the bank, and with a thrill of anticipation, cast my line into the dark water. To me it was the crowning day of the year, with its brazen sun and tumbling clouds, but why is it the end never seems like the end, even at the moment of ending?

Four lazy hours and three fine trout later, I ate my sandwich and varied apples, some sour and some sweet. Pocketing my hooks and flies, I chose a different route of return following a trace along the far side of Black Creek where I'd never walked before.

I explored for a while and judging I was about two miles from the farmhouse crossed the creek at a place of shallow eddy in a dark crescent of woodland. Here, I chanced upon a small graveyard. Seven stones tilted and sinking, from a household long gone to dust. A lone bird chattered in the leaves above me, moving from branch to branch as I tore away the overgrown grasses from the faces of the stones to examine them.

Joel Chamberlain the tallest stone read with a death date of fifty years before. *Eunice* said a smaller stone beside it in rude lettering, and another with the letters *S.C.*, more primitive yet, doubtless wrought by some home-owned chisel. The others were left blank, their identities either sunk out of sight or weathered away.

I sat down in the thick grass, fumbling a single stalk of it between my forefingers and listening to the particular pre-autumn whistle of the wind in the air around me. I'd known people of the surname *Chamberlain* in Boston and reasoned these were some of the same blood, probably come west after the Revolution looking for better land.

The sunlight slanting through the trees made a shadowy dappled pattern in the somber place which still maintained a great dignity even in abandonment. I thought then of Toby, grandfather's man, grandfather's slave, buried under his own anonymous marker, indistinguishable from the dogs.

How horrified I'd been when Aunt Susan blurted out his name last year in Boston, bringing back a long-buried shame. For of course I'd realized Toby was a slave or at least assumed it, as I knew him when I was a boy.

Lord knows how old Toby was back in those days of my own childhood, but I imagine he was close to my grandfather's age which would put him near seventy years. I remember his deep-lined face and the pouches under his eyes which seemed as big as pockets. He had a high domed forehead scattered with a few freckles which fascinated me to see on black skin and dense grey side-whiskers of which I believe he was a bit vain.

I and other boys of my acquaintance felt free to tease Toby in those days prompted by his status and relative oddness, and I am appalled to remember just what a lot of shit-arses we were. To his credit, Toby reacted with an amused detachment as he knew we were damned fools, but boys of that age are cruel. "Black as Toby's ass," we would often taunt when in Toby's hearing and out of range of my grandfather's, and I seem to recall pelting poor Toby with chestnut conkers one autumn.

What I do know for certain was how I would rue my words and actions only hours after engaging in them, and after the other boys had gone home would skulk back around Toby's quarters in some sort of inarticulate contrition. He lived in the clapboard ell of my grandfather's large red brick house which overlooked the mill in Winslow Falls, in a room of extreme bareness.

Other than when he sat with my grandfather or helped with household chores, this spartan room was where I remember him, with a particular vision of his tremulous and knobby old hands loading his small stove with squares of wood he'd taken from the pile laid out for the cook in the kitchen. I also remember him singing, a rich baritone springing in surprising robustness from his thin frame, the same crooked hands keeping tune in a soft slapping on his knees. In recent years, I have tried to remember these songs more clearly and in my days in Louisiana tried to match them with songs I'd heard from the slaves and Black soldiers but Toby's singing was not the same. I know now his songs reached back to where he began, and besides memory, were the only pathway he could use to take himself there.

In those days of my youth, I wondered if Toby were lonely with no wife, no friends of his own kind, in the stark room away from the rest of the house. Today, I realize he was not bound to stay in Winslow Falls, as slavery was abolished years before I was born, but where would he have gone?

I asked Toby one day, regretful after making jokes with the other boys about boot blacking, where he was from.

Toby shrugged as if the question could not possibly matter. "I don't know," he answered. "Around Rhode Island way, I guess.

That's where old Mr. Winslow got me. I was to be companion to your grandfather."

So Toby was a gift, from father to son. My grandfather both knew Toby and owned him. The notion that a man could be a present, something traded like a puppy or a horse, stunned and mortified me. That was the day of my own epiphany, the day which made me as I am.

I shook my mind free from these thoughts and back to the lonely graveyard. Here buried were forgotten Chamberlains, most likely men whose family died out, but whose forefathers could be traced in some attic Bible. My own family went backward from Winslow to Winslow until we reached the ones who came on the Mayflower. I could not as a young boy—nor even today—imagine not knowing where one came from or who one's family was, nor even begin to conceive the terrible solitary life of Toby, if that was even his real name.

A shudder ran through me as I stood and looked once more at the forlorn stones attesting to seven individual lives, overgrown and disappearing in a dense and waiting stillness so insistent it made me feel as if something was about to be said. So convinced was I, that I strained to detect a syllable in the silent air. If I had Cora's ears, perhaps I would have heard someone.

Arriving back at the farmhouse, I dressed my fish and fried them in batter myself, eating them on the back steps where I'd been banished, my only companion a barn cat from Beaulieu's who'd come around to beg from me.

At about 4 the following morning, our daughter was born. *Henrietta Lydia Winslow*. I was a father for the second time or the first, depending on which way you want to consider it.

The only blemish on our beautiful summer of 1866 was the terrible news out of New Orleans of the massacre at the Mechanics' Institute in July. Cora and I did not hear of the awful event until several weeks after it transpired, so secluded were we in our dreamlike world. Even today I rebuke myself with thinking, what shady lane was I walking, what chair was I lazing in, while men I once knew were being slaughtered?

Discouraged that the goal of voting rights for Black men remained elusive, activists both White and colored called for reconvening the 1864 Louisiana Convention in hopes these rights might be gained. Remarkably, Louisiana's Governor James Wells, whose opinions might blow in any direction along with the prevailing wind, acceded to the demand, but the mayor of New Orleans and his police force made up of erstwhile Rebels had other ideas. The fateful Convention was to be held in the Mechanics' Institute on Canal Street.

As we learned, while the delegates inside the Institute were preparing their business, a rally of more than two hundred veterans of our old Louisiana Native Guard Regiments paraded through the French Quarter with drums and banners to support the cause. By all accounts these former soldiers, many of whom I knew, were cheered as they marched, but when they reached the center of Canal Street, the former dividing line between the French and the Americans, all hell broke loose. A White mob unleashed gunfire, brickbats and even swords harbored from their days in the Rebel army, and by day's end scores were killed. The marching soldiers were gunned down, the men inside the Institute ambushed and shot, before the self-styled "police" vigilantes fanned out over the nearby streets attacking and murdering Black men at random. Many of the newspapers have called the incident a riot, but it was no riot—it was a massacre, destitute of any justifiable cause, and carried out without any regard to human life!

There has been great joy in my household over the long winter since Cora and I traveled from the Black Creek farmhouse to Boston, and she was welcomed as daughter and sister to my family with a hundred affections. Falling into easy sympathy, the women of my life laugh and tease one another and walk the streets of Boston with their arms entwined, while beautiful little Etta, as we all call her, thrives and charms us all.

But in all these months, I have burned with other ambitions wishing to take a more active role in pursuing the rights of the colored men. Up until this time I had been working with Oliver Howard at the Freedmen's Bureau, writing as a correspondent, lobbying and pressing politicians to appropriate funds for Freedmen's schools and land grants, activities which seem benign since Mechanics' Institute. I knew Louisiana and the sort of enemy that lurked there, thirsting to regain all the evils the war deprived them of. I wished for the chance to travel south and take these unrepentant brutes in hand and have pressed all the men of influence I am acquainted with to help me find a tangible way to serve.

I confess I may have even allowed my keenness to become visible as Cora and Sophia caught me just last week standing before the long mirror in the upstairs hall dressed in my old military uniform. I'd had an urge to try it on again, and just as the two were climbing the stairs, they spied me. They paused and smiled at one another, but only Cora spoke.

"It suits you," was all she said.

Mrs. Beaulieu

1866

How the floorboards creaked and the fifth stair tread on the so'ward side and the door of the jelly cupboard in my pantry! Bacon frying in the iron spider, where my own boudin once sizzled and laundry dancing on the line, where for the last few years the farm had been alone and silent.

Certainly it was not the farm of Octave and Rosa with the ample gardens, forty hens, two hogs, the milk cows and the beeves, for she only stayed the summer, but to have mon Ange pregnant and brought to bed in my farmhouse caused a joyful leap in my heart. Our hearts do leap sometimes, even here. For all we now know in the Summerland, there are things which surprise us still.

Mon Dieu! Mon Ange roaming the path behind the milk house, pausing near the barn door, shelling peas in her apron on the porch by the trumpet vine. I was in those places too, hulling berries, lugging the beehive boxes, setting my ax aside the woodpile. I, too, have shifted sleepless and big-bellied on my own bedstead in the front room, just as Cora does. My son's wife, too, and another woman ten years hence, and another in the coming century, each one knowing things I will never know, each different and each the same, one soul atop another, a spool of unwrit names. You pass through my very self, daughters and sisters, and call it daylight! You will pass through one another calling our sadness midnight and our joy noon, for nothing...nothing ever goes away, and the sigh you hear will not be just your own.

You think my fears and wishes in the night are gone? My longing? My love? It is evaporated, but not disappeared; invisible, but never lost. Do you think all things live only in the moments of their breathing? Nothing is quelled; all is vouchsafed. The soul turns and turns.

I watch as you too will someday watch your beloveds—Cora at the dry sink, Cora washing her hair on the longest day of the year, Cora hanging her apron on the peg, Cora with her arms around her husband's neck, in the magic time of marriage before the days become noisy with children. For all is evident, and there is nothing now that is new to me.

My eyes see Cora's man too, exploring my orchards in Octave's old straw hat. He is a man hot with ideas and intentions, which I have no desire to pry into.

On the last day however, curiosity bested me, and I followed him as he strode toward the creek with his fish pole, the uncut grass bending beneath his hasty tread. He fished for some hours and crossed the creek at the site of the old Chamberlain homestead, stumbling upon the burial place of the unfortunate clan. They were mon Bouton's people from long ago, felled by illnesses I cannot now recall. Grippe, fever, consumption, or suchlike. Where I live now, death is trifling, just a turning on the stair, a sooner or later, a last lingering hour before a daybreak.

How vexed and uneasy he seemed seated before the gravestones, a frowning forehead and hands soft and pale as a priest's worrying a tassel of timothy. I had the urge to speak; I almost whispered the counsel on my lips, but I remembered myself. My business is not with him.

Years and years, I watch my babes, mes petits, those born in my hands, and the distances I must go to be among them cannot be mapped.

With mon Ange the oratress, to the platforms and lyceums. With mon Hibou the sailor, to the wharves and seas of the world where I climb with him in the rigging. Ma Souris, the thief and liar, I cajole to decent doorways but follow him anyway to places of shame and squalor, for the corrupt are as precious as any, and goodness is not my concern.

Each one I follow; each one I counsel and caution. The wicked, the righteous, the hapless. I will stay close to them until the day they bear their own babes, and I let slip their hands. This or until they themselves let go, as mon Bouton did. One moment running behind a flag in a blue uniform with a rifle fixed with bayonet, and the next, exploded! Lost in a horrible shower of metal and powder and himself.

It was Gettysburg, he later told me, and painless, but this modern death makes me shudder. I never even had a chance to watch him close his eyes.

So, mon Ange and I will be parting on this night of the Hunter's Moon as soon as the girl-child she is carrying is born. I shall sit out the birth with my pipe in this same room where I gave birth to children of my own. I had dear Octave, and Cora has her friend Lydia to attend her. Lydia is pregnant too but does not yet know it, a joy for a future season. Cora will sense I am with her, will smell my pipe she knows so well, but won't feel my hand when it drops hers, or hear the sound of my egress over the cries of her firstborn. "You," I will whisper a final time, "I know you," and I will be gone.

I will emerge from Cora's birthing chamber lighter, as I am lighter every time one of my babes moves onward. Each time something of me is loosed into the heavens, and I become more pervious. Some atom of me changes to light. Already my fingers glow and sparkle like the gleam of love in an eye. My whisper grows softer, but each of my words become a syllable of some huge and ancient song, each glitter a flash of some endless light. When my sight is done, this light is what my eyes will be watching. I cannot explain it, but if I had to give it a name, I would call it love. I want to hope it is love, but now I beware the old catechisms, taught by the priests and bishops, and forgo hope.

Faith and love are twin sisters, but hope is a trickster. Every hope contains a plan of man. I am a mere midwife, but have noted it is only hope which dies stillborn.

**“Ils ne sont pas *morts*.
Parlez-leur; ils vous répondront.”**

Joseph Barthet
Le Spititualiste de la Nouvelle-Orleans

“They are not dead.
Talk to them; they will answer you.”

Cora

1867

"Seven months and seven days side by side," I said while pondering the two infants sleeping in their little baskets on a thick rug on the bedroom floor.

"Just to think of it!" Lydia added, "I'd no idea I was pregnant when I was with you at Black Creek when Etta was born, and now we are both mothers."

"Of course Clara is just a week old, so she'll do little but sleep, but I'm a bit amazed my Etta is finally napping. Now she has the notion of sitting up by herself, she seems determined to keep trying."

Lydia rolled her eyes. "Just wait until she starts crawling, then you will have your hands full, and besides, it's Mae who's tired Etta out, chattering and fussing with her."

"For five years she's had her mother to herself, and now there are two babies in the house. Of course she is fascinated."

"Well, thankfully, Charles has taken her for an afternoon at Union Square, so we may all have a little peace," Lydia said smiling.

Lydia pulled her dressing gown more tightly around herself and began to rise from the low chair where she'd been seated, grasping the corner of the headboard for support. Stepping to her side I took her elbow. "Are you still sore, dear?"

Lydia bit her lip before she answered. "Yes, somewhat," she confessed.

Pressing Lydia's shoulder lightly and easing her back into her chair, I reached to the nearby dresser where a hairbrush sat with a comb wedged into its bristles. "Then rest now, and let me do your hair."

I gently removed the tie from the bottom of Lydia's hair and unpicked the braid it held. Our friendship was so close, such an exchange was established routine, and Lydia closed her eyes in pleasure as I brushed, holding the thick tress up and away from her nape. Lydia let her head fall backward, but turned her gaze once again in the direction of our two babies, Henrietta Lydia Winslow and Clara Alice Austin, as they slept.

"Clara likes her basket," Lydia observed. "She looks like a little Moses nestled there."

I'd finished with the brushing, and was twisting and folding Lydia's hair, then plunging hairpins into the chignon to hold it fast. "I don't think you could float it down the Nile," I said, with one hand cradling the half-pinned hair, "but it is handy on the train cars for carrying a little one. I admit it is a selfish gift."

"Selfish?" Lydia questioned.

I smoothed my hand across Lydia's forehead and gave her shoulders a quick pat to signal the hairdressing was complete. "I'm hoping it will carry Clara when you and Charles come to visit us in the South," I said.

"When will you leave for New Orleans?"

"In about a month. Not long after I return from here. Nathan is anxious to get started. He's to be Register under the Bankruptcy Act, managing the claims of local debtors. He feels he can be a monitor for fraud and abuse and continue to advocate for the rights of the Freedmen."

"Goodness!" Lydia exclaimed. "Have you married a politician?"

"No, well yes…possibly." I answered. "Oh Lydia, you can't know how he is. He is goodness itself, and has such modesty and patience, and how grateful I am to finally be in the hands of someone of virtue."

"What of Sophia?" Lydia asked. "Will she be joining you? She is from New Orleans herself, is she not?"

I moved from my standing position to sit on the bed and hoped Lydia did not notice how her question discomfited me. I often puzzled on Nathan and Sophia and their strange relation, the one part of our marriage which seemed to have nothing to do with me. Sophia's silence about her terrible past in the days of slavery and Nathan's adoption of a daughter he did not treat with typical fatherly affection. Of course their situation was a strange one, an unlikely consequence of the war, but stranger was the way I sometimes saw Nathan looking at the girl, chastened and shamefaced, as if she were some sort of crime he were guilty of. So too, did I wonder if what Nathan was offering Sophia was what the girl actually wanted for herself.

"The entire family are off to the Nahant cottage for the hot months now," I replied as offhandedly as possible, "but I think Sophia means to stay in Boston. Nathan certainly encourages her studies and the girl seems devoted to her tutor. I gather there are some bad memories for her in New Orleans. The war, her family…I am not sure…and haven't been bold enough to ask."

"I can't imagine," Lydia said. "It must be difficult for her in surroundings so strange. You know Sojourner has often asked after Sophia in her letters. Apparently the girl caught her eye back in Washington City."

"Well, Nathan and Sophia did make a notable pair in those days, and you can tell Sojourner that Sophia thrives in every aspect as far as I can see. My goodness, I am told she is even learning Italian. She's a lovely girl, and I'm awfully taken with her. Her humor is winning and well, look!"

I slid off the bed and crept to my trunk propped open in the corner. I pulled out a length of white fabric and placed it in Lydia's lap. It was an exquisite infant's dress with elaborate smocking worked in two colors of thread. "Sophia made this for Etta. She is a marvelous seamstress. I could never possess such talent."

Lydia studied the garment for a long moment running her hand across the detailed stitchery. "It is a beautiful thing, but don't undervalue yourself, Cora. Your talents are in words. I assume Nathan encourages your lectures."

"Oh yes, but I am too much of a wife and mother at present to entertain any of that," I said, taking the dress from Lydia and refolding it carefully. "Perhaps when I am done with nursing."

Lydia placed her own hand on top of her dressing gown at the level of her breasts and looked down. "Yes," she agreed, "there is that."

* * *

Our conversation paused, I let my eyes wander around the room. Irving Place, my old refuge, and Lydia, my finest friend. I remembered arriving here covered in blood, sitting with Sojourner in complete uncertainty, and the happy day searching dress patterns from magazines on the parlor floor. All the old fragments of life one leaves behind, none of which lose their color in the passing.

Now, we were two young mothers with sleeping babes before us. I recalled how Lydia told me once how calm the sight of her newborn child made her feel. For me, it was the opposite. An insistent, anxious sensation had come to live in my brain since Etta's birth. I wondered if it were worry or responsibility gnawing but suspected it was just motherhood, which in the end was probably the same thing.

"Lydia, what you said earlier made me think of something I wanted to tell you, about my lectures."

Lydia glanced with a single eyebrow raised.

"I've long wanted to lecture in my own words, instead of those of the spirits," I said.

Lydia seemed unfazed. "Why don't you?"

"I don't think I could. As I've told you before, the moment I step to the platform and fall into the sounds of the audience, the spirits begin their racket. There is no other word for it. They shout, they plead, they sing, anything to get my attention. It is unpleasant, and the reason I prefer to work in smaller circles, with séance not trance. The difficulty in trance lies in grasping one voice from the hundreds. I literally cannot hear myself think. I'm afraid the spirits would drown out whatever I thought to say, except..."

"Except?" Lydia questioned.

"I did it one time. Spoke my own words before an audience," I confessed.

"When?"

"It was just after Nathan and I married. I hadn't planned to do it, I just seized a chance."

"Why was this time different?" Lydia asked.

"The audience was not very large, and mostly colored people, but it was their silence which allowed it. I've never stood before an audience who waited in such silence, and I believe this quiet gave the spirits no chance to slip in. Nathan had lectured just before me about the rights of the freedmen. I wanted to do well and wanted him to be proud of me, and when I stepped to the platform, I was filled with my own ideas about suffrage and equality. When I first realized I could hear no spirit voices, I panicked but recovered myself and just began saying the things I believed.

"No one suspected? No one was able to detect the difference?"

I shrugged. "Everyone applauded. Nathan was ecstatic."

"Why that's wonderful," Lydia said.

"No, it's not wonderful. I shan't try it again because it wouldn't be truthful. People that evening assumed a spirit was speaking, but worse was what they also assumed. For years now, I've spoken on the platform to praise and applause. Yet in all the articles written about me, all the proclamations of my wonderful gift, no one has ever suspected me of using my own words or attributed the lectures to me."

Lydia shook her head, not understanding. "Of course not, Cora. Your audiences can see you are truthful."

"This is what troubles me so," I complained. "People assume the words come from the spirit, not only because they believe me truthful, but because they don't believe I am capable of devising them. They don't think any young woman capable of such a thing."

I'd been warned of the heat but found the air pleasant when stepping to the docks of New Orleans after the stuffy cabins of the steamboat *Ruth*, which had been our home for so many days. From the top of the gangway, I could see the products of the region, stacks of lumber, bales of cotton, wagons heaped with their drayage, sacks of grain and coffee, barrels of sugar and turpentine.

The din was not unlike the voices of my trance spirits, a half-dozen languages, stevedores and teamsters barking and scolding, crates of poultry squawking, hooting boat horns and churning paddles thrashing the mud-brown river water and the rubbish floating in it.

The large wooden dock was built above a sloped levee, slick with mud and swill, and foul-smelling, but in the distance I could make out the city itself, long streets running back from the river, grand slate rooftops shimmering in the sun and, in the haze, a cathedral spire.

Our journey was not an easy one, particularly with baby Etta. The worst had been progressing overland on stages and trains from Boston to Pittsburgh, but once aboard the steamboat, my interest in the surroundings far outweighed any exhaustion.

I would always remember the calm magnificence of the Ohio, with tidy towns set up against its banks and the beautiful Indian names of the sister rivers, *Kanawha*, *Muskingum*, *Kinneconick*. So, too, the clever workings of the canals and locks interested me, and the variety of shipping cruising beside us. Nathan never tired of pointing out these other vessels—keelboats and sloops, snagboats and luggers. My favorite were the small flatboats with a shack built atop them—cooking smoke pouring from a pipe stuck through the roof or a fire built directly on the deck—and men dressing, playing cards and shaving themselves in full view as they glided along. The other passengers aboard the *Ruth* were worthy of observation too—drummers and dentists, traveling ministers, and wealthy families with their servants.

Once we were steaming far down the great Mississippi however, the scenery and the aspect changed. Thick morning fogs enveloped us, and the glaring sun throbbed like a headache. The small family farms of the Ohio River became dense jungles, forbidding cypress swamps and fields extended to the horizons planted with crops I'd never seen, indigo, cotton and eventually sugar cane. The trees were filled with strange birds with calls like screams, and once I saw a large black snake swimming in the river beside us.

Even the passengers seemed different, changed from the innocuous to the underhand—the dentist become gambler, the drummer a confidence man, the minister a sinister land agent with his beard stained with tobacco. Were these the same men who'd boarded with us on the upper river, or had I imagined them differently at the first?

With the steamboat tied up for wooding at Vicksburg, I saw the first scenes I equated with slavery, sweaty Black men loading cordwood, singing mournful songs in a language I could not decipher. Nights, this same race of men would sleep on the deck of the *Ruth*, the only place they were allowed passage.

Yet, the foliage and flowers presented a luxurious beauty which exceeded my imagination. Blossoms which would require careful nursing in a sunny window in New York burst forth here like weeds. Splendid palms tossed themselves like wild dancers in any hint of wind. Nathan said there were oranges, figs, pomegranates. I had already seen huge banana leaves resembling a fringed blanket and magnificent white jasmine tumbling in great sweet cascades. The rivers had beautiful names here too, *Ouachita*, *Atchafalaya*.

Now at the docks in the city which was to be our home, Nathan pulled me against him and hoisted Henrietta upon his hip. He gestured with a nod of his head toward a wide street which lay before us stretching from the edge of the river where the steamboats lay nosed to the wharf, as far as my eyes could see.

"Look at Canal Street, Etta," Nathan said, addressing his statement to our daughter in his arms. "The widest street in the United States. Managed differently, this city could rival New York."

I already knew Nathan could travel a long way on this sort of thinking, but felt a tug of dread. What would be the result of Reconstruction? Would Louisiana be the place of the black snake or the white jasmine, or some mixture of both?

'It is a great honor," Nathan proclaimed after he'd read the letter I'd received asking me to be one of the speakers at a commemoration marking the first anniversary of the Mechanics' Institute Massacre.

I took the letter from Nathan's hands and returned it to its envelope. "Yes, but I don't know if I should accept."

"Why ever not?" Nathan questioned. "The massacre is among the most fiendish acts ever to occur in this city. If we are to support the cause of Reconstruction giving such a speech is more than an honor, it is very nearly a duty."

"It makes me fearful."

Nathan lowered his head, and I could see he was considering my sentiment. "Yes, I suppose there is a risk of another melee, as those against us are still seething with rage, but I am told the organizers have planned a force of security to be stationed outside the hall."

I waved away his words. "I have no physical fear. I just don't wish to speak in trance this time."

Nathan frowned. "Why is this instance any different than the others?" he asked.

"I don't feel confident lecturing in trance any longer," I confessed. "It is exhausting, and I am helpless while in that state. How would you feel standing before hundreds of people not knowing precisely what words you are saying."

"You truly have no realization?"

"Very little," I answered, "and in a room where so much horror and death erupted only last year, I'm just as likely to be overtaken by the voice of one of the murderers."

Nathan appeared shocked. "Surely such men are not to be found in the same afterlife as the innocent."

I reached my hand out and smoothed his hair away from his forehead. I liked the feeling of its crisp dryness, the subtle strength it evinced by always retaining its natural curl, but often wondered if Nathan's idealism was just as intractable. "The heavens do not seem to be ordered by man's moralities," I said.

He fell silent and motionless but for his fingers with which he twisted his wedding ring. "Is there anything I can do to help you?" he asked.

I let my hand travel from his forehead to his restless hands and stilled them in a clasp.

"If I am to speak at Mechanics' Institute, I will use my own words."

"How?" Nathan said blankly.

How weary it made me feel, the sting that he, too, believed me incapable. "I will pick up my pen and write them," I said. My answer was more than a declaration, it was a vow.

* * *

The truth was I'd picked up my pen long ago. I had never stopped thinking of Nettie Colburn's mysterious voice at the White House or my own success in speaking at the Asbury Methodist Church, but it was baby Etta who'd finally brought me to my desk.

In the days after my pregnancy was certain and once I felt my child's first movements, I noted these events in a journal purchased for the purpose. I had a hazy notion of presenting my child with this account in the far future as a record, but it was not long before these little milestones were overwritten with my own ideas and enthusiasms. Poems, essays, short stories, my words poured out, to the extent that even in Black Creek when I'd filled the book, I began cross-writing in the journal to get it all down. A child was not the only thing I felt I had to deliver that year.

Now on the day I was to read the poem I'd written for the occasion, I sat with the other speakers on the platform at Mechanics' Institute and watched my hands shake.

The composition itself had not been difficult, though I'd far less time to devote now little Etta was creeping about the floor and hitching herself up against my skirts. Nathan did all he could in tending to the baby, giving me time to work on the writing. In the end, the entire poem came to me on a single afternoon, a rare cool and wet day where the words spilled easily from my pen and the rain pattered pleasantly on the leaves of a banana tree just outside my open window.

Yet I was uneasy for the first time ever, awaiting my turn to speak in the great hall. Even though I intended to read my poem from the pages I carried to the podium, I did not know if I could prevent myself from falling into trance. After all the years I'd feared the spirits might abandon me, I now worried they would not leave me alone.

The Institute was like others where I'd lectured in the past, except it was draped in mourning. I'd not seen such swags of black crepe since president Lincoln's death. A great drape of silver and black hung on a catafalque centered in the middle of the space with the words "In Memory of the Martyrs of the 30th of July 1866" placed upon it, and a grisly blood-stained American flag which had hung in the Institute on the day of the massacre was displayed.

Nathan bought me a new dress for the occasion, black as jet and made up quickly by a seamstress last week and within which I already felt the prickling of sweat. The sensation brought to mind Lovey and the dressing rooms of the New York days, memories interrupted when I heard my own name introduced.

A man named Waples, a U.S. Attorney, had spoken previous to me, and the audience, demurred from applause by the mournful occasion but still murmuring their approval at his oration, were stirring in their seats in the interlude. It was the old recipe of my transformation, the familiar aural pathway to my world of trance. The scraping of chairs, the soft whispers, the fluttering of paper programs. Trying to resist the sounds, I stepped across the stage to take my place at the podium.

The singing had come first, dropping from someplace overhead, a soldiers' song, marching, drums, a shaggy-haired youth in the jacket of a Zouave, then a terrible whimpering, someone old and bandaged and in pain, a blacksmith with intense eyes repeating my name, a chorus of scolding women, the cry of a child. In between the voices, visions flashed or hovered, insistent and just past the edge of my full perception.

I raised my eyes to the transom windows near the ceiling, tilted to full open position in the hot July afternoon and saw through them humid skies colored a shopworn grey. The trees in the nearby square rustled as if to quiet me. Shhh, shhh, shhh, they seemed to be saying. Looking down at the poem I'd written, the ink was smudged and the pages dampened in my sweaty hands. I was already taking too long to begin, and only moments from losing the patience of the audience. Only their expectation was holding the instant together.

"Toll, toll, toll!" I began,
we have need of mournful bells,
need of penitence and tears..."

A carillon then sounded, dozens of bells as if to mock my efforts, the sight of two horses on a tether, a man drumming his fists upon a table and speaking of the end of the earth, a foreign woman jabbering some long complaint, all of it roiling and thrashing like the water which had run under the wheels of the mill at Hope Grove and which every adult in town had warned me to stay clear of. The same awful undertow.

"grief grows strong with lengthening years,
But no grief hath cause so strong—
no year of woe, no drear so long…"

Some sound of hammering from outside the hall. A mob at the doors? On the street? More murderers come to avenge themselves? Or just workmen? The audience appeared composed so perhaps it was nothing. A man at my elbow, tugging gently, "I am a philosopher," he said, "I am a philosopher." Shaking him away in my mind, still another replaced him, bald but for two curly white puffs above his ears. "You would not cause him to be hung?" he questioned in an urgent voice. They were all urgent, as always, a sound swarming my ears, and so tangled with the past and the present I could not sort them. I feared I was losing myself.

"As that which brings us pale with pain,
To weep at death's dark door again…"

A sharp slash of pain across my eyes, like a cut from a carelessly handled knife, and a light so bright it seemed I would find myself blind or burned as by a curtain of wind-fanned fire. Then—silence and the strangest of visions.

A crowd of human spirits in complete subjugation, stretching back into the farthest parts of my vision, or in my memory, or perhaps in all memory of all mankind, they seemed so endless… somehow quelled and abated by the effort of a single spirit.

I regarded the spirit's face and his brown eyes never left me, standing before the multitude with his arms held out to restrain them in stillness and silence. The holes in his clothing were utterly familiar, the bloody shirtfront as I'd seen it before, only the square of ragged cloth tied about his shoulder seemed strange, fluttering sharply and silently in what I assumed must be a breeze-less place.

I sobbed—a great loud gasp of emotion I believed startled the audience—but realized shortly had come out only as a pause in my reading.

"by those slaughtered murdered ones,
Freedom's latest franchised sons,
By the tombs o'er which we pray,
By tardy justice long delay, He will repay"

Outside when the program was finished and the crowd dispersed, Nathan and I stood alone on the steps. The air was still hot on my skin, and out on Canal Street, a pair of mules pulled a streetcar full of nodding passengers. The day was waning, and the sidewalks under the galleries on the opposite side of the street were already beginning to fall into shadow.

Nathan drew me to him and held me in a hard embrace, his face buried in my hair, his words spoken to the curve of my throat. "I am so proud of you," he said.

Yet, my thoughts were on another man. Silently, I gave a prayer of thanks and love to Robert, and took a moment to be proud of myself too.

The Ceremony at the Mechanics' Institute

We would call attention of our readers to the
very beautiful poem printed in its entirety
in another part of our paper entitled "In Memoriam"
written by Mrs. Cora Winslow
and read in her sonorous voice
at the magnificent ceremony.

—*The New Orleans Tribune* July 31, 1867

Hollis
1867

What fauna there is to be found in South Louisiana! I have seen turtles with odd shells, large fishing birds which scoop their bounty using pouches in their bills, and a shambling creature which appears to be armored for war, like the knights of old England. There are said to be alligators too, but I have not met up with one of those yet.

My favorite are the small and cunning lizards which live in the nooks and crevices around Cora's house. Sleek and of a rather showy Paris green color, they bask with pleasure in sun-warmed spots. I keep their company on the sultry brickwork or in the cool lush foliage as my invisible presence does not startle them and I am indifferent to either sunshine or shadow.

Cora's home is located in a district of gardens, with much green space between houses of all sizes. Hers is a snug cottage, with four windows across the face, a center hall doorway, and six wooden columns supporting the porch. The only oddity to New England eyes is the fact of its raised position, the entire structure supported to the height of my shoulders with a forest of brick piers, in anticipation of floodwater, I assume, but providing a good cover for some the creatures I've already mentioned.

It is a fine and respectable residence as far as I can compare, Nathan evidently not as adverse to supporting a wife as Benjamin had been, and I suspect Cora is pleased with it. For the rooms of Cora's life have always been transitory, belonging to other people, with nary a furnishing which held evidence of her presence. I like to see her with ornaments and books. I like to watch her passing through the chambers carrying little Etta, sweeping a floor, boiling a pot for tea.

I especially like to see her seated at her desk engaged in her writing. She has many journals now, tied with string or marked with scraps of paper. Clinging to the stalk of the banana tree outside her window with my saurian friends, I watch her working steadily, the lineaments of her features serious and just as I remember her as a child, sorting printing type in those last days of what I once thought of as my life.

I am often in the house. I watch over little Etta, and although she can not hear me as Cora does, I sing songs to her, those I remember my own mother singing to me. I see Cora cooking, or poised over her journal with ink stained fingers, Etta hitching herself around the floor nearly ready to take her first steps, and the games she and her mother play together, pat-a-cake, peekaboo. Through the summer Cora tended a pair of potted roses, and even when rigged-out in a work apron and kerchief, she made a handsome sight.

There were other times with a different mood. Times when Nathan would travel away from the house for as long as a week, sometimes with other men in a buckboard, others by himself setting off with his own packed kit on a saddle horse. He traveled to conduct his business for the Bankruptcy Act, often to districts which might be hostile to his presence, and Cora feared for him.

Those days, I would observe Cora watching from the window with her face taut and anxious as her husband rode away. Those nights, even if it were hot, she would still close her doors and windows carefully, securing them firmly, and walk the porch latching every shutter one by one.

There are those who might guess I hung around the house to provide protection; others who might conjecture I remained for the pleasing views of Cora sauntering through her pretty rooms. Neither would be accurate. I simply wanted to linger in this place as long as I could before everything else which was to come.

Two sisters they were, risen from their birthplace in the calm waters to do the work of God. Newborn but old as the eons, their ancestors occupying places closer than all others to the Lord, bearing swords of sacred flame and a thousand eyes, no strangers to the prophet Isaiah, from the tribe of Aedini, each carrying a lyre upon their breasts. "Holy! Holy! Holy!" they cry one to the other, a sound indistinct to human ears, heard only as a wordless keening.

While Cora sat writing at her desk a month ago, these sisters were already with her, drifting in their cradle of rainwater dripped from the broad leaves of the banana tree to the upturned saucers of the pots of roses set near the house. Here they rested swaddled in the softness where their mother laid them, breathing gently and growing wings for their ascent.

Here they slipped their sheathing and climbed upon the dews of the morning to become airborne, swarming in billows of their brethren, patrolling the perimeter of their dominion, eschewing only the brightest hours of the sun in shady crevices of leaves where they spread their wings and lay still.

With the twilight, the sound of a wingbeat, the hum of the one word paean of glory, as they embark, tasting the air against Cora's latched shutters, the glass of the locked door, fumbling along the jambs and muntins, thwarted by a tight sash and finally finding the small transom Cora left ajar to provide a breath of air.

Indoors, the sisters traverse again, feeling for heat, their thousand eyes seeing the floor, the ceiling, the walls, the hallway, the bedstead all at once. Clasping with barbed feet the netting draped to exclude them, they flutter, more determined than ever in their quest to find the single rent in the fabric, the opening that allows them to fall through. Holy! Holy! Holy!

Then the unexpected lull, the sisters slowing, almost drifting, downward to the sleeping figures mother and child, in a tangle of sheets from the humid night. The sisters choose by chance, and silencing their near-constant song, alight separately on each of the sleepers. Tiptoe on soft skin, parting the tiny hairs to find a place for their awful swords. I would close my eyes now, if I had them, for I know what is to happen.

I know better than any of the living, for we spirits can see parts of the future in our spectral state. Small glimpses of the mysteries and amazements and inconceivable mechanisms of the universe. That some of the most numerous, the most odious and reviled sit nearest to the throne of God! Each a divine Seraph who delivers flames and who carries within them even smaller sparks of God's creation which devastate and transform, unseen to even the wisest among the living.

You might think all that remains for mankind is pity.

The following morning, I watched as Cora was awakened by Etta fussing, kicking and pawing the air with her little arms and legs. Parting the mosquito curtains, Cora rose from the bed and walked to the dresser to retrieve a fresh napkin for the baby, absent-mindedly scratching the insect bite on the back of her own hand. The napkin changed, she cuddled her child and unbuttoned her nightdress for nursing.

It was not until the child's face was snuggled against her breast that Cora noticed the red welt on Etta's temple. "Oh dear," Cora said, touching the tiny mark. "You've got a little bite, Etta. Is it itchy?"

Once the child was done feeding, Cora carried her to the dining table and sat her daughter in the high chair. Etta had begun to wiggle again and whimper, and Cora hurried to her baking cabinet and fished around for the tin of soda. Wetting a pinch of the soda and mixing it with a spoon in a tumbler, she brought it to the chair and smiled at her child. After carefully holding the baby's head and daubing the soda paste on the small red bite with her fingertip, Cora finished and kissed her daughter's lips.

"There my dearest," she said, "Gone in a few days."

Oh, Cora. Oh, oh Cora.

Onset

1867–1869

Cora

1867–1868

I was the first to disappear into the dark tangle of the illness. A day of headache and nausea, and while crossing the porch to toss a basin of Etta's bathwater into the hedgerow, the vomiting began. I leaned against the wall of the house retching with spasms so powerful my body was knocked off balance, and I dropped to the porch floorboards. I was aware of Nathan dashing through the doorway to my aid; I was aware of the start of Etta's crying. She's been startled by the sound of the basin falling, I thought as the smell of my vomit filled my nose, but Etta never stopped crying for days and days.

How long is a day in the ferment of fever? Months with the sodden heavy desire to vomit, months in the wet shivering and thrumming of headache, which felt like a paring knife coring out my eyes. A moment only when Nathan stood over me heavy with helplessness, a mere moment as I felt life cloud over and become brighter again, like a weak sun straining behind a louring sky.

I knew I was passing through danger. Sometimes I felt close enough to it to be afraid, and other times as if I wanted to take the danger by its hand and follow wherever it led me. Either way, I held onto the sound of Etta, her ceaseless crying. Early on I was terrorized by the child's sobbing, sure my daughter was perishing, but later found my ears sought out the wails, realizing it meant Etta still lived.

What was the time? What was the day of the week? Small sounds grew very large—the wooden shutters opening and closing, the fruit seller in the street calling his wares, footsteps of someone entering the room or pausing by the door. At one point the scrape of a chamber pot startled me, and after the great effort of opening my swollen eyelids, I saw Mrs. Dostie carrying it.

My mind swam with confusion at the presence of the lady. Poor Mrs. Dostie was a widow, her husband one of the innocents murdered at Mechanics' Institute. I could only reason Nathan had asked Mrs. Dostie to care for me. How kind Mrs. Dostie was, but how sick this meant I must be.

Indeed, it was difficult to apprehend all those who attended me. I'd lived in the hazy home of the spirits but never before in the blind black of illness. Yet, the two worlds were similar, inhabited by things heard but not seen, others seen but not heard.

Nathan came and went, and Mrs. Dostie. In some late and exhausted hour, Captain Walker returned, this time not brandishing his hand to gain my attention but using it to hold mine. I knew it was him as the touch was familiar, and he sat with me for a long, comforting time as I traced with feverish fingers the letters *SS* raised in scars on his cold palm. A lady in old fashioned dress who said she was Lydia's mother came and re-arranged my bedding. A strange man's voice hovered overhead and spoke the words "yellow fever" and "the prevailing epidemic." Many times Hollis whispered to me in his familiar murmuring voice. At least, I thought it was Hollis. It may have been the rain. I was sure I heard rain.

Or was it hiccups? Yes, it was Etta with the hiccups. Surely Mrs. Dostie knew what to do—rub the baby's back or give her some gripe water. Perhaps Etta needed to be turned in her cot. She was often colicky just after feeding. But, who was feeding her? My God, all these days no one had fed Etta!

I tried to rise and call out, but no words came from my mouth, only a gush of vomit, black and alarming. I drew my knees up, the damp sheets sticking to my body, the heat of fever rising into the dead air. I needed to feed Etta. There was crying again, the great gulping sobs Etta sometimes made when she was exhausted. Or, perhaps it was hiccups. Etta often got hiccups after eating, so someone must be feeding her. It was hard to discern against the sighing sound of the rain. I was sure I heard rain.

* * *

Through bewildered eyes, I saw pallid light creeping along the wall from the slits in the shutters. Was the day ending or beginning? Either way something in the illness had opened and pushed me through. My mouth tasted like metal, and a wave of some awful fear rose in me. The sudden terrible suspicion that consciousness might be worse than the fever had been, and as I'd once fought for coherence, I now resisted awareness. I wanted to turn and go back. There was a loud and persistent sound, something toneless and terrible. I tried not to listen, but it pushed at me. It was the sound of the present world—or rather the overpowering absence of sound. Both this world and Etta were silent.

Nathan who'd been sleeping on folded arms atop the bedclothes lifted his head to appraise me. "Thank God," he said, taking my hands in his, "I thought I had lost both of you."

So, as mercilessly as that, I learned Etta was gone, utterly gone. She'd died in the midst of my illness, and with the hot weather and nature of the disease, was buried the same day. I found myself returned to health in a world I barely recognized. The pointless listening for a child rendered forever silent, the lost daily schedule, the feedings, the bathing. During the fever my breasts had gone dry, and my current sleep was riddled with terrible dreams from which I would wake breathless and trembling.

Someone had taken Etta's little cot away, probably to spare me, but her high chair still stood against the wall by the table and sick with longing, I placed my hand on the small seat where my daughter was not. Not only was Etta gone, she was still disappearing.

I did recognize the face in my mirror. It was not just my face but a face I'd seen on others, and one I now realized I'd never had enough experience to comprehend. The skin was pale, the eyes were glazed with grief, the inner will too heavy to carry further. Mary Greeley, Mary Todd Lincoln, and now, myself.

Despair came in gusts, sometimes so strong it seemed it would topple me. I might sit for hours in a motionless heap of pain or could sometimes barely restrain myself from tearing at the air or my own clothing in anger, because of what I wanted returned to me, what I wanted to possess again, what I just wanted and wanted.

That I would not get my wish, any more than the other women, I understood; but what tortured me was my inability to use my powers of spirit communication to see or hear my own child. Try as I did over and over in those early days, Etta remained silent.

Of course, unlike the others, my child was not grown. Etta had not yet learned to speak and knew no words, so how could she communicate? Yet the girl never appeared as a vision either, and when I gave myself the same glib explanation I'd given every other woman—spirits come in their own time, spirits cannot be bidden—I felt furious. Furious and shamed. I believed I knew all about grief, until grief came to keep company with me.

A few days before Christmas, Mrs. Dostie came for a visit, on an afternoon when Nathan was still in the city working. Of course, the good lady had been back since Etta's death a number of times. She'd already told me what she knew of the particulars of those terrible days, and we'd even gone together to visit the place of Etta's burial, but this time Mrs. Dostie bore a different sort of offering.

She passed me a small envelope which contained a lock of Etta's hair.

"I wanted to wait a while," she said, "until the first bad days were over. And I confess I cut it without Mr. Winslow's knowing. It is no near substitute I know, but it is not the sort of thing a man would think of saving."

I placed my forefinger on the miraculous little curl, laid atop the envelope it was delivered in. I knew it well enough to recognize it as one of the curls which grew beside my daughter's ears. The color of my own hair but the texture of Nathan's. I pressed the curl gently, and when I released it, it sprang back into its curved shape. As if it still rested against Etta's cheek. As if it did not realize it was dead.

* * *

During the long nights of the remainder of winter and into the early spring, Nathan and I often lay sleepless. Though side by side, there seemed to be a far distance between us, a space neither knew how to cross. So, too, was something in our conversation compromised. There was no anger or particular arguments, but there did not seem to be much to say. Speech felt self-conscious, and silence was simpler. Nathan lingered with his associates in the city. I wrote apathetically in my journals or sat by the window. It was as if we were walking through a winter storm without mentioning the weather.

I tried to recall what we'd talked about while we were courting, those days in the fancy Washington City parlors when Nathan had proposed marriage with the clever paper puzzle he'd constructed himself. We were full of ideas for reform then, spurred on by others from the Freedmen's Bureau—Oliver Howard, Sojourner Truth and the rest. The prizes of the Union victory seemed so ready to grasp at the time, but now those ideals had worn a little thin, more difficult in practice than in promise.

I'd become pregnant so soon after our marriage that much of our talk was of the coming child. Those laughing days of thinking up names and dreaming of the future.

Wistfully, I returned in my thoughts to our romantic summer at Black Creek, that season which seemed to last forever, and this memory brought back those old longings. The same flush of desire could still overtake me when I looked at Nathan, and when I recalled the nights in the old cove-ceilinged bedroom of the dear little farmhouse, the flirting, the swimming in the creek.

Yet, such feelings were quickly shut down by our odd new shyness and my near constant fear. I was newly suspicious of all that was around me. The lush foliage and flowers seemed possibly poisonous. The humid air perhaps the bearer of the terrible scourge that killed Etta. Like everyone else, I did not know where the contagion came from or what to do to prevent it.

Nathan claimed that during the war the yellow fever had disappeared and insisted it was only present in the filthy areas of the city. Mrs. Dostie told me local people called it the *Stranger's Disease*, and only persons from other places fell victim to it. Our home was clean, and yet, were we not strangers?

Last summer, city officials burned pots of tar in many places filling the air with acrid smoke, and the streets in the business districts stank of the carbolic acid which was swabbed in them, but I'd not let such portents rattle me then. My new life with Nathan and Etta stood before me, and the great work of Reconstruction. Now, stripped of my child and scarred by the fever itself, I felt differently.

I wanted to leave New Orleans for the hot months as others did, but Nathan resisted, considering his duty too important, as if setting the world to right was something only he could do. The chafing between us was growing, and Etta was no longer there to soften it.

"You shan't have the fever again," Nathan said. "There is general agreement a person can not be affected twice."

"I know, but what of you? Traveling overland as you do."

"I suffered many fevers while in the army," he said. "It's likely one of them was a mild case."

"Nathan, it frightens me. What of another child? I could not bring myself to expose another baby to the danger," I argued. He did not seem to hear this concern. "I thought you might wish to resume public speaking. The men from the Mutual Assistance Society have told me they would be greatly interested in hearing your words at the Economy Hall."

I could not even bear to think of public speaking and shook my head as I spoke. "I haven't the heart," I said.

The weather was the same that May of 1868 as it was the day we arrived a year before. We even stood near the same part of the dock where we'd first stepped off the steamboat *Ruth*. This time though, I was outbound for New York, which was not as Nathan envisioned. He assumed I would want to spend the summer with his family in Nahant, but I insisted on going to Charles and Lydia Austin. He'd not argued with me, declaring it would be selfish to dictate after all I'd suffered. My tears had come fast, and we embraced almost wearily at the foot of the gangplank. He was unhappy to see me go. "My dear Cora," he implored, "don't let our loss cause us to lose one another."

"I just don't know how I feel, Lydia," I said. "Whenever I try to speak from my heart, I come up wordless." We were resting in cane armchairs on the veranda at the Austin summer home overlooking the Hudson River upstate from New York City. We'd been potting flowers from little plants brought by a farmer in small wooden trays and pausing from our labors.

Lydia swatted at a passing fly with a gloved hand. "It's grief, dear. It will take some time before you are accustomed to it.

"I don't know that I ever want to be accustomed to it," I mused.

Lydia nodded with a sympathetic smile. "Perhaps "accustomed" is the wrong word, as grief never goes away. It just becomes lighter to carry. Take my word, there are days to come when you will take less notice of its weight."

"I also don't think I shall ever be brave enough to live in New Orleans during the fever season."

"Why you very nearly died there!" Lydia said. "No one would fault you if you didn't return."

"Nathan means to stay," I said.

"His war service probably conditioned him to the climate, and you have said many families leave during the dangerous season. Certainly Charles and I would always be glad to have you stay with us here in Hudson, and the girls adore your presence."

I scanned the surroundings, the modest cottage with its broad view of the river, the roofed porch covered with evidence of our project, pots and spades and spilled soil. Mae was out in her own little garden on the shady side of the grassy lawn which sloped up to the place the local people called *Parade Hill*. Charles had constructed a four-sided area out of old timbers and had the space filled with sand. "My sand garden," Mae called her play space, and she worked there now wearing a blue sunbonnet, brandishing her little spoons and buckets.

Lydia followed my eyes. "I've been afraid the presence of Mae and Clara might cause you pain."

"Goodness no!" I said, expressing the truth. Although the sight of Lydia's children did bring a twinge at times, I loved them too much to feel envy. "My thoughts tend to drift to the hope these little ones grow up in a better world."

Lydia stood and lifted one of the finished pots of flowers to its place on the porch railing. "With the war in our past, it's hard not to believe the future cannot be better," she said.

Later, with only two pots remaining to fill, Lydia dug her gloved hands deep into the soil around one of the last few plants in the tray. She passed the plant to me, and I tucked the green and purple coleus into the soil of the pot and pressed gently around it. Something now troubled me, something occasioned by our earlier conversation which stirred all that felt unsettled inside me.

"It was last August I think," I began, "not long after I read my poem at Mechanics' Institute. It was beastly hot and humid, one of the New Orleans days we Northerners are warned about. Our house was positioned for good breezes either from the lake or the river, but sometimes the air hung so heavy with moisture it seemed possible to take it in your hands and wring it out. Etta was cutting the first of her teeth, a tiny little pearl on the bottom and she was fussing. She liked me to rub her gums with my little finger but whenever I stopped she would resume crying."

"She'll have a notable speaking voice like her mother," Nathan said, plugging his ears in jest.

"I hope she has a bigger voice than that," I replied, "I am looking forward to Etta being able to cast a ballot when she grows up."

"It's why we must work to ensure the Black man retains his right to vote," Nathan replied. "Once his ballot is secure we'll have enough votes to guarantee all our desired reforms. Give the Black man suffrage and the rights of women will follow."

"I don't see why voting rights for both cannot be achieved together," I told him. "In my own observation most men White or colored are unlikely to give a woman a chance to speak."

"You know I want you to speak Cora! More than anything, I wish you would take to the platforms of every city. You could begin tomorrow at the request of the men of Economy Hall."

"At the time, I didn't say any more. Etta was fussing, and there was supper to get ready, but I knew the topic of the speech Nathan was urging was not to be women's suffrage. It troubles me Lydia, this aspect of our marriage. I feel as if I was dearly loved by someone entirely incapable of seeing me."

Lydia passed me the very last of the plants from tray. "How so?" she asked.

"I have no doubt of Nathan's grief," I explained. "Mrs. Dostie told me he cried like a child when Etta died, and his actions since have spoken of his heartache, but he does not suffer the same way I do. I feel as if my heart has been torn from my chest and left a gaping hole. In my own vocation, I know better than to console a grieving mother with the suggestion she could have another child, but of course, Nathan has hinted at this many times. This I attribute to the clumsiness of a man's solace, and I understand men are encouraged to stoicism, but Nathan seems to view Etta's death almost as a sort of...setback. I have no better word for it."

Lydia remained quiet. She moved softly across the porch carrying the last flower pot down the steps and placed it in its appointed spot. She then seated herself next to me on the top step, took a deep breath and scanned the far distance shading her eyes with one hand. With the other she clasped one of mine. The Hudson River lay far below us, curving around a long bend and disappearing beneath a shoreline of forest and a horizon of blue-grey mountains. A boat made slow progress upstream, trailing a long v-shaped wake. Closer at hand, Mae puttered in her sand garden, decorating a wet mound with twigs and dandelion blossoms. In the tree above her, the soft syllable of a bird sounded.

"I did have an inkling I might be pregnant when Etta was born at Black Creek," Lydia began. "In fact, it was the very day of her birth. I'd been feeling a bit ill in the mornings beforehand, which I then ascribed to excitement and travel, but on that day, I became nearly sure.

You'd already been laboring for several hours, and for some reason, I went downstairs to the kitchen. Nathan was there frying fish he'd caught that afternoon. It was the smell of the cooking fish which caught me, that awful strong smell, and I gagged, vomiting up a bit of my lunch. I'd nowhere to catch it but in my hand, and as I stood wavering in the doorway of the room with a palm full of vomit and the sudden suspicion I might be pregnant, Nathan looked at me.

I'll never forget his odd expression. He made no move to assist me. He never spoke a word to question my well-being. He just placed on me a cold, quizzical stare; the corners of his mouth in a tiny lift of...mockery. If I had to describe his manner, I would call it cruel, yet I know Nathan is not cruel. It was strange and it frightened me. I grew brave, though, and scolded him. "You might want to take that smell out-of-doors, considering the circumstance," I told him. I elbowed past him to reach for a dishtowel to clean my hand, turned, and walked away.

The war has damaged our men, Cora, I am sure of it. They've returned to us as different people. Charles has changed too. Not in a significant way, but subtly. Sometimes he is so sad I cannot pierce the gloom surrounding him, though I am absolutely sure of his love and protection. They will not be the same men our fathers were. How could they? As soldiers, they experienced terrible things."

I purchased my Chinese lanterns. After the clerk at Macy and Wing Variety Store parceled them, I strolled back to my quarters through the charming streets of Onset village to get ready for the special evening.

It had been a pleasant summer in the seaside Spiritualist retreat, and I was glad I'd accepted the invitation from the Onset Bay Grove Association to visit from July to September. I'd agreed to performing a weekly lecture, not in trance, and was also to offer private spirit circles to the growing audience of visitors and residents at the new Massachusetts resort devoted to Spiritualism. I'd been provided a good rate of rent on a pretty cottage on the bluff overlooking Onset Bay and was returning there after my morning shopping excursion.

Though of the same tone as other Spiritualist summer camp meeting places like Lake Pleasant and Cassadaga, Onset had achieved astounding popularity. I supposed it was the proximity of the village to Boston and Providence. Onset was even an easy railway journey from Lydia's cottage in Hudson, New York when I arrived in early July, but as I walked along the streets it was clear to see the entire mood of the place was delightful.

The awnings of the storefronts buckled softly in the cool breeze, and out on the bay, catboats with multi-colored sails glided through sun-struck seas. Three big steam launches, the *Calla*, the *Favorite* and the *Electric Spark* wheeled grandly, loaded with eager passengers.

In early days, visitors to Onset came for just a few weeks and were housed in stout tents, but now many permanent cottages had been built, and the season lasted the entire summer. Little porches were hung with swinging hammocks and boxes of flowers, and the cottages themselves boasted quaint fretwork and scroll-sawn bargeboards painted in gay and playful colors. Pleasant promenades meandered through the vicinity, and the main streets were paved with crushed oyster shells which made them appear almost white with snow. The outdoor speaking pavilion where I lectured was decorated with fancy cut shingles. There was a dance hall, a carousel, a large temple building. Wet sea bathers ran laughing from the beach directly to their nearby cottages, and the smell of the cooking of shore dinners drifted through the salty tang of the air. Ice cream, candy, and taffy were purveyed; picnic groups dressed in light summer clothing clustered in the many groves.

Walking back along South Boulevard to the cottage, I strode upon tidy asphalted sidewalks, chalked with advertisements for the many mediums who plied their skills in the houses abutting them. *"Mrs. Allyn—Seance Circle—sharp noon,"* one read, and I stepped over another stating *"Giles Twing—Spirit Paintings and Slate Writings."* Thankfully, I found no need to advertise. My position of prominence as a scheduled speaker and reputation from Dodsworth's Hall held me in good stead, although people still insisted in addressing me with my old married name, Cora Carter.

All in all, Onset was a scene of endless interest and on this day appeared even more animated. The entire village was in a state of excitement anticipating Illumination Night, which was to commence at dusk. Ladders were set up, and from the piazzas of the hotels and dwellings, the noise of hammering issued forth. Fireworks were being prepared. Bunting and banners were being hung, streamers and strings of Chinese paper lanterns were hoisted, for they would all be lit tonight, casting the village and the harbor into a magnificent spectacle.

Indeed, nightfall was a beautiful sight and one which invited reflection as I sat on my porch beneath the glowing lanterns I'd strung from the ceiling. The sky was glossy black which accentuated the thousands of lights in view, flickering on hotel piazzas and cottage windows, suspended in branches of trees and the rigging of sailboats, arcing and sparkling in a display of fireworks and blazing in dozens of little beach fires built along the shore all the way to Shell Point.

Hollis always said spirits were called to earth by fire, and I could feel them this night. The atmosphere was thick with their presence, hovering close around their beloveds who'd traveled to this village to seek them, homing in by the light of the thousand tiny flames. Waiting to be remembered, yearning to make themselves known, drifting among the overheard conversations on porches, eavesdropping on laughter from boat decks, fragments of talk and whispers of those they'd left behind.

I was going to be sad to leave Onset and the gracious gifts of the past summer. My comfortable cottage was on high ground just beyond the Prospect Hotel, and on many days, I'd gazed with restful pleasure at the silvery sea. Onset Bay was warm and shallow, its waves merely wrinkles in a soft watery fabric with sun glittering across the dimpled surface. I often watched the beachgoers—city sports in fishing togs angling for bluefish and children with buckets and sunhats. One day I saw a brother and sister hand in hand wading in the turning tide, the girl in a yellow dress and the boy so like

Hollis it stung a raw memory. Waving at the pair, they returned my greeting, but in seeing their young upturned faces, I felt the sharp twist of loss. My Etta, my own childhood, even the precise features of Hollis, treasured as all lost and precious things always are but hidden in a dark and secret place by doing so.

In the front room of the cottage, I passed my spare hours making notes for my lectures and writing. I was even able to finish a poem I'd started the year before, entitled *Hesperia*. In wielding a pen, my life reopened to a pleasure I'd left behind since my illness. How I loved committing ideas to words which were meant to be read and not heard. *Hesperia* was an allegory, a poem rather than a pronouncement, to foster the growth of man by the understanding of spirit, fixed and certain in ink and not scattered impermanently into the air as speech on a platform.

On other days, I held private seances in this same room usually at a table set before the odd corner fireplace where I sometimes built a small fire to warm a foggy afternoon. It was here the great miracle of the summer unfolded. As I comforted and consoled my clients, hunting out their dear ones in the Summerland and relaying their spirit messages, I found myself comforted too. As I sat with a grieving mother and gave the woman evidence of the happiness of the hereafter, a mother I now understood at my own terrible cost, I too, began to heal.

I would be leaving Onset in three weeks, stopping to see the Winslows in Boston and then for another week with Lydia in New York. Missing Nathan body and soul, I could hardly wait to tell him what the dear little village by the sea had done for me. At Onset, I was able to both give and receive solace nearly every day.

By ten o'clock, the tide had turned and leaned against the beach. The evening dew was falling and the sea-damp enclosed each of the thousand lights in its own hazy nimbus. Lanterns on the piazza of the Prospect Hotel bobbed in a blur of light, a prenumbral glow that defined their varied shapes, oblongs, globes and stars. Groups of sailboats on the bay were rafting up, and from some far-off point, perhaps the bandstand, a single cornet played in slow tempo *In The Sweet By and By*. The lighthearted days of summer were waning, signaling that for me, too, it was time for sleep.

I was just extinguishing the last of the lanterns when I noted another sound, finding it confusing at first because as often as I had heard the familiar crunch, as often as I'd sat alone anxiously awaiting it, it was a sound of New Orleans not Onset. Crushed oyster shells covered the pathways of both this cottage and the house in Louisiana, but my husband's step sounded the same in either place. Turning to look, he was just a shadowy figure in my dooryard, but it was certainly Nathan, dark and somewhat disheveled but with the same intense aspect I'd seen in the Washington City parlor two years before.

I dropped the lantern which fell weightlessly at my feet and dashed down the shell gravel path to Nathan, throwing my arms about his neck. He stiffened in my embrace, and I pulled away in some alarm trying to recalculate the meaning of his cold hesitation.

"My little gypsy. You haven't kept a fixed address all summer," he said. "I've had to track you all over the Northeast."

Had Nathan traveled so far just to be churlish? It seemed unbelievable, yet his eyes held a spark of menace, and I felt tension in him, a current of angry impatience alive beneath his smile. And what of the word "gypsy"—was it insult or endearment? "That's not true, Nathan," I countered. "I've had your letters here for a month and hope you've received mine. Why ever are you here? Is everyone all right?"

Nathan did not answer but stepped around me on the path, gesturing to indicate the cottage. "Is this really where you live?" he asked. I was sure of his anger now and considered if he'd been drinking, but knowing his horror of anything immoderate dismissed the notion.

Before I could answer, there was a sharp whistle and a popping sound as a Roman candle launched into the air from down on the beach. Some of the local revelers were still abroad and celebrating, and Nathan looked balefully at the blazing white arc and the shower of sparks dissolving into the darkness.

"I didn't realize the Spiritualists embraced such amusements," he said "I thought they left this sort of thing to the Methodists."

How heartless he could be! And how aware I was that in our circle, I'd be the only one to notice it. I'd heard these kind of comments from him and his radical fellows before, their self-assured superiority so calmly and reasonably stated no one took offense to them or seemed aware of the prejudice inherent in their words. If he'd made such a proclamation in a room of Washington City reformists, they would have chuckled and continued their conversation, confident in their opinion of which religion or race or creed deserved justice and which could be disparaged, unaware of the difference between hypocrisy and morality, and certain of their own integrity.

Furthermore, these were my people he was mocking—not wealthy mill-owners, or the unfortunate members of an oppressed race—but simple people of middling means and decent intentions, gathering with the like-minded in a small village to worship and receive confirmation of the afterlife. These people were as worthy as any, and I meant to stand by them A cold needle of disgust pushed through me, and something awful rattled in my heart, like hate was trying the door.

Perhaps I'd been seduced by Nathan too, confusing his polished, sophistic arguments in favor of Black equality with moral integrity, and although unsure what his sudden appearance now meant, I was certain an argument lay ahead.

Awaiting some kind of response, Nathan gave me a questioning look. His face remained contorted in the same fixed angry smile, or was it a grimace? Either way his teeth were bared, and I feared for a brief second he might be about to strike me as Benjamin had.

Only moments before, running to embrace him brought forth another longing, one which recalled our beautiful first summer. Now I felt washed over with emotion, but was this desire or dread? I knew I loved him, but something calm had come to live in my heart during my Onset summer, and this rested beside my love. Part of me did want him to seize me, force me bodily to his will, but I knew he would not do it. Nathan Waldo Winslow's passions were reserved for moral retribution. Another part of me could not reconcile how to live with him. Would we ever be able to make our different pieces fit together to shape a life? During this summer, my own heart seemed to have cooled to his temperature.

"You'd better come in," I said, while climbing the porch steps.

Nathan

1868

I saw her before she saw me and gazed for a moment in admiration at her face illuminated by the glowing paper lantern, caught in the instant before she blew out the candle inside it. She was calm and her movements graceful, and I thought it terrifying how the mere sight of her could thrash my heart, distressed she might already have the advantage.

Now, after she'd invited me inside I followed her, suppressing the urge to crouch while passing through the doorway as the cottage seemed so odd and elfin, like the denizen of some fairy tale sorceress which perhaps, it was. I was cautious of Cora, as I knew her powerful presence, and have witnessed much about her I cannot explain. Yet once inside the structure, the magic fell away and I relaxed.

The entire village was a newly-built town of similar inexpensive gaudy cottages, tarted up in colors and designs like circus wagons with oddly shaped doors and windows which no doubt leaked damp air in a stiff wind. Cora's place was a kind of New Jerusalem cabin, with shiplapped walls tacked with Japanese paper fans and foxed pictures, windows hung with fringed curtains, and a disconcerting angled fireplace built in the corner of the room with a lunette mirror set above its mantle shelf. I caught a glimpse of myself in this mirror while taking the seat Cora offered me. I did not look well.

Cora lit a lamp and placed herself in a chair across the room from me, and although the distance was small, I noted uncomfortably I could not make out her eyes. Her letters from Onset unsettled me, long paragraphs in her looping feminine script describing how much she enjoyed the village and the activities. I had not heard such happiness in her voice since before Etta died.

In my travels from New Orleans, I'd rehearsed the sequence of this confrontation. I would cajole, insist, and if need be, demand she return with me to Louisiana. I'd developed several convincing arguments. I envisioned tears and shouting, but ultimately, capitulation. I'd even allowed myself to imagine the pleasant activity of making up, as I still felt her kisses of greeting on my face, but I'd never allowed for the woman seated across from me now, her eyes pools of darkness, her face still and remote. Perhaps I ought not to have come at all. Perhaps I'd already made a mistake. In the event, I had no idea how to proceed in dislodging my wife from this plebeian and cultish place.

Realizing I was picking at the fingernails on my fidgeting hands, I stilled them. "I thought you might show me the Onset sights for a few days," I said, "but I have tickets for our return to New Orleans on Friday morning."

Cora was silent for so long I knew she was calculating her answer. "I will be glad to show you Onset, but I won't be accompanying you on Friday," she replied.

"I don't know why not!" I snapped more harshly than I intended. "The fever season is nearly over—or will be by the time we arrive, as I've planned several touring stops."

"I have plans of my own," Cora said, "and lectures until the end of September when the camp closes."

Could she not see her ridiculous position? "I rather think those can be disregarded."

"I've signed a contract," Cora said eyeing me distastefully.

"That your husband will see you are able to rescind."

Cora stood from her chair angrily and stepped toward me. "You'll do nothing of the kind. I have a contract, and I enjoy my work. We've already negotiated our pact. I will be in New Orleans from November until May and the remaining months here in the North."

Her brow darkened, and I felt a muscle in my jaw twitching, "You should be speaking to worthy audiences, not wasting yourself in this poky town of occult dabblers," I said sourly.

"I know what you want," she cried. "A constant companion to preach lectures like those of Asbury Church and Mechanics' Institute and nothing else! There is much support for Black equality here, and I have lectured twice on the subject."

Just picturing her perched on the silly seaside platform speaking to an audience of rapt ignobles chewing on their shore dinners made me want to laugh. "They say preaching to the converted is a useless office."

"And preaching to the unconverted is a thankless office," Cora countered.

It was very late. My head felt hollow and exhausted. Cora turned, as if wishing to keep her eyes away from me, but I could still see my reflection glaring at her back in the mirror above the fireplace. "I will finish my lectures and then visit your mother and Sophia in Boston, as we agreed. One week with Lydia and I will be in New Orleans by November."

"You won't find Sophia in Boston," I said.

"No? We'd planned a visit to the Athenaeum in our last letter."

"She will be off to Oliver Howard's University by the end of September."

Finally I had surprised her. I noted too the slight envy in her face and admit I took a small pleasure in it. Cora once told me how she wished she'd had more education and that she felt the want of her vocabulary and broader knowledge. A comeuppance was perhaps just what she deserved.

"Why that's wonderful," she said. "I'd no idea she was even entertaining such a step."

"There is much you don't know about Sophia," I taunted. "Her rise has been amazing. She speaks four languages now and to think her previous destiny would have left her mind fallow! You have no idea what it is like to have been put to a life of work when just a small child."

The look she then fixed upon me was murderous, more than murderous; I even quailed a bit before it, perhaps even stepped back. "Actually I have every idea of what it is like to be put to work as a child, as I was placed on the platform while still wearing short dresses," she said with a calm and vicious savagery.

Nor was she through. Something had come to her, I could see her mind working on it—a knowledge which altered her face and at which I could only wonder until she flung it at me.

"Does Sophia want to attend Howard's University, or is this your idea?"

Her question irritated me, and I fear I responded with a mere sputter.

"For all your talk of equality," she continued, "I find you as inclined to issuing orders as any tyrant."

"Sophia loves her schooling," I growled, tired of this conversation. "Sophia has even left Nahant early to get her trunks packed. She seems excited to return to Washington City."

I jumped up then, so abruptly my chair crashed to the floor, grasped Cora by her wrist and dragged her to me. "This is ridiculous!" I heard myself shout. "I have never loved you so much as in these weeks you've been gone from me. You must give this foolish whim up!"

Again her expression frightened me. I held her by the wrist, twisted in such a way it probably hurt, but she responded only with a vague smile, her eyes passing through me as if I were just another of her wispy spirits, as if there were nothing personal between us. I wanted to force her and physically impose my will, but her gaze defeated me, reminding me there had always been something in Cora just beyond my reach. I let her wrist slip from my hand.

"It is the duty of a wife to remain with her husband," I snarled.

Cora sniffed. "It might also be said it is the duty of a husband to remain with his wife."

"Is it your idea I should give up the nation's work of Reconstruction to mingle with table-tippers, mesmerists, and grieving widows?" With hands on my hips, I shook my head in disbelief. "You are simply addicted to the attention you receive from this... this...sect. I believe Spiritualism has disordered your mind!"

With that I gave up my efforts, lunging through the door which I pushed open with my palms, letting it bang harshly against the outer wall, and stalking off with my teeth clenched, turning back to see if Cora was following me only when certain I was hidden by the darkness of the dense night.

She did not leave the house. Framed by the rectangle of the doorway, made glowing by the interior lamps and the garish, fantastic scrollwork of the porch, she reached out for the open door and closed it carefully, extinguishing herself in a slash of blackness. Like a magician disappearing behind a curtain. Like a theater stage going dark.

One summer when I was a boy, I caught a bird in my bare hands. It was an impulsive moment. The bird leapt from its grassy hiding place and took flight, and I reached out for it and grasped it with a success I would never have realized had it been planned. There was no doubt the capture surprised us both, and I would always remember the feel of the little brown bird in my hands—its resistance, its struggle and its final quieting as it poised itself for any chance of escape. I'd dropped to my haunches in the tall grass, feeling my hands clasped around the quivering feathers and bones. I contemplated the helplessness of the creature but also its feral will, and I found myself powerfully affected both by my certainty the bird should be released and my sorrow at the creature's absolute desire to be free of me. I dreaded the bolt of joy and relief the bird would have in wresting itself away.

Now, concealed in the dark shadows in Onset, I recalled holding Cora at the steamer dock in New Orleans the day she left me in the spring. How her small body reminded me of that long-ago bird, her frail shoulders, the tiny cage of her corset inside her shirtwaist, her thin fingers lacing my own.

With the bird in my hands those many years ago, I parted my fingers slightly to look at it. There was a rush of futile pressure and a straining by the captive against the tiny hole I'd made in my clasp, before the creature again relented. Still, I detected a small eye peering up, fixing me with a look of disdain and defiance.

I'd drawn back from Cora as the New Orleans steamboat blew its last whistle and lifted her chin in my hands to face her directly.

Her eyes were streaming tears. She was making no secret of her sorrow. There was then no hint of disdain or defiance, but her quick step to the gangplank sounded like the flutter of wings, and the sharp flick of her wrist, as she pulled it from my encircling fingers, had all the feel of a wrestling away.

1868
Washington, D.C.

My Dear Madame and Friend,

I was expecting to visit New York early this month and intended to call and thank you for your beautiful and valued gift of "Hesperia"—but finding I shall not now go for two or three weeks, I write to acknowledge the receipt of the poem and to say that when I come on, I shall personally call and pay my respects.

Walt Whitman

Cora
1868

He was a florid and shaggy man, his beard gone further to grey and disregard than the last time I spoke with him in Washington just after the war, yet his blue eyes maintained their dreamy character, and I was overjoyed to see him. In fact, I'd delayed my return to New Orleans by two weeks so I would be able to visit with Mr. Whitman at Irving Place.

His *Leaves of Grass* touched and inspired me, never having read any other poetry of the like. That Mr. Whitman encouraged my own writing and declared he'd enjoyed my poem *Hesperia*, cheered me, as he was a writer of both fame and publication. There were those who said his words were improper, but I disagreed. To me, his poems were as all the voices of America speaking, not unlike the utterings of my spirit chorus, and when I told him this, he was pleased. Mr. Whitman was interested in the world of spirits and those able to communicate with them, an ability he'd told me he wished to learn, but attempted with no success.

"When I was younger I believed access to spirit voices was available to all," I told him, "but now I am unsure if all persons have the aptitude. It requires a stilling of the mind, a special kind of listening."

"Spirits do retain their nature," he asked, "on the other side?"

"Oh yes," I replied, to what I saw was his relief. "Talkative or taciturn, spirits remain as they were in life."

"During the war, when I worked as a nurse in the army hospitals," he began, "I noted soldiers were mostly of three minds. The majority talked as normal, no more or less speech than was needed or enjoyed.

Others jabbered constantly, tugging at my sleeve seeking a converse as I passed through the wards and pestering their fellows as soon as I was gone. Still others turned their faces to the wall and said nothing."

I was glad he'd come around to the subject of the wounded soldiers. I knew from his writings and his talk how the sufferings of these men moved him. "You have spent as much time with the dying as I have with the grieving," I said. "Do you think every soldier suffered some kind of damage from the war, even those who escaped physically unscathed?"

Mr. Whitman took his hat from where he placed it earlier on the side table and held it on his knees, turning it in a slow circle by the brim. "Like the iron in a forge, no man escaped untouched by that fire," he said.

The telegraph message from New Orleans came the day after Mr. Whitman had, snatching me from the pleasant thoughts of our conversation to the despair of a long-dreaded fear. Nathan was ill with yellow fever, and I was being sent for.

The message, signed by Mr. William Baggett, a fellow Reconstructionist Republican I remembered from our days in Louisiana, was grim. At the first sign of illness, Nathan was taken upriver from New Orleans to Baggett's home near Baton Rouge. Nathan was gravely ill and asking for my return. The tone of the message implied I should prepare for the worst.

After four days in train cars accompanied by my hastily packed trunk, I arrived in Baton Rouge at nightfall. With trembling hands I opened a message awaiting me at the Harney House Hotel finding it contained no bad news, only a ticket and instructions for the remainder of my journey. I was to board the steam packet *Alice* for a trip down the Mississippi and would alight in a place called St. Gabriel where Mr. Baggett would meet me.

I first saw the smoke just after the *Alice* passed Bayou Plaquemine. Billowing far ahead on the port side of the steamboat, a larger cloud than any which could come from the burning of a structure— large enough it seemed the entire countryside was afire. There was something awesome in the sight, beautiful but for the alarming color, vast black clouds roiling with fierce energy.

Set down at the empty and forlorn St. Gabriel landing as the only passenger debarking, I felt as if I'd been brought to the edge of hell's inferno, and indeed, after trudging to the top of the levee, I was hit with the hot rush of heat, the fire's own wind whipping the air into eddies which caused my skirts to snap and flutter like a loose sail. Clutching my bonnet tightly and surveying the scene, the view presented a landscape entirely filled with smoke and flames eating into the greenery and leaving behind charred remains. Tall smears of smoke rose into the sky, and after topping the levee, the sound of the conflagration emerged, crackling through foliage like a great creature chewing, the unburnt leaves quaking with a fretful sound as if they understood they were next to be destroyed.

Two men from the steamboat lugged my trunk over the levee and set it down on the grassy bank beside me.

"St. Gabriel," one of them shouted, his voice nearly lost in the din of the fire, and slapping his hand on the trunk to indicate his job was done.

It was the first moment of my unease. Something seemed unsafe and wrong. "Is this sugarcane?" I asked the man, remembering Nathan once told me the leaves were burned away before cutting the harvest.

Looking at me as if I'd just pointed overhead and asked if it were the sky, he nodded in the affirmative. "It's grinding season," he answered, shaking his head and turning away.

Five hundred feet off, I noticed a buckboard pulled onto the verge of the road which bounded the levee. A pale colored mule with his ears laid back was in the harness, and a young man scrambled from the seat and hurried toward me. When he got close, I could see from his vacant eyes and peculiar cheerfulness he was slow-witted. Fair-haired with the faint start of a mustache, he stood before me smiling and rocking back and forth on barefoot heels. This was not Mr. Baggett.

"Where is Mr. Baggett?" I asked.

"They said I was to git you," he replied.

"Did Mr. Winslow send you?" My question clearly prompted some dim memory, and the boy foraged his pockets and thrust into my hand a crumpled square of paper. *Mrs. Cora Winslow* it read, in Nathan's handwriting!

"Is Mr. Winslow feeling well?" I asked, with a sigh of relief.

"Everybody's feelin' well," the boy answered grinning and hoisting my trunk. I hoped it was true but realized I could not put perfect trust in any information coming from this boy's perpetually sunny world.

We walked to the buckboard where the boy stowed the trunk as I climbed to the spring seat. The fire had burned away from the levee road by now, though the smoky air stung my eyes.

"What's your name," I asked the boy as he nickered to the mule, and we started off.

"Yip"

"You're called Yip?"

"Yip," he answered, and I understood.

Mr. Baggett's house was a broad white temple, ionic of pillar and a bit over-tall in the architrave to have perfect proportion, like a pretty girl with too high a forehead. It lacked a pediment too, being more in the style of the double gallery homes of New Orleans but grandly horizontal with matching service buildings sprawled at each side, rich with pilasters. I supposed it had been a sugar plantation before the war, but now the land around it lay fallow for many miles, though the grass in the front was trimmed and tidy, and the second floor gallery probably had a view of the river. Which of the tall windows were Nathan's? In what state of illness would I find him? Since receiving the telegraph, I'd prayed he would be spared and regarded our last awful encounter with a bitter rue.

Although we'd just spent an hour in the buckboard, Yip disappeared moments after we arrived promising to bring my trunk up presently. There was no sugarcane burning nearby, but a hot haze hung over the barren fields, and the facade of the house lay silent and sunstruck in late afternoon light. An elderly woman seated in a summerhouse in a grove of live oaks on the opposite side of the property took no note of my arrival. As the lady was at too far a distance for greeting, I instead turned to the front door and spied a crack in one of the curtains in a second floor window close quickly.

Inside, there was the feeling of time arrested and then lost. The spaces were orderly, but in the way of all rooms of the war-ravaged South, everything seemed withered and gnawed at the root. Fly-spotted mirrors reflected dully: the near-empty shelves of the large mahogany furniture gaped like startled eyes, while side chairs and lesser tables clumped in uncertain groupings, as if they were unfamiliar with one another. The walls were recently distempered, but the curtains were sunned to a dusty hue, soot streaked around the fireplaces, and the decorations scattered here and there, like odd lots, seemed placed upon the flat surfaces simply to give them something to do.

It was easy to imagine these rooms fifty years hence gone completely to ruin. Windows broken and leaves blown in, plaster fallen on the stairway, collapsed chimneys, for how could such a place endure, succored on slavery and surrounded each year by a hellfire of intentional burning? Already there was the sharp sour smell of some decay. Illness? Deterioration? Something run to seed.

"Welcome to Woodland," said a man who appeared straight away. "I am Mr. Newell Decker."

He was plump and soft, neither old nor young, and smiled at me as if we were old friends, but I did not recognize him.

"I am Cora Winslow. I am here for my husband, Nathan, or Mr. Baggett."

A heavyset colored man emerged from under the stairs at the far side of the room, fumbling with a broom and dustpan, but so ineffectually I believed he was eavesdropping. Mr. Decker took what seemed an inordinate period of time removing his gold-rimmed spectacles and placing them upon the nearest table. He had the small, dainty hands of a woman.

"Neither man is here," Decker finally said.

Before I could question his statement, another voice interrupted.

"Ah, ah, ha," it seemed to say, or some inarticulate utterance come from overhead at the top of the stairs. Sounds were loose and echoing in this house, the rooms were so big, the ceilings so high. My eyes followed the sound to the source, a stooped and blanketed figure with a nest of grey hair, being tugged away from the balustrade by a cruel-eyed housemaid. The blanket was odd given the heat of the day, but the figure was certainly not Nathan.

"Where is my husband?" I insisted with a rising dread.

"In the city of New Orleans, I gather," Mr. Decker replied circumspectly.

"Is he not gravely ill? Mr. Baggett sent me a dire message."

"Not at our last communication, which was yesterday morning," Mr. Decker said.

I did not like the man's furtive eyes, all at odds with his smiling face. "Then Nathan is well?" I pressed.

"Well enough to send the message," Decker replied, giving the big man with the broom a quick glance. "There seems to be some confusion Mrs. Winslow. We heard from your husband just yesterday and have been expecting you, but were given to understand it is you who are unwell and will be staying here with us."

I snatched at the realization with both terror and clarity. The desolate house, the forlorn inhabitants, the brute of a guard sent to hover the room in case I proved to be any trouble. The memory of Nathan's assertion in Onset that Spiritualism was disordering my mind.

I was now an inmate.

My first impulse was to run, but then remembered the pointlessness of even trying it. "What is this place?" I cried.

"We are neither hospital or institution," Decker explained, both menacing and unctuous at the same time, "and you will be most kindly treated. We are a home for rest. Goodness knows, these past years have taxed the strongest of minds."

* * *

I lay in my room at Woodland stunned and tearless for the first few days, but my heart was a furnace of fury at Nathan's betrayal. His false summons, which had caused me to cross the entire country alone and fearing for his death, was one thing, but this trickery and imprisonment was a heartlessness unimaginable.

On my arrival Mr. Decker had given me a packet of Nathan's letters, three missives on his expensive stationery I'd felt too exhausted to even examine. I feared the sight of his handwriting might send me staggering back into old longings, the desire for a lost happiness.

When I finally opened them, they were just as I might have expected. In his words I "needed to rest and release myself from delusions, and take time to reconsider my life free from outside influencers and possible exploiters." In the last paragraphs, his prose would grow sweet, expressing depths of feeling I never knew he had. The missives were the perfect vehicle for him, allowing only his arguments and no dissent. His soft commands issued in the uphill slant of his writing, his small letters balled tightly and often opaque with ink like tiny fists, yet his ascenders were overly tall and long tails reached out with grasping curls from the end of his sentences, the tenacious caprice of his idealism visible even in his pen strokes.

After reading Nathan's words, I even found I went so far as to wish for the simple corruption of Benjamin again, his false smile, his devious huckster's heart. He was merely a swindler and a survivor, practicing his immorality as visibly as Nathan did his out of sight. Radical, suffragist, abolitionist, social reformer. Which man was the more shameless?

On the third day, I rose from my bed at Woodland, finished with my state of injured piteousness. At the washing basin, I poured water in the bowl and let my hands rest in its coolness. Wetting a towel I washed my face and neck. There was no mirror in the room, but my fingers knew how to plait and pin my hair, and the movements recalled Lovey fashioning my old New York ringlets. How long ago that seemed.

Every morning one of the maids, Emeline or Nellie, walked the galleries and creaked open the shutters, filling my room with brassy sunlight. In the view from this window, which overlooked the area behind the house, were several other structures declining from disuse. A large vine-raddled brick barn with a square chimney, and beyond across the fields, a row of miserable cabins I assumed were the former homes of the slaves, sinking into years of lavish overgrowth and overshadowed by live oaks dangling sinister wisps of moss.

The presence of these awful dwellings provided me the explanation as to why I felt no spirits of those who'd once lived here. Woodland existed in the sterility of evil. No soul who'd passed though here remained. No soul wanted anything to do with this place.

Is there any way to mend the harm that has been done? Wondering this, I realized the question could also be asked of my condition. Downriver in New Orleans, Nathan was busy working for the rights of colored men and at the same time jailing his wife on a former plantation. Some things are beyond apology.

The days were a slow and comfortable horror, if such a thing was possible. The meals were ample and tasty, my linens and clothing kept pristine, but nothing overcame the awareness of captivity. I tried to concentrate on methods of escape, but often found I could not think at all. I slept poorly. Sometimes the wind rattled the window frames, or sometimes it was the hollow quiet in the unfamiliar house which kept me tossing through the night. Sometimes rain would wake me; other times I would wake unbidden and stand at the shuttered window, peering through a crack at the moonlit lawns, still and brilliant, with the stout prickly grass of the South picked out in sharp detail. The calls of night birds were unusual and shrill. One night I was sure I heard the keening of the demented woman who never left her room, and once when I believed I heard the laughter of a woman from the barn, the view from my shutter crack yielded the sight of a small lantern or candle flickering in the huge outbuilding's interior.

Day times, I wrote letters to Lydia and Charles, Uncle Arthur and Aunt Ellen, and even Sojourner, expressing my plight—letters which I was sure ended up in the pile of trash Luther, the big guard I'd met on my first day, routinely burned in the back fields. Watching him from the gallery, he returned my gaze with a hostile scowl and stirred the ashes with a shovel.

Luther's menacing twin was the maid Nellie Tew, who dragged through the halls carrying a meal tray or bed linens at a slothful pace, treating me as though she bore me an honest grievance. Nellie cleaned my room with the indifference of a slattern and was careless in her efforts of supplying me with water—water which tasted strange and possibly tainted, giving me the fear it might be poisoned or drugged. I tried to be extra pleasant to the woman but was met every time with a nasty look. *Luther is foul*, I thought, but *Nellie hates me*.

Mr. Decker, when he did appear, was both fawning and dismissive, evading any question I posed, but sharply watchful. He replied to most of my inquiries by placing another of Nathan's letters in my hand, the only mail I received, which contained a different assemblage of the same words and admonitions as his first three. I assumed both men were seeking my declaration that I was "well."

"I don't think I'd be giving any thought to running away if I was you," the forthright voice behind me said. It was Vinnie Wick, the elderly lady I'd first seen seated in the summerhouse the day I arrived at Woodland. By this time, I had met most of my fellow inmates at mealtimes—the talkative duo Belle McNairy and Narcissa Bard who spent their days promenading arm-in-arm and playing whist, and the pretty but brazen Sybil Dix—but Vinnie was both blind and quiet and kept to herself. It was thus embarrassingly easy to overlook Vinnie's presence, and this is what I'd done while walking on the lawn surveying the border of the property on this day. It bothered me to realize my thoughts were so obvious, especially to someone who had the disadvantage of blindness, and I replied more snappishly than was proper. "Are you a mind-reader then?"

"No," Vinnie answered, "but they say you are. Is that true?"

"No, it is not true."

"But you are something of the like. A fortune teller or maybe a witch," Vinnie ventured.

"If I were any of those, would I need to plot my escape?" I replied.

Vinnie gave a colorless laugh. "You are pretty though. Even prettier than Sybil."

This talk annoyed me. I did not like Vinnie's familiarity. "How would you know?" I asked.

"I hear how Sybil sniffs and huffs when you come or go, and she's larded the perfume ever since your arrival. I also overheard Newell Decker saying if you was his wife he'd keep you locked up in the bedroom, not a hundred miles away on some plantation. People are always running their mouth around me. I am blind, but they also seem to think I'm deaf."

Decker's words angered me. "Who did Mr. Decker say this to?"

"Luther. That big brute pushing the broom around, but he's more guard than butler, I'll tell you. You want to keep watch on him. He's a mean one. He broke Lorena's wrist."

Lorena was the mysterious figure I had seen wrapped in a blanket speaking gibberish, a victim I now knew, of the lunacy that sometimes comes with old age. "Why that is terrible! What cause would he have to do such a thing?"

"Senility comes both wild and calm. Belle McNairy is calm. She remembers nothing except how to play cards. Those that work here are content to let Narcissa keep watch of her. The two are like sisters. But Lorena's wild. Emeline and Nellie wrestle with her regularly and keep her to her room. I've heard that commotion many times. I suppose her wrist just got broke in some tussle, but Luther isn't gentle. None of them are," Vinnie said.

"What about Lorena's family?"

"Pffft! You are a babe," Vinnie sniffed. "We're all forsaken! Dropped off and forgotten, usually by some male kin or in-laws. Not a one of us truly crazy either, just inconvenient."

"I suppose you are right," I said, moving away from my vantage place to sit beside Vinnie in the summerhouse. "But what of Sybil? Surely she has no ailment."

Vinnie sniffed again. "Her! I might take back what I said about crazy, for if any one of us is, it's her. She's locked up by her man for adultery."

"Truly?"

"You look at her," Vinnie said "You're the one with eyes. I don't imagine she looks much different than she smells and sounds, all that perfume and flouncing about. Not to mention sneaking off with Decker to the sugarhouse at night. That Sybil is up for a bad end."

I pondered Vinnie's tale. It did account for the sounds and light I'd seen through my shutters in that building at night. "Why does William Baggett allow such behavior in his house?"

Vinnie usually kept her eyes closed, but occasionally one flickered open as it did now. "What Baggett?" she asked.

"William Baggett of New Orleans," I replied. "The man who owns this house."

"There's no Baggett," Vinnie said, "This is Decker land and has been for years. It belongs to Newell Decker, now that Justus is dead. Justus was his elder brother; he was the sugar man, rich and handsome and mean as a snake. He was a great one for horses and ruled this place like the devil, riding through the cane on a huge stallion named *Helon* and sparing no slave the bullwhip. The day he rode off to the war, half the belles of the vicinity were hanging on his stirrups bawling, but Chickamauga finished him. He's buried right under us you know."

I jumped and glanced at my feet.

"Well," said Vinnie, "not right here, just under the tree yonder. They built this summerhouse for Callie, their mother. Newell never went to war. He stayed in New Orleans with women and bourbon, letting this place go to ruin. They say they had to send someone down to New Orleans and pull Newell off a Girod Street whore to get him to come and tend to his mother once she started talking."

"Talking?"

"Night and day, sitting right here in this summerhouse talking to Justus. She wasn't an awful lot older than he was. Couldn't have been much more than fourteen or fifteen when she had him."

"Was there a father?" I asked.

"Died of lockjaw, November of 1852," Vinnie answered. "Anyway, Newell did as he should have in the end and lived here with his mother. I think it is where he got the idea."

"Idea?"

"Why Callie Decker was the first of Woodland's invalids, until the grippe took her last year. Newell knew no other way to keep this house going then to paint the walls and call it a rest home. He knew nothing of farming, and the family money was lost in the war. It was just him and Yip and Callie when the war ended."

"Yip is a brother?" I asked.

"His name is Alonzo. Imagine having a name you don't have sense enough to pronounce. Some say he is Newell's brother; others say he is Callie and Justus' son.

I took some time thinking through this statement. "You mean...?"

Vinnie interrupted me. "How old would you say Yip is?"

"Fifteen, maybe," I answered.

"Just subtract and you get to 1853," Vinnie answered with a leery sort of grin, "No one knows. There are always odd doings in a house like this."

Vinnie raised her face to the distant fields and sighed deeply just as though she enjoyed the view, and I wondered suddenly if she could.

"I take it you once lived nearby," I said.

"Yes."

"How near?" I asked, not caring if my voice showed suspicion.

"Not that near," Vinnie said, "but near enough. My daughter was one of the fools hanging on Justus' stirrups."

Vinnie began to stand upright taking her time as the elderly do, feeling for the arm of the seat with an uncertain hand, and making sure her legs were well under her before putting weight on them. I stood too, guiding the woman's elbow with a loose grip.

"Don't go running in them fields, Cora," Vinnie said. "Play your husband for the fool I know he is, and when he lets you out of here, then do your running. You try going out of here overland and you won't make it. There's miles of swamps and cane to the north and east and the river to the west. There's alligators and snakes, even bears. Every man in the area, including those on the river, knows well what Decker'll pay for your return. Take my advice."

"You didn't say what was to the south," I said.

Vinnie shook her head in discouragement."If you are lucky enough to make it through the miles of cane and swamps, then you'll end up at the leper colony."

Vinnie's warning pushed me near to panic. In my room that evening, I stood by the shuttered window with my arms wrapped tightly around myself in an effort to still my pounding heart, gulping at the shred of cooler air sifting through the shutters bearing the smell of the river, the silt and mud of this bottomland. I'd hoped I could get to the water's edge, perhaps flag down a passing boat, but never considered the men of the area were already apprised of such a circumstance. I knew Vinnie's tales of the leper colony were true too, as I had seen the ominous red-painted wagon in New Orleans last winter and was told it transported victims of the disease to a place of forced quarantine upriver. Those who stepped inside it were said to never return.

Still, I needed to keep myself in hand, as any outburst would be taken advantage of. For all these weeks, I'd not argued or resisted for fear of being subjected to a more restrictive form of restraint.

Needless to say, I'd already considered Vinnie's other advice—setting myself free by deceiving Nathan—but was unsure I'd be able to convince him and thought it likely he would always have me watched and confined. Merely imagining the constant conflict made me feel heavy and tired, with every day of my future threatening to be a hopeless prison.

My spirits were with me of course, with all their gestures of comfort. I could feel them close around me, Captain Walker and Hollis by the bedside, and I'd even woken once in an hour past midnight to Robert's gold sunlight glittering in front of the closed door as the protective sentinel he'd always been. The elderly woman was completely absent, gone since before Etta died, and I missed the touch of her female spirit and the husky tone of her endearments, but Hollis' voice was rarer too. When Hollis did speak, his voice sounded thin and muted, as though he, too, were confined and calling out from some dark and distant corner of the enormous house. Yet what could they do? Spirits performed many miracles, but I did not think them capable of transporting a person to freedom.

My mind clutched on a final idea, and I sat at my desk one night to carry it out. I would write a letter asking for help and giving my whereabouts, address it in bold handwriting to Nathan in New Orleans, but place Mrs. Dostie's street address on the second line, hoping Newell Decker would overlook the difference and Mrs. Dostie might receive the letter and understand.

The following morning I awoke stiff and with a sharp headache, still at the desk in my room at Woodland. I'd fallen asleep on my crossed arms, my pen and ink untouched, and my letter to Mrs. Dostie unwritten. Chastising myself and rubbing my sleep-blurred eyes, I noticed a square of paper set at a slant against the lamp on the desktop. I squinted at the odd handwriting on the paper. It was a one word message, and I knew exactly who had sent it.

SUMMER BREEZES AT ONSET BAY GROVE

A more perfect season than that of 1868 was never before seen. Upwards of five thousand have been known to converge at Onset Bay on any given Sunday from the opening day festivities in June to the final harvest Moon celebration in late September.

No small part of the popularity of the 1868 season was the lecture series provided by Mrs. Cora Winslow, the noted trance medium, who filled the Grove amphitheater to bursting at each of her addresses.

As those familiar with Mrs. Winslow will know, she is possessed of a clear, pleasant diction blazing with impressive enunciation and poetic metaphors. Although she seems to have entirely disappeared to her home in the south-land for the winter months, it is hoped by many that she will return to join our "little band" in future summers.

—*The Onset Dot* Newspaper
October 5, 1868

Hollis

1868

We reckon time differently, the quick and the dead. For the living, time is always either hastening or loitering, but we spirits know time keeps no tally in eternity. Here, we all persist in what I can only describe as an unending instant, a state unlikely to be understood by those in the earthly world.

I almost wanted to call the earthly world the real world, but I cannot think of it that way any longer. I find myself in readiness for a different sphere, and when I look back over my shoulder, the earth already appears blurred and ill-defined, just as though I were viewing it through tears.

There is a boy, a very young boy, standing on the bridge at Hope Grove, barefoot, shirt puckered into his trousers, one of his braces loose and slipping off his shoulder. How do I resemble him? I no longer have his teeth or hair, even his heart lies shrunk and shriveled, going to the same pieces as the rest of him in a grave across the river. So what remains? What possible thing am I?

If I were only memory would I be here to talk of myself? No, I am made of sturdier stuff, the strongest and yet most ethereal of all materials, the soul. For what prison can hold a soul, what power can overcome it? Even death can not keep its grasp upon it. A soul cannot be diminished or destroyed, nothing can consume or exhaust it. The soul is, in its way, identical to love.

So the boy I was, the earthly boy, was told trout lived in the stream which ran beneath the bridge, and for days he searched for them. Wading with his cuffs rolled to his knees, poking about with a stick, all to no avail. It was not until he'd given up and was resting dejectedly against the bridge rail that he saw them. Plain as day, if he'd only understood they had to be seen in their disguises, their speckled skin nearly indistinguishable from the stony stream bed.

How joyful the discovery made him, and how fixed in his memory was the moment. The July sky, the speckled fish suspended in the current, the cicada's long song in the nearby trees, the cracked and peeling paint of the bridge rail, his grubby and boyish fingers gripping it. Even as an older boy, when the bridge rail reached to his waist rather than his chin, he would still take time to stop and seek out the descendants of those first trout.

Finding the fish was my first remembered happiness.

There were others. The day I feigned illness and mother allowed me to stay at home in bed rather than go to school and the taste of the raisin cookies she made for me. The winter morning I finally mastered ice skating. The fateful afternoon when I chanced upon a traveling drummer at the store in the village. The old salesman peddled toys and novelties and the wonders he produced from his leather-trimmed grip changed the direction of my future hopes. The memory of the smell of the paint on a paper mask he gave me still can jolt my heart into a happy daydream.

My time on earth was not long, so I did not taste much of manhood, but cherish the day I first felt my maturity. That episode of tomfoolery in Boston, my fellows jostling and teasing me with no little envy after I'd made the impetuous purchase of a yellow waistcoat with an entire months allowance. It was my favorite possession, my little badge of frivolity and free choice.

Thus eternity is not an endless tract or a perpetual span; it is as I said, more of an unending instant. Eternity is made of moments such as the fish and the paper mask, and these moments are the seeds of your soul. Each of us slips the earth with our own small hoard of them, for even in a long life moments strong enough to build eternities are few, and you will not test their power until you join me here in the world of spirits. I can only say this, what looks like an end is never an end, and all things die, but they do not perish.

Out of modesty perhaps, I have not yet mentioned the most significant of my moments, or the name of the single person present in each of them but I suspect it is not even necessary.

Cora Page, Cora Carter, Cora Winslow. Whatever man may claim her, her name was written first on my heart. Written, I now know, from the day she climbed the stool at the print shop and read the type in the composing stick perfectly. My fondness began when I was far too old for her, and now it has warmed into love I am far too…dead. So, too, am I leaving.

I am in a state of departure whether I like it or not. The spirit world is not a static place, no drowsy vale of repose and soft music. Rather, it is an animated crossroads with much coming and going, souls changing their containers as the living change their dress and wandering in various centuries as diverse as earthy weather. I can only describe my change as a lightening, an odd description since I am presumably weightless. At any rate, I am coming loose from something which has held me and at the very moment Cora seems to most need my help. Our minds are uncoupling, and I wonder if Cora can feel this. I am dead, but she is a living thing and still senses pain; *Forgive me!* I try to say but find I can no longer speak to her. I cannot even see her clearly as she is just a dim profile pacing the room of that awful plantation prison. My spirit is rising to meet its translation, a reason for joyfulness, but had I known I was to lose Cora in my vision, I would have taken a last look; had I known I was to lose our communication, I would try to voice a last word.

I do not go alone. I rise with another. Our hands hold fast to each other as we both drift and quiver, fluttering like a banner attached to a pole by a single thread.

I have in my clasp a child. A girl of about six years in a yellow dress, who bids fair to rival the precociousness of her mother. Much grown from when I saw her last, as is usual in the spirit world where all souls proceed from their death to verbal sentience so they can be themselves, we will ascend to a higher sphere together.

When Etta was presented to me by Mrs. Beaulieu, I was astonished to learn the girl remembered all the little songs I'd sung to her cradled self while I haunted Cora's house in New Orleans. Could she hear me as her mother could? I cannot say, and she is too young to answer, but it is a mystery. Perhaps we are all ghosts, even the living, simply a different shade of shade.

"Etta is in need of a teacher," Mrs. Beaulieu said, in her unarguable way.

As my heart leapt at the thought of teaching Cora's child and my head lectured me on my lack of experience, I dithered. Why do I even have a heart and a head to trouble me when I no longer possess either? "I-I-I never finished school," I stammered, "I don't think I can teach."

There is no one in the spirit world who can outdo Rosalie Beaulieu for a withering glance, and I received it in full force. "Ça alors! A father then," she said rolling her eyes, "as it amounts to the same thing."

Etta stood between us, quiet and patient. I placed my hand on her fair hair, brushing back the curls from her forehead, recalling Cora's winsome braids. Where does a love go that has no home, I once asked myself. Where indeed.

A father. Yes, this sounded right. To become the very thing I might have been. Oh what the heart affords itself, even long after it is gone.

I took Etta's hand and have not let go of it since. If she were older, I might try her first on the word "incorporeal," but since we are both such, I will only smile at the memory.

"Are you ready to visit your mother?" I asked her.

"Yes!" Etta said.

"You have many things to learn before then. Do you think your mother will recognize us?"

Etta nodded.

It will be well beyond fifty years of earth time and after Cora's own death before she meets the two of us waiting to greet her, but for Etta and I the time will be merely an instant. Still, I will wear my yellow waistcoat, just in case.

Goodnight, goodnight, dear Cora. We will see you on a different morning.

Cora

1868

I had never seen spirit handwriting. I'd heard of it, even met several mediums who claimed to evince it, but such manifestations were unknown to me. Yet here was a word in Hollis' hand, scratched on a sheet of paper presumably with my ink and pen! There was no salutation and no signature, but that was unnecessary, for the manner in which the word was written revealed its author. The single word WAIT written upside down and backward, just as if it were type in a printer's composing stick.

I felt something close to elation. Those in the world of spirit have a range of vision far broader than the living, even into the future, and I took Hollis' entreaty with all seriousness. I would wait, and I would watch.

After another two weeks passed however, my confidence was shaken. Nothing in my situation changed, and nothing new presented itself. I'd gone ahead and written the letter to Mrs. Dostie's New Orleans address to no evident effect. I had been confined at Woodland for nearly two months without word from anyone I knew, outside of Nathan's coaxing letters. Surely others would have missed me by now. Lydia and Charles, my family in Cadytown. All would think my silence unnatural. What was Nathan telling them?

Soon it would be Christmas. The daylight was short, and even here in this tropical climate, leaves were drying into brown twists and falling from trees, and the grasses around the summerhouse had been burned in an overnight frost. Was it Nathan's intention I pass the winter here?

Worst of all was Hollis' silence. I'd not heard his voice or felt his presence since the day of the handwritten message, despite pleading to him to make things clear to me. In the past, he was sometimes absent for short periods, but never when I posed him a question.

My speculation was agonizing. Was there some significance I misunderstood, or was fear merely depriving me of common sense?

As with many other things in my life, assistance came from a place where it seemed least likely. During her rounds distributing nighttime chamber pots, Nellie Tew shuffled into my room. After giving the pot a rough slide beneath the bed with her foot, Nellie turned, and with a nimble flash, withdrew a small packet from somewhere on her person, pressing it into my palm.

"Wha-?" I began to say, but closed my mouth around the question and swallowed it, as Nellie scowled fiercely. For a long moment we faced one another in silence, nothing passing between us but Nellie's provoking glare.

"Thank you," I said, though feeling almost as if I should have apologized, as Nellie turned and stalked away. The woman was the bearer of my deliverance, but I would not have been surprised if she had spit on the chamber floor.

Once the house was quiet, I sat on the bed in the light of a single candle and opened the message carefully, taking it apart fold by fold. Creased into a tight and tiny square and much handled, the spread-out page was an octavo of worn foolscap with a few terse words. The handwriting was obscure, plain block letters probably meant to disguise the author, who I was sure was not Hollis.

DECEMBER 14
AFTER MIDNIGHT
WALK DOWNSTREAM ON RIVER ROAD
WILL MEET YOU
BRING ONLY WHAT YOU CAN CARRY
BURN THIS.

December 14 was two days away. There was no doubt in my mind I would comply with the instructions, and I put the paper in the candle's flame.

I prepared myself by paying special attention to the features of Woodland, taking note of places where the floors or stair treads squeaked, plotting the most inconspicuous route across the property to the river road. Nothing was locked in the great house, as its very isolation promoted the property as a prison. Long ago, I'd sewn the remaining money I'd carried from New York into the bodice of my dress and resolved to take little else with me. Some clothing, as well as the small envelope of Etta's hair which now also contained the WAIT message from Hollis, the latter items being the only two remaining scraps of my life where my love could rest.

December 14th was moonless, which I assumed was intentionally planned. After the rest of the house had fallen into the quiet of sleep, I changed into my black dress, the one Nathan gifted me for the event at the Mechanics' Institute. To think I had worn the dress in 1867 at my New Orleans triumph, not knowing I'd be packing it in a trunk a year later fearing it might be needed for my sick husband's funeral. Now it was the costume of my escape, as dark as the night I was about to venture into.

Closing the mosquito net around my bed and fluffing the bedclothes to appear like my sleeping shape, I crept into the hallway where in the dense quiet I could hear nothing but the soft sounds of others sleeping. I descended the stairs avoiding the tread that creaked and winced at the groan of the door handle which sounded like an onlooker clearing his throat.

Tiptoeing across the gravel of the drive, I crept into the silence of the grass, moving into the shelter of shrubs and trees, praying for obscurity, and waiting for my eyes to adjust to the blackness of the night. Once I'd made it to the river road, I turned to the left walking quickly, almost at a run, transporting myself to a memory from the past—my breathless dash from the Tontine Hotel with a bloody eye. It seemed I must start fresh once again, but since those days I had learned a thing or two about hope.

The landscape which seemed straightforward during the day became more forbidding at night, and my fears caught up with my initial daring. It had rained that morning, a short heavy storm which flooded the fields and puddled the roads. By the end of the day, the sun baked away most of the moisture, but a few ruts of standing water were present. I imagined snakes and alligators. I knew little of the natural world but remembered snakes came out at night to warm themselves on the roadways, and I'd once seen an alligator, hanging dead in a butcher's stall at the Poydras Street Market. It was a huge thing, as long as I was tall, with a mouth of sharp white teeth. Shuddering, I felt the quickening pace of my heartbeat.

There were other fears. I was quite exposed on the open road, and the broad fields of cane stubble and widely scattered trees gave little place to hide. What if someone came? What, too, if this were another trick of Nathan's? Woodland was not an asylum. Nathan would never have risked the shame to his family of placing me in such an institution, but how far would he go if I continued to defy him? My eyes watered but I refused to cry, and instead, turned my face to the stars overhead and hurried along. Orion with his bright belt climbing to the top of the sky hunting a quarry he never catches, the Milky Way streaming behind him.

Far ahead, a faint orb of light bobbed and hovered and a scrap of sound found my ears. The jangling of a harness and soft clatter of turning wheels accompanied by a strange tone for a lonely midnight, the soft notes of a man's song floating in the impenetrable darkness. I wondered if this were a sound from the living, as the abiding feature of my life was the task of separating the real from things spectral or imagined. Because it was sung, the voice was like a glimmer, rising and fading, allowing no clue to its meaning, only releasing a word here and there. "Sweet, carry, coming." A streak of something passed through me, nostalgia or perhaps simple remembrance, but it felt like heartache. I peered into the gloom, scarcely breathing and spellbound.

"I looked over Jordan and what did I see?
A band of angels coming after me,
Coming for to carry me home."

The singer wore a soft brimmed hat and was driving a box-backed wagon pulled by a pair of large mules. The trio drew up beside me, the man modifying his song from lyrics to simple humming, as he got closer. He was an old man, his face a pattern of sags and wrinkles and a deep 'V' of rumination or consternation etched in the middle of his forehead. Grey hair like fleecy wool and a goatee framed his tired face. Tired of what, I could not tell. I supposed the man had been a slave and was probably just tired from the hard work of forgetting.

He pulled off his hat and held it to his chest. "I'm Pliny Layton," he said. "Are you Cora?"

There was only the lantern suspended from the roof of the wagon to provide any light for examination, but once surveying the wagon, I recognized it. Painted an alarming red—even to the spokes of its wheels—the vehicle was a chilling sight on the streets of New Orleans and always led observers to uncomfortable speculation. *LLH* were the letters stenciled on the sides of the enclosed wooden van. Louisiana Leper Home.

"Yes, I'm Cora."

Pliny slid from the wagon seat and stood on the road. "Then I am here for you." He walked to the rear of the vehicle and opened the pair of doors, indicating I should climb into the back.

"Who sent you?" I asked.

"They don't tell me names. It's better that way. People from the North. I'm supposed to deliver you to New Orleans where they are waiting."

Charles and Lydia! Mrs. Dostie must have contacted them. But why would they send such a wagon? Or was it another deception from Nathan, sending me to the lepers or somewhere worse? I knew I must have looked uneasy. "I'm meant to ride in this?" I asked.

Pliny's wrinkles broke into a broad smile."I'm the only camel you're apt to find in this desert."

Some tight little mechanism unlatched in my chest at the sight of Pliny's smile, but I'd read of leprosy, the contagion, the awful disfigurement. "Is it safe?"

Pliny held out his hand for my balance when climbing the wagon step. "I've carried lepers since before the war. 'Taint as contagious as people think. Besides in your particular case, you are as safe here as anywhere in south Louisiana. No one harasses this chariot. Most people won't get ten yards of it." Pliny smiled again mischievous and twinkling, and I relented and climbed into the wagon, not entirely because of the smile but also because of the way his voice sounded when he was singing.

"We'll be some hours riding," Pliny said, as though he knew the oddity of it and meant to make me feel more comfortable about the journey. I perceived his concern, the peculiarity and outright impropriety of our situation. A young White woman riding in a Black man's wagon, avoiding detection. I positioned myself deep inside the wagon box up close to the wall nearest Pliny, where he had slid open a window blind behind him so he and I could talk and I could see the road ahead. In Louisiana, there were probably laws against our actions, and although I mulled my incaution, I nevertheless felt assured. I trusted the situation precisely because it made little sense.

We kept to the river road initially passing miles of empty fields. There were few buildings, most of which seemed abandoned, some tracts of cut and burned cane and broad swaths of tall grass, where clusters of trees appeared like shadows on the land. We saw no living thing apart from a lone dog with an injured hind leg drawn up against his belly loping along the roadside and a family of wild hogs thrashing in a brushy thicket. About an hour along, Pliny began to sing again, low sad songs that matched the color of the night.

I felt we could have gone on endlessly, all quiet but for the singing and footfalls of the mules and the leathery sound of their ears flicking, all my future decisions suspended in the act of escape. Such was the taste of freedom in my heart, until my reverie was broken by the brightening of the sky. The black of the night softened to a deep violet and was being pushed back from the horizon by the tide of the daylight. Pliny steered the wagon down a gentle incline and along a creek bank where the mules feet sunk and sucked in mud or ooze. Then they pushed through a break in a tract of dense willows, grown so close together they slapped the sides of the wagon box like a hundred hands applauding, to greet the surprising sight of the Mississippi River. I hadn't any idea it was there, nearly silent and expectant, like a great creature holding its breath in the wilderness.

After we'd both stood down from the wagon, Pliny spoke. "It's a bit over ten more miles to get to my cabin. My wife Adah is there. It won't be long before you are discovered missing at Woodland. We should lay up for the daytime and head out again tonight. I've opened the side grates, but now the sun's up it will be hot inside the wagon."

"I'll be all right," I assured him.

Pliny nodded and looked as if some preconception had been confirmed. "I took you to be a tough one," he said.

I wondered at his meaning. "Not so tough I don't need to make a visit to the bushes." I confessed, and made a rather awkward foray into the nearby brush to relieve myself. Pliny scrambled to the rivers' edge and drew a bucket of water for the mules, allowing them some time to feed in the grass along the road's edge.

Returning from my toilet, smoothing my hair and sweeping leaves and grass from my skirts, I spoke in a concise voice, hoping to regain my poise. "You seem to be very familiar with the vicinity."

"I come from Ohio, free born, where I always worked with livestock. I made the mistake of coming down the river with a flat-boat loaded with mules in the spring of '61 and found I could not get back during the war. I landed here with the Sisters of Charity at the Leper Home and stayed because of my wife Adah. My whole life got changed by a woman, a war, and a load of mules."

I smiled and approached his animals. They seemed near-twins, both dark colored with pale muzzles, but the larger of the two had a crooked blaze running from his nose to one eye which gave him a quizzical expression. I reached out to stroke this mule's neck. "What are their names?"

"The one you're handling is Honest Abe. The other is Horace."

"Is he honest?" I asked smiling.

Pliny laughed his soundless laugh, with which I was becoming familiar. A quick intake of breath, followed by a smiling open mouth and a dip of his chin in agreement. "He's always honest, 'til I've got my back turned."

As Pliny, indicated we traveled another two hours in the wagon, moving away from the river on a two-track lane that cut along a flat place of palmettos and into a watery country of cypress swamp. Grey moss hung from trees with ragged branches which shadowed the pale gravel on the road. The wagon box was hot and close, full of heavy stale air, and my eyes swarmed with fatigue and headache. Despite Pliny's assurance, I fretted with the thought of contagion. I was relieved when we finally came to a stop in a shady clearing. From the tiny window, I saw Pliny's cabin, a small sturdy wooden structure with a mud chimney, mossy roof shingles, the furs of muskrats drying on an outside wall and chickens in the dooryard.

A woman, presumably Adah, stepped into the doorway shading her eyes to take a look and turned back inside. She was tall and long-shanked, taller than either myself or Pliny, and even in a simple cotton house dress moved with confident grace, her gestures unhurried and her features unmoved, as though her husband's arrival after an overnight ride with a White female escapee were common practice.

While Pliny took care of the mules, I washed myself, changed my chemise and put on my cotton wrapper, hanging my black dress on a peg to air. The cabin was one large room, with a ladder tilted to a loft-like space overhead, and I was given a cot cushioned with blankets on which to sleep. Since Pliny and I would be leaving again that evening, I thought to pin my black veil to my bonnet as a further disguise.

Adah came to sit beside me. She was a stately woman, queenly even, probably forty years old to Pliny's sixty. Despite streaks of grey in her hair, her skin remained flawless, soft and nearly shimmering, but there was something about her which seemed familiar.

"That veil is a good idea," Adah said, watching me wind it around the bonnet.

I sighed. "The only reason I have it is because two months ago I believed I might be attending my husband's funeral."

Adah smiled sadly. "Do you need some pins?" she asked.

"I couldn't take your pins!" I said. "I have four or five of my own, and that should do."

"You should sleep a while if you can," Adah advised, as she stood. "It is still many hours to New Orleans."

"Adah," I said. "I have five dollars. I would like to give it to Pliny for all his trouble but have the idea he won't take it. Is there something you could use, or something you might buy for him?"

Adah shook her head. "We haven't much need for money."

"For the house, then, or for Honest Abe and Horace?"

"Pffft," Adah said smiling broadly, a beautiful smile. "Those mules already live like kings."

I barely recalled lying down on the cot but awoke in the darkness to the smell of good cooking, realizing I was very hungry. Adah was busy at the fireplace and had a skillet sputtering with griddle cakes and pork lard. Pliny had risen from his own nap and stood before the fire with his suspenders hanging down around his waist and his hands pressed at the base of his arched back.

"May I help?" I asked. "Set the table?" Adah gestured toward an open cupboard which contained the needed utensils.

"Cold weather coming tonight," Pliny said. "We'll need to take some blankets."

At first, we three ate our supper in the silence of unfamiliarity, but it was not long before Adah broke the quiet with a strange question. "Are you afraid, Cora?"

As the question was unexpected, I took a moment to answer "No...no. I am concerned for the future, but my present here with you and Pliny is quite pleasant."

"Woodland is an evil place," said Adah.

"I could sense the wickedness and the awful buried secrets," I said. "I was terrified of the confinement and didn't trust a single person, but everyone was outwardly kind to me except..."

"Except who?" asked Pliny.

"A housemaid named Nellie Tew."

Abandoning his soundless laugh, Pliny roared and slapped his hand on the table. "Ha! I knew it! She is a mean one. Mean as ptomaine."

"I'm afraid she didn't like me," I said.

"Oh, but she did," said Adah smiling.

"Nellie is Adah's older sister," Pliny explained.

I am sure my eyes were as wide as saucers as I gaped at the couple, but the revelation went a long way toward explaining the familiarity I'd noted in Adah's face.

"If she hadn't liked you, she would never have delivered the note Pliny wrote," said Adah.

"You wrote it?" I said to Pliny.

"Yes, but we weren't sure if Nellie would deliver it. She's an independent one."

"Most of it is an act," Pliny said. "About noontime today there was hell to pay at Woodland while old Decker tried to figure out how you slipped away, and who might have helped you. Nasty Nellie would be the last one he'd suspect."

Adah made a huff of contempt. "Surely true. They suspect us of laziness, of stealing, of every bad thing, but they never suspect us of watching and understanding."

The plan was for Pliny to take me in the leper wagon all the way into New Orleans, where he'd drop me off at St. Patrick's Church on Camp Street. There I hoped Charles or Lydia would meet me. We left Pliny's cabin at some hour before midnight, and now it was near noontime the following day. The journey seemed endless. I slept in fits and starts swaying like a lumpen bag of freight over the uneven roads. We stopped twice to rest and water the mules, and eat a bit of the chicken and cornbread Adah packed for us. When the wagon finally came to a stop before the tall Gothic church, I was consumed by a jumpy exhaustion, as if I could neither move nor stay still.

Nevertheless, clad once again in the black mourning dress, I stepped down from the wagon and stood on the banquette facing Pliny. The air had breezed up, a harbinger of one of the frequent winter rains, rippling my widow's veil around my hidden face.

"I have nothing to give you," I said, "but please carry away my deepest thanks to you and Adah both. I will always remember your kindness to me." My voice snagged in my throat, and it was all I could do to resist weeping, some waterfall of ceaseless tears, for this city, my unimaginable future, my dead Etta, the uptown cottage, the mules, and Pliny, my briefly known helmsman.

"I thank you for raising your voice for my people," Pliny said. "We know how much stomach it took to stand and speak in Mechanics' Institute where you could have been killed just as the others were. We know Mr. Winslow's efforts too, but cannot accept his putting you under lock and key.

"You say "we"?" I asked, not understanding the plural.

Pliny looked away, almost dreamily before he answered. "It has been some years since I last transported anyone on this railroad," he said and then offered a small smile, "and never a White woman."

Suddenly understanding, I stared at Pliny with amazement—The clever ploy of the leper wagon which no one dared approach, Pliny's calling the wagon a chariot and his singing. "You are the Undergroun…?" I began, but he silenced me with a finger to his lips.

At the same moment, I was silenced even further by what I saw over Pliny's shoulder on the far corner of the street, and a shock of terror jolted me. Two men walking in opposite directions had met and were beginning a jovial conversation. One of the men took off his hat, brushed back his hair over a balding pate and stared at the sky, no doubt predicting the coming rain, and the other stood smiling, both hands in his pockets. The smiling man was Nathan. I scanned everyone in my line of sight for treachery, but there was none. Nathan's office was not far from this corner, and his appearance was probably an uncanny and awful chance.

"Pliny!" I whispered. "Mr. Winslow is on the opposite corner!

Pliny seemed alarmed for a moment but covered his emotion quickly and suppressed the urge to look behind him.

"Just act as natural," he instructed me. "There hasn't been time for him to know of your escape and Decker will keep it quiet until every corner is searched. Mr. Winslow will keep his distance from this wagon as everyone else does."

Pliny was right. No matter that I was fifty feet from my husband. No matter that I was dressed in the very gown he'd ordered made for me, which I'd worn at Mechanics Institute on the day he probably loved me the most, Nathan did as everyone else who encountered the wagon from the Leper Home. The last time I ever saw Nathan, he was looking at me in disgust.

I had never been in a Catholic church. Before Pliny drove away, he told me to wait inside for an hour and then return to the street where a carriage would be arriving. The carriage would have closed curtains and the driver would be a Black man wearing a mourning armband around his upper sleeve.

St. Patrick's was cold and stone-tiled and seemingly unoccupied by anyone other than myself. The outside of the huge structure was all vertical lines, and the loftiness continued within, tall veined columns breaking into arches overhead which curved like the stems of plants. I felt as a small creature in a garden gazing upward to the undersides of leaves. The roof above the altar was a half-dome of stained glass, very grand, and on it, I could hear a tapping sound like the drumming of fingers. The threatening rainstorm had arrived.

Walking a few steps up the center aisle, I took a seat in one of the last rows of pews. Decorative colonnades ran the length of either side enclosing stepped racks of burning candles and little cabinets, indicating unfamiliar rituals. Glancing behind myself several times, I feared Nathan's appearance or the arrival of someone who would know I was a Protestant interloper.

There was the odor of wax and something sweeter like perfume, and the space was dense with the air of ruminative suspension all churches possess. Every gleam of light filtered by colored glass, the very air quelled and contained as if each breath ever taken here was still trapped inside. I imagined the vapors of songs and sermons rising to the rafters, the prayers of earlier thousands floating in the air, but found I was unable to pray. I would bow my head and begin, but it always seemed shameful to ask for something for myself.

Shame was my dominant feeling. Once again, I was destined to flee to the shelter of Lydia and Charles, escaping the consequences of another poor decision, but Pliny's words seeded another suspicion. He'd hinted at the Underground Railroad. Was my rescue to be from that brave band? Sojourner Truth or her friend Amy Post? Even the Reverend Lyman who'd hidden Negro fugitives on their journey north at Hope Grove in the years before the war. But why? And how would they have known I was missing or where to find me?

I looked down at my hands crossed in my lap. I saw evidence of their aging and felt a sharp nostalgia for their lost girlishness and for a past life which seemed hard to believe ever existed. The skin around the knuckles more puckered, the veins trailing feebly to my wrists.

I had changed so much. Benjamin was a deceiver, but Nathan had robbed me of my very liberty, forcing me to become a new person—a person I realized I was going to have to learn to understand. It was a task I could not yet grasp. I was now so changed that no place to which I might return—not Nathan, not Cadytown or Lydia, not even dear Onset—would be anything like the place I had left.

How long is an hour? A slice of sunlight beamed through the domed glass ceiling and cast itself on the altar like one of the old limelights of my platform days. The quick storm had passed and outside the streets were steaming in the sun as I stepped into the bright air. Glancing about for Nathan, I saw he and the other man were gone, probably to a lunch in some eatery near the market. The promised carriage stood before me. The driver wore the described armband and did not descend from his seat but met my gaze and nodded almost imperceptibly. A corner of curtain inside the carriage drew quickly back and snapped shut. The door opened, unlatched by the passenger inside, beckoning my entrance. The passenger was Sophia.

Sophia
1868

I was not prepared for the veil hiding Cora's face. In all my imaginings of our reunion, we would gaze wide-eyed at one another, and in the moment of this gaze, all would be understood.

Instead, Cora drew back, and I realized she believed I might be an agent of Mr. Winslow, so I was obliged to alter my plan. "I am running away too," I said, and watched as her head tilted in question and misgiving.

I tapped my hand lightly on the seat beside me. "Come inside and sit with me," I said.

Still she held back, and from what I knew of her circumstance I could not blame her. "I am not sent by Mr. Winslow. He has no idea I am here," I explained.

With this assurance, Cora climbed in the carriage beside me, pulling back the veil and draping it over her bonnet. It had been many months since I'd seen Cora and she was altered. She looked older, her face weary and watchful and her body grown thinner.

"Do you know Nathan…Mr. Winslow was here only an hour ago?" she said.

"What!"

"I saw him standing on the opposite corner when I first arrived. I was shocked, but he did not see me. I think he was just out from his office taking lunch."

I opened the window on my side of the carriage and called out to the driver, "René, sil te plaît emméne-nous sur les quais." I've asked him to take us to the wharves," I translated. "Somewhere out of the way near the river warehouses so we can talk."

"Sophia," Cora said in the tone of a vexed mother, "why are you here and what is happening?"

"First of all…I must confess my name is not Sophia." I slid my arm around hers and pulled her close to me, as the carriage turned down Poydras Street toward the river.

"I am Sophie Dumas," I began, after the carriage was stopped in an alley between two freight warehouses along the levee, and René the driver had taken shelter in a nearby doorway. The rain had returned and was spattering lightly on the canvas roof enclosing us in close quarters which reminded me, especially in my current state, of the church confessionals of my youth.

"I was born in Paris and brought by my parents to the United States when I was three years old. My father was Hypolite Dumas and my mother was Felicite Bertonneau, but everyone called her Lissy. It was Mr. Winslow who called me Sophia, and as it was close enough to what I was accustomed, I never corrected him."

I stopped after this to allow what I'd said, which was so opposite of what Cora believed, to have its full effect.

"I thought you'd been a slave," Cora said.

"As did everyone. It was Mr. Winslow's fancy. Out of the most wretched slave pen rises Sophia, civilized and speaking four languages, suitable after sufficient education and proper costume for any high class parlor soiree. I am sick to death of it."

Cora's eyes flickered with interest then, as though I'd said something she already knew. "So you lied?" she asked.

"I don't think I ever did, at least I tried not to, but Mr. Winslow did, and I suppose I was complicit because I never exposed him. Yet, what was I to do, dependent on his people and not yet arrived at my majority?"

"You were never a slave, you never lived on a plantation?"

I suppose Cora fixed on the deception because she'd been so convinced of it. Yet knowing I had another thunderbolt to launch, one I feared might cause Cora to hate me, I bit my lip and then continued. "No I was never a slave, and yes, I lived on my father's plantation with the hundred slaves our family owned."

Cora regarded me with a look of vast and uncomprehending amazement. I suspected she'd perhaps suffered too many revelations in the past days, but I knew no way to soften the truth.

"My God," was all she said.

I feared her rage, but wanted to explain further. "I must tell you my story," I said. "My family's story."

"Where are your family now? Cora asked. "Have they survived?"

"Everyone is gone since the war, but we were lost years before it even started."

The rain had petered out again as it does in New Orleans, replaced moments later by a hot sun, which was beginning to make our closed carriage uncomfortable. I could see Cora was exhausted and wished to take her to my rooms elsewhere in the city.

"Will you come with me to the other side of the city?" I asked.

Cora closed her eyes and nodded yes.

René steered the carriage to the opposite side of the city, and once we'd crossed Canal Street I felt free to open the curtains and windows of the carriage. We moved along Royal Street past the doorways of the fancy stores I'd known as a girl, diminished now since the war, and so different then the staid streets of Boston.

"I've never been to this part of the city," Cora remarked.

"Mr. Winslow's people would be unlikely here," I told her as we turned onto Esplanade and stopped before a house not far from the corner.

"It's all right," I reassured Cora as we entered the premises, climbing the grand curved staircase and stepping into a suite of elaborate but barren rooms. A single bed, a battered wardrobe, a sofa, and my two trunks were the only furnishings in the vast, dusty space.

Cora looked in wonder around her. "Is this your parents house?"

"No, it belongs to friends, but in the last years before the war, I lived with my father in a place just like this. By 1861 our plantation Belle Clair was a shadow of what it had been and mortgaged for nearly all its value to a New York bank. Still the home of a hundred slaves, because my father was too soft-hearted to sell them, and manumission was impossible in Louisiana at the time. These slaves had nowhere to go and were nearly all subsisting on the property by their own efforts. My father and I stayed mostly on Toulouse Street in near-empty rooms that bore the marks of sold furniture and paintings on the walls and floors. Our box at the opera and my tuition at the Couvent School were the last things to go, two small vestiges which allowed us to pretend we were as we'd always been."

We sat down on the bed, and for the first time, Cora took my hand. "Tell me everything please, so I can understand."

"My father was the younger of a pair of brothers and probably sealed his fate by being the merrier of the two. Exasperating his own father, he lived the life of *le flaneur*, as opposed to his brother Etienne, who was diligently studying medicine at the Sorbonne.

Our family had been from Saint-Domingue but left there in 1790; so for two generations, Paris was the family home. My grandfather Pierre was a successful wine merchant and expected his sons would follow similar pursuits, but no occupation seemed to suit my father.

Grandfather Pierre had a brother named Mathurin, who, though born in Paris, dreamed of running a sugar plantation like those he'd heard of in Saint-Domingue. In those days, free men of color, as my forebears were, thought nothing of owning slaves. We may have been as dark skinned as they, but those people were uneducated and from a different class. There was no notion of the equality given credence today. At any rate, Mathurin removed to America to the river parishes of Louisiana and ran a thriving sugar plantation all his life.

When I was two years old, Mathurin died without heirs and left all his Louisiana property to my father. It was immediately suggested, or as my father would later say, dictated, that he relinquish his youthful dithering and take the reins of the enterprise uncle Mathurin gifted him. It was said since he already had a wife and two daughters it was time for him to become a man.

The plantation named Belle Clair was extensive. When we arrived in 1850, there were a hundred and fifty slaves, many acres under cultivation, a sugar mill, a fine house and furnishings, another house in French New Orleans, and a box at the opera. It took almost no time for things to begin to fall apart.

At first our ruination moved slowly—a poor crop, an unwise loan, money frittered on the balls and parties of a New Orleans season. It was with the death of my mother and sister the following winter of 1851 when the descent really began. A breakout of yellow fever at Belle Clair took them both in the space of a fortnight along with a dozen slaves. My father was devastated. Widowed and unmoored in a foreign land where he'd no skill for farming or taste for slavery."

Cora barely moved in all the time it took me to relate my tale but began to speak in the low, marvelous voice I remembered. It was such a gift, Cora's voice, and how I envied it, as it seemed to me a remarkable and potent weapon capable of issuing any emotion, capable of wounding or consoling, healing or hating, all with the slightest tenor of tone. "I am so very sorry," she said, and I was certain of it. With her words, I felt her sympathy as if a cool hand had passed across my forehead. "Of course I had no idea," she continued, "Nathan admired your father immensely. How much of this did he know?"

"Very little, I suspect. I think Mr. Winslow loved my father for what he represented. Handsome, urbane, educated, all the things he was convinced colored people could be if they only had the opportunity. Of course, for my father, Colonel Winslow was a silver lining."

Cora's brow furrowed in confusion. "How so?"

"My father was a Spiritualist. I'm guessing this surprises you, but for the *gens de couleur*—freemen like ourselves this was not unusual. These days I hear people use the words "freemen" and "freedmen" as though they were the same thing, but for us, there was a world of difference. We were free, we owned property, we were educated and skilled, many of us were wealthy, and many of us owned slaves. We had nothing in common with our enslaved brothers but darkness of skin. Before Louisiana was American, there was a place for us, but later the line between us and the slaves began to blur. The French and Spanish thought differently, but Americans saw no difference between one Negro and another.

We lost much in the war, but what we *gens de couleur* most lamented was our loss of status. It was a bitter reality for all my people. We were squeezed on both sides.

My father and a group of his friends gathered together in a séance circle where they met semi-secretly to contact our ancestors for solace and advice. They called their group *Le Cercle Harmonique*—The Harmonious Circle.

Through the influence of this circle and the advice given by the spirit ancestors, my father and the others began to understand they must not fight against their enslaved brothers but join with them to assert the rights of all Black men. So when the Federals arrived and with them Colonel Winslow, the solution to my father's problems became clear.

Hypolite Dumas finally found the occupation he was destined for. Being a soldier excited his passions as nothing else ever had, and the Union army presented him with a solution for both himself and his slaves. Despite their abolitionist pretensions, the New York bankers to whom my father was in debt would have been more than happy for him to sell his slaves and turn the proceeds over to them in 1860, but by 1862, the tables had turned.

After talking with the slaves at Belle Clair, my father and the men he'd owned presented themselves to the Federals and they enlisted in the Union army. There were enough of them to start a regiment, which became the *Corps d'Afrique*. Thus, my father protected his honor and set in motion the events which would end his life. During the war he died of fever with Colonel Winslow by his side."

Cora sighed heavily and shook her head. "All you say takes my breath away. You've come to rescue me, but I feel I should comfort you," she said.

"I need no comfort," I said, "but both of us are in trouble and need to get away. Do you know how I found you?"

"It is one of many of my questions," Cora said, venturing the first smile I had seen from her, and setting my own heart at some ease.

"I was alone in Boston packing to be sent off to Howard University, when Mr. Winslow came storming in. I say "storming," because it was obvious he was in a fury. I thought he was in Onset with you, but he looked as though he'd been out all night.

He said very little except you were to remain in Onset, and he was to return to New Orleans. He changed his schedule so we traveled together to Washington City. We parted there, and he continued south, but by that time, I'd apprised the situation.

Mr. Winslow received three telegrams before we left Boston which gave me a bad feeling, and I admit I peeked at one and learned his terrible intentions. He believed you insane and planned on having you committed to an asylum."

"Did you know he tricked me to Woodland by having someone write and suggest he was ill and possibly dying?" Cora asked.

"No," I answered, "but it is no surprise. He thinks anyone insane who does not follow his own line of thinking. I had no more desire to attend Howard University than I did to go to the moon, except it would give me the privacy to keep on with my search."

"Your search?"

"All these years since the war, I have been seeking my Uncle Etienne, my only relative, whose proper address died with my father. Here in these United States—if they can even now be considered "united"—there is nothing for me. I can see what is still happening to Black people here. I want my real home. I want my family, Cora."

"Have you found him?"

"Yes!" I said grinning, for I was quite pleased with myself. "I found both of you in the same week. All I knew was you were to be taken upriver, and thus I wrote to the State Asylum in Jackson. Learning you were not there, I sent letters to the few people I remembered from New Orleans. During the war, my father left me to live with a woman named Adele Menard. Mrs. Menard, like all of us freemen had come down in the world, reduced to taking in sewing after once having the grandest box at the French Opera House. She was not overly disposed to being kindly but was always a good one for gossip, so I wrote first to her. It didn't take long. Imagine of all the places you could have been, finding you at Belle Clair!"

"Belle Clair?" Cora asked.

"Or near enough," I replied, "Belle Clair is the plantation adjacent to Woodland. My family once owned Adah Layton. She was my childhood nursemaid."

Cora placed her head in her hands and shook it. "My head is spinning," she said. "And Pliny? Did you own him too?"

"Lord no. He was a mule trader out of Kentucky or Tennessee or some such."

"Is it true they were part of the Underground Railroad?" Cora asked.

I smiled, but declined to answer. "All I will say on the subject is Pliny is mule trader on the outside and shrewd operator within. I knew you'd be safe with him."

"How did you find your Uncle Etienne?"

"Spiritualism. The ancestors. When I was all out of options, I sat in my room in Washington City and did as you do. Dimmed the lights, lit a candle and asked for the help of the spirits."

"I know they answered," Cora said. "What did they say?"

"They didn't answer, not in the way the spirits talk to you. I was hugely disappointed and went to bed sorrowing. In the morning, just as I awoke, I heard a single voice. I don't even know if the voice was male or female. I simply heard the words *Rue du Bac*. The letter I then wrote to Etienne Dumas, Rue du Bac, Paris France was answered by my uncle. It was the correct address! Etienne and his wife Jeanne had been seeking my father and I since the war."

Cora laughed, "So you have the gift."

"I don't think so," I said. "I asked of your whereabouts too, and the voice was silent. I owe finding you to the gossipy tongue of Adele Menard."

"So you plan to reunite?"

"I sail tonight on the *Charlemagne*, and have a ticket for you if you will join me."

Cora's pause was long enough I knew she was considering and not rejecting my offer. For what was she to do and where was she to go that Mr. Winslow would not follow her?

"I could not burden the generosity of your uncle and his wife," she said.

"They have invited you and would be grateful to know I was accompanied," I replied.

"I don't speak French."

"I will teach you. I don't think learning languages is likely to be difficult for you," I said laughing.

"I have no clothing except what I carried in my arms."

I stepped to one of the two trunks on the floor in the room and opened it, revealing the neatly folded garments. "I am enough of a seamstress to have remembered your size and have things packed for both of us." I was not going to let her wiggle away because of a practical matter.

"It is not just your family. It is also you. Your wisdom and resourcefulness astonish me, not to mention your kind heart. There is nothing I can do to repay what you have done."

"Yes," I said as seriously as I could sound. "there is."

Again Cora looked askance.

"I am fluent in four languages. When I was delivered to Mr. Winslow, I knew only French and spoken English. The others I've learned at his behest and benevolence. Yet despite my fluency, I'm barely allowed to speak. I have been tutored beyond the educational level of any woman I know, White or Black, but have been made to understand I am to forever hide the fact I was free and not a slave. I do not want to be a silent ornament to my race. I feel like a trained puppet brought out to demonstrate Mr. Winslow's ideals.

When I was in Washington City on the night I first saw you, I also met Sojourner Truth. In one evening I saw two women who had stood before the world and spoken their thoughts. I want to speak as the two of you have, and I believe you can teach me how."

Cora studied me as if to gauge my earnestness. "Yes," Cora said, "that I can do."

* * *

A great deluge of rain returned and poured like a waterfall on the townhouse gallery, while a sweep of wind rattled the windows, whirling the rain against them.

"Are you sure, Sophie?" Cora asked. "He will never forgive this."

"Mr. Winslow loves us only because he thinks he can invent us. I don't want to spend my life proving someone else's point. I am tired of being his example."

Cora was quiet for some time before lowering her head and brushing a tear from her eye. I'd never seen her cry; frankly, she did not seem the sort of woman for tears.

"Are you all right?" I asked.

She nodded. "You've jogged my memory is all. Once long ago someone told me the same thing. A young man who felt trapped by his father's wishes. I suddenly feel as though I have been all around the world, just to return to where I began."

Cora

1869

I pause for a moment at the window seeking the figure of Sophie passing beneath the streetlamp at the curve of the Rue du Bac. The street shines with moisture from a light rain in this hour of dusk, but even on a dry day at broad noon, the skies are always grey, a lustrous dome of quicksilver above the old city.

Paris is standing on the sharp edge of winter, with Christmas only a few weeks away, its big buildings tall, steep-roofed and many chimneyed, their upper regions swathed in frosty wood smoke from the fires burning within. I tend our fire now and pull my new shawl tightly around my shoulders. It is fringed and the color of an emerald—a gift from Sophie who is partial to luxuries and fripperies—but can well afford them with the popularity of her lectures.

I do not see her yet, but she can be expected at almost any hour, and I like to keep watch for her. I enjoy imagining her as she probably is now, not caught in the rain but cozy in some cafe, enchanting a listener with her words.

My afternoon has been occupied with writing letters and making parcels of the book Sophie and I have written together. Seated at our desk enfolding the small volume in brown paper for mailing, the smell of the glue of its dark blue binding, the pretty gold lettering on the face, *Le Spiritualiste de Paris*. How excited we were when the delivery boy from the publisher brought a dozen copies for us the day it appeared. "It's in the windows of all the shops," the lad declared, and so it was. It has been a success, and a second printing is already being planned.

December 4, 1869
Rue du Bac, Paris

Dear Lydia et al.,

I am enclosing for you and your father each a copy of the book written by Sophie and I. It has been judged successful by all, and I am so pleased the efforts of my pen have finally borne fruit.

After this year of study, I now feel competent in my French, particularly in reading and writing, though I am still a bit awkward at speaking outside of simple conversation. One result of this addition to my education is I am now able to understand the words of French-speaking spirits. They have the same messages for we living beings as the English speakers, and in part, listening to their words has helped me learn the language. Still, it is through Sophie's instruction I owe any proficiency. Many a night we have sat in our rooms sewing and practicing conjugation.

I have not heard anything from or of Nathan since our legal parting in September. I had hoped it would not be this way, that we might still find something to say to one another, if only in the memory of Etta, but it seems impossible. I look back on our days together as a very different time, and I do not blame him for anything. I have tried to do away with blaming anyone in this life, except, of course for, myself—but all humans are prone to that.

I don't know when I shall return. There are those I miss. All of you of course, and I should like to see my relations in Cadytown, but the idea of America makes me feel skittish just now. Oddly it seems best to pass these strange and changeful times in a place that also feels strange. The unfamiliar brings me comfort.

Give my love to Charles and your father and many hugs and kisses to Mae and Clara. You will find I have also enclosed a package of sweets for them which I have been assured will survive the journey. You can tell the girls they are bonbons from the confiseur, and I am sure this will make them taste even better.

Love,
Cora

Rising to poke at the fire and add another log, I pass by the ghost who sits at the doorway, costumed from another century and sleeping in our chair. If my ears have always been teeming with voices, so too has my vision been peopled with ghosts. They are fixtures in my line of sight, silent and numerous, and found in places where the living would not expect them. In any silent graveyard or deepest forest, you'll hardly find a trace, but the markets, railway stations, hotels and highways are teeming with their presence. As with all spirits, some seem to appeal to us while others seem unaware of our existence. Daily the living and dead pass through one another like clouds across the sun.

Why do spirits show themselves so? Why does this antique man travel between the afterlife and my room merely to sleep in a chair? Perhaps he is not a true spirit but the trace of a moment, the etch of a footprint, which I've the gift to see, but not the wisdom to understand. Perhaps the vision is merely his outline, some translucent and discarded costume once worn by his soul.

I could suppose the variety of spirits mirrors the variety of mankind. Those who speak and those who are silent. Those who touch and those who make mischief. And what of Hollis, where is he? Gone from me since I was trapped at Woodland, and after all our long conversations leaving me with just a one-word appeal to wait.

Of all spirits, he was my lodestone, and I grieve his loss only a bit less than my loss of Etta. Some days I forget their absence, but grief is a visitor who is slow in going home, returning again and again, just when you hoped it was gone for good.

I pray I will see them again and believe I will. I sometimes think Hollis did not mean for my waiting to refer to my deliverance from Woodland but rather as a request for patience until I see him again. I like to imagine he and Etta are risen to some higher sphere in the kingdom of spirits and now live where Robert does—passed to a world where not even a skilled medium can follow them.

December 4, 1869
Rue du Bac, Paris

Dear Sojourner,

I know of your tireless travels to persuade the government to supply western lands for the freedmen, so know not when this letter will find you. I am hoping you are taking a rest for the winter, which must be well along now in Michigan, and hope you might be home for Christmas.

Thus, I am enclosing for you a small memento in the form of a book written by Sophie and myself. Sophie has inscribed it especially to you, and we both hope you will find someone to read it for you, perhaps, on one of your long railway journeys.

Oh Sojourner, you should see Sophie! She is a young woman in her element, with so much depth and richness. I gave her what teaching I could, the old rules of elocution as tendered to me by the Reverend Lyman when I was a girl, and the manners I've taught myself from years of speaking—the cadence of the voice, how to gauge an audience, enliven a flagging subject etc...all things you know well yourself.

I have attended her lectures, and she dazzles her audiences with her words but also I daresay, with a style neither you or I would have considered in our day. She is tinder and flint all at once, and I delight in observing her costume, usually a dramatic dress she has sewn herself and always the traditional tignon headwrap of the free woman of color she wears so proudly. At first I feared she might be considered a mere spectacle; but her audiences have grown larger, and she regales them with a heady mix of stories of America, the war, New Orleans, spiritualism and ancestors—what Sophie calls her "gumbo" of subjects. In every lecture she advocates for women and Blacks, suffrage and equal rights for all. The girl will live a life she will be proud of.

I know I have told you before how inspired Sophie has been by you, but I must repeat my thoughts. When I see her on the platform, in her headdress and beautiful skin, storytelling her way to her message of equality and to the hearts of her listeners, I think of you.

No matter your success or failure with the intractable government, or those who fail to make the most of the freedom they have won, or those who would continue to suppress that freedom, you should know what your influence has changed. In Sophie, you have a daughter you never bore. In time, you will have a thousand such daughters who share your message but not a drop of your blood.

Stay well and take care my friend.
Love,
Cora

So we have reached the end, and you believe you have heard my voice. But have you?

Supple it has been called, rich and emotive, limpid and measured, but those have been the reports of others, other voices, and whose can be most believed? Indeed, what charlatan calls forth a spirit, what fraud guides the gullible, what coercer coaxes the credulous?

Moreover, each of these voices has been delivered here by another, set in print for the reader, in much the same way spirit voices were delivered by me to my listeners. Did my own imagination shape what I heard and yours what you read? It bears keeping in mind while listening or reading. How much do we know which has not come to us through someone else? Do we know what we think we know or is everything a bit of trickery, for all stories get twisted in the telling?

Yet, here is my voice. And not here. Incorporeal… yes, that is the word.

Is it wise, then, that spirits and their voices be doubted? How many things live beside us unseen but of which we remain certain? Music, joy, gravity, heat, electricity… and science will find more. What soul could ever leave the world without a deed unfinished, a secret untold, a final word crackling like a spark in the air?

Perhaps it is better after all to make friends with wonder. What if wisdom comes not from being certain, but from being able to accept the uncertain?

Shhhh, I hear Sophie's steps on the stairs. I know it is her because she takes them two at a time, in the rush of youth, where wonder still thrives. She will drop her parcels and coat on the chair near the doorway in the lap of the sleeping ghost she does not see and chatter excitedly of the events of her day. Perhaps in some measure, Sophie is my daughter too, and I will let her do all the talking.

Living here for so many months with the inability to speak the language has caused me to cherish this opportunity for silence. Because I have not called on them, my spirits are hushed and placid, and like friends grown fond and familiar, we have learnt how to be quiet with one another. Each morning I wake with the glad knowledge I finally have nothing to say. After all these years of never being allowed to stop speaking, I am wordless at last.

Or so I can imagine. For the past week there has been the pressure of a new hand on my shoulder. Whose it is, I do not yet know.

Afterword

The black biplane approached unsteadily, quickly losing altitude as it passed across the large field behind my parent's house. Although this was 1959, such a plane was even then antique, scarcely seen and notable.

"Look at that," my mother said, pointing in the plane's direction. An otherwise practical and undramatic woman, my mother was quite agitated. My father and grandmother, who were standing beside her, scanned the sky and indicated their confusion. "What?" They saw nothing.

As the plane plunged toward the ground, my mother could hear the faltering engine, see the leather-helmeted head of the pilot. "My God, he's going to crash!" my mother cried.

Again the others questioned her. "Can't you see it?" she exclaimed, still pointing. "It's right there!" Then it disappeared.

I suppose I was aware of the biplane also, to some degree, as my mother was five months pregnant with me the day she saw it. I like to think I heard her muffled cries and felt the certainty of her vision. In any regard, I heard her tell the tale all my life, tracing a line with her finger in the backyard sky to denote her memory of the pathway of the airplane, seen to no one but her.

Thus the black airplane has become to me, along with a handful of other experiences in my life an example of the power of the inexplicable.

There is probably no human soul who has not had such an experience. Something seen or heard and not logically explained. There is certainly no human culture without a word for a spirit or ghost or a vision, and most make room for such phenomena. Yet in our scientific and secular age, the supernatural is not seriously discussed, except around the campfire or on cable TV. It was not always so. In the middle decades of the 19th century, such experiences were absolutely nurtured.

Those decades, set within a larger time period now known as the "Great Awakenings," were a period when new ideas and the pursuit of social reforms took center stage in movements often led by the middle-classes with a deep belief in the perfectibility of mankind. It was a time of many "isms," with transcendentalism, Mormonism, vegetarianism, abolitionism, Adventism, suffragism either being born or maturing. New religions were formed, Utopian communities organized, established norms were challenged, and millions of American Spiritualists routinely talked with the dead.

Spiritualism rose quickly in the fertile soil of these years, with its followers believing the dead could be contacted by the living, particularly through gifted mediums, and might impart advice and comfort. Given the frequency of child mortality and the mass carnage of the Civil War, as well as the recent introduction of the telegraph which could communicate messages instantly across oceans, it is not surprising such communication would be desired and considered possible.

The Seraph is a work of fiction set in these remarkable times and inspired by the life of one of the most famous Spiritualist mediums of the day. Cora L.V. Scott—1840-1923 (Cora Page/Carter/Winslow) was a scarcely educated farm girl from western New York when she encountered her first taste of fame. Many Spiritualist mediums and lecturers were young women, as they were considered pure and uncorrupted, and Cora checked every box for audience approval. Blonde, beautiful, and with a calm manner and a melodious voice, she entranced audiences seeking both the words of the dead and those others desiring an enticing woman to look at.

In our visual age, it is probably impossible to emphasize the significance and celebrity given to proficient public speakers in the 19th century, and if there were a sexualized aspect to this prominence, it would be little different than the ogling of female stars in our own day. More important is the barriers these women broke. In speaking as they did for their causes and beliefs, Cora and her cohorts found themselves where no other women of the past or even of their own present could be—at a podium with an audience interested in what they had to say. They were the first such women in America to taste this power, and once they had it, they never let it go. With her platform secured, Cora went on to a lifetime of advocating for spiritualism, abolition of slavery, Native American and worker's rights and many other worthwhile reforms.

It is notable that Cora's impressive stage presence was such that her legacy in literature is not confined to *The Seraph* alone. As early as 1863, author Henry James wrote to a friend that he'd attended one of Cora's New York lectures and took special note of her unsavory manager. More than 20 years later, she was apparently still on his mind as he penned his novel *The Bostonians* with a beautiful feminist lecturer named Verena Tarrant trailed by a repugnant father who managed her speeches.

Cora Scott's personal life was compelling. Four times married, she first found herself wed to a grifting manipulative husband named Benjamin Franklin Hatch—1817-1877 (Benjamin Chandler Carter) who was apparently the figure observed by Henry James. Married to Hatch when just in her teens they were soon to part. Their divorce was scandalous and public, and reported with eager salaciousness in the newspapers of the time.

Her second marriage to Nathan Waldo Daniels—1836-1867 (Nathan Waldo Winslow) was well-matched but destined also for sorrow. Nathan was a reform-minded Union army officer with whom Cora had a daughter named Henrietta in 1866.

She soon married for a third time to another Union army military man, Samuel F. Tappan—1831-1913 (also Nathan Waldo Winslow as an alter ego). Samuel was a veteran of western theaters of the Civil War and afterward worked for the betterment of Native Americans, ostensibly believing in their right to self-determination. A member of a staunch and storied New England family of abolitionists and social reformers, Samuel displayed a high degree of moral certainty which seemed at times to veer into dogmatism. In 1867, he adopted an orphaned Cheyenne girl, changed her name to Minnie Tappan and left her in the care of female relatives in Boston to be raised and educated. When Minnie came of age, Samuel contacted his friend General Oliver Otis Howard and had Minnie enrolled in the preparatory academy which became Howard University. Minnie died of disease in 1873, and shortly afterward, Samuel abandoned Cora. Their marriage had lasted less than five years.

Cora's last marriage in 1877 to William Richmond—1845-1909, was quiet and long lasting. William, who had been a member of the Chicago Spiritualist church where Cora served as pastor, helped his wife transcribe her sermons and writings and manually recorded her lectures for publication.

Despite its unconventionality, Cora Scott's life was one of service, both to others and to her own beliefs. Unlike many of her peers, she was never exposed as a fraud or ridiculed into silence, and unlike the fictional Cora Page of *The Seraph* and some other female Spiritualist speakers, she was never institutionalized by her family. It is perhaps fitting that Cora L.V. Scott came to a quiet end after a tumultuous beginning, finding her own voice in writing, helping to found the National Spiritualist Association of Churches in the United States and acting as personal counsel to her own parishioners.

In 1859, Cora Scott gave a lecture at New York's Cooper Union in which she famously declared "You cannot direct the wind, but you can trim your sails." In her own way, she did just that.

Abolitionism, Feminism, and Spiritualism traveled through the mid 19th century hand in hand, and Cora's circle of associates advocated for all three causes. One such friend was the redoubtable Sojourner Truth—c. 1797-1883, the character in *The Seraph* who remains the most famous today. An illiterate Dutch-speaking woman who had spent much of her life enslaved in the American

North, she became one of the most profound speakers of her time.

Unfortunately, as she was unable to write down any of her words, she has been transcribed by a multitude of others (including myself) who have no true idea of how she actually sounded or precisely what words she used in her expression. Some recorders even attributed an exaggerated Southern Black dialect to her words; something which would be impossible due to her native speech. What is known is her speech sounded "peculiar" to many listeners, probably because of her Dutch accent, and that she often left her listeners laughing at her quick wit.

There are accounts of her resistance to well-meaning friends who made her "sound more proper" in the letters they wrote for her, or suggested she learn to read and write or give up smoking her pipe. Such testimony hints at the power of Sojourner Truth's personality and convictions. I think it likely that the "self" she fought so hard to retain and preserve after years of being regarded as mere chattel, was precious to her.

Mindful that the real Sojourner Truth is likely lost behind her legend, I have tried in *The Seraph* to honor her raw, powerful and, doubtless, imperfect speech in which she employed emotion, song, humor, plain-spokenness, and parable, all extemporaneously and to world-changing and enduring effect.

In 1866 Cora Scott wrote of her friend Sojourner "...her words are like pearls cast from the crown of truth. She is a noble old hero, and the world will long remember her when other names are forgotten." So it has proved to be.

Despite her many marriages, undoubtedly the love of Cora's life was her second husband, Nathan Waldo Daniels—1836-1867 (Nathan Waldo Winslow). The real-life Nathan was a Spiritualist, Union Army officer and Freedmen's Bureau advocate. Beginning his career as an Ohio lawyer with abolitionist sympathies when the Civil War broke out, he was placed in charge of the African American 2nd Regiment of the Louisiana Native Guard. Stationed at points in Louisiana and Mississippi, he regularly advocated for his troops' welfare and recognition, recording his views in a diary which has since been edited and published.

Nathan and Cora met in Washington D.C. the summer of 1865 and were immediately smitten. Both were young and handsome, and they shared reformist ideals. The war had just ended with their hoped-for result, and the world must have seemed as though it was soon to be made anew. Marrying that same year, their daughter Henrietta was born just over nine months later.

The little family soon found themselves working in New Orleans, Louisiana, with Nathan advocating and writing to promote Reconstruction and Cora giving her famous speech honoring the victims of the Mechanics' Institute Massacre. Sadly, this time of happiness and purpose was short, as Nathan fell ill with yellow fever and died in the fall of 1867 with little Henrietta also dying of the same sickness just 8 days later. Only Cora survived.

In examining the pages of Nathan W. Daniel's wartime diaries, which are today held in the Library of Congress, another remarkable individual appears from history's shadows. Nathan had mounted several cherished photographs in his book and, in one of these, he appears seated closely beside a good friend. The men sit shoulder to shoulder with their military jackets unbuttoned and their hair uncombed as though they'd just popped into a photographer's studio while on leave. This friend was Francis Ernest Dumas—1837-1901 (Hypolite Dumas) a wealthy Louisiana planter and slave owner who spoke five languages and was also Black. Prior to the taking of this photograph Francis had done an amazing thing. With their consent, he enlisted more than 100 of his slaves in the Union army, where he then fought beside men he once owned. During the war, he saw combat in the Western Theater and achieved the rank of Major, one of the highest held by an African American during the war. He was later to be candidate for both Lieutenant Governor and Secretary of State for Louisiana.

The Seraph abounds with such true-life characters, misfits all, strange to both their century and ours. Spirit-talkers and a Black slaveholder, a passionate female speaker who could not read the words she was uttering, charlatan mesmerists, abolitionist utopians whose community, nonetheless, depended on a machine that loomed cotton and a man whose face was less famous than the palm of his hand.

Yet, America turned for the better under the efforts of such singular individuals and their complex journeys through their glorious and terrible times.

And what of my mother's black airplane? She herself never knew. It was the only such vision she ever experienced. The family home she was standing behind when she saw the plane was just being constructed in 1959, and for fifty years the field over which the airplane once swooped remained empty. Only recently was the acreage built upon, with a sprawling one-story hospital rehabilitation center. My mother died there while *The Seraph* was being written, in a room located in the same place in the field where the crashing airplane of her vision disappeared.

Acknowledgments

Every book has many midwives and all authors owe a host of thanks for a successful birth.

Firstly, I wish to thank the institutions for access to their enlightening collections. The Bancroft Memorial Library, and Little Red Shop Museum in Hopedale, Massachusetts gave great insight into the Utopian community which once thrived there. The Massachusetts Historical Society, and Historic New Orleans Collection housed photographs and manuscripts which spoke eloquently of some of the characters in this novel and their times.

Libraries played their vital role. The Library of Congress, Wareham Public Library, New Orleans Public Library and the Boston Athenaeum all provided material for my imagination. Trips to the Lily Dale Assembly grounds in Cassadaga, New York and the On-I-Set Wigwam Spiritualist Camp in Onset, Massachusetts provided the flavor of the 19th century Spiritualist camp experience.

Although the Carville Leprosy Hospital, which opened in 1894, was not in existence during Cora's time in Louisiana, my inclusion of its history and geography fit well into the narrative of banishment and exclusion in the novel. Today, one may make a visit to the National Hansen's Disease Museum on the site and explore one of America's most fascinating museums and collections.

Likewise, the nearby St. Joseph's Plantation showcases the social and agricultural history of the time. It was here I was taught the basics of the farming of sugar cane.

I am grateful to Michelle Leckert of Neal Auction Company of New Orleans for permission to use the fabulous work of painter Jacques Amans (1801-1888) for the cover.

Lastly, at the library of the University of Rochester's collection of Amy Post's correspondence, I was able to hold in my own hands some of the letters of Cora Scott Hatch Daniels. In these missives sent to Mrs. Post from Cora's home in New Orleans, I was able to see Cora's delicate precise handwriting and read her words advocating feminism, abolitionism, and Spiritualism, as well as her praise of her friend Sojourner Truth.

I also owe thanks to many supportive individuals, all who provided suggestions, editing and good cheer. Thus I am grateful to Kara Goodrich, James van Pernis, James Beyor, Wren Schmith, Anne Dentino, Shelby Gates Legere, Jeanne Schinto, Tripp Evans, Sandra Goroff, Robin Clifford Wood, John Lindberg, Eleanor Edmondson and Gigi Wilmers. I memorialize Cathy Fuss who was the first reader of the manuscript.

A Note on the Type

The text of this book was set in the present-day version of Bembo, recut in 1929 by Stanley Morison from the original face designed by Francesco Griffo for Aldus Manutius, the renowned Venetian printer. First used in a Renaissance travel book written by Pietro Bembo, the typeface was named for this author, who later became a cardinal. Bembo is a typeface of remarkable clarity, both elegant and beautifully proportioned.

The chapter-headings and cover type were created nearly 300 years later by an unknown gravestone carver in coastal Maine. Set alongside carved images of winged skulls and hourglasses, these peculiar yet dignified cuttings caught the eye of type designer Brian Willson of Three Islands Press and inspired his *Castine* font, named for the town where the anonymous carver plied his trade.

It is perhaps worthy to note that the gravestone cutter and the 19th century spiritualist medium pursued the same goal—to transmit messages and information from the dead to the living.